I0822382

CHAINS OF FATE

A Novel

MELISSA COLE

ISBN-10 (e-book): 979-8-9899976-3-3

ISBN-10 (print book): 979-8-9899976-4-0

ISBN-10 (hardcover): 979-8-9899976-5-7

Library of Congress Control Number: 2024911233

Printed in the United States of America.

To those who suffered from injustice in the past and those still facing it today, we honor your strength and promise to keep fighting for freedom for everyone.

That man who is the property of another, is his mere chattel, though he continue a man.

— ARISTOTLE

Foreword

Thomas Everhart personifies the countless individuals who faced the grim realities of being treated as property and denied freedom. His story is a tribute to the resilience of the human spirit and the enduring power of hope, even in the darkest times. While Thomas's tale is fictional, it is inspired by the genuine struggles of those who endured unimaginable hardships. In the annals of history, they stand as some of the bravest souls to have graced the earth, a testament to the fact that even in the darkest of times, light can always guide the way. As we consider our lives, let us honor the sacrifices of those who preceded us, drawing strength from their resilience. May we serve as beacons for those still lurking in the shadows, aspiring to brighter days.

Chapter One

In the shadowy alleys of eighteenth-century London, Thomas Everhart moved like a ghost. His footsteps were whisper-soft against the uneven cobblestones of Essex Street. With practiced stealth, he navigated through a tumultuous sea of carts and horses, each jostling and braying in the morning uproar. Each breath he took formed icy puffs in the crisp morning air. He knew one wrong step could deliver him into the clutches of ruthless criminals on the hunt for vulnerable souls like his. Every day was a desperate search for scraps, each moment a silent plea to the fickle gods of fate.

It was 1770, and the pale winter sun cast weak rays over the city, barely warming the cobbled streets and the cold, huddled masses within. The light illuminated the young orphan's face, revealing a visage weathered too soon by the harshness of street life. His unkempt brown hair, matted and tangled, framed his face like a makeshift curtain, partially concealing the determined glint in his piercing blue eyes. His eyes, bright and keen, betrayed a resilience forged from constant vigilance and the pursuit of survival.

At fifteen, Thomas's frame was lean and wiry, shaped by the scarcity of his meals and the physical demands of his daily struggles. His clothes were a patchwork of repairs, with fabric worn thin at the elbows and knees, while his clogs were scuffed and barely holding together. Despite these signs of wear, there was an air of stubborn defiance about him, as if he refused to let the world crush his spirit.

The streets of London thrummed with life and chaos. Street vendors shouted their wares with boisterous enthusiasm, their cries slicing through the air as they hawked everything from ripe fruit to tattered books. Horse-drawn carts rumbled and clattered over ancient cobblestones, their wheels echoing against the close-knit buildings and narrow thoroughfares. Every so often, the gruff voice of a nightwatchman cut through the commotion, his orders sharp and commanding.

The air was a tapestry woven with the city's scents: the warm, yeasty aroma of freshly baked bread from the bakery mingled with the acrid stench of sewage lurking in the shadows. Overlaying it all was the pervasive smog of coal smoke billowing from countless chimneys. The city was a living, breathing entity teeming with life and activity, yet it was a battleground for Thomas. Each day was a fight for survival.

"Oi, watch where you're going, lad!" A gruff voice jolted Thomas from his thoughts. He narrowly avoided a man whose muscular arms strained under the weight of a basket overflowing with fish. The man's face, weathered like an old sea chart, twisted into a scowl, accentuating the deep lines etched around his eyes. His rough hands, scarred from nets and hooks, clung tightly to the basket. Thomas quickly muttered an apology and sidestepped the man. His lean frame slipped effortlessly back into the flow of pedestrians crowding the narrow streets.

As he navigated through the crowd, the stench of rotting garbage overwhelmed him. Turning a corner, Thomas slipped into Clements Inn Passageway, finding brief respite from the throng. The passageway narrowed, its ancient cobblestones slick with muck that squelched under his clogs. The walls, darkened with soot and neglect, seemed to swallow the scant light, casting elongated shadows around him.

At the end of the alley, Thomas stumbled upon a sack of discarded vegetables, likely cast aside by someone from Clements Inn. His stomach roared with hunger. He pounced on the sack, his rough, calloused hands fumbling with the knots. Inside, he found a few withered carrots, a bruised apple, and some wilted greens—not exactly a feast, but to someone as hungry as him, they were as precious as gold. He swiftly pocketed the food, casting wary glances around to make sure no one was watching.

His relief was short-lived. A sudden commotion up ahead caught his attention. A gang of ruffians was harassing an elderly woman. Their laughter echoed off the brick walls. The frail woman, visibly shaken, held her basket close as if it could protect her from their cruel jeers and rough handling. Thomas froze, torn between the impulse to help and the need to remain unseen. His fists clenched, nails digging into his palms. The sight of the woman's terror-stricken face tugged at his heartstrings, but he knew better than to step in. Helping her would only get him a beating—or worse. Altruism was a luxury he couldn't afford. He had to think of his survival, even if it pained him to walk away.

Just then, a burly man with a filthy cap pulled low over his brow rounded the corner, blocking Thomas's path. The man's hulking figure cast a long shadow, and a leering grin revealed his blackened, broken teeth. The man swayed slightly, clearly drunk from his stint at the George Tavern. His breath, heavy with the stench of potent spirits, filled the air.

"Aye, lad. Got any coin to spare?" the man growled, stepping closer. The dim light revealed the pockmarks and scars marring his weathered face, a testament to a life marked by violence and crime.

Thomas's heart pounded, but he forced himself to stay calm. "Sorry, mister. I've got nothing. Feel free to search me if ya like."

The man's eyes narrowed, suspicion and greed flickering within them. "Is that so?" he sneered, grabbing Thomas by the collar with a grimy hand. His grip was iron-strong. His filthy nails dug into Thomas's shirt. "I'll search ya alright, and when I find what's mine, I'll—." he spat, his breath rancid.

Thomas didn't wait to hear the rest. With a burst of desperate energy, he wriggled free from the man's grasp and ducked under his arm. His lungs burned as he gulped down the cold air, each breath sharper than the last. He darted through the alleys, trying to remember every twist and turn. He knew the city's underbelly well, but panic made everything seem strange and threatening.

He ducked into Devereux Court Alley near Twining's Tea Shop on Strand, pressing his back against the damp, cold wall. The smell of tea and biscuits wafted from the shop, making his stomach rumble. He held his breath, listening for the thief. The footsteps grew louder, slowly fading as the man gave up, muttering curses.

Thomas paused to catch his breath, his chest heaving as he leaned against the wall. The encounter had been too close, a reminder of the dangers lurking in every shadow. After checking that the coast was clear, he carefully returned to his hideout. He stuck to the shadows, avoiding the main streets. The tolling of Paul's bells echoed through the city, reminding him of his struggle to survive. The cold air nipped at his skin, and the clatter of horse hooves on cobblestones added to the eerie atmosphere. He kept his footsteps light, moving quickly through the alleys as the city sounds surrounded him.

For a moment, he imagined a life away from the filth, where he didn't have to look over his shoulder constantly, but he couldn't stay there daydreaming. His stomach growled, louder this time. Thomas stood up, determined to find food for himself and the other orphans. He maneuvered through the alleys, sidestepping drunks and dodging rats, until he reached their makeshift home in a dilapidated Southwark warehouse. The air inside was stale, tinged with decay and mold, yet it offered more shelter than the harsh streets. Weathered wooden beams and dusty rafters stretched to the ceiling. Along the walls, empty wooden crates and discarded barrels were piled up. The floor was a patchwork of cracked concrete and scattered debris, including old papers, bits of cloth, and broken glass. Large, unshuttered windows allowed in only a scant amount of light. In a corner, he saw his street family, other urchins like him, huddled together for warmth.

"Oi, Tom!" a familiar voice called out.

Thomas's eyes brightened as Charlie, one of the younger orphans who couldn't be more than six, stepped out from the shadows. Pale and gaunt, his face was streaked with soot, and his worn shirt draped loosely over his slight frame. His blond hair, matted with dirt and grime, framed his face in messy tufts. Despite his rough appearance, Charlie's bright blue eyes sparkled with an unquenchable curiosity and resilience. His bare feet, calloused from navigating the unforgiving streets, and his small, agile hands, always ready to lend aid, testified to his survival skills. Despite his hardships, Charlie had an infectious smile that could still thaw the coldest hearts.

"What'd ya bring home?" he asked, eyes hopeful.

Thomas handed over a small slice of bread and watched as Charlie tore into it, his tiny body shaking with hunger. He waited for Charlie to finish eating before asking, "Anything happen while I was gone?"

Charlie shook his head. "Same as every day. Jimmy got caught nickin' again, and Feebles is sick."

Thomas's stomach dropped. Jimmy might hang this time, and Feebles—no one survived long on the streets when they got sick. Suddenly, they heard unfamiliar voices outside, making them exchange worried glances.

"The Press Gang's back," whispered Charlie, his eyes wide with fear.

Thomas's heart pounded. The Press Gang was their worst nightmare, constantly scouring for young boys to conscript into the King's Navy. Notorious for snatching people from the streets, taverns, or even the safety of their homes, they forced them into naval service, sometimes for years or even for a lifetime.

"Quick, hide!" Thomas hissed, shoving Charlie behind a crate. He followed suit, heart hammering in his chest as boots stomped closer.

"We know you're in there, lads!" a gruff voice bellowed. "Come out peaceful-like, and we'll go easy on ya!"

Thomas clenched his fists. They both knew it was a lie. Minutes passed like hours, but finally, the footsteps receded.

"That was a close one," Charlie breathed, coming out from the hiding spot.

"Too close," Thomas replied as he nodded.

The air inside the abandoned building smelled of unwashed bodies. Baths were a luxury long forgotten, and Thomas couldn't remember what it felt like to soak in a tub. It had been too long. Exhausted from a day spent scavenging for food, he collapsed onto his threadbare straw mattress. A fierce loyalty to the other orphans, who had become his family, burned within him. They were all he had left in the world, and he would do anything to protect them, even if it meant putting himself in danger.

"Tom," William whispered as they lay there, "do ya ever think 'bout what life'd be like if we weren't here? If we didn't 'ave to nick and scrap to survive?

"Sometimes," Thomas admitted, pondering. "But this is our life, and we've got to deal with it."

"I'm tired of nickin' and scrappin' to survive," William murmured, his voice barely a whisper. "We get by, somehow. Maybe one day we'll find a better life than this."

"Maybe," Thomas said softly, knowing it was a long shot.

As he lay there, Thomas's thoughts wandered back to his past, memories as faded as the ragged blanket that scarcely kept him warm. He vaguely remembered the warmth of his mother's embrace and his father's hearty laughter. But those memories were dimming, like worn pages of an old book. Fate had snatched them away, leaving him to fend for himself on the harsh city streets.

"Tommy," he imagined his father saying, his voice like a warm embrace, "one day you'll see, life won't always be this hard. You're destined for extraordinary things, my boy."

Thomas clung to memories of his father, the last remnants of life before hunger and fear dominated. In his dreams, he found an escape from his grim reality. He saw himself standing upright and proud alongside his parents. His brown hair was neatly combed. His mother was dressed in one of her cherished floral dresses, her light brown hair neatly tied with a bow. His father, tall and lean with blonde hair and blue eyes, was clad in his finest Sunday suits.

"Oi, Tommy! What ya dreamin' about?" teased James, one of the orphans close to Thomas's age, who had been stirred awake by Thomas's restless movements.

"Nothing worth mentioning," Thomas replied, trying to hide the sudden feeling of vulnerability.

"Alright then, keep yer secrets," James muttered, rolling over and burying his face in his arms.

Closing his eyes, Thomas tried to block out the gnawing ache in his belly and the chill creeping into his bones. He took refuge in his imagination. In his mind, he was no longer a street urchin but a fearless adventurer, embarking on grand quests and daring rescues. In his dreams, he could escape, if only for a moment.

Was it foolish to believe he could break free from his life? Would he always be stuck in this squalid place, forced to steal and fight to survive?

"Maybe one day we'll find a way out," William's words echoed in his mind, bringing a flicker of hope. "A better life for all of us."

"Maybe," Thomas whispered into the darkness as if saying it aloud could make it real. Yet deep down, he knew dreams wouldn't be enough to save him or his makeshift family. They needed more than hope; they needed a plan and the bravery to carry it out.

Chapter Two

Thomas shifted uneasily on the gritty warehouse floor, a sense of dread washing over him as he faced another grueling day on London's unforgiving streets. Cold air seeped through the window cracks, sending shivers down his spine despite the thin blanket draped over him. The musty scent of damp wood and mildew filled his nostrils, clinging to the air like a sinister presence. His breath formed a mist in the chilly morning air, a bleak reminder of the life he faced outside.

Glancing at the other orphans, still deep in sleep, he decided against rousing them. Their thin blankets provided scant warmth against the chilling air, and signs of exhaustion were etched into their faces even in slumber. He couldn't help but envy their ability to find peace, even for a short while. As he rolled over, a sharp pang shot through his ankle—a reminder of yesterday's encounter with the thief. He winced, biting back the pain. It wasn't like he had anything to steal anyway. He gently rubbed the bruised area, hoping to ease the ache.

He shut his eyes, trying to escape the grim reality of the streets and his empty belly. Laughter echoed in his mind, drawing him back to the cozy living room of his childhood home. He felt the fireplace's warmth and saw the soft flicker of firelight painting shadows on the walls. His mother's gentle chuckles and his father's booming laughter wrapped him in a cozy embrace. The smell of his mother's cooking filled the air, making his mouth water.

The memory was so vivid, so achingly real, that for a fleeting moment, he believed he could reach out and touch it. He could almost feel the rough texture of the quilt his mother had made, the warmth of the fire caressing his face, and the solid presence of his father's reassuring embrace.

"Tommy, my boy, come here," his father called, gesturing toward the worktable in the far corner of the room. His strong, calloused hands cradled a piece of wood and a carving knife. The beginnings of a toy began to take shape beneath his skilled fingers. "Let me show you how it's done."

Thomas edged forward, his eyes alight with curiosity and excitement as he approached his father. He reached out to grasp the knife, noting its heft, and looked up at his father eagerly, ready to learn.

"Watch closely," his father instructed, covering Thomas's hand with his own and guiding the knife through the wood with practiced ease. "First, you carve out the rough shape, then you refine the details. It's all about patience and precision, son."

"Look, Pa!" Thomas exclaimed, holding up the finished toy with pride. "I did it!"

His father's laughter rang out again, filling the room with warmth. "Well done, Thomas! I knew you could do it."

The smell of stew wafted through the cozy kitchen as Thomas's mother, a petite woman with kind eyes and an ever-present smile, tended to the stove. Her gentle humming filled the room, infusing it with a warmth that seemed to seep into every corner.

"Thomas," she beckoned. Her voice was a soft melody that filled the warm kitchen. "Could you fetch the dishes from the cupboard?" Her words were gentle yet firm, wrapping around him like a familiar hug, offering comfort and security.

He glanced up from his doodles, the late afternoon sun casting the kitchen in a warm, golden glow.

"Sure thing, Ma," he answered, rising from his chair. Barefoot, he padded across the room, lured by the comforting scent that filled the air.

The cupboard stood like a sentinel in the kitchen, its sturdy frame bearing the marks of years of service. As he reached for the handle, his fingers traced the grooves worn into the wood, feeling the coolness of its polished surface. With a gentle tug, the door creaked open, revealing the neatly arranged dishes inside. Each dish gleamed in the soft light, inviting him to take hold. Grasping the top bowl, he felt its smooth surface against his fingertips.

He saw his mother as he turned to carry the dishes to the table. She was stirring a pot on the stove, her movements graceful. Her light brown hair was neatly pulled back with a bow, and her face, though lined with the cares of daily life, was lit with a serene smile. Her dress swayed gently as she moved, a testament to her simple elegance.

Thomas set the bowls down on the table, arranging them with care. He loved these moments in the kitchen, where the outside world seemed to fade away, leaving only the warmth and comfort of home.

His mother turned from the stove, giving him an approving wink. "Thank you, Thomas," she said, her smile widening. "You've always been such a great help."

His mother's words filled his heart with pride. He returned to his seat and watched her stir the stew; everything felt perfect. "Do you remember the story I used to tell you about the brave knight and the dragon?" she asked, her voice tinged with nostalgia.

Thomas nodded eagerly, his eyes lighting up. "Yes, Ma. I remember every word."

She smiled, a faraway look in her eyes. "I used to tell you that story every night before bed. You always asked so many questions about the knight and his adventures."

He grinned, recalling those nights spent curled up under the covers, listening to her weave tales of courage and heroism. "I still think about those stories," he admitted, his voice soft. "They always made me feel brave, like I could face anything."

She reached out, placing a hand on his shoulder. "And you can, Thomas. You have a brave heart. Never forget that."

"Why don't you say grace, Tommy," his father suggested.

They all bowed their heads as Thomas began the

prayer. "Thank you, Lord, for this meal and the love in our home," he said as gratitude swelled within him. He looked up to meet his parents' proud and approving gazes. "Great job, son," his father praised, his voice brimming with love.

His mother smiled and gently patted his hand, her touch tender. "Are we ready to eat? I know I am." Although their supper was modest, it felt abundant to Thomas. The small wooden table, polished by years of use, gleamed under the soft light. Mismatched plates and cups graced its surface, each with its own story. A pot of stew brimmed with meat and vegetables at the center, while freshly baked bread sat beside it. The scent of herbs wafted through the air, enticing his senses. Times were hard in England, yet his mother always provided a comforting meal.

His mother looked at him with a twinkle and scooped a generous helping of stew into his bowl. The simmering broth and tender meat made his mouth water. With a gentle tug, she pulled out a worn wooden chair, its surface smoothed by years of use, and settled into it. As she did, his father began to share stories, his deep voice weaving captivating tales for their small family.

"Did you hear about the latest rumors circulating about the New World?" his father asked, his eyes alight with excitement as he leaned forward, anticipation etching his face. "They say it's a land of vast opportunities, with endless possibilities beckoning those brave enough to seek them out. Imagine, Tommy, a place where dreams can take root and grow as tall as the towering trees in the forests."

Thomas leaned in, his eyes sparkling with wonder as his father vividly described the New World. His imagination took flight, conjuring images of towering forests alive with chirping birds, vast fields stretching as far as the eye could see, and bustling towns buzzing with the energy of new beginnings. His father's words fueled Thomas's dreams of adventure and discovery, igniting a spark within him.

"The New World," his father continued, his voice brimming with excitement, "is a place where anyone can carve out their path without the rules holding them back. It's full of opportunities and dreams just waiting to be chased."

"Did the Smith family go to the New World?" Thomas inquired eagerly, his eyes alight with curiosity.

"Indeed, Thomas," his father nodded, a thoughtful expression on his face. "Many folks are setting sail across the sea, looking to escape religious troubles and carve out fresh beginnings."

His mother's brows furrowed with worry. "How dangerous that must be!"

"I heard that some are going there to work."

"That's true, son. The journey is dangerous, but for those seeking a better life, the New World offers a chance to start over."

"Maybe we can see the New World one day."

"Perhaps, son, but for now, let's finish this wonderful meal your mother cooked for us."

Thomas fought back tears, longing for the warmth and laughter of his parents. He yearned to return to their simple life, but now survival was his only option. He clung to his father's teachings, moving forward like the hands of a clock, marking time.

As he drifted back to sleep, memories of his mother's soothing voice washed over him. He was a young boy again, snuggled under a threadbare quilt as his mother sat beside him. Her work-worn hands gently smoothed back his hair as she sang a lullaby, her voice sweet and clear. Thomas's eyelids grew heavy, the day's activities tiring his tiny body. His father entered the room quietly, planting a whiskery kiss on his forehead.

"Sleep well, my boy," his father's deep voice rumbled.

His mother's voice faded as she leaned in to kiss his cheek gently. "We love you more than anything," she whispered.

Haunting memories shattered his brief joy. In his mind, he saw the flames engulfing his childhood home, twisting like sinister spirits in the night. The flames' wicked fingers reached out to grasp the Everhart home's wooden beams and thatched roofs. The smoke thickened the air, staining the sky black. He heard a shout in the distance, maybe his mother or father, but it was hard to tell in the chaos.

Thomas woke suddenly, his heart racing like a frightened animal. Smoke filled the air, choking him with each breath. Confusion clouded his mind as he struggled to understand what was happening. Slowly, the fog of sleep lifted, revealing the terrifying truth: his world was on fire. He stumbled forward. His lungs burned as he inhaled the smoke that filled the air. His heart raced with fear and confusion, but above all else, he was driven by a single purpose: to find his parents.

"Ma! Pa!" he screamed, his voice barely heard amid

the raging fire. The intense heat made it hard for him to think, but he still pushed forward. "Where are you?"

Thomas's eyes darted around the room, searching for his parents. Time was running out, and the fire was beginning to engulf him.

"Please," he whispered, choking back tears, "I need you both."

As he staggered through the blazing inferno, panic gripped his chest. He called out for his parents once more, his throat raw and burning, but received no reply. Only the merciless crackling of flames echoed, a cruel companion to his agony.

Where are they? His thoughts raced, frantic and desperate. Why can't I find them?

Without warning, the floor beneath him moaned and gave way, hurling him to the ground. Embers cascaded around him like fiery raindrops, scorching his skin and filling his senses with the acrid stench of burnt wood and ash.

Enough. Thomas thought, his mind numb with grief and despair. I have to get out of here.

With a final, anguished cry, he dragged himself to his feet, stumbling blindly towards a gaping hole in the wall. Then, reality hit him with the force of a sledgehammer: he was alone. He sobbed, tears streaming down his blackened face as he stumbled out of the burning house and into the night.

"Please," he whispered into the darkness, "please don't leave me." But there was no answer, only the mocking laughter of the flames as they danced and twirled amidst the ruins of his shattered world.

The warmth of his family and the comfort of their home had faded into memories, replaced by the harsh reality of his dismal surroundings at the warehouse. Sitting on his worn blanket, Thomas held onto a small wooden toy, a precious relic of happier days. Each scratch and mark on its surface told a story of the life he once knew, now lost to him forever.

"Pa," Thomas whispered into the quiet, his voice filled with yearning. "I wish you were here." Outside, the wind stirred, shaking the feeble shutters against the window. "No point dwelling on it," he muttered, fighting back tears. "Got no choice but to keep going."

A sudden noise outside snapped Thomas back to reality. The loud clatter of a horse-drawn cart and the shouts of vendors signaled the city's awakening. Thomas sighed, rising from the floor, his muscles stiff and sore from the cold, hard ground. He surveyed the dimly lit warehouse. Their few possessions lay in a corner: threadbare blankets, a chipped cup, and a battered kettle. These were their meager belongings, all they had to call their own.

Thomas walked softly, careful not to wake the others. He slid into his worn-out clogs and draped his threadbare coat over his shoulders. Stepping out into the narrow alley, the chill nipped at his cheeks. The city unfolded before him, a labyrinth of shadowed paths and bustling streets. Despite its hardships, it was familiar ground, every nook and cranny etched into his young soul. By now, he knew the routine well: steal or starve, cheat or be cheated. This unforgiving code ruled the lives of the forgotten and forsaken.

As he wove through the winding streets, memories of

his parents flooded his mind. He clung to those precious moments, using them as a shield against the harshness of his reality. They were a reminder of what he had lost and a source of strength. No matter how difficult life became, those memories fueled his determination to survive and, one day, carve out a better life for himself.

Chapter Three

Footsteps echoed outside the squalid dwelling where Thomas and the others huddled together. It was the dead of the night. All the orphans were accounted for; none was missing. Nobody was expected at such a late hour, leaving him on edge. He hoped it was merely a drunkard lost in the alleyways or a stray cat wandering by. He struggled to control his breathing. Each breath came out in rapid, shallow puffs, visible in the frigid air of the dimly lit room. The cold fog of his exhalations mirrored the anxiety gripping his chest. He fought to stay calm.

Quietly, Thomas rose from his bed and crossed the room to where William and James slept, intent on waking them. His eyes flicked nervously toward the door at every creak and murmur from the streets outside, each sound heightening his anxiety.

"Who do ya think it is?" whispered Charlie, his eyes wide with fear.

"Hush now," Thomas whispered in a calm and steady voice. He reached out and hugged the younger boy tightly. His heart felt like it was beating a thousand times a minute, but he refused to let fear take over.

Thomas had survived countless hardships on the streets and was determined to protect those who depended on him. Emily, the only girl in the group, a bit older than Charlie, quickly tiptoed over and plopped beside him on the mattress. The floor was cold, and the mattress didn't provide much protection from it. He draped his blanket around Emily's shoulders and huddled close to her. She was cold and scared, and he wanted to protect her. She was like a little sister to him. Not long ago, he had tried to convince her to stay in one of the orphanages, but she refused. Emily insisted that Thomas and the others were her family, and family sticks together no matter what. She was right, but it didn't make life less dangerous for her on the street.

The door flew open without warning, revealing Silas Baines, one of the most menacing figures Thomas had ever encountered. His burly frame filled the doorway, casting a dark shadow across the room. Weathered and lined, his face bore deep creases that seemed to accentuate the cruelty in his cold, steel-like eyes. His attire marked him as a man who had lived a rugged and lawless life. A faded bandana was tied around his head, the fabric frayed from years of use. Once white, his loose, billowy shirt had turned a dull gray. Over it, he wore a dark waistcoat with what buttons remained mismatched. A brightly colored sash around his waist was a belt and a place to tuck a pistol. His knee-length breeches were tucked into tall, weathered leather boots, their tops folded down.

"Evenin', children," he sneered, taking slow, deliberate steps into the room. "Hope I ain't interruptin' nothin'."

Thomas swallowed hard, trying to muster courage. "What do you want with us?" he demanded.

"Ah, a brave little runt speaks," mocked Baines, his lips curling into a sinister grin. "Well, if ye must know, I've come for some recruits."

"Recruits for what? Who comes looking for recruits at this time of night?" Thomas asked, his mind racing with thoughts of what horrors could possibly await them.

"The New World, o' course," he replied. "Some workers we need, and I thought ye lot would do nicely."

Has he been watching us? How did he know we were here? Thomas wondered.

"Workers for who?" William asked.

"Ye'll find out soon enuff," Baines snickered.

A shiver ran down Thomas's spine. He had heard whispers of kidnappers who snatched orphans off the streets, selling them into servitude. The mere thought of his friends enduring such a fate was unbearable. As he scrambled to his feet, the room grew colder and darker, with shadows closing around him. His chest heaved, and every creak of the floorboards, every murmur from outside, amplified his dread. Thomas knew he had to act quickly to protect the only family he had left.

"Stay put!" Baines barked, his voice cutting through the air like a whip. "Ye move when I tell ye, boy."

Thomas clenched his fists, his nails digging into his palms. He saw Charlie and Emily trembling, but they remained still as Baines had commanded. Thomas hoped the older boys, William and James, wouldn't try anything rash. He knew they stood no chance against someone as menacing as Silas Baines. Emily gripped his hand, her fingers shaking. He reached over and pulled Charlie close, wrapping his arms around their shoulders. Charlie looked up at him, eyes wide, shining brighter than the moonlight peeking through the windows. His mind raced. He needed to stay calm and think clearly. He couldn't let Baines see any of his inner turmoil. Protecting Emily and Charlie was all that mattered.

"Good," Baines said, casting a cold, disdainful glance over the children. "Now, let's make sure ye won't cause any trouble."

Two hulking figures emerged from the shadows behind Baines as if on cue. They bore no resemblance to one another except for the malicious sneers on their lips. One had a jagged scar running from the corner of his mouth to near his eye, a testament to a life filled with violence and danger. His eyes were cold and calculating, glittering with a dangerous glint as he assessed the scene before him. The scar twisted his mouth into a permanent sneer, giving him a sinister appearance that made Thomas's skin crawl.

The other man reeked of alcohol and dirt, his clothes stained and tattered, hanging loosely off his broad frame. He looked as if he had just been dragged out of a tavern. His breath came in heavy, sour gusts that hit Thomas like a physical blow, causing him to take an involuntary step back. His hair, the color of mud, was a matted tangle of grime, and his bloodshot eyes struggled to focus, reflecting a dull, predatory hunger. His unsteady gait suggested he was no stranger to the bottle. Yet, beneath the surface, there seemed to be a sadness in his demeanor, a shadow of regret that lingered in his eyes.

Both men moved with a predator's grace, their muscles rippling under their coarse clothing as they advanced. The one with the scar cracked his knuckles, the sound echoing ominously in the confined space. He flexed his fingers, knuckles scarred and calloused from countless fights.

Thomas's heart pounded in his chest. Every instinct screamed at him to run, but there was nowhere to go. He tightened his grip on Charlie and Emily, feeling their small bodies tremble against him. The room seemed to shrink, the walls closing in as the danger approached.

"Who's this then?" Scar sneered, his voice a gravelly rumble. "Looks like we found ourselves some lost pups."

Alcohol and Dirt chuckled. "Lost pups fetch a good coin. Ain't that right, Baines?"

Baines nodded, his eyes never leaving Thomas. "They ain't just any strays. These ones be special."

Thomas swallowed hard, his mind racing. Special? What did Baines mean by that? He had to think fast and find a way to protect the children. His eyes darted around the room, searching for anything he could use as a weapon.

"Wot's goin' to 'appen to us, Tommy?" Charlie whimpered.

"I don't know, Charlie, but I'll be right by your side, and so will Jimmy and Will," Thomas replied, glancing over at the older boys. They nodded in agreement.

Thomas knew they were all brave, especially William. As the oldest of the crew, William was James's older brother, and the two had been orphans since they were little. They had been in and out of orphanages, but none had ever worked out for one reason or another. Their father loved the bottle, and he too often beat their mother. One night, he left in a drunken rage and never came home. Unable to cope with the burden, their mother couldn't take care of them anymore, leaving them to fend for themselves. William's eyes, as blue as the ocean, always hinted at sadness. But now, as Thomas looked at him, he saw uncertainty flickering. And something else—anger.

Thomas swallowed hard. He knew they were in for a tough fight, but he felt a little stronger with William and James beside him. "We stick together, no matter what," he said firmly, trying to instill confidence in the group.

William's jaw tightened. "If I don't wring 'em first," he said, his voice steady but his eyes betraying the storm of emotions inside him.

Thomas nodded, squeezing Charlie's shoulder reassuringly. "Just stay close," he whispered.

Suddenly, Baines pointed at Thomas and the others. "Bind 'em," he barked. The two men moved swiftly, grabbing the orphans one by one and binding their wrists and ankles with rough, coarse rope. The ropes bit into their skin, leaving red marks.

Emily began crying, tears streaking through the dirt on her face. Gags were shoved into their mouths, stifling their cries of pain and protest.

"Please," Thomas managed to choke out before a gag was forced between his lips. "Don't do this!"

"Quiet, boy," Baines snapped, his eyes narrowing with contempt. "Ye'll learn soon enuff that silence be golden."

An oppressive silence filled the room. Thomas looked

around at his friends, his heart racing as he strained against the tight ropes binding his wrists and ankles. Sweat trickled down his brow. The room was a whirlwind of chaos and desperation. The other orphans twisted and writhed in their restraints, trying to escape the cruel hands of their captors.

The air grew thick with tension. Every rustle of clothing, every muffled cry, seemed to amplify it. Thomas's mind raced. He had to find a way out. They all did.

William, usually so stoic, struggled violently against his bonds, his eyes blazing with fury. James, though younger, mirrored his brother's defiance, his jaw clenched tight. James's red hair, a striking contrast to his pale skin, was tousled and unkempt, and freckles dotted his cheeks and nose, giving him a deceptively innocent appearance. The fierce determination in his eyes told a different story, one of resilience and an unyielding spirit.

Emily's sobs were heartbreaking, her small frame shaking with each muffled cry. Thomas's protective instincts flared, but he was powerless, trapped by the ropes cutting into his flesh.

Baines watched them with a sneer, enjoying their suffering. "Ye think ye can escape? Think again. Ye're naught but helpless brats."

Thomas's anger surged. He couldn't let this monster break them. He glanced at William, who caught his eye and gave a barely perceptible nod. The room grew colder, the shadows longer. Time seemed to stretch, every second an eternity. Thomas's breath came in shallow gasps, his mind frantically searching for a plan. But for now, all he could do was endure. They all had to endure, biding their time, waiting for a chance. Any chance.

“Enough!” Baines barked, his voice booming like thunder, causing the room to fall silent. His menacing gaze swept over the faces of the young captives before settling on Thomas again. “Ye lot are worth naught more than the dirt beneath me boots, but ye'll serve yer purpose,” he sneered, gesturing for his men to gather the bound children.

“Get 'em on their feet! We ain't got all night!” Baines commanded, his eyes never leaving Thomas's defiant stare.

The henchmen obeyed, yanking the trembling orphans upright. As they did, Thomas stumbled forward. The rough hands of the man with the scar gripped his arm tightly, forcing him to remain standing. A storm of thoughts and emotions swirled inside his mind. Anger at the injustice of it all, sorrow for himself and his friends, and a fierce determination to resist and survive.

Baines stepped toward William, his sneer widening, hand resting on his pistol. “Ye think ye can defy me, boy? Ye're naught. Less than naught.”

William's jaw clenched. He wouldn't give Baines the satisfaction he sought. He muttered his defiance despite his mouth being gagged.

Baines's eyes narrowed as he pulled the gag away from William's mouth. “What did ye say?”

“We're more than ya think, ya old dirty fool,” William repeated, louder this time.

A cruel laugh escaped Baines's lips. “We'll see 'bout that.” He turned to his men. “Move out. Now.”

The men began to drag them towards the door.

Thomas's heart pounded as he was forced to march alongside his friends, their fates uncertain.

"Move faster!" Baines growled, shoving Thomas and the others roughly.

As they were led out into the cold night air, their breaths formed misty clouds before their faces, their frail bodies shivering from the chill. They had no thick coats, only thin clothing to protect them from the biting cold. Though winter was nearly over and spring was on the horizon, the air remained bitterly cold. Emily's teeth chattered, and Thomas's heart sank. He hated seeing her suffer. She was so small, too young to be treated this harshly. She'd been on her own, drifting in and out of orphanages, ever since her mother died shortly after her birth.

"Keep movin'!" snarled Alcohol and Dirt, shoving Thomas roughly forward. Catching a glimpse of the brute, he couldn't help but notice the sadness in his eyes.

"Please," whispered Emily, her voice barely audible from the gag in her mouth. "Where're they takin' us?"

"Shh," Thomas urged her, his eyes darting nervously. He didn't have an answer for her, but he knew letting their captors hear their concerns would do no good.

They approached a waiting carriage. Baines grunted, "In ye go!" and shoved them headfirst through the open door, slamming it shut behind them. The sound sent a shudder down Thomas's spine. Though their gags were removed, the ropes around their hands and ankles remained. It was a slight relief to speak freely again. The air inside the carriage was stifling, making it hard for them to breathe. He glanced around at his friends. They were just urchins who had once been full of laughter and dreams. Now, they were reduced to frightened shadows.

The carriage jerked forward, its wheels clattering over the uneven cobblestones, and Thomas's heart sank with every jolt. He peered through a tiny gap in the wooden panel and saw they were heading towards Ratcliffe Highway. He caught one last glimpse of the warehouse they called home before it disappeared from view. The dim glow of lanterns flickered. Long shadows danced across the buildings, making the city seem alive and menacing. They were being taken away from everything they had ever known.

The interior of the carriage was cramped. The hard wooden benches dug into their backs, and the constant jostling made it impossible to find comfort. The others huddled close, their faces pale and eyes wide with fear. Each bump and turn of the carriage only heightened their sense of impending doom.

"Oi, Tommy," whispered Charlie, his voice trembling. "Ya think we're goin' to end up like them stories—sold to the highest bidder?"

Thomas clenched his jaw and swallowed hard, feeling the heavy weight of responsibility pressing down on him. He knew he had to stay strong for the younger ones. With determination shining in his blue eyes, he looked at Charlie and said, "We won't let them win."

"Damn right, they won't," William added, anger flashing in his eyes.

"We've got to be careful and not do anything we'll regret. Baines has a pistol, and he looks like the type to use it," Thomas said, his voice barely louder than the creaking of the carriage and the clattering of the horses' hooves.

He reached out and took Charlie's tiny hand, squeezing it to reassure him. William placed a hand on Thomas's shoulder, his grip firm. "Yeah, Tom, but if they try to 'urt one of us, I'm goin' to fight. If it's between us and them, I'll do what I hav'ta do."

Emily shook her head, her eyes fierce but frustrated. "What if we can't find a way out this time?"

"Don't worry about that right now, Em," Thomas replied firmly.

"I'm with Will. I'll wring the bastards' necks if they hurt one of ya," James added.

Suddenly, the carriage hit a hole in the road, causing everyone to lurch forward. Thomas steadied Charlie, his resolve hardening. "Don't do anything rash, James. I hear ya, but we have to play it smart."

"What if this time, we don't make it?" Charlie's voice wavered, his tough exterior cracking.

"Shut up with yer whinin', all of ya," William said, anger rising. "Yer gettin' on me nerves."

The outside world passed by in a blur, but the tension was palpable inside the carriage. Minutes felt like hours as the carriage rattled on. Thomas could feel the strain in his muscles and the anticipation gnawing at him, but he refused to let it show.

"Tommy, are ya sure they won't hurt us?" Emily's small voice broke the silence.

"If they try, we scrap," Thomas said, squeezing her hand tighter.

With each passing moment, he forced himself to cling

to hope. He was determined to survive and protect those he loved like family. As the carriage carried them further into the unknown, Thomas held tightly to his friends, knowing their bond was the only thing standing between them and the cold, cruel grip of men like Silas Baines.

Chapter Four

The sudden jolt as the carriage came to a halt shook Thomas from his thoughts. He braced himself against the seat, his heart pounding in his chest. The doors swung open with a loud creak, revealing Baines and his men. Their faces were hard and cruel as shifting shadows played across them in the flickering light.

Rough hands seized the orphans, yanking them into the biting night air. The piercing cold cut through their thin garments, causing their bodies to tremble as they stumbled over the icy cobblestone streets. Snowflakes danced in the air, settling softly on the ground, creating a thick, treacherous surface. The sharp scent of rain mingled with the earthy stench of muck, filling the night as they struggled to keep their footing on the slippery stones.

The narrow street where they had been dumped, Wapping High Street, was barely lit, flanked by towering buildings that leaned in like old men whispering dark secrets. The air was thick with the smell of damp stone and decaying wood, mingling with the distant brine of the river. As they made their way toward the Wapping Docks, the faint glow of tavern lights pierced the darkness, spilling onto the cobblestones where sailors, worn out from their labors or too much drink, lay sprawled in doorways. The echo of distant laughter and coarse voices filtered through the narrow alleyways, blending with the faint creak of ships moored in the nearby docks, adding an ominous undercurrent to the already foreboding atmosphere.

Baines sneered as he loomed over them. "Get in line, ye rats," he barked. "Ye'll do as I says. Best keep that in mind if ye wanna stay breathin'."

Emily gave him a fierce look. "We got to scarper," she whispered to Thomas.

"Yer mouths, keep 'em shut," Baines snapped. "No talkin'."

Thomas felt a surge of anger. "We won't be your pawns forever," he said under his breath, low enough that only his friends could hear.

Thomas felt a hand clamp down on his shoulder, the grip like a vice. He turned to see Baines, his face twisted into a sadistic grin. "Ye think you're tough, don't ye, boy?" Baines hissed, his breath hot and foul. "Well, we'll see how long that be lastin'."

Thomas met his gaze with defiance, his heart pounding so hard he thought it might burst from his chest. "We'll do what we have to," he said, his voice steady.

Baines laughed, a harsh, mirthless sound that echoed in the street. "We'll see 'bout that. Now, move it!"

"Move it, ye rats!" shouted Scar, shoving Thomas and

the others toward their destination—an enormous ship, a dark, foreboding fortress on the water's edge at the docks. Like a hungry beast, its massive bulk seemed to devour the moonlight, casting eerie shadows on the water below.

As they stumbled forward, Emily whispered, "Tommy, what're we gon' do?"

Thomas didn't answer right away. His mind was racing, searching for a way out of this nightmare. "We'll work something out," he whispered, his voice barely audible. "Just stay close to me."

William, walking behind them, said in a low voice, "If we get split up, let's try and find each other again. Best we stick together."

Scar turned and snarled, "No talkin'!" He shoved William hard, causing him to stumble and almost fall.

Thomas's anger flared, but he swallowed it down. As they marched closer, the ship's hulking silhouette came into view, a fortress of weathered planks groaning under the weight of years and untold misery. The wood was dark, nearly black, slick with rain and sea spray, and seemed to absorb the dim light, creating an ominous silhouette against the night sky. A chill ran down Thomas's spine as he imagined the countless souls who had endured unspeakable horrors within its depths, their cries for help swallowed by the vast, indifferent ocean.

"Get up there!" barked Baines, shoving Thomas towards the gangplank. His heart thundered in his chest, but he remembered his promise to be strong for Charlie and Emily. He glanced at William and Jack and gave them a reassuring nod.

"Take a gander at this, mates," called James, a forced cheer in his voice. "We're about to sail."

"Keep quiet," growled Scar, giving James a rough shove.

Thomas clenched his teeth. A storm of anger and resentment swirled beneath his calm exterior. Each step up the gangplank felt like a march toward his doom. The smell of salt grew more pungent, filling his nostrils and stinging his eyes. When he finally reached the deck, the River Thames stretched before them, dark and unwelcoming. The ship creaked and groaned, swaying on the waves like a living beast preparing to swallow them whole. The deck was a flurry of activity: sailors coiled ropes, secured supplies, and clambered up the rigging with the agility of monkeys, their muscles straining under the effort. The ship's captain stood at the helm, his weathered face stern as he barked orders, his eyes scanning the horizon with determination and wariness. The wooden planks beneath Thomas's feet were damp and slightly slippery, forcing him to move cautiously as he took in the scene around him.

"Never been on a ship before, have ye?" Alcohol and Dirt asked, noticing his wide-eyed stare.

"Only in my dreams," Thomas replied with quiet defiance, his heart racing as he gazed upon the seemingly endless horizon.

"How long ye been on yer own, lad?" the man asked with a touch of kindness.

Thomas remembered the hint of sadness in the man's eyes at the warehouse and wondered if he regretted his actions. "Not long, mister. My parents died a couple of years ago. Been on my own since then. What do you care, anyway?"

The man shifted uncomfortably, his rough exterior softening for a moment. "More than ye think, boy. More than ye think." His voice was gruff, but there was a flicker of something gentler beneath the surface. He turned away, looking over the water as if lost in thought.

Thomas studied the man's profile, noting the deep lines etched into his face and the haunted look in his eyes. There was more to this man than met the eye, and for a moment, Thomas felt a pang of pity for him. The ship rocked gently on the waves, and the rhythmic motion seemed to lull the two into a shared, uneasy silence. The deck beneath his feet felt unstable, as if the ground might give way. They were then herded toward a narrow hatchway.

"Down ye go!" barked Scar. With a sudden shove, Thomas stumbled down the narrow wooden stairs below deck. The air grew thicker as he descended, each step taking him deeper into the ship's bowels.

The dim light below deck was barely enough to see by. Thomas blinked, struggling to make sense of his surroundings. The space was cramped and foul, filled with the smell of sweat, salt, and something far worse. The floor was damp and slick, and muffled sobs and quiet prayers echoed through the darkness.

"Tommy!" Charlie's voice trembled as he called out.

"I'm right here, Charlie," Thomas answered, reaching out to find his friend. He felt a small hand grip his tightly and squeeze back, offering what little comfort he could.

They were shoved into a corner, huddling together like

frightened animals. The wooden walls seemed to close in on them, the oppressive heat making it hard to breathe. Thomas looked around at his friends, their faces pale and eyes wide with fear. Nothing could have prepared them for what they saw.

"Move faster!" growled Baines, shoving Charlie forward. The cramped space was filled with people. A foul stench of unwashed bodies hung in the air. Rows upon rows of filthy people in tattered clothes, shackled at the hands and feet, lined the walls.

"Find yerselves a spot," Baines ordered coldly. "Women to the left, men to the right. Yer goin' to be in separate areas!"

"Is this where we're stayin'?" Emily asked, her voice trembling. "I can't breathe in 'ere," she added, her eyes wide with a growing panic at the thought of being separated from Thomas in such a confined and unfamiliar place.

Thomas reached out, briefly grasping her hand and giving it a reassuring squeeze before they had to part. "It's going to be alright, Em," he whispered, trying to infuse his voice with a calm he didn't feel. "Just stay strong. We're not far apart, and I'll find a way to keep checking on you."

As Emily's eyes filled with tears, a woman noticed her distress and moved closer. She was an older figure, likely in her mid-thirties, with a matronly presence. Dressed in a simple yet sturdy dress, she exuded a quiet authority. Her strawberry blond hair was neatly pulled back, and her blue eyes, though gentle, held an unwavering resolve. With a kind, understanding smile, she introduced herself. "I'm Harriet," she said, her voice soft but carrying a strength that seemed to ground her. "I see you're finding this hard. Don't you worry, child. I'll watch over you. Let's stick together now, hm?"

Comforted by Harriet's presence, Emily nodded, managing a small, grateful smile. With one last glance at Thomas, she allowed Harriet to lead her to the women's area, feeling slightly less alone with her new protector by her side. Harriet, who had once worked as a caretaker in London, had faced her share of hardships. Her husband's sudden death had plunged her into crippling debt, and instead of debtor's prison, she had been sent into indenture.

Suddenly, the ship's hull door creaked open, and the captain descended the stairs.

"I am Captain Robert Crowe," he introduced himself, his voice booming through the cramped space. "This here is the Planter, and she's ready to set sail. Yer to mind the crew. So, be on your best behavior, or you'll be wishin' you were back where you came from."

The Captain then turned to his first mate, a stern-looking man with sun-kissed skin. "Get everyone's name and write them in the Ship's Register," Captain Crowe ordered. "We need to keep track of 'em."

The first mate nodded and began moving through the group, jotting down each name in the worn leather-bound logbook. The quill's scratch across the parchment added a somber note to the tense atmosphere.

Captain Crowe was a tall, imposing figure, standing well over six feet with broad shoulders that seemed to fill the narrow space of the ship's hull. His face was weathered, etched with deep lines that told of many battles at sea. His eyes were a piercing blue, sharp and cold like the ocean on a stormy day, and they seemed to bore into anyone who met his gaze. His hair, as dark as coal, was slicked back under a navy blue tricorn hat adorned with a single silver feather. He wore a long, deep black coat trimmed with gold braiding along the edges and cuffs. Beneath the coat, he wore a white linen shirt, slightly open at the collar. His trousers were a dark brown, tucked into knee-high black leather boots that were meticulously maintained. With his stern demeanor, Captain Crowe exuded an air of command, a sense that he was used to being obeyed without question. His presence, coupled with the authority in his voice, left no doubt that he was a force to be reckoned with on this ship.

The ship swayed with the rise and fall of the water outside. Each creak of the timbers, each whisper of the wind against the hull, reminded him that this nightmare was all too real. A flicker of light inched through the slats above, casting eerie shadows that danced like specters on the faces around him—strangers, all marked by the same fear and confusion gripping his heart. Their faces were sallow, eyes wide and searching for any sign of comfort. But there was none to be found within these walls encrusted with salt and sorrow.

There was hardly any room for Thomas and his friends to sit. The ship was packed with the wretched and the damned, all crammed together like cattle. He stepped aside, letting Charlie take a seat against the bulkhead. He leaned against the ship's side, the cold seeping through his shirt and chilling his back where it pressed against the damp wood. The planks were rough against his skin, but he welcomed the sensation. It reminded him that he was still alive, still capable of feeling something beyond the dread that threatened to consume him. Exhaustion weighed heavily on him, and he closed his eyes, letting the darkness behind his lids engulf him.

He thought about the others, especially the younger orphans. He made a silent vow, promising to survive this and do whatever was needed to protect his friends. No matter how far they took him or what trials lay ahead, he would not let this ship, this ocean, or the men who claimed dominion over his fate quench the fire that now burned within him.

The ship creaked and groaned as if protesting the weight it bore while the rumbling shouts of sailors echoed above. Thomas clenched his jaw, trying to block out the deafening roar of the waves crashing against the hull. He was too exhausted to move.

"Where are they takin' us?" whispered Charlie, his eyes filled with terror.

"America," William replied, his voice low and steady.

"The New World?" James asked.

"Will we ever see London again?" asked Charlie, his tiny hands trembling.

"I don't know," Thomas admitted. His heart constricted at the thought of never returning to their home.

William stood up from where he was sitting and moved to sit next to Thomas. He wore a brave face, but uncertainty gnawed at him deep down. Beneath his tough exterior, he was kindhearted. Even now, despite the fear of being kidnapped and taken to an unknown land, his blue eyes shone with concern.

"Tom," William said hesitantly, glancing around at the others before locking his gaze on him. "What do ya reckon our chances of survivin' this ship ride are?"

"Hard to say, Will," Thomas answered without hesitation. "Wish we were sailing on this ship under better circumstances."

They were leaving behind the familiar shores of England and plunging into a vast, uncharted abyss. Thomas braced himself against the wall of the ship's hold. His heart pounded with the rhythm of the waves as he felt the last remnants of his old life slipping away.

Chapter Five

The *Planter* unfurled its sails, the aging timbers creaking and groaning as it began its slow journey down the River Thames. The ship carefully navigated the winding river, its hull cutting through the murky waters that reflected the overcast sky above. Towering warehouses and crowded docksides slipped by, giving way to the sprawling marshlands and open fields that bordered the river. Eventually, the *Planter* would reach the English Channel, where it would face the vast, unforgiving expanse of the Atlantic Ocean.

The journey to the Atlantic took days as the ship maneuvered through the congested waters of the channel, teeming with vessels of all kinds. Majestic galleons, merchant ships laden with goods, and small fishing boats jostled for space, each carving its path through the narrow strait. The air was thick with the scent of saltwater, mingling with the smoke from the nearby ports. Seagulls circled overhead, their cries drowned out by the cacophony of sailors shouting orders and the constant creaking of wood under strain. As the *Planter* pressed onward, the familiar shores of England slowly receded into the mist, and the crew prepared themselves for the open ocean ahead.

The ship's hull groaned a low, mournful sound that echoed through the confined space. The stench was unbearable—a thick, choking haze of sweat, vomit, urine, and shit. Every breath Thomas took assaulted his senses, making his stomach churn and head spin. The ship rocked violently, intensifying his nausea and disorientation. Thomas struggled to keep his footing as the boat pitched and rolled. He felt like he might pass out any minute, and he yearned for his tattered blanket in the old warehouse where he used to live with the other orphans. The memory of that place, as grim as it had been, offered a fleeting comfort amidst the horror.

They were now on their way across the ocean, being taken to a foreign land. Thomas's mind raced with the uncertainty of their fate. He looked over at the women's area, searching for Emily. Panic gripped him when he couldn't spot her among the huddled figures. His heart pounded in his chest, each beat a desperate plea. He frantically scanned the crowded space until his eyes finally found her. She sat next to Harriet, whose arms wrapped protectively around Emily. Relief washed over him, almost making his knees buckle.

Emily's eyes were closed, her face pale and drawn, yet even in her weariness, there was a certain grace about her. Despite everything, her kindness and compassion shone through, making her one-of-a-kind. Thomas remembered how she shared her meager food with a stray cat just days before their capture. That was Emily—always thinking of others, even when she had nothing to give.

"God help us," whispered a man to his left, his voice barely audible above the groans and labored breathing of the others. He held his son close, trying to protect him from the surrounding misery. Thomas felt a pang in his chest at the sight, remembering how his father had once held him before he died in the fire that destroyed his childhood.

The ship's hold below the main deck was a chamber of horrors. Dark and poorly ventilated, with barely any light coming through, it felt like a tomb. Days passed since they were kidnapped. He knew he was headed to a life of servitude, but what that looked like was still a mystery. He wasn't sure if it was better to have been free on the streets or to be crammed below deck, shackled alongside countless others.

"Tommy," came a weak voice from beside him. He turned to see Charlie, his face pale and his body trembling with fever. Once bright and full of life, his eyes were dull, sending a shiver down his spine.

"Charlie," he whispered, moving closer to him. "Hold on. We'll get through this." He gently touched his forehead, feeling the heat radiating from his skin. He felt a sharp pang of helplessness, knowing he couldn't do much to ease his pain.

"It's hard to breathe," Charlie gasped, his chest heaving.

"Try to think about something else," Thomas said.

"Remember the stories I told you? About the beautiful gardens in London?"

"They were just stories, Tommy," Charlie replied weakly. "I don't think I'll ever see those gardens."

Thomas's heart ached as he looked at Charlie, so small and fragile. He tried to muster the strength to remain hopeful, but the oppressive stench, the relentless rocking of the ship, and the sight of his sick friend tested his resolve. A gnawing fear crept in, whispering that maybe Charlie was right—they might never escape this nightmare.

He couldn't let Charlie see his doubts. "We'll see those gardens, Charlie," Thomas insisted, his voice trembling slightly. "We'll run through the grass and smell the flowers. I promise."

Looking over, he recognized James a few places away. His red hair was matted, tangled from neglect, and streaked with grime. Tears filled his haunted eyes, tracing wet paths down his dirt-streaked cheeks.

"Damn these chains!" James choked out through his sobs, tugging at the iron shackles that bit into his ankles. The metal rattled against the wooden floor, a harsh sound that amplified the despair in the cramped hold. Since they were brought onto the ship, they had been bound by shackles, with only brief moments of freedom when allowed to use the latrine. His despair echoed through the close quarters, reverberating off the damp, rotting planks.

"We're never gettin' out of here," James continued, his voice a broken whisper. "This ship is our tomb. Look around! There's nothin' but sufferin' and misery here. And, look at Charlie—he's sick!"

"We're trapped here and goin' to be sold as servants.

That's if we make it that far," William cut in. His voice, usually steady and reassuring, was edged with a bitterness and fear that Thomas had never heard before.

Thomas felt the weight of their words pressing down on him. The rough, splintered wood of the ship's floor bit into his skin as he shifted, trying to find a more comfortable position. The cold seeped through his thin clothes, chilling him to the bone. His stomach churned, not just from the nauseating sway of the ship but from the hopelessness that threatened to consume them all. He looked at Charlie, whose petite frame was wracked with shivers. His cheeks were flushed with fever, and his breaths came in labored, wheezing gasps. The sound of his suffering pierced through the background noise of creaking wood and distant, muffled voices.

A sudden burst of anger startled Thomas. It was James. He lunged forward, fists clenched tight, his face twisted with rage. Spittle flew from his lips as he cursed their captors. "Damn 'em all to hell!" He snarled. "I'd give anythin' to be back on the streets of London, even if it meant livin' in the filth and squalor of the gutters!"

The air in the hold grew thicker, heavy with the choking stench of sweat and despair. The other captives shrank back, their eyes wide with fear and hopelessness. The dim light flickered, casting eerie shadows on the wooden walls. The ship groaned and rocked, adding to the chaos.

Thomas felt the tension rising, a wave of panic threatening to break. He took a deep breath, trying to steady his nerves as the damp, musty air filled his lungs. "James," he said, gripping his friend's shoulder. "You must calm down.

Being angry at our captors won't help us and will only worsen things. If they think we're causing trouble, they'll punish us hard. We don't want that."

"Leave me alone," James spat, pushing Thomas's hand off his shoulder. "Where's yer hope now, eh, Thomas? Look at where we are! Even if we make it outta this hellish ship, what then? We'll still be the property of some rich bloke, Tom. We'll never be free."

"Then we fight," Thomas said, his eyes fierce. "We fight for our freedom, our lives, and the lives of everyone here."

"Even if it costs us everythin'?" James challenged, his eyes narrowing.

"Especially then," Thomas replied. "It's the only way we'll ever be truly free, Jim."

James stared at Thomas, breathing hard, his chest rising and falling with his emotions. Slowly, the anger in his eyes faded. He nodded at Thomas with a determined look. "Alright, Tom. I'll try. For all of us, I'll try. We need to find a way to help Charlie."

Suddenly, the heavy door to the hold creaked open, allowing a thin beam of light to pierce the darkness. A gruff voice shattered the silence, barking commands that bounced off the damp walls. They heard something heavy being dragged across the deck above. Time seemed to stand still, except for the one time they got food each day. Moments later, a crude basket was lowered into their midst, containing only moldy bread and brackish water.

"Take yer share and be quick about it!" The rough, commanding voice cut through the stale air of the hold, dripping with contempt. It sounded like one of Baines's henchmen, Scar. He moved from person to person, unlocking their shackles and giving them brief relief from the rigid metal digging into their skin.

Like starving animals, they scrambled frantically, driven by the gnawing ache of hunger. With trembling hands, they reached for the meager provisions. The smell of the stale bread and the salty water mixed with the dank air made their hunger even more painful. Thomas grabbed a small piece of bread, his stomach churning at the damp, cold texture. He hesitated for just a second, then broke off a larger piece. Charlie needed it more. Glancing at his shivering frame, he slipped the morsel into his hand. Their eyes met, sharing a silent moment of gratitude.

"Here, drink this," Thomas said, pressing the cup of murky water to Charlie's lips. He steadied his shaking hands as he gulped down the foul liquid. His face twisted in disgust at the taste.

"Thanks," Charlie whispered hoarsely, his voice just a faint sound over the creaking ship and hushed conversations around them. "Dunno what I'd do without ya." He managed a small smile, his eyes shining with a glimmer of hope as he leaned against Thomas. To Charlie, Thomas was like a big brother, and he was grateful for his presence. He knew Thomas would look out for him, no matter what.

In an instant, the ship lurched violently, plunging everyone into chaos. The sudden movement sent the captives tumbling across the slick, weathered planks of the hold, their bodies hitting the floor with sickening thuds. Thomas gasped, fighting to regain his balance as his stomach churned against the relentless rocking of the vessel. Panic swept through the hold. Thomas clutched the rough wooden boards, his fingers digging into the grooves as he tried to steady himself. Around him, cries of pain and alarm filled the cramped space, echoing off the damp, dark walls. The ship creaked and groaned as if protesting the turbulent seas.

Most unfortunate souls on the ship were destined to be sold against their will, but some had willingly sold themselves for a chance at a new life. He remembered hearing his parents whisper about people signing indenture contracts, though he had never understood what it meant. Now, he was beginning to grasp the grim reality of it all.

Chapter Six

Weeks slipped by, and time blurred into one long haze of agony. Huddled against the damp railing on the ship's deck, Thomas shivered in his tattered clothing. The captain had them on deck five hours a day, where the wind cut through them like a knife, and the salt spray stung their eyes. Although Charlie's fever had subsided, he remained weak, his small frame leaning heavily against the railing as he struggled to regain his strength.

Thomas glanced around the deck and noticed Emily standing beside Harriet on the ship's starboard side. The two figures were huddled together, their faces pale and drawn, trying to find warmth and comfort in each other's presence. Harriet's protective arm was wrapped around Emily's shoulders, and despite the harsh conditions, a faint glimmer of determination shone in their eyes. He motioned for Emily to come over. She hesitated momentarily, then carefully crossed the swaying deck to stand beside him, with Harriet following closely behind, her watchful eyes never leaving Emily.

"Look at that!" Emily exclaimed, pointing to the ocean where sleek, gray shapes broke the water's surface.

"What do you think those are?" Thomas asked, his curiosity piqued despite their dire circumstances. The creatures seemed to dance through the waves, graceful and carefree.

"I dunno," James said, squinting at the mysterious shapes. "Never seen anythin' like that before."

Just then, Alcohol and Dirt came over, his gait unsteady but his eyes sharp. "Them's dolphins," he said, a hint of a smile on his grizzled face. "Pretty critters, ain't they? They follow ships sometimes like they're keepin' us company."

They watched in awe as the dolphins continued to play in the waves, their spirits momentarily lifted by the unexpected spectacle. The sight of the dolphins brought a tiny spark of joy to their otherwise bleak existence, a reminder that there was still beauty in the world.

As time passed, Thomas noticed the change in the air. Despite the stifling atmosphere and the constant rocking of the ship, a chill settled over the captives. Moans filled the hold, and he feared they wouldn't make it. They had already lost one passenger to thirst, and it was days before anyone noticed he was gone. The horrible smell was the only clue. Harriet alerted Captain Crowe, who had one of his crew wrap the body in a sheet and toss it overboard. The indifference reminded Thomas of how people ignored him when he begged for food on the streets. Sometimes, he wondered if life was a cruel joke.

The ship became a floating nightmare when dysentery, known among the captives as "the flux," broke out. It started slowly, with just a few people complaining of stomach cramps and frequent trips to the makeshift latrines. Soon, the cramped, filthy conditions of the ship's hold exacerbated the spread of the disease. The sounds of suffering were everywhere. People groaned and whimpered in pain, their cries punctuated by the sickening splatter of diarrhea hitting the wooden floors. The already stifling air grew even fouler, making each breath feel like inhaling poison. Flies buzzed incessantly, drawn to the filth and decay, landing on faces, food, and open sores.

Thomas's heart ached with helplessness as he watched his friends suffer. Charlie, who had just started to regain his strength, now lay listless and feverish once more, his tiny body wracked with uncontrollable shivers. Emily clung to Harriet, her eyes wide with fear, as Harriet tried to soothe her while fighting off the illness herself.

One of the older captives, his face gaunt and eyes hollow, muttered weakly, "The flux, it's got us all. We're done for." His words, though whispered, seemed to echo through the hold, a grim acknowledgment of their dire situation.

Captain Crowe and his crew showed little concern for the suffering below deck. They tossed food and water down sporadically, their faces twisted in disgust at the sight and smell of the human misery they had wrought. The sickness took its toll swiftly and mercilessly. About eight people died, their bodies becoming lifeless reminders of the cruelty of their condition. Each time, the crew would come, wrap the bodies in sheets, and unceremoniously throw them overboard. The splash of the bodies hitting the water echoed through the hold, a sound that haunted Thomas's nightmares.

Recognizing the severity of the outbreak, Captain Crowe eventually decided to bring those who weren't too sick up to the deck, hoping the fresh air might stem the spread of the disease. The healthier captives were allowed to stay on deck for hours each day, away from the foul air of the hold. Over time, this seemed to help, and the sickness dissipated among those left below. The fresh air seemed to work miracles. As the days passed, Charlie gradually regained some color, his breathing steadied, and the flicker of hope in his eyes grew stronger. One day, as if in answer to Thomas's prayers, he felt a small hand touch his arm—it was Charlie, stirring in his sleep, showing signs of improvement.

"Tommy, d'ya think it'll be better there? In that new land?" Charlie's voice was weak but hopeful, breaking the heavy silence over them.

"Charlie!" Thomas said, relief washing over him like a wave. "How are you feeling? Your fever seems to be going down." He brushed a stray lock of hair from Charlie's forehead.

"Better, I think," Charlie replied, his voice husky but steadier than before. He tried a small smile, which warmed Thomas's heart like the first rays of sunlight after a stormy night.

"Here, drink some water," Thomas urged, holding a tattered tin cup to Charlie's cracked lips. He was relieved to see signs of improvement. The feverish glaze had left

Charlie's eyes, and though still pale, his cheeks no longer burned with fever.

"Thank you, Tommy," Charlie whispered, his grip tightening around the cup.

"Never mind that now," Thomas said, brushing away a stray tear. He knew Charlie was going to survive.

"Tommy? Do you miss 'em? Yer parents?"

"Every day," Thomas said, allowing himself a moment of vulnerability. "But I know they'd want me to keep moving forward, to make something of myself. That's what I intend to do."

"Me too."

"Get some rest, Charlie. We'll need our strength for what's ahead."

A few weeks went by, and the wave of dysentery abated. The air in the hold became slightly less oppressive, and the moans grew fewer. Those who didn't survive were thrown overboard. Each splash of a body hitting the water echoed in Thomas's mind, a haunting reminder of the thin line between life and death. The survivors, though weakened and traumatized, began to show signs of recovery. Charlie's fever had finally broken, and he was starting to regain strength, though his movements were still slow and labored.

One morning, Thomas was abruptly awakened by a key turning in the lock. Baines, his face twisted into a sneer, unlocked Thomas's shackles and kicked him in the shins to rouse him fully. The pain shot up Thomas's leg, and he winced, quickly scrambling to his feet to avoid another blow.

"Get up, boy. Time to move," Baines barked, his voice a harsh rasp. "Cap'n wants you on deck."

His face was even more menacing than Thomas remembered. He wondered what happened in Baines's life that turned him into a cruel tyrant. Surely, he wasn't born that way. Maybe he was. Perhaps some people are just born mean.

Thomas and the other captives clumsily scrambled to their feet. Their limbs trembled with each movement. Endless weeks of confinement had weakened their muscles, making them stiff and uncoordinated. Just standing felt like a monumental effort, their legs shaky and unreliable. They gripped each other for support, swaying unsteadily.

"Alright, you scum, up to the top deck," Baines shouted, his voice cutting through the damp air like a whip. "There's no time for lollygagging around. Move!"

Everyone scrambled to their feet. The urgency in Baines's voice left no room for hesitation. The ship groaned and creaked as it sliced through the murky waters of its destination, its wooden hull straining against the current. The sails billowed in the breeze like the heavy breaths of a tired beast, the fabric snapping sharply with each gust of wind.

Thomas climbed the narrow steps to the top deck, the wood beneath his feet slick with seawater. He stood at the edge of the deck, his fingers gripping the weathered rail as he stared across the expanse of water. A shiver ran down his spine as he took in the sight before him: the muddy shoreline, dense forests that seemed to swallow everything in their shadows, and the haphazard cluster of buildings. It was nothing like he imagined, and it was nothing like London.

"Look at that," William said, standing beside Thomas. His voice held a mix of awe and apprehension. "We're almost there."

"Don't look like much," muttered James, his arms folded over his chest, his eyes dark with anger and mistrust. His usually cheerful demeanor had been replaced by a brooding silence since their capture.

"Maybe not," William reasoned, his tone more hopeful. "But it's our best chance at startin' anew. We can't change the past but can make the most of this opportunity."

"Opportunity? What bloody opportunity?" James snapped, stepping closer to William, his fists clenched. "We're still prisoners. Nothin's changed!"

"Stop bein' so damn negative, Jimmy!" William shot back, his patience wearing thin. "We have to believe things can get better. It's all we've got left."

"Believe?" James sneered, his face twisting in anger. "Believin' don't change facts, Will. We're gonna be worked to death or worse. You think things will be different just because we're on a new land? You're foolin' yourself!"

Thomas stepped between them, trying to diffuse the tension. "Calm down, both of you. Fighting amongst ourselves won't help."

"Stay out of this, Tommy!" James growled, shoving him aside. "I'm sick of all this false hope. We need to face reality!"

"Reality is what we make it," William said through

gritted teeth. "We can't just give up. We've survived this far, haven't we?"

James's eyes narrowed. "Maybe some of us have just been lucky. But luck runs out."

"But what if it's worse than we thought? I'm scared. What if we're separated?" Emily asked, her small frame trembling. She looked up at the older boys with wide, fearful eyes.

"Now, don't you worry about that, Emily," Harriet said, placing a reassuring hand on Emily's shoulder. "I'll do my best to make sure we stay together." She remembered her days working at an all-girls orphanage in Scotland. Emily reminded her of the girls she had cared for, and she vowed to look after her.

"Harriet's right," Thomas said, his voice steady despite his uncertainty. He looked around at the others and saw the same fear and hope in their faces.

"Remember," Harriet said, turning her gaze from the shore to the faces of the children around her, "our strength lies not in the circumstances we find ourselves in but in the bonds we share and our choices. No matter what awaits us on those shores, we have each other."

The wind picked up, rustling the leaves of the towering trees that lined the riverbank. Birds called out from the forest, their songs contrasting the grim thoughts occupying Thomas's mind. He looked at Jamestown, its wooden structures clustered together like a refuge against the wilderness. Smoke rose from chimneys, hinting at the life and activity within the settlement.

The sight before him was a blend of rustic charm and harsh reality. The wooden houses, with their thatched roofs and sturdy logs, stood resilient against the elements. Each structure seemed to tell a story of survival and determination. Some houses were weather-beaten, their timbers darkened by years of exposure, while others were newer, their wood still pale and fresh, representing the settlers' ongoing efforts to build a stable life in this new world.

The sharp, acrid smell of wood smoke mingled with the earthy aroma of freshly turned soil from nearby gardens. Occasionally, the breeze carried the faint, salty tang of the river, blending with the more pungent smells of livestock and human habitation. The marketplace was a hive of activity. Stalls were laden with various goods—brightly colored fabrics, handmade tools, and freshly harvested produce. The mingling aromas of spices and herbs added a fragrant note. Nearby, the clucking of chickens and lowing of cattle punctuated the din.

"Let's just hope it's not too awful," James grumbled, his skepticism evident.

"Even if it is," Thomas said, turning his gaze back toward Jamestown, his heart swelling with determination, "it's up to us to find a way to overcome it."

The ship moved slowly forward, the sounds of the crew preparing to dock mixing with the river's natural symphony. The gentle lapping of the James River against the hull was interspersed with the creaking of the ship's timbers and the rhythmic calls of the sailors as they maneuvered the vessel toward the dock. Thomas took a deep breath, the mingling scents of salty water and forested riverbanks filling his lungs and calming his nerves.

As they approached the bustling dock, the sight of other ships anchored along the river came into view. Some were large, with tall masts and billowing sails, while others were smaller, utilitarian vessels. Each boat was bustling with activity, crews unloading cargo and passengers, their shouts and laughter mingling with the cries of gulls circling overhead. The dock itself was a scene of organized chaos. Workers moved crates and barrels with practiced efficiency, their movements quick and sure. The air was filled with the earthy smell of wet wood and the tang of tar and rope. Vendors called out, selling fresh produce, salted fish, and other goods, their voices a lively counterpoint to the grunts of laborers and the clatter of carts on the wooden planks.

Thomas felt a mixture of awe and trepidation as the ship finally docked. Baines barked orders, his voice cutting through the noise, pushing the captives forward. The gangplank was lowered with a heavy thud, bridging the gap between the ship and the shore. He stayed close to his friends, his eyes fixed on the shore. As his feet touched solid ground for the first time in weeks, a wave of dizziness washed over him.

He looked toward Jamestown, his heart pounding with anticipation and drcad. Thc unknown loomcd bcforc him, a terrifying abyss that could swallow him whole. Yet within that darkness, he glimpsed the faint glimmer of a new beginning.

Chapter Seven

The air of Jamestown, Virginia, hit Thomas's face as the shipmasters and Silas Baines herded him and his companions off the ship. It was late May, and the warmth of the spring sun was softened by a gentle breeze carrying the scent of blooming flowers and freshly turned earth. The air was thick with humidity, clinging to their skin and making their clothes feel heavier. The sky above was a brilliant blue, dotted with fluffy white clouds drifting lazily, seemingly indifferent to the hardships unfolding below.

The Virginia countryside was in full bloom, its lush greenery vibrant and alive. The trees, adorned with fresh green leaves, swayed gently in the breeze, casting dappled shadows on the ground. The sweet scent of magnolia and honeysuckle filled the air, mingling with the earthy aroma of the moist soil. Birds chirped melodiously from their perches, and the occasional rustle in the underbrush hinted at small animals going about their day.

Thomas could hear the distant murmur of the James River, its waters glistening under the midday sun. The sound of the river was a soothing backdrop to the otherwise harsh circumstances they faced. The fields around them were a patchwork of green and brown, some already tilled and planted with the season's first crops, others still awaiting the touch of the plow.

Their wrists were bound in chains that rattled with every step, a constant reminder of their captivity. The metallic clinking echoed in the otherwise serene surroundings, contrasting the landscape's natural beauty. Fear and uncertainty gnawed at Thomas as he glanced at the others. Dread was visible on their faces, knowing their fates were now entirely out of their control.

"Move it, you scum! Faster!" Baines sneered, his voice dripping with disdain as he roughly shoved Thomas forward. His piercing eyes betrayed the satisfaction he took in his cruel task.

The shore was a chaotic scene. Men, women, and children of all ages and backgrounds huddled together, their faces etched with suffering and exhaustion. Chains rattled, and ropes dug into their flesh, binding hands and feet. Tall hardwood trees draped with moss loomed over them, the vibrant greens of pines and cedars strikingly out of place. The ground beneath Thomas's feet was soft and damp, covered with a carpet of pine needles. He found the land beautiful. Too beautiful. It seemed wrong for such a pretty place to hold such misery.

Thomas noticed other ships docked along the riverbank, their decks crowded with dark-skinned people being herded off in a similar manner. He had never seen so many people with dark skin in his life. He wondered what they were doing there, their faces mirroring his fear and confusion. Baines and the other overseers barked orders, directing the new arrivals into pens behind tall wooden slats.

Baines placed Thomas and his companions in one of the pens alongside the dark-skinned people. The pens were makeshift enclosures, their wooden walls high and imposing, offering no hope of escape. Everyone was afraid, their eyes darting around, searching for any sign of what awaited them next.

Baines scowled at them with visible disgust. "You're filthy and smellin' somethin' awful. Ain't nobody goin' to want to be around you like this. You'll get cleaned up first." He pointed to a bucket of water. "There's a bar of lye and a rag over there. Use 'em to wash up. Get cleaned up. You'll get clean clothes after."

Reluctantly, they began to strip off their dirty, ragged clothes. The lye soap was harsh and abrasive, burning as they scrubbed away the grime of their journey. The water was cold, a sharp contrast to the warm air, and the scent of the soap stung their nostrils. After they had cleaned themselves as best they could, they were handed clean clothes. The fabric was coarse but felt better than their previous rags. The change of clothes did little to alleviate their fear, but it was a small comfort in the face of uncertainty.

The dull thud of heavy boots arrived. It was Baines. His presence sent a shiver down Thomas's spine. Baines's eyes scanned the group with disdain and satisfaction, his lips curling into a cruel smile. "Time to move," he barked, his voice grating against the backdrop of the serene landscape. He unlocked the pen gate with a metallic clink, swinging it open wide. "Out, all of ya. Line up!"

Thomas and his companions hesitated, exchanging nervous glances before slowly filing out of the pen. As they stepped forward, Baines methodically locked the wrist and ankle chains back on, the cold metal biting into their skin and adding weight to their every step. Baines pushed Thomas forward roughly, his grip like iron. "Faster!" he snapped. The sensation of Baines's hands on his back made Thomas's skin crawl, but he forced himself to keep moving.

Rows of chairs surrounded a platform, each occupied by well-dressed individuals fanning themselves as they chatted and exchanged the latest gossip. In the middle of the second row, Thomas noticed a woman in a floral linen dress of yellows and blue with a large skirt and lace petticoat. A matching floral hat perched elegantly on her head. Beside her sat her husband. His jet-black hair lay flat against his head, accentuating the narrowness of his face. Long, slender sideburns extended down his cheeks, making his features appear even more angular. A hooked, hawklike nose jutted out above a wide, firm-set mouth, giving him a stern and commanding presence.

As they were herded to a large platform, Thomas felt like a lamb being led to slaughter. Hunger gnawed at his stomach, leaving him weak and lethargic.

"Please," Emily whispered, her voice trembling as she caught Thomas's gaze. "Tell me there's a way out."

Thomas wanted to assure her, to promise that they would somehow escape this nightmare, but the crushing weight of reality silenced him. Instead, he squeezed her hand, trying to convey what words could not.

Emily nodded, biting her lip to hold back the tears. "I trust you, Tommy. I don't know how much more of this I can take."

"We don't have a choice, Em. Remember all those times when you were scared on the ship or when you were sick, and everything turned out alright? Try to focus on that and try not to worry," Thomas said firmly, though his voice wavered.

James, overhearing their conversation, added, "Tom is right. We've survived this long because we've stayed together like a family. We've been through a lot together. You're stronger than you think, Emily."

"Keep moving!" Baines snarled, yanking the rope that held them together.

With each step toward the platform, the knot in Thomas's stomach tightened. The onlookers' eyes followed them, scrutinizing them like pieces of meat. A man in fine silk robes stroked his beard, eyeing Emily and Harriet with unsettling interest. A portly man with a sneer seemed to be calculating the profit he could make from James's muscular frame.

They were a pitiful sight, gaunt and malnourished from the journey. Harriet stooped over, barely able to stand. Thomas wished he could help her, but his hands were tied. Emily stood solemnly, fear in her eyes. Charlie, still sick, looked ashen. The cruelty of it all made Thomas want to scream.

"Step right up, ladies and gentlemen!" The auctioneer bellowed to the crowd. "Feast your eyes on this fine selection of servants—hardworking, strong, and capable of enduring even the harshest conditions!"

"Look at them," a woman with a parasol whispered to her husband, disgust creeping into her voice. "How could anyone bear to have such filthy creatures in their home?"

"Desperate times call for desperate measures, my dear," he replied, his gaze lingering on James and William. "We need more hands to work the fields."

These people see us as animals, he thought. He clenched his fists, anger rising within him. How could they treat human beings so callously?

"Begin the bidding!" the auctioneer shouted, slamming his gavel down.

"Two shillings for the young lass!" called out a silk-robed merchant, pointing at Emily.

"Three for that strapping lad!" countered the portly man, nodding towards James.

"Five shillings for the older woman!" someone else yelled, gesturing at Harriet. "She'll be useful if she can read and write."

Inside, Thomas was screaming. They were being sold like cattle, their futures in the hands of strangers. His heart felt crushed under the weight of despair. He told himself to stay strong, focusing on his heartbeat. *I have to get out of here. This is wrong.*

Sweat trickled down his face as he stood on the auction platform with his friends. The sun beat down mercilessly, but the cold, calculating stares from the buyers were far worse. Years on the streets of London had been terrifying, but nothing compared with this—being treated as less than human by the wealthy plantation owners.

"Five shillings for the boy with the brown hair!" a stout man in a waistcoat shouted, pointing at Thomas. His voice was tinged with excitement, like a child selecting a toy from a shop.

"Six shillings!" countered a thin woman in a bonnet, her eyes narrowing as she sized up Emily. They all stood there, trying to maintain dignity in their tattered clothes while the buyers circled like vultures.

"Seven shillings for the older woman!" chimed in another bidder, gesturing towards Harriet. Her lips were pressed tightly together, her eyes flashing with defiance. But Thomas knew that beneath her brave exterior, she too felt the fear gnawing at her insides.

The bidding droned on, each price called out like a death sentence, crushing any hope of escape. Thomas watched his friends exchange anxious glances, wondering who would be next. As the numbers climbed higher, so did the tension in the air.

"Eight shillings for the lad with the bright red hair!" a middle-aged man bellowed, pointing at Charlie. He looked back at Thomas with wide, frightened eyes, but Thomas could only manage a weak nod of encouragement.

"Nine shillings for that one at the end with the dark skin!" a woman with a parasol declared, eyeing one of the Africans closely.

"Sixty shillings," a gruff voice called out from the back of the crowd, "for all of them." The man pointed to Thomas and his friends.

Thomas's heart leaped into his throat. Could it be possible? Would they stay together? He scanned the sea of faces. Hope battled with fear over what kind of person would want all six of them. It was the burly man with the woman in the floral dress—the odd couple.

"Sixty shillings going once . . . Going twice . . ." The auctioneer paused, raising his gavel as the crowd breathed.

Thomas's gaze locked onto the man who made the bid. A cold shiver ran down his spine as the man stared at them, his dark eyes calculating and unyielding. It was as if a predator was sizing up its prey.

"Sold to Lord Reginald Blackwood!" The gavel slammed down with a loud crack, sealing their fate.

Lord Blackwood approached his new servants, casting long shadows across the dirt road. His imposing figure was a dark silhouette against the golden hues of the setting sun. His presence drained any hope they had, leaving them feeling powerless. Beside him stood Lady Constance Blackwood, quiet and demure.

"Follow me," Lord Blackwood ordered, yanking the rope that bound them. He led them away from the bustling market, his strides long and confident. The group hurried and stumbled to keep up, exchanging fearful glances. Each step from the platform felt heavier, weighed down by the knowledge that they were now bound in servitude to this man, who seemed to hold their lives in his hands.

Once they reached the edge of the market, Lord Blackwood directed them towards a large, horse-drawn cart. The wooden structure was crude but sturdy, and its wheels were already caked with mud from the journey. With a curt gesture, Blackwood signaled for them to climb in.

"Get in," he commanded, his tone allowing no room for disobedience. They scrambled into the cart one by one, the rough wood digging into their hands as they hoisted themselves up. The cart's interior was bare, offering no comfort for the long ride ahead. The horses snorted and stamped their hooves impatiently as they waited. The smell of sweat and hay filled the air, mingling with the more pungent scent of fear that clung to the new servants. Thomas took his place among the others, feeling the cart sway slightly under their combined weight.

Blackwood climbed onto the driver's seat and cracked the whip. Lady Blackwood sat beside him, silent. The horses lurched forward, the cart jolting into motion. The wheels creaked, and the rhythmic clopping of hooves on the dirt road provided a monotonous backdrop to their dread.

Their journey took them deeper into Virginia, from the chaos of the port town to rolling fields and dense forests. Towering birch trees and pines gradually gave way to vast tobacco fields, their broad green leaves shimmering like emeralds under the waning sunlight. It was a breathtaking sight, marred by the reality of the labor force tending to it. Row upon row of green fields stretched to the horizon, leaves swaying gently in the warm breeze. Thomas glanced at his friends. Emily's knuckles were white as she gripped her arm for comfort while Charlie stared blankly at the ground, lost in thought. James and William exchanged worried glances, their concern evident in their eyes.

As they entered the plantation, the scale of their new lives became apparent. Row after row of corn and other crops stretched before them, a testament to the back-breaking labor awaiting them. In the distance, men, women, and even children hunched over, harvesting with practiced hands.

"It is a lovely sight, is it not?" Lord Blackwood said, noticing Thomas's lingering gaze on the workers.

"I've never seen anything like it before," Thomas muttered through gritted teeth. He forced himself to show deference, even as his heart cried out for rebellion. His words tasted bitter, like ash in his mouth. Lord Blackwood didn't even glance his way. Thomas struggled to keep his anger in check, feeling a growing dread as the cart rumbled down the path. This was their new life, a reality he was forced to accept. He wondered what lay ahead for them.

Someone will remember us, I say, in another time, he thought, clinging to the hope that their suffering would not be in vain.

Chapter Eight

Blackwood Plantation was enormous, a sprawling testament to wealth and power. As the main house came into view, nestled among the vast fields, Thomas was stunned by its size. He'd never seen anything like it before. The two-story, Georgian-style brick structure featured stately columns, decorative moldings, and a steeply pitched roof with chimneys at each end. A meticulously manicured garden surrounded the home, its vibrant blooms adding color to the landscaped grounds. The sheer majesty of the home commanded attention from afar. Thomas squinted against the sun, taking in what was now his new home.

The size of the plantation filled him with both awe and fear. Beyond the main house and the servants' cabins were tobacco barns, a butchery, a smokehouse, a separate kitchen, a dairy, stables, carriage houses, and a laundry. All of these were for the use of servants whom Lord Blackwood owned.

The horse-drawn wagon suddenly halted, jolting Thomas and the others. With a curt nod, Lord Blackwood signaled for them to disembark. Thomas's legs trembled beneath him as they stepped onto the ground. The weeks at sea had left him utterly exhausted, hungry, and weak from malnutrition. The promise of rest and a warm meal felt like a distant dream.

As they disembarked from the wagon, a man with a commanding presence approached them. He was tall and broad-shouldered, his face weathered by the sun and marked by lines of authority. His dark brown hair was combed back meticulously, and his eyes, the color of dirt, scanned the new arrivals with a stern and intimidating gaze. He wore a long-sleeved white linen shirt, brown trousers, leather boots, and a wide-brimmed hat.

"You two," he pointed at Harriet and Emily, "you'll be workin' in the main house." Then he gestured to Thomas and the other boys. "You four will be in the tobacco fields. I'm Mister Edmund Lawson, and I oversee things 'round here. Follow instructions, do what you're told, and we won't have no problems." He directed Harriet and Emily to follow Lady Constance into the main house, where they would be assigned their living quarters. Then, he motioned for the four boys to follow him to their quarters.

Thomas felt a tightening in his chest, as if someone were pounding on his heart. The boys trudged after the overseer toward the tiny log cabin that would become their quarters. With each step, his old life seemed to slip further away, replaced by this strange new world. It felt like walking toward an abyss. He recalled how his neighbors spoke of the New World, filled with dreams of freedom.

But now, it was hard to believe that freedom could come in chains.

The log cabins were a short distance from the main house yet close enough to the fields where they would work. Constructed from rough-hewn wooden planks and shingles, the cabins were small, making it hard to imagine everyone fitting inside. As they approached, Thomas noticed something else—tiny gardens near the servants' quarters, little patches of earth where vegetables grew in neat rows. A few slaves tended to them, their hands gently working the soil, while chickens clucked and pecked nearby.

"Here are yer uniforms," Lawson grunted, thrusting a set of rough, coarse garments in their hands. The clothes were made from threadbare fabric, faded from repeated washing, and stained with sweat and dirt. The tunics were simple and loose-fitting, paired with equally worn trousers that had been patched in several places. The shirts had no collars, and the trousers were cinched with frayed rope instead of belts.

"Thank you, sir," Thomas said, knowing better than to show any sign of defiance.

Lawson gave a curt nod and walked away, his heavy boots crunching on the gravel as he headed back toward the main house.

"Sir?" James echoed incredulously as the overseer turned to leave. "He ain't any better than us just 'cause he's got authority."

"You best keep that thought to yerself, mate," William warned, his eyes filled with concern. "We got to pick our fights smart-like."

"Will's right, Jimmy. We don't want to draw attention to ourselves," Thomas said.

James, still fuming over the situation, reluctantly nodded. He agreed to keep quiet but silently vowed to seek justice one day. He kicked the dirt floor, stirring up a cloud of dust that made Charlie cough. Concerned, Thomas walked over to the makeshift kitchen, filled a cup with water, and handed it to Charlie, urging him to take a sip. Charlie's pallid complexion worried everyone. Even though his fever was gone, he still wasn't back to his usual self.

As they dressed, James glanced over at Thomas, his brow furrowed in thought. "What do you reckon life will be like on this plantation? If it's anythin' like the ship, I don't think I'm ready for it."

Thomas scowled. "It'll be just as bad, if not worse, and by the look of Mr. Lawson, they'll make sure we know our place."

James's voice rose, frustration bubbling over. "It ain't right! We're treated like animals, and for what? So they can make a profit off our backs?"

Charlie, barely able to hold himself up, added with a pained edge to his voice. "Feels like we're goin' from one hell to another."

James plopped down on a rickety chair in the kitchen, his face flushed with anger. "They ain't got no right to treat us like this! Can't believe we're s'posed to be grateful for this. If they think we'll roll over and accept it, they've got another thing comin'."

Their conversation was abruptly cut short as Lawson's gruff voice echoed from outside. "You lot! Get a move on and come to the main house." The commanding tone left no room for delay or dissent.

James glanced at the others before heaving himself up from the chair. "Guess we better get goin'," he muttered, his anger still simmering as they headed toward the main house.

Thomas and his companions made their way toward the grand plantation house. Along their path, the estate revealed its daily rhythm: dairy cows meandered slowly in a nearby pasture, chickens clucked contentedly, and the occasional bray of a mule punctuated the air. In the distance, weathered barns and outbuildings loomed, their wooden frames sagging with the burden of time.

As they neared the main house, its imposing facade loomed even more formidable in the dimming light of dusk. With a blend of apprehension and awe, they trudged toward the house, their steps weighed down by anxiety. The distant chirping of crickets and the rustling of leaves heightened the tension, amplifying their growing unease as they approached the uncertain future that awaited them.

Silence enveloped the room as they stepped into the grand parlor, heavy and suffocating. The air was thick with anticipation, tinged with the faint scent of polished wood and lingering tobacco smoke. Luxurious drapes framed the tall windows, while the soft glow of oil lamps cast dancing shadows across ornately carved furniture, each piece glistening.

The group, still huddled near the entrance, gazed in awe at their opulent surroundings. Frescoes adorned the tall ceiling, depicting idyllic scenes of pastoral bliss. Thomas glanced at Emily, who stood slightly apart with a rigid posture. He knew she was frightened. She was now dressed in a servant's dress instead of her tattered street clothes. He felt a slight tinge of gratitude. Yet, despite their fresh clothing, they were still just the property of Lord Blackwood.

Suddenly, the faint rustle of silk broke the room's stillness. All eyes turned instinctively toward the ornate staircase as Lady Constance appeared. She gracefully descended the steps, each movement fluid and assured, casting a soft glow upon the room as the light caught the delicate fabric of her gown. Her dress, an exquisite creation of pale blue silk interwoven with subtle silver threads, shimmered like morning dew under the chandelier's soft luminescence. Pearls adorned her neck, each reflecting the light and mirroring the subtle strength in her poised stature.

Her hair, a cascade of golden curls, tumbled elegantly around her shoulders, softly framing her face and catching the light with every step. The lustrous strands were swept back from her face, revealing her striking features and the vivid blue of her eyes, which were as deep and stirring as the ocean. Her eyes, starkly contrasting with her gentle smile, flickered with a complex blend of emotions, hinting at a depth of sorrow that seemed at odds with the composed image she presented.

"Welcome to Blackwood Manor," she said, her voice soft and melodious. Thomas could've sworn he saw her wink at them, a moment of private camaraderie from their new master's wife. He remembered how uncomfortable she appeared as she sat among the buyers during their auction, her face etched with quiet shame.

"As you find yourselves in this new beginning," Lady Constance continued, her tone turning earnest as she paced slowly in front of the newcomers, "it is important you understand where you stand. Here, amidst these fields and within these walls, you will be asked to give much of yourselves."

She paused, her eyes scanning the room, meeting the gazes of those gathered before her. "The work is by no means light," she admitted, her voice carrying a note of regret. "The tobacco fields require diligence and resilience, and you are expected to rise with the sun and rest only when it sets. You will be provided with rations of cornmeal, salt pork, and molasses, which will be for your meals. On Sundays, work ceases at the noon hour. Time is allotted for rest and, for those inclined, prayer or quiet reflection."

"Thank you, Constance," Lord Blackwood's voice sliced through the tension like a knife, his presence filling the room with authority. His icy stare pierced the air, settling on the servants with disdain as if sizing them up like mere commodities. "Remember, you are here to discharge your debts. You are to report to our overseer, Mr. Lawson, to begin your duties tomorrow morning. Any semblance of disobedience shall meet with due correction."

Thomas's fists clenched, his knuckles white with suppressed rage. The injustice burned within him like a smoldering flame, knowing they owed no debts—they had been taken against their will. Beside him, Emily's hand quivered as it grasped his, her touch a beacon of solace in his storm of emotions. Amidst the turmoil, he clung to her warmth, drawing strength from their shared history and friendship. He looked at the others and caught Harriet's gaze; she nodded and offered him a subtle, reassuring wink.

"You must be famished," Lady Constance interjected, compassion evident in her eyes. "I shall have our chief cook conduct you to the servants' dining hall and provide you with a warm meal there."

She paused, signaling with a graceful hand towards a figure approaching from the end of the hallway. "And allow me to introduce George, our head butler, who shall be instrumental in your transition here at Blackwood Manor."

As he stepped forward, the chandeliers above cast a warm glow on his figure. George was a tall, imposing man with a confident stride that spoke of years managing the manorial intricacies. His outfit was impeccably tailored: a dark coat with sharp lines and polished brass buttons that gleamed under the soft light paired with a crisp, white waistcoat. A neatly tied cravat added to his dignified appearance.

His sandy blond hair was combed back, revealing a broad forehead and light eyes that scanned the room discerningly. Though light in color, the eyes held a depth of experience and an unspoken knowledge of the many secrets concealed within the manor's walls.

"George will conduct you to the servants' dining area and help acclimate you to the workings of the estate," Lady Constance continued, her voice smooth and reassuring. "He has been with us for many years and holds the trust of every soul within these walls."

With a polite nod, George stepped forward, ready to assume his role as guide and guardian for the newcomers. He signaled for them to follow, leading them down the hallways. As Thomas walked, he marveled at the opulent decorations. Grand portraits of the Blackwood family, each capturing generations of their lineage, graced the walls. Deer antlers and mounted trophies from Lord Blackwood's hunts were prominently displayed in the study, visible even from the hallway.

Down the hall, through an arched doorway, they passed the servants' kitchen. Flames danced in a large fire where a cauldron hung, and the scent of bread wafted from a brick oven. Sacks and barrels lined one wall, while shelves sagged under the weight of pots and jars. Inside, several servants sat on makeshift stools, their foreheads glistening with sweat. They entered a small room with a wooden table and mismatched chairs—the servants' eating area. The space was hot and cramped, contrasting the elegant dining area reserved for the Blackwood family and their guests.

"Have a seat. You all look tired and hungry," George said. He surveyed the group, ensuring everyone was comfortably settled before he turned to address another member of the household staff. "Allow me a moment to introduce you to one of our esteemed cooks," he announced, signaling towards the kitchen. With a swift motion, he beckoned to a figure busy at the room's far end.

A moment later, a robust woman with a kindly demeanor approached. She wiped her hands on her apron, which was as white as the cap atop her head, her face lighting up with a welcoming smile as she neared the newcomers. "This is Henrietta, our senior cook. She will be taking good care of you this evening."

Henrietta, a warm and motherly black woman, greeted each new face with a nod, her eyes twinkling with both mirth and maternal care. "Pleased to meet y'all. We done prepared a hearty stew tonight, and I hope it bring you some comfort as you settle in," she said, her voice rich with a comforting lilt.

Thomas and the others sat down. They were exhausted and hungry and couldn't wait to eat something other than the moldy bread served far too often on the ship.

Henrietta placed bowls down in front of the newcomers. "We'll get time for meetin' and greetin' later. Eat first," Henrietta said as she ladled soup into the bowls.

The scent of herbs and cooked meat filled the air, overwhelming Thomas. He glanced at Emily and saw a smile on her face. It had been ages since they'd enjoyed anything like this. The six of them, including Harriet, eagerly devoured the flavorful stew. Charlie used a thick slice of crusty bread to soak up every last bit of the soup, ensuring no drop was wasted.

They didn't talk much during the meal; there were just some happy murmurs here and there and the familiar sound of utensils on plates. When they finished, the six friends leaned back in their chairs, full and feeling brighter after sharing a good meal.

As they rose, their chairs scraped softly against the wooden floor. Thomas glanced over at Harriet and Emily, his smile reflecting the warmth of their shared meal. "Goodnight, Harriet, Emily," he said, his voice carrying a note of reluctance to part. Harriet and Emily nodded, smiling softly as they returned the farewell. The group then went their separate ways: Harriet and Emily headed to their quarters in the main house, while Thomas and the others left to return to the small cabin that was now their new home.

That night, under the dim glow of a flickering oil lamp, Thomas lay on the straw mattress, finding scant comfort in the cramped quarters. The weight of their new reality pressed down on him like a heavy burden. Amidst the soft snores and restless shifts of his companions, Thomas allowed himself a moment of introspection. His thoughts swirled between resignation and anger, like eddies in a turbulent river. Yet, amidst the darkness, a spark of determination refused to be extinguished.

"Tomorrow is a new day," Thomas whispered into the darkness, his voice barely audible above the gentle sigh of the wind outside. With that thought, he drifted off to sleep, dreaming of a brighter future beyond the horizon.

Chapter Nine

The following day dawned clear and crisp. The cool air was a welcome relief as it filtered through the small openings in the walls of the servant's quarter, which was now his new home. Thomas awoke to the soft light of the early sun pouring in, casting gentle shadows on the floor. The fresh, clean scent of morning drifted in with the scant breeze. It was the first official morning of his new life in a world thousands of miles away from the streets of London.

His stomach growled from hunger, the emptiness gnawing at him like a persistent ache. Despite the hearty stew they had eaten the night before, the memory of the last eight weeks on the ship—weeks spent with hardly any food—left him still feeling malnourished and weak. He stood up slowly, his legs shaky and unsteady, and stumbled into the makeshift kitchen area at the far end of the shack.

The faint sounds of birds chirping and the rustle of leaves outside added a strange serenity to the morning. He rubbed his eyes and sat up, taking in the unfamiliar surroundings. As he stretched, he noticed his friends stirring about. He sat up, stretching his sore arms and legs. His muscles ached. The thin straw mattress offered little comfort, and his back protested as he swung his legs over the side of the bed.

A familiar tune filled the air as Thomas went about his morning routine. It was one of his mother's favorite songs, a melody etched into his memory from countless nights of her lullabies. The lyrics, a bittersweet reminder of his past, took him back to his childhood. He could almost feel his mother's hands tucking him into bed, her voice soothing him to sleep.

The water is wide, I cannot get o'er,
And neither have I wings to fly.
Give me a boat that can carry two,
And both shall row, my love and I.
A ship there is and she sails the sea,
She's loaded deep as deep can be,
But not so deep as the love I'm in,
I know not if I sink or swim.

The others were already busy with their morning routines. The living space was cramped—a single large room that served as a kitchen, dining area, living space, and sleeping quarters. A worn wooden table stood in the center. Against the walls were makeshift beds with straw mattresses. It wasn't the best living situation, but he reminded himself it could be worse. At least he had a bed to sleep in at night.

"Mornin', Tommy," Charlie said, interrupting Thomas from his thoughts.

Thomas reached over and patted Charlie on the shoulder. "Morning, Charlie. How did you sleep?"

"I tossed and turned all night," Charlie replied, his voice weary. Dark circles under his eyes betrayed the restless night he had endured. "Kept dreamin' about the ship and all them awful weeks we spent on it. What was that song I heard you singin', Tommy?"

"One of my Ma's favorite songs. She used to sing it to me as she tucked me into sleep at night."

"I like it. Maybe one day you can teach it to me."

"I will, Charlie. Now go on and get dressed."

Just then, a loud knock echoed through the cabin, jolting them. The door creaked open, revealing the stern face of the overseer. "Time to get to work," Lawson barked. "Henrietta's cooked some cornbread and milk for ya. Eat quickly and meet me outside in five minutes."

The four of them—Thomas, James, William, and Charlie—quickly dressed and gulped down the cornbread. As they finished breakfast, Thomas stood and stretched, feeling the pull of sore muscles. He glanced at the others, already on their feet, ready to face whatever the day would bring. They grabbed their hats and stepped outside into the morning air. The plantation was already coming to life, with workers moving about and the sounds of nature mingling with the bustle of activity. The morning light illuminated the fields, casting long shadows and highlighting the dew that clung to the grass.

Lawson stood waiting, a coiled whip wrapped on his

shoulder, his expression impatient. "Follow me," he ordered, striding away, turning on his heel.

As they walked, Lawson led them through the plantation grounds, pointing out various tasks and responsibilities. They passed workers milking cows, the rhythmic swishing sound of milk hitting the pail mingling with the lowing of the cattle. Nearby, women gathered eggs from the chicken coop, their chatter blending with the clucking of the hens. Others tended to rows of vegetables in the garden, their hands moving deftly through the plants. Some workers were busy with the maintenance of equipment. Finally, they reached the fields where they would be working. Rows upon rows of young tobacco plants stretched out before them, a vast expanse of green against the rich, dark soil. Lawson stopped and turned to face them.

"Today, you'll be transplantin' these young tobacco plants out in the fields," he said, his tone making it clear he wasn't messing around. "It's tough work, but it's what you're here for."

Thomas and the others followed Lawson, shuffling toward the fields. As they walked, Thomas noticed white and black servants already working hard. The fields were a hive of activity. Men and women worked side by side, their faces set in grim determination as they completed their tasks. Thomas could hear the rustle of leaves, the clink of tools, and the low murmur of conversation carried on the breeze.

Lawson pointed to an empty spot when they reached the rows of young tobacco plants. "Stand here," he instructed. "Watch what they're doin' and copy it."

Thomas and his friends positioned themselves next to some of the seasoned workers. They watched closely as the experienced hands deftly transplanted the fragile plants into the rich soil. The process was methodical—digging small holes, gently placing the plants, covering the roots, and patting the soil down firmly. He bent down and mimicked the actions of the enslaved man beside him. His hands were initially clumsy, unused to the delicate work, but he quickly adapted.

Hours passed, and the sun was a relentless force bearing down on the vast tobacco fields. Thomas wiped the sweat from his brow with the back of his hand. His fingers were stained green from the leaves he had been transplanting since dawn. He squinted against the glare, scanning the horizon for any respite. There was none. He looked around, taking in the scene. His fellow workers, bent and weary, moved methodically through the rows of crops. Further down the field, he saw other enslaved people, faces etched with exhaustion, bodies glistening with sweat. The overseer paced on horseback, whip coiled and ready, eyes scanning for any sign of slacking.

"You're doin' it all wrong!" barked Lawson. He loomed over Thomas, his shadow engulfing everything around him. "Transplant properly, or you'll ruin the crop!"

Thomas wiped his forehead with the corner of his shirt. Sweat trickled down his neck and back. "Sorry, sir," he mumbled, trying to steady his trembling fingers. One mistake could cost him dearly. Lawson's ever-watchful gaze made it all the more difficult. There was so much to learn, and the pressure was relentless.

"Leave the boy alone," a gruff voice called nearby.

Thomas saw a tall, enslaved black boy standing up for him. He was thin but muscular, a testament to his life working the land. His skin glistened with sweat, and his hands were rough and calloused. Despite his youth, he carried himself with a quiet dignity and strength beyond his years. Not much older than Thomas, he immediately took the new servants under his wing. "He's new. Give 'em time."

Lawson spat on the ground, his eyes narrowing into slits. "Stay out of it, boy," he snarled, his voice low and dangerous. "You'll get the same if you cross me." But without another word, he turned on his heel and stalked away. Thomas breathed a sigh of relief, grateful for the intervention.

"Thank you," Thomas said quietly, wiping the sweat from his brow with the back of his hand. He felt a mixture of gratitude and embarrassment, not wanting to appear weak in front of the others.

The boy nodded, offering a small, comforting smile. "You welcome. Name's Elijah. We all been where you standin' now. It gets easier, I promise." He extended a hand to Thomas, helping him to his feet. "Come on, I'll show you how we do things 'round here."

"Nice to meet you, Elijah. I'm Thomas," Thomas responded.

Thomas followed Elijah through the fields. The land stretched out in every direction, a patchwork of green and brown. Workers moved among the rows of crops. It seemed as if hundreds of people were out there in the fields. Thomas couldn't imagine a world where hundreds of people were enslaved, but that was his new reality.

"Elijah, why did you stick up for me?" Thomas asked.

Elijah shrugged, his expression thoughtful. "We got to look out for each other. Out here, we all we got. Besides, I been in your spot before. Ain't easy bein' new and tryin' to learn all this."

Thomas nodded. The kindness was unexpected but deeply appreciated. "I'm just trying to keep up," he admitted. "It's all so different from what I'm used to."

Elijah chuckled. "You'll catch on soon enough. Just mind ya pace and keep ya head straight. And don't let Mr. Lawson rattle ya none. He all bark and no bite, long as you handle ya business right."

They reached a section of the field where William and James were bent over, pulling weeds. Elijah showed Thomas how to properly hoe the soil and remove weeds without damaging the crops.

"See? Just like this," Elijah instructed, demonstrating the technique. Thomas mimicked his movements, struggling at first but gradually finding a rhythm.

"Thanks, Elijah," Thomas said, feeling more confident with each passing moment. "I appreciate your help."

"Anytime," Elijah replied, his tone sincere.

As the sun rose higher in the sky, they took a brief break in the shade of a large oak tree. The cool shade was a welcome relief, and they shared a small meal of cornbread and water.

"So, where you from, Thomas?" Elijah asked, leaning back against the tree trunk.

"London," Thomas replied, taking a sip of water. "We were on the streets, trying to survive. Then, one night, some men took us from the building where we were sleeping, put us on a ship, and then sold us once we got here."

Elijah nodded, his expression sympathetic. "I was born here, but my folks were took from Africa. It's a hard life, but you learn to get by."

Thomas felt a connection forming, a bond forged through shared hardship and mutual respect. "Do you ever think about leaving? Finding a way to be free?"

Elijah's eyes darkened, a shadow of pain crossing his face. "Every day," he admitted quietly. "But it's dangerous. Them overseers and patrollers always watchin'. You got to be careful. Just so ya know, the overseer expects us to have fifty plants transplantin' before sundown. When we harvestin' the tobacco in summer, they weigh our bags at the end of the day to make sure we hit that mark. Miss it, and there's hell to pay."

As Thomas glanced around the plantation, he saw that Elijah wasn't the only one watching their exchange. The other workers, their faces etched with exhaustion or wary curiosity, observed the newcomers. Among them was a young woman with fiery red hair that caught the sunlight like a beacon. She was in the house kitchen garden, her hands busy picking vegetables and herbs, adding vibrant greens and earthy roots to her basket. She flashed Thomas a reassuring grin, and his heart fluttered. She was beautiful, with freckles scattered across her nose and a glint of mischief in her green eyes, hinting at a spirit unbroken by their harsh circumstances.

"How ya doin', handsome," she called out, her voice tinged with humor and warmth. She removed her hat and wiped her sweat-dampened brow with her sleeve. The sight of her, so vibrant and alive despite everything, filled Thomas with admiration.

Elijah, who had been watching the exchange with a knowing smile, nudged Thomas gently. "That's Marianne. She one of the good ones," he said quietly.

The cool evening breeze brought welcome relief as dusk settled and the sun dipped below the horizon. The sky turned a deep shade of purple, dotted with the night's first stars. Thomas hurried to complete his work. He was exhausted. The overseer began to retreat. His shouts and commands faded into the background as the workers returned to their quarters.

"Thank you, Elijah," Thomas said, his voice raw with emotion. The day's labor had taken its toll, but he felt a sense of solidarity that bolstered his spirits.

Elijah clasped Thomas's shoulder. "My momma always cooks a good meal. Come on over to my cabin for supper. We's the first one on the second row."

Thomas nodded, a faint smile breaking through his tired expression. "I'd like that. It's been a long day, and a good meal sounds perfect."

Elijah grinned. "Trust me, ya won't regret it. Momma's stew is the best. We'll get ya fed an' rested."

Thomas turned to James, William, and Charlie, who were finishing up their work nearby. "Hey, you lads up for a good meal at Elijah's cabin?"

James wiped the sweat from his brow and nodded. "Sounds like just what we need. We could use a break after today, for sure."

William and Charlie nodded their agreement, their faces lighting up at the prospect of a hearty meal.

"Good," Elijah said, leading the way. "Follow me. Ya'll in for a treat."

They followed Elijah to his cabin, the sun setting and casting a warm, golden glow over the plantation. The evening air was cooler, bringing a welcome relief from the day's heat. As they approached the cabin, the comforting smell of stew wafted through the air, making their mouths water. Inside, Elijah's mother greeted them with a warm smile. "Welcome, boys. Sit down and make yourselves comfortable. Supper's almost ready."

Thomas recognized her instantly—Henrietta, the kind woman who had fed them last night in the main house. He felt a sense of relief wash over him, knowing they were in good hands.

"Henrietta," Thomas said with a smile, "I didn't know you were Elijah's mother."

Henrietta chuckled warmly. "Yes, Elijah's my boy. I'm glad y'all came. Sit down an' rest them tired bones. Y'all had a long day."

As they ate, the conversation flowed easily, the camaraderie growing stronger with each passing moment. For a little while, they could forget their worries and enjoy the company of friends and the kindness of Henrietta and Elijah.

Chapter Ten

August brought a change in weather to the plantation. The sweltering heat of the summer months gave way to a more bearable warmth, though the air remained thick with humidity. Mornings were cooler, blessed by a gentle breeze that rustled the leaves of the tall maple trees, offering a brief reprieve before the sun climbed higher. The brilliant blue sky was often dotted with fluffy white clouds that cast moving shadows over the fields. The scent of rich, tilled earth and growing crops filled the air, mingling with the sweet aroma of ripening fruit in the nearby orchards.

A few months had passed since Thomas and his friends arrived at the plantation. During that time, they learned the rhythms and demands of their new life. What began as shock and fear gradually shifted to a grim acceptance. The plantation's vastness and the sheer number of servants became part of their daily existence. Workdays were long and grueling, with little time for rest. Thomas came to realize that Virginia's economy was heavily reliant on forced labor, with the lives of many people, both black and white, bound to the relentless demands of the plantation.

Back in London, Thomas's life had been vastly different. As a street urchin, and even when he lived with his parents before they died, the concept of indentured servitude or slavery was foreign to him. In the crowded streets of London, poverty was rampant, but the struggles people like Thomas and his family faced were different. They lived on the fringes of society, scraping by through petty theft, begging, and odd jobs. The poor of London faced harsh realities, but the bound labor and ownership that defined life on the plantation was not a part of his world.

Each day, he woke up to the unrelenting demands of his new existence, where the grueling work of the plantation dictated every hour. Today was no different. The cool morning air offered little comfort as Thomas prepared for another grueling day in the fields. He quickly dressed, grabbed his usual breakfast of cornbread and milk, donned his hat, and headed to the tobacco fields. Today's task was harvesting tobacco, a laborious endeavor that marked the season. The fields stretched before him, the tobacco plants tall and lush with broad, deep green leaves. Harvesting was backbreaking work, requiring precision and stamina. Each plant had to be cut at the base, the leaves carefully handled to avoid bruising, then gathered and transported for curing.

Lawson, the overseer, was already there, his stern gaze sweeping over the workers. "It's harvest season," he barked. "We need to get those leaves in before the sun gets too high. No slackin' off. We're on a tight schedule. I'll be weighin' your bags at the end of the day. I expect each of ya to have at least seventy-five pounds in your bag."

Thomas looked at Charlie to see how he was doing. The boy had been struggling ever since they arrived at the plantation. Charlie swore that today was his birthday. He wasn't sure of the exact date of his birth, only that it fell during the hottest time of the year, which meant sometime in the summer. Thomas wanted to make sure Charlie had a good day, even if today wasn't the exact day he was born years ago in a hovel in London's East End.

Charlie's birth had been fraught with challenges. Born with eyes the color of the ocean, a striking blue that stood out even in the dim light of their hovel, his mother had been unsure if he would survive. He was born early, a tiny, fragile thing that seemed too delicate for their harsh world. His mother, unmarried and already struggling to make ends meet, faced immense pressure from her family and society. Unable to provide for him, she was forced to give him up. Thomas often wondered if she had ever thought of Charlie and if she knew about the hardships her son was now facing.

Back in London, Charlie always had a knack for making Thomas laugh. One day, while they were begging near Covent Garden, Charlie had spotted a group of well-dressed ladies exiting a carriage. With a mischievous grin, he had begun imitating their high-pitched voices and exaggerated mannerisms, much to the amusement of passersby. Even the stern coachman had cracked a smile. Thomas could still hear the laughter ringing in his ears. Today, just like in the past, Charlie seemed to be in a mischievous spirit.

Just as they were almost finished harvesting one row of tobacco, Emily came walking over from the kitchen garden. Her steps were light and purposeful, the gentle rustle of her skirt blending with the whispering leaves. Thomas looked up and noticed the hint of a smile on her lips, a rare sight that momentarily lifted the weight of the day's labor. The rich aroma of ripe tomatoes and freshly cut basil wafted from the basket as she reached them.

Charlie's eyes lit up at the sight of the fresh produce. "Blimey, that looks good," he said, his voice full of wonder. He took a deep breath, savoring the smell.

"Thought you'd like it," Emily said with a smile. She handed Charlie a small cucumber, its coolness a welcome relief against the day's lingering heat. "Happy birthday, Charlie," she added softly.

Charlie grinned and held up the cucumber like a prized possession. "Well, ain't this a fancy birthday gift! Almost better than that time I found a half-eaten apple in the trash back in London!" he joked, his eyes twinkling with mischief.

Thomas chuckled, shaking his head. "You and your treasure hunts, Charlie. You always did have a knack for finding the best scraps."

Emily's laughter rang out, light and melodic. "You boys are hopeless," she said with a playful roll of her eyes. "But I suppose a cucumber will have to do for now."

Charlie took a dramatic bite of the cucumber, chewing with exaggerated slowness. "Mmm, tastes like victory," he said, grinning from ear to ear. "Best birthday ever."

Emily punched Charlie in the arm and returned to the

garden where she was working. "Don't get too cheeky now," she teased, shaking her head.

Charlie watched her go, the mischief in his eyes softening into a look of fondness. "She always looks out for me, even when I'm bein' a right nuisance," he said, turning back to Thomas with a grin.

Just as they settled back into the picking rhythm, James walked over, his face a mask of anger. His steps were heavy, and his jaw was set tight. "What's all this muckin' about?" he growled, his eyes flashing with frustration. "We ain't got time for foolin' around."

Thomas straightened up, meeting James's glare with a steady look. "We're working, James. Just taking a break is all."

James crossed his arms over his chest, his expression hard. "We don't get breaks. You know that. We got to keep at it, or we'll catch hell."

Charlie, sensing the tension, stepped in. "We're just tryin' to get through the day. Ain't no harm in a bit of cheer, right? It's my birthday, mate. Want a cucumber? I'll trade ya for a pinch of that tobacco I know you carry around in yer pocket."

James tousled Charlie's hair, a small smile breaking his stern demeanor. "Alright, alright, you little rascal. Happy birthday, then."

The three of them laughed. But just as they began to return to their work, they overheard a commotion in another plantation area. Raised voices and heated words drifted through the air, catching their attention. Thomas glanced over, his eyes narrowing as he saw a group of slaves arguing. It looked like Elijah and William were at the center of the conflict, their voices loud and angry. Elijah's face was flushed with anger, his hands gesturing wildly, while William stood rigid, his expression equally intense. They made their way over to where William and Elijah were working. As they approached, the voices became more apparent.

"You think you's better than us, William?" Elijah spat, his eyes blazing. "Just 'cause you got some fancy ideas don't mean you can boss us around!"

William's jaw tightened, his fists clenched at his sides. "I ain't tryin' to boss no one around, Elijah. I'm just sayin' we need to work smarter."

Elijah sneered, his anger barely contained. "Work smarter? You been here a few months and think you know more than us. I been here my whole life, workin' from the time I wake up to when I go to sleep. You white indentures come here and think you better than us negroes. Well, you ain't."

William's eyes narrowed, his voice rising in frustration as he scoffed. "Better than y'all? Ain't no one better than another. Indenture? You think there's any real difference? Property is property, Elijah. You call it what you want, I guess. I'm just sayin' we need to work smarter, and here you are gettin' all worked up about it!"

Before Elijah could respond, the sound of hooves thundered towards them. Lawson appeared on his horse, his face twisted in anger. He cracked his whip in the air, the sharp sound slicing through the tension.

"Get back to work!" Lawson bellowed, his eyes glaring down at them. "Ain't no time for fightin'! You lot think this is a social club? Move it!"

The sharp crack of Lawson's whip cut through the humid air, scattering the workers back to their tasks. The tension between Elijah and William simmered, replaced by the urgency to avoid the overseer's wrath. The afternoon sun dipped lower, casting long shadows over the fields as they toiled silently, each retreating into their thoughts. Thomas found a moment to approach Elijah. He could still see the frustration etched on his friend's face, the weight of the day's argument lingering in the air.

"Elijah, can we talk for a moment?" Thomas asked, his voice low and careful. He didn't want to draw Lawson's attention.

Elijah looked up, his eyes still blazing with residual anger but softened slightly at Thomas's approach. "What is it?"

"I just wanted to smooth things over between you and William. It's tough enough out here without us fighting amongst ourselves," Thomas began, carefully choosing his words.

Elijah sighed, running a hand over his face. "It ain't 'bout William, not really. It's this whole situation. Bein' a slave. . . it eats at ya every day."

Thomas nodded, his expression empathetic. "I understand. It's a hard life, harder than anything we knew back in London. But what's got you so riled up today? More than usual, I mean."

Elijah's jaw clenched. "Blackwood done sold one of my friends this mornin'. He was a good man and a hard worker. And just like that, he gone. Taken from his family, from everythin' he knows. It's like we ain't even people to them. Just property to be bought and sold."

Thomas's heart ached at the pain in Elijah's voice. "I'm sorry, Elijah. It's not right, what they do to us. It's inhuman."

Elijah shook his head, his frustration evident. "Every time I start to think maybe we can make it through, somethin' like this happens. It's like they remindin' us we ain't got no control over our own lives."

As the sun finally began to set, casting a golden hue over the fields, they gathered their tobacco bags and shuffled towards the old barn. The weight of the day's labor hung heavily on their shoulders as they prepared to have their harvest weighed, ensuring they each met their quota. Once done with the weighing, they made their way toward Elijah's cabin, where the promise of a small celebration awaited them. The warm, inviting light from the cabin's wall opening made Thomas smile. He knew the night was important to Charlie. Inside, Henrietta bustled about, her warm smile and twinkling eyes greeting them as they entered. A few minutes later, Emily and Harriet arrived from the main house. Emily cradled a small package under her arm.

Charlie's eyes were wide with excitement as they gathered around the table. The sweet aroma of molasses cookies and hoecakes filled the air. Henrietta had gone out of her way to make this special for him, saving up extra ingredients from her work as the head cook at the main house. Every crumb and every spoonful of molasses had been carefully hoarded over time, a testament to her love.

Henrietta set the plate before him. "Happy birthday, Charlie," she said with a smile, her voice filled with love. Emily handed Charlie a small gift, her face beaming with pride. "I knitted these for you," she said softly, watching Charlie unwrap the package to reveal a pair of warm, woolen socks.

Just then, Elijah brought out his fiddle, a grin spreading across his face. "To one more year," he said, positioning the fiddle under his chin. The lively tunes filled the cabin, and everyone joined in, dancing and singing songs in honor of Charlie.

Chapter Eleven

Christmas season arrived at Blackwood Plantation, bringing a rare sense of anticipation and bittersweet cheer among the servants. The usually quiet, melancholic air of the plantation seemed to hum with a subtle change as if even the land sensed the season's significance. For Thomas, this was his first holiday in Virginia, a time that should have been filled with warmth and celebration, now tainted by the bitter reality that he was no longer free.

The first signs of the season arrived with the crisp, biting chill in the air, a cold that seeped through the thin walls of the slave cabins and nipped at their skin. Frost clung to the bare branches of the trees, glistening like a dusting of sugar in the pale winter sun. The ground was hard beneath their feet, each step crunching on the frozen earth as they made their way to their daily tasks.

The plantation, with its sprawling, frost-covered grounds and the distant, imposing main house, felt like a world away from the bustling, chaotic streets of London where he once roamed free. Back in London, even the poorest found some semblance of cheer during Christmas. The roads were crowded with people, the air thick with the mingling scents of roasting chestnuts and the tang of coal smoke. Candles flickered in windows, and the sound of church bells rang out over rooftops. Despite the cold, the city seemed to glow with warmth from the shop windows adorned with festive decorations, the laughter of children, and the cheerful carols sung by groups on the corners. The dark, winding alleys and cramped hovels might have been bleak, but there was always a sense of life, of movement, even if it was driven by desperation.

Yet here, at Blackwood Plantation, Christmas was different. It was quieter, more subdued, and the cheer among the servants was tinged with the bitter reality of their enslavement. Though decorated with whatever greenery could be scavenged, the cabins were a far cry from London's warm hearths and bustling markets. The chill seeped into every corner, and no amount of small fires or layered clothing could keep it at bay. It was as though the cold was a physical manifestation of the emptiness that now filled his heart.

Thomas felt the sting of his new life with every breath he took. He was no longer a scrappy street urchin with the freedom to roam, hustle for a scrap of bread, and find warmth wherever he could, but he was now someone else's property. His life was dictated by the whims of a man who saw him as nothing more than a tool, a means to an end. This awareness gnawed at him, making the holiday that had once been a source of joy and comfort feel hollow and distant.

As winter set in and Christmas Day approached, Lawson assigned some of the servants the grueling task of gathering firewood for the main house. The chill in the air grew sharper by the day, and the need for warmth in the grand rooms of Blackwood Plantation became more urgent. Thomas, James, William, Charlie, and Elijah were sent into the woods, their hands stiff and aching from the cold as they felled trees from dawn until dusk, chopped the wood, and hauled it back to the plantation.

Meanwhile, Emily, Harriet, and Marianne gathered evergreens—holly, pine, and cedar—from the nearby woods. They wove them into garlands and wreaths, their fingers numb from the cold. Lady Constance, dressed in a thick, fur-lined cloak, oversaw their work with a critical eye. She walked through the main house, pointing out where each garland should be hung and how the wreaths should be placed on the doors. The main house slowly transformed under their hands, each room taking on a festive air despite the barrenness of winter. The garlands draped over the mantels, the wreaths on the doors, and the pine-wrapped banisters brought a semblance of cheer to the otherwise grand and imposing home. Lady Constance walked through the halls, nodding approvingly at their work.

A few days after gathering firewood, Thomas and Elijah were assigned to repair a fence on the north end of the property. The cold had settled deeply into the land, making the work slow and difficult. Their breath fogged in the air as they hammered nails into place, the rhythmic pounding echoing across the frost-covered fields. As they worked, they heard the crunch of footsteps approaching. Turning, they saw Lady Constance walking toward them, her thick, fur-lined cloak wrapped tightly around her against the biting wind. Her presence was unusual in this part of the plantation, and Thomas and Elijah straightened up, wary of what she might want.

"Thomas, Elijah," Lady Constance called out, her voice imbued with her station's gentle yet unmistakable authority, softened by the chill of the winter air. "I require the both of you to make haste into town. There are several provisions to be procured before Christmas festivities commence. You are to acquire one pound of flour, one pound of sugar, a bottle of sweet sherry wine, a modest portion of marzipan, a measure of cinnamon, and sugar plums. I trust you will discharge this task with due diligence and return without delay."

"Yes, my lady," Thomas replied, his voice steady as he inclined his head slightly in acknowledgment.

Lady Constance, her gaze lingering on them, nodded approvingly. "Very well," she continued, her tone as formal as ever. "Elijah," she added, reaching into the folds of her cloak and pulling out a folded piece of parchment, "you will need this for your trip." She handed Elijah a slave pass, her gloved hand brushing against his as he accepted it. It contained Elijah's name and cited the owner as Reginald Blackwood of Blackwood Plantation in Virginia. The pass requested that if the slave were found after today or heading anywhere but into town and in the direction back toward the Plantation, he be taken into custody immediately. A reward was offered.

Thomas watched the exchange, confusion flickering in his eyes. As Elijah tucked the pass carefully into his pocket, Thomas couldn't help but wonder why he hadn't been given one as well. They were both going into town, after all. Lady Constance offered no explanation, her gaze drifting away as if the matter required no further discussion.

"Return promptly, both of you," she concluded, her words leaving no room for delay or error.

Lady Constance turned, the hem of her cloak sweeping the ground as she began to walk back toward the main house. Thomas hesitated for a moment, then turned to Elijah, his brow furrowed with curiosity. "Why were you given a slave pass, Elijah?" he asked, genuine confusion in his voice. "I wasn't given one."

Elijah glanced around to ensure they were out of earshot before replying. "Thomas, us black folks got to carry a pass when we go into town for our masters. It's proof we belong to somebody, that we got permission to be out there," he explained.

Thomas's confusion deepened. "But why wasn't I given one? We're both servants here, aren't we?"

Elijah sighed, shaking his head slightly. "It ain't the same, Thomas. You's an indentured servant. That means you work for a set number of years, then you free to go. Me? I'm a slave for life, and so's my children if I ever have any. That pass is just one of the ways they keep us in our place, to remind us that we ain't ever gone be free."

Thomas felt a heavy knot of unease settle in his stomach as Elijah's words sank in. The difference between their circumstances, though they both labored on the same plantation, was stark and unsettling. The thought gnawed at him as they prepared to leave for town, a newfound understanding of the harsh realities Elijah lived with every day weighing heavily on his mind.

As Thomas and Elijah set off on their walk into town, the sky above them darkened, heavy with the promise of rain. Sure enough, within minutes, a fine drizzle began to fall, the cold droplets soaking through their worn coats and chilling them to the bone. The path before them grew slick with mud, and the snow that had gathered in patches on the ground began to melt, making their journey even more difficult. Each step was an effort, the cold seeping into their boots, the wetness clinging to their clothes and weighing them down.

Despite the harsh weather, they pressed on, heads bowed against the drizzle, their breath visible in the frosty air. The landscape around them was bleak and barren, the once vibrant fields now covered in snow, and the trees standing bare and skeletal against the gray sky. The silence of the countryside was broken only by the sound of their footsteps and the occasional call of a distant bird. After what felt like hours, their destination came into view: a small collection of buildings huddled together against the cold. The town was quiet, and the streets were mostly deserted as people sought refuge from the weather. Smoke curled from the chimneys of the houses and shops, a welcome sight that promised warmth and shelter.

They walked through the muddy streets, their feet slipping occasionally on the icy patches, until they reached Jamestown Mercantile & Supply. The wooden sign above the door creaked in the wind, and the warm glow of firelight spilled out through the windows, beckoning them inside.

As they stepped through the door, the warmth of the fire hit them like a wave, the sudden change in temperature almost dizzying after the cold of the walk. They shook off the wetness as best they could, their coats heavy and dripping, and moved closer to the fire that crackled in the large stone hearth at the back of the store. The heat was a welcome relief, and they stood there momentarily, letting it seep into their bones.

The interior of Jamestown Mercantile & Supply was a cozy, cluttered space filled with the smells of dried herbs, fresh wood, and the faint sweetness of molasses. The walls were lined with shelves that held everything from sacks of flour and sugar to bolts of fabric, jars of preserves, and barrels of dried goods. In one corner, a small selection of tools and farming equipment was stacked neatly, and in another, crates filled with bottles of wine, including the sweet sherry wine that Lady Constance had requested.

Behind the counter stood Mister Townsend, the store's proprietor. He was a tall, wiry man with graying hair and a neatly trimmed beard. His sharp and shrewd eyes softened with a smile as he recognized Elijah.

"Elijah, good to see you," Mister Townsend greeted him, his voice warm and friendly. He looked like a man who had spent a lifetime in his store, his clothes well-worn but tidy, and his hands rough from years of handling goods and stock. "What brings you into town on such a miserable day?"

"Afternoon, Mister Townsend. Lady Constance sent

us to fetch some supplies for Christmas. This here's Thomas," Elijah said as he pointed to Thomas.

Mister Townsend nodded, his expression thoughtful as he took in their wet clothes and the tired lines on their faces. "A cold day for such errands, but I suppose Christmas waits for no one." He motioned for them to follow him as he began gathering the items on their list, his movements efficient and practiced. "You're welcome to warm yourselves by the fire while I get everything together."

As Mister Townsend moved about the store, Thomas took the opportunity to look around. The store was a world of its own, filled with goods and luxuries that he could only have dreamed of back in London when he was a street urchin. The jars of marzipan, the bottles of wine, and the sacks of sugar and flour were far from the meager scraps he had once scavenged for on the streets. The sight of such abundance was almost overwhelming, a stark reminder of how far he was from the life he had once known.

The town of Jamestown itself was small, with buildings made of brick and wood, their windows fogged with the warmth from within. The streets were narrow and lined with cobblestones, now slick with snow and rain. The town square, visible through the store's windows, was dominated by a large, barren tree, its branches heavy with snow. Even in its simplicity, the place had a sense of history and permanence, a stark contrast to the transient life Thomas had led.

Thomas felt a strange mix of emotions as they waited for Mister Townsend to finish gathering the supplies. The store's warmth was comforting, the smells and sights almost familiar, but there was also an undercurrent of unease, a reminder that this was not his world. The life he had known was gone, replaced by this new reality he was still struggling to understand.

After warming themselves by the fire for a few minutes, Thomas and Elijah watched as Mister Townsend returned with the needed items. He carried a sturdy canvas bag filled with the requested supplies: a pound of flour, a pound of sugar, a bottle of sweet sherry wine, a small portion of marzipan wrapped carefully in wax paper, a stick of cinnamon, and a handful of sugar plums tucked into a cloth pouch.

"Here you are," Mister Townsend said, smiling, placing the bag on the counter. "That should be everything you need. Mind your step back—the roads are slick today."

Elijah nodded, grateful for the man's kindness. "Thank ya, Mister Townsend. We gon' be careful."

Thomas lifted the bag, surprised by its weight but determined not to show it. "Thank you, sir," he added.

Mister Townsend gave them a nod. "You boys, take care now and give my regards to Lady Constance."

With their farewells exchanged, Thomas and Elijah turned to leave the cozy warmth of the store. The drizzle outside had lessened, but the cold was still biting as they stepped back onto the muddy streets of Jamestown. The town, now slightly more active as the afternoon wore on, had a quiet energy. A few townsfolk passed by, wrapped in heavy cloaks and hats, their breaths visible in the cold air. The buildings, with their weathered wood and brick facades, stood as silent witnesses to the comings and goings of the townspeople. Thomas and Elijah walked side by side, their pace steady despite the slippery ground beneath them. The journey back to Blackwood Plantation felt more extended than before. The supplies were heavy, and it slowed them down. The drizzle had turned into a fine mist, coating everything with a damp sheen, making the cold seem even more penetrating.

They didn't speak much as they trudged along the path, their boots sinking into the snow. By the time they reached the plantation, the sky was beginning to darken, the gray clouds overhead thickening. They made their way to the main house. The warmth from within the house was visible through the windows. They reached the kitchen entrance, where Henrietta greeted them and took the supplies from their hands.

Christmas Day came and went, leaving behind a muted sense of relief and a brief respite from the relentless routine. Lord Blackwood and Lady Constance granted the servants a few days' rest, a rare allowance. Many chose to use it to visit family on neighboring plantations. Each one was given a set of extra clothing—a small but practical gift received with quiet gratitude.

Henrietta, always resourceful, had spent the past year squirreling away extra ingredients from the main house's kitchen. With these, she prepared a special meal for the servants. The scent of roasted meats, stewed vegetables, and freshly baked cornbread filled the air, mingling with the sweetness of molasses cakes she had carefully saved for this occasion.

As night fell, the servants gathered in one of the cabins for a Christmas service. The dim light of a few lanterns cast flickering shadows on the walls, but the voices brought the room to life. They sang songs of hope and freedom, their harmonies rising and falling like the breath of the weary yet unbroken. The melodies blended old spirituals and hymns passed down through generations, their words speaking of faith, perseverance, and a yearning for deliverance from their bondage.

Chapter Twelve

Months passed, and the harsh winter gave way to the first signs of spring. The servants labored tirelessly as the season changed, preparing the fields for the year ahead. Tobacco plants had been carefully seeded and nurtured, ensuring a promising start. As summer arrived, the fields were dotted with vibrant green tobacco plants, their leaves reaching eagerly toward the sun.

As the morning sun crept over the horizon, golden rays were cast onto the sprawling tobacco fields. The heat of the summer was relentless, settling over the plantation like a thick, suffocating blanket. The air was heavy with the scent of earth and growing plants, and the sounds of cicadas filled the morning stillness, their incessant drone a reminder of the long, hot day ahead.

Lady Constance, in her crisp morning gown adorned with intricate lace and soft, pastel hues, adjusted a vase of fresh flowers on a polished mahogany table. Her housemaids bustled around her, attending to various tasks. Emily, Harriet, and other maids meticulously mended clothes, prepared breakfast, and tidied the living quarters. Their hands moved with practiced efficiency, their eyes occasionally darting toward Lady Constance, whose gaze was sharp and discerning.

"Remember to keep the linens spotless," Lady Constance instructed, her voice smooth but carrying an undercurrent of authority. "We cannot afford to have any imperfections."

"Yes, my lady," Emily responded.

In the kitchen, Henrietta worked with a quiet determination. Bacon and eggs were sizzling in the skillet. She moved swiftly between the hearth and the table, her hands expertly stirring pots, flipping bacon, and arranging dishes. Harriet joined her, her presence a welcome addition to the bustling kitchen. She carefully kneaded the dough for the biscuits, her hands moving with practiced ease. The two women worked side by side, their actions synchronized.

Henrietta glanced at the clock on the wall, ensuring everything was timed right. Breakfast was to be served at the same time every morning. She pulled the biscuits from the oven, their crisp surfaces steaming slightly in the kitchen's cool air. The scent of fresh bread filled the room, mingling with the aroma of bacon. She placed them on a cooling rack.

Harriet glanced over at Henrietta, arranging the food on the ornate tray. "How're the biscuits comin', Henrietta? Do we still have time before breakfast?"

Henrietta wiped her hands on her apron. "About done,

Harriet. Them biscuits is out and coolin'. We on track to have everythin' ready on time, just like usual."

With breakfast prepared and the final touches complete, Harriet carefully carried the tray through the grand corridors of the plantation house. Their shoes clacking on the polished wooden floors echoed softly in the quiet halls. They approached the dining room, where Lady Constance and Lord Blackwood were already seated, engaged in a calm conversation.

Lady Constance looked up with a practiced smile. "Good morning, Harriet. Everything looks wonderful. Please set it down here."

Harriet quietly placed the tray on the table, meticulously arranging the dishes and utensils. Lord Blackwood, a tall man with a commanding presence, had a stern face softened by a few faint lines of age and wisdom. His dark eyes, set beneath a heavy brow, were momentarily cast upon Harriet, assessing her with a critical yet appreciative glance. He then returned to his conversation with Lady Constance, his posture relaxed but authoritative.

As they began their breakfast, Lady Constance took a delicate bite of biscuit, nodding in approval. "This is quite delightful, Harriet. You and Henrietta have outdone yourselves."

Harriet bowed her head slightly in acknowledgment and then turned to return to the kitchen. "Thank you, my lady," she said before hurrying back to the kitchen to help with the day's tasks.

Lady Constance smiled warmly at her husband. "Mornings like this remind me of how fortunate we are. I do appreciate the little touches that make our days more pleasant."

Lord Blackwood's expression softened, and he reached across the table to take her hand. "And I appreciate your unwavering support, Constance."

Their conversation was interrupted by an excited bark. Scout, their foxhound, burst into the room, his tail wagging furiously. He bounded over to Lord Blackwood, whose face lit up with genuine happiness.

"Ah, Scout!" Lord Blackwood exclaimed, kneeling to greet his dog. "You have come to join us, have you?"

Scout leaped into his lap, his nose nuzzling against Blackwood's face. The warmth and affection between them were palpable, and Lord Blackwood laughed heartily, his usual stern demeanor melting away in the presence of his beloved pet.

"Seems Scout is as eager for the day as we are," Lady Constance remarked with a gentle laugh, observing the lively hound with a fond smile. "He certainly possesses a talent for lifting one's spirits."

Lord Blackwood set Scout gently down and adjusted his chair. "Indeed, he does. There is something about his unwavering loyalty and boundless energy that provides a refreshing perspective."

Lady Constance took a thoughtful sip of her tip before continuing. "How fare the tobacco fields? I have received varied reports from Mister Lawson regarding their progress."

"The harvest appears to be quite promising this season. The weather has been favorable, and the fields are thriving.

I am optimistic that we shall achieve a substantial yield for export."

"That is indeed splendid news. A prosperous harvest would ensure considerable profits and elevate our standing among the other planters. Have you reached any conclusions regarding the management of this year's crop?"

"I have been contemplating an expansion of our export ventures. We have received proposals from several new markets, and should the yield meet our expectations, it could greatly augment our revenue."

Lady Constance's gaze grew distant, her thoughts turning to their upcoming journey. "I have been reflecting upon our forthcoming journey to England. It will offer a marked departure from our usual daily routine here."

"Indeed, the journey shall present an opportunity to establish new connections and, perhaps, secure advantageous contracts. It will also afford us a respite from the pressures of our daily affairs, allowing us to enjoy a measure of leisure and refinement."

After their meal, Lady Constance and Lord Blackwood stood and walked to the grand foyer. The room was beautifully decorated with polished wood and rich velvet curtains hanging from the windows. Looking through the windows, they saw the workers laboring in the fields under the sun.

Emily walked down the stairs into the main foyer, her gaze sweeping over the grand staircase and the opulent furnishings. Her nerves were evident, and she gave a somewhat clumsy curtsey to her mistress.

With a practiced smile, Lady Constance looked at Emily, giving her instructions. "Today, I need you to attend to the laundry. The basket is in the service quarters. Please ensure you clean, iron, and fold everything neatly. The linens and garments must be in perfect order by the end of the day. We cannot afford any lapses in presentation."

Emily nodded quickly, her hands clutching the edges of her apron. "Of course, my lady. I'll get right on it."

Lady Constance gave a nod of approval. "Very well. Please tell Henrietta we will be dining for lunch promptly at noon."

Her apron neatly tied and hair pinned up, Emily made her way out of the house with a basket in hand, heading towards the service quarters. The midmorning sun's heat was almost unbearable, casting a shimmering haze over the fields. The sound of the workers in the tobacco fields was a constant backdrop as she walked. As she approached the edge of the field, she spotted Thomas and Charlie bent over the tobacco plants. Their movements were steady but slowed by the oppressive heat. Thomas glanced up, catching sight of her.

"Morning, Emily!" Thomas called out, shading his eyes from the sun. "How's your day coming along?"

Emily smiled wearily and took a moment to catch her breath. "Just started, Thomas. Lady Constance has me on laundry duty today. It's so hot out here. Are y'all managin' alright?"

Thomas wiped the sweat from his brow, nodding. "We're getting by. It's rough today, hotter than usual."

Emily's brow furrowed with concern as she looked at Charlie. "You don't look too good, Charlie. Are you sure you're alright?"

Charlie waved off her concern, though his face was

pale. "I'm fine, Em. Just need a sec to catch me breath."

Emily nodded, but her worry didn't ease. "Alright, I'll be back soon. Goin' to get some water."

As she turned back toward the house, Emily focused on how she could best assist the workers enduring the sweltering heat. She quickened her pace, determined to bring some relief to Charlie and the others. In the kitchen, Emily swiftly filled a large jug with water, her hands trembling slightly with urgency. Engrossed in her tasks, Harriet looked up and gave Emily a brief, concerned glance.

"Everything alright?" Harriet asked, noting Emily's urgency.

"Got to take this water out to the field," Emily panted. "Charlie's havin' a rough time with the heat. I want to make sure he and the others get some water."

With the jug of water in hand, Emily made her way back to the field. As she reached the tobacco rows, the sight of the water was a welcome relief for the weary workers. She approached Thomas and Charlie, who toiled under the relentless sun.

"Got some water for ya," Emily said. She handed the jug to Thomas, who took it with a grateful nod. Charlie, on the other hand, looked pale and sweat-soaked.

"Thanks, Em," Thomas said, taking a long drink before passing the jug to Charlie. "You're a real help."

Charlie managed a weak smile as he drank deeply, but his face remained flushed, and his breaths came in labored gasps. Emily's concern grew as she observed him.

"You alright, Charlie?" she asked, her brow furrowed.

Charlie wiped his brow, trying to muster a reassuring

smile. "Yeah, just need a sec. It's hotter than the devil's furnace out here."

Emily watched as Charlie continued to work, but the heat was taking its toll. His movements became sluggish, and he stumbled slightly as he tried to lift a bundle of tobacco leaves.

"Charlie, you should take a break," Emily urged, her voice filled with worry. "You're lookin' worse for wear."

Thomas glanced at Charlie with concern. "Emily's right. You're not looking so good. Maybe you should rest a bit."

Charlie shook his head though his strength was waning. "I'm fine. Just need to finish this row."

Emily returned the jug to the main house and watched from afar as Charlie struggled to maintain his pace. The heat was nearly unbearable after a few hours under the relentless sun. Harvesting tobacco was grueling. The workers had to cut the mature leaves from the plants, carefully handling them to avoid damage. Each leaf was then tied into bundles and set aside to dry. The constant bending and lifting and the sweltering heat made the work exhausting.

Before long, Charlie's condition deteriorated. He leaned heavily on his cutting tool before collapsing onto the ground, his face pale and his breathing labored.

Thomas rushed to Charlie's side, his face etched with alarm. "Charlie! Are you alright?" he asked, kneeling beside him. Without waiting for a response, he sprinted toward the laundry house, where he spotted Emily immersed in her work. Panting and with his breath coming in ragged gasps, he approached her urgently."Emily!"

Thomas called out, his voice tinged with panic. "Charlie isn't doing so good. He collapsed out there in the field. We need some more water. Can you help?"

Emily's eyes widened with concern as she quickly abandoned her work. "What happened to him?" she asked, her voice trembling slightly.

"I reckon' it's the heat that got to him," Thomas said, his hands shaking.

Hearing the commotion, Harriet hurried over from where she'd been working. "I'll get a bucket of water," she said, her face pale with worry. "You two go on with that water jug, and I'll catch up with you."

Emily and Thomas dashed back to the field, their urgency mounting with each step. They reached the tobacco fields to find Charlie lying on the ground, his face ashen and sweat-soaked. Thomas knelt beside him, checking his pulse while Emily hurried to pour water over Charlie's face and offer him a drink.

Harriet arrived and knelt beside Charlie, her face lined with worry. "We need to get him cooled down and rested. This heat isn't anything to mess with."

Thomas, with grim determination, nodded. "I'll take him and place him under a tree. We need to make him comfortable and try to get him cooled down."

Carefully, Thomas laid Charlie down in the shade beneath a nearby tree. The reprieve from the sun was minimal, but it was the best they could manage. Harriet hurried towards the main house to fetch a hand fan and washcloths. As she worked quickly to retrieve the items, the overseer arrived, his face dark with displeasure. He stormed towards the scene, his gaze shifting from Thomas to the prostrate Charlie.

"What in blazes is goin' on here?" Lawson bellowed, his voice cutting through the air. "Why are ya'll not workin'? Get back to the fields!"

Thomas stood up, his face flushed with anger and frustration. "Charlie's suffering from the heat. He's in bad shape. We're trying to cool him down."

Lawson's eyes narrowed, and his hand gripped the whip. "I don't care about your excuses. We've got work to do. You're all wastin' time. Get back to it!"

Thomas's eyes blazed with defiance as he squared up to the overseer. "You can whip me if you want, but I'm not leaving Charlie here. He needs help. He's just a kid, you bastard."

Emily stepped forward, her face pale with worry. "We're tryin' to do what we can, sir. Charlie's in a bad way, and we need to keep him cool and get him to drink more water. He's fightin' for his life."

Harriet returned, breathless but determined, carrying the hand fan and washcloths. She quickly applied the cool cloths to Charlie's forehead and neck, while Thomas worked the fan to create a gentle breeze. Emily stood nearby, her hands trembling as she helped with the water and tried to provide whatever comfort she could.

The heat had taken its toll on Charlie's body. His skin was flushed and damp, and he began to moan softly, his discomfort evident. As the minutes ticked by, his condition worsened. Charlie's breathing became increasingly difficult, punctuated by harsh, ragged gasps. His body began to convulse slightly, and then he started to vomit, the result of the intense heat and dehydration. The sight of his distress was heart-wrenching.

Thomas, Harriet, and Emily worked frantically to help him. Harriet gently wiped Charlie's face with the cool cloths, trying to alleviate some of his suffering, while Thomas continued to fan him with steady, rhythmic strokes. Emily dabbed at his mouth with a damp cloth, her heart aching as she watched the scene unfold.

Despite their efforts, Charlie's condition continued to deteriorate. He was growing increasingly unresponsive. His movements became sluggish, and his eyes, once filled with life, stared blankly at the sky. The symptoms of heat stroke were taking their cruel toll: extreme fatigue, confusion, nausea, and now, unconsciousness.

Lawson's face twisted with anger, but he hesitated. The sight of Charlie's weakened state, coupled with Thomas's desperate efforts, seemed to give him pause. He glared at them, the threat of his whip hanging in the air. After a tense moment, he released an exasperated growl and turned on his heel. "Fine. But this better not affect the day's work. Get it sorted, or there will be consequences."

As Lawson turned and walked away, Thomas, Harriet, and Emily stayed close by Charlie's side, their faces marked with grim resolve. Emily kept trying to give him water, though he could not swallow. Harriet's hands trembled as she kept applying the cool cloths to his burning skin, and Thomas's frantic waving of the hand fan seemed to grow more urgent with each passing moment.

Charlie's breathing grew shallower, and his body became still. Despite their desperate efforts to revive him, it became painfully clear that he was succumbing to the heat and exhaustion. The relentless sun and his weakened state had overtaken him, and their attempts to save him grew ever more futile. It was clear that Charlie was slipping away. Finally, with a final, ragged gasp, Charlie's body went completely limp.

Thomas stood back, his eyes wide with grief and disbelief. His anguished cry broke the heavy silence, "He didn't deserve to die like this. He was just a kid."

Chapter Thirteen

It had been nearly a year since Charlie died. The year was 1772, and the winter chill gave way to spring's gentle warmth. Thomas was slowly finding his rhythm on Blackwood Plantation. The work was grueling, especially under the hot Virginia sun. Each day began just before dawn and usually ended at sundown, with rare early reprieves. He quickly learned that even if the servants did their work without complaint, there was no guarantee the overseer would show them mercy.

Since Thomas's arrival at the plantation, Baines had brought in more unfortunate souls. The quarters for the servants were now overpacked, making their already cramped living spaces even tighter. Both indentured servants and the enslaved worked the plantation, and all were treated as if their lives didn't matter.

When they weren't planting or harvesting tobacco, there were always other chores. There was never a dull moment, and work was plentiful. As time passed, Thomas got to know the other servants on the plantation. Entire families worked side by side for years. His friendship with Elijah had grown stronger, as Elijah had a knack for lightening the day. Born under Lord Blackwood's rule, Elijah's parents were enslaved before his birth, ensuring he would be bound to the same fate.

Despite these horrific circumstances, Elijah's strength and optimism inspired Thomas, especially after Charlie's death. His support and ability to find light even in the darkest moments helped Thomas cope with his grief. Elijah's laughter, jokes, and stories were always a welcome escape.

The frost had melted from the ground, and spring had breathed new life into the fields. The sun beat down on the workers as they toiled over the freshly turned soil, planting tobacco seedlings. Sweat dripped from Thomas's brow, mingling with the dust on his skin. A gentle breeze rustled through the trees, making the leaves dance in the wind. Despite the relentless strain of the work, Thomas found a certain solace in the beauty of the springtime landscape, where the promise of renewal mingled with the demands of the season.

"Another day in this hell," Thomas muttered, wiping sweat from his brow with his dirty sleeve.

"Don't talk too loud," Elijah warned, glancing around nervously. "You never know when Lawson might show up. It's like he always prowlin', lookin' for a reason to whoop us. I swear, he got ears like a fox."

"I'll never forget the screams from ole man Johnny

when they caught him after he ran away," James interjected, his voice sad.

"It's best we don't bring no attention to ourselves," Elijah added, looking around nervously. "I done felt them lashes myself 'fore you got here."

"What happened?" James asked.

"It was awful," Elijah said, his voice low. "Lawson caught me restin'. I was tired, just closed my eyes for a second. Next thing I knew, he had me tied up and lashed twenty times. Pain felt like fire on my back. I still got the scars. Ain't no mercy in this place."

Thomas's face grew somber, the memory of Charlie's death last summer weighing heavily on him. "Charlie was just a boy," he said quietly. "He died out there in the fields from the heat. I swore I'd protect him, but I couldn't save him from the sun, the work. I feel like I failed him."

James placed a hand on Thomas's shoulder, his voice soft but firm. "You didn't fail him, Tom. None of us could've changed what happened."

Thomas shook his head, the pain still fresh. "I remember asking for more water for him. He was sweating buckets, looking pale. I begged Lawson to let us take a break, just a minute to get some water. But he wouldn't hear any of it. Said we'd lose too much time and had to keep working. Charlie struggled, but we kept on, and he fell out there."

Elijah's expression hardened. "Lawson's got no mercy. He's got his demons, I reckon, and he takes 'em out on us. We know it's wrong, but there's nothin' we can do but survive."

James nodded. "We all know it's hard, Tom. But remember, Charlie would want us to keep pushin' through. He wouldn't want us to let his memory be a weight that drags us down."

Elijah's face darkened further as he spoke of his pain. "Y'all ain't the only ones who lost someone you love. When my sister was just a baby, they sold my daddy, and I ain't seen him since. Then, two years back, my lil' sister, Lucy, died from the pneumonia. Master Blackwood wouldn't bother with a doctor, and Momma tried all sorts of home-made remedies. Lady Constance did give Momma some-thin' to help her bring up the mucus, but it was too late. We lost her, and Momma cried for days on end. Lawson don't care none about our sufferin'. We just here to work, and if we drop, they'll replace us like we was never here."

Thomas looked at Elijah, his face full of sympathy. "I'm sorry to hear that, Elijah. I had no idea about your sister. Losing Charlie's been hard enough, but hearing what you went through, well, I can't even imagine."

Elijah took a deep breath and knelt, his eyes scanning for any sign of trouble. "Thomas, I seen men give up hope, and it ain't pretty. Without it, we just empty shells, waitin' for death," he said solemnly. "We gotta keep goin', no matter how hard it gets. Plus, I ain't ready to be no empty shell just yet. Got too much life in me for that."

Thomas let out a slight chuckle. "Sometimes I wonder if there's even a point to life." Thomas stared at the ground, his voice cracking with emotion. He had never felt so powerless in his life.

"Listen to me," Elijah said, touching Thomas's shoulder and locking eyes with him. "One day, we gon' be free from this place and these chains. Till then, we got to stay strong. And hey, if we stick together, maybe we can find a way to make this place a little less miserable in the meantime. Ain't nobody can take our spirit if we keep laughin' and hopin'."

As Elijah spoke, William walked over to the field where Thomas, James, and Elijah were planting seeds. The sun was high, casting a warm glow over their work.

"How y'all gettin' on with the seed plantin'?" William asked, wiping sweat from his brow with his hand.

"We're makin' progress," Elijah replied, still on his knees, his fingers deftly working the soil. "Just tryin' to keep our spirits up."

William nodded, glancing at the rows of freshly planted seeds. "Glad to hear it, mates. You mind if I give ya a hand?"

"Not at all," Thomas said, looking up. "Could use the extra help."

William picked up a small bag of seeds from the ground. "Well, if one of y'all could hand me a handful of those seeds, I'll get to plantin'. We've still got a lot of ground to cover."

James grabbed a handful of seeds and passed them over to William. "Here ya go. Appreciate the help, Will."

William took James's seeds and began to plant them. James, always ready with a quip to tease his brother, leaned against a nearby row of plants and watched.

"You know, Will," James said with a smirk, "I'm startin' to think you might enjoy this. Look at you—plantin' seeds like you're born to it."

William shot James a sideways glance, a grin playing

on his lips. "Well, I reckon I'd rather be plantin' seeds than listenin' to you complainin' all day. At least the seeds don't talk back."

James laughed. "True, but if they did, they'd probably complain about your technique. You've got the slowest plantin' method I've ever seen. I swear, you're out here movin' at a tortoise's pace."

William chuckled, shaking his head. "Oh yeah? And who was it not long ago who couldn't tell a weed from a tobacco plant? Had me fixin' up your mess more times than I can count."

James put on a mock, hurt expression. "Hey now, I was doin' my best! Besides, if you were a bit quicker, maybe I wouldn't need to make so many mistakes."

William chuckled, shaking his head. "You keep tellin' yourself that, little brother. Just don't expect any medals for your so-called 'best.'"

The sun was setting, casting a golden glow over the fields as the last seeds were carefully planted. The work was nearly done for the day, the rows of newly sown seeds stretching out before them. William and James continued their banter, the camaraderie a welcome distraction from the endless toil. However, as the evening settled in, a sudden commotion arose from the direction of the main house. Lord Blackwood appeared at the far end of the field, his imposing figure silhouetted against the fading light. His gaze was fixed intently on Thomas and the others, and the usual chill of his presence settled over the workers.

Anxiety churned in Thomas's gut, and he felt he couldn't breathe. He nudged William and whispered, "Look over there."

William followed Thomas's gaze and immediately stiffened, his eyes narrowing. "What do you think he wants?" he asked, his voice tense and cautious.

"Can't be anything good," Thomas replied, his throat tight as Blackwood approached them.

"I don't like him," James said.

"Nor I, Jim, but you got to admit that it's nice not to havin' to beg for food every day," William replied, trying to find a silver lining.

"Food ain't much better here than the scraps we got back then," James shot back, his voice laced with bitterness. "I'd rather be starvin' with some dignity than stuffin' my belly with this slop and still feel like a dog."

"You're tellin' me," James continued, his anger simmering. "Every day, we work our bones to dust, and for what? To get just enough to keep us from droppin' dead in the fields. It's like they want us weak and miserable to break our spirits."

William gave James a sympathetic look. "I hear you, but complainin' won't change much. We got to keep our heads up, if for nothin' else than our sanity."

James snorted, "Sanity? I'm done with just scrapin' by. I want more than a scrap of comfort. I want to be treated like a man, not a beast of burden. And if we're not gettin' that, then I say we don't let them think we're satisfied."

As the sun descended, Lord Blackwood approached, his steps measured, the overseer's whip draped over his arms like a sleeping serpent. Thomas felt the shadow before he saw it, a chilling contrast to the heat radiating from the earth.

"Do any of you boys possess knowledge beyond tilling

the fields and harvesting tobacco? The plantation requires an individual skilled in coopering and building tobacco barrels," Blackwood's voice rang out with commanding authority, each word a sharp jab.

Thomas lifted his gaze to meet Lord Blackwood's stern face. His eyes locked with Blackwood's, holding the gaze longer than was wise.

"Aye," Thomas replied, his voice steady despite the storm of emotions inside him. "I've got some skill with wood. My father's lessons stuck with me."

"Woodworking, is it?" Lord Blackwood's lips twisted into something that could have been a smile or a sneer. Thomas couldn't tell which and wasn't sure he wanted to.

"Taught me before he died," Thomas added. "Carving and joinery, sir."

"Woodworking," Blackwood mused, stroking his chin thoughtfully. The silence between them stretched, causing Thomas's heart to race with dread and anticipation. "Very well. Starting tomorrow, you'll work in the cooperage. It's time those hands served a purpose beyond laboring in the dirt."

Relief swept through Thomas, swift and unexpected, but he dared not show it. Escaping the fields was a rare mercy, but he was not so naïve as to believe it was purely a stroke of luck. Lord Blackwood's motives ran as deep and twisted as the roots of the old oaks around the plantation.

"Thank you, sir," Thomas murmured, bowing respectfully. In the back of his mind, he wondered if his father, wherever he might be, would feel pride about this sudden change.

As Blackwood walked away, the future spread out before Thomas like a new map—still tricky and uncertain, but now with the possibility of something more than survival.

"What does that mean, Tom?" William asked.

"I don't know for sure, but it sounds like he wants me to work on the tobacco barrels," Thomas replied.

"I heard ole Samuel, the cooper, ain't easy to work with," Elijah said. "He been been here a long while, come as an indenture 'bout seven years back. Sold hisself for a new life in these parts. Used to be a carpenter back in the Old World but couldn't find no work, so he chose to be an indenture."

"Well, I hope he isn't too bad. Besides, he can't be worse than dealing with Mister Lawson, the overseer," Thomas replied.

Elijah snorted, "The only one worse than Lawson is Lord Blackwood hisself."

"I'm starving. Let's pack up and call it a day," Thomas said, reaching over and patting Elijah. "I hope your momma is cooking hoecakes and collards again, Elijah. They're delicious."

"Me too, Tom. Me too."

As the four of them finished their work for the day, Thomas felt a surge of excitement about returning to woodworking. Yet, a pang of sadness tugged at him as he thought about being away from the others. His mind wandered to Emily and Harriet, wondering how they were doing. He hardly saw them now, except when Emily was collecting eggs on the farm. He missed her gentle presence, but she seemed happy the last time they talked. She told him Lady Constance was kind to her and Harriet, and Harriet had taught her how to wash laundry by hand and beat dust out of rugs. She seemed to be fitting in, and for that, Thomas was grateful.

Chapter Fourteen

As dawn crept across the sky, roosters announced the new day with loud crowing. Perched on the fence, they stretched their necks and let out piercing crows that echoed through the quiet morning air. The sharp, insistent sound woke everyone up. Around the farm, doors opened, and sleepy faces appeared, resigned to the early wake-up call from the farm's natural alarm clock.

With excitement and nerves, Thomas stretched and yawned as he woke up. Today marked the start of his new role in the cooperage, and he was determined not to be late. Sliding off his straw mattress, he quickly dressed in his linen shirt, work pants, and shoes. The others were still asleep, their light snores filling the room. He moved quietly around the tiny log cabin, careful not to disturb them. They had a long day in the fields ahead and needed all the rest they could get.

As he walked past the tobacco fields, the smell filled his nostrils. He thought of his father and hoped he would be proud. Pulling the toy soldier his father carved from his pocket, he whispered a secret wish that his woodworking skills could free him from bondage. He passed the garden plots where the servants grew their food and made his way down the dirt path toward the stables.

Thomas pushed open the heavy wooden door of the cooperage, the iron hinges groaning in protest. He stepped inside and was immediately hit by a symphony of sounds: hammers striking iron hoops, saws biting into timber, and the rhythmic pounding of mallets. The air was thick with the rich smell of freshly cut wood, mingling with the tang of sweat and the faint, acrid scent of smoke. Barrels in various stages of completion lined the walls, their wooden staves held together by shiny new hoops, while others lay in pieces, waiting to be assembled. Sawdust covered the floor, crunching under his shoes as he walked further in, taking in the bustling activity of the cooperage.

His eyes darted around the workshop, taking in every detail. The place was full of men, most older than him. Thomas realized he was the youngest there, and nervous tension rose, making him want to return to the fields with his friends. In the center of the room, an older man with gray streaks in his hair worked on a barrel. His skilled hands moved with the practiced precision of a master craftsman. The man's focus was intense, and the rhythmic sounds of his work seemed to set the pace for the whole workshop.

He looked up from his work. His arms were muscular, with thick veins showing beneath his dirt-streaked skin. Despite the grime and sawdust on his face, there was a kindness in his eyes. His wild mane of golden hair framed a weathered face that softened when he saw Thomas. "A bit young, ain't you, lad?" he asked.

"I might be young, but I'm eager to learn," Thomas replied. He could sense the tension in the air and the eyes of the other workers on him.

He paused, his gaze lingering on Thomas. After a moment, he nodded, "Very well, as long as you do your work, we won't have a problem. My name's Samuel. Did Lord Blackwood send you here?"

"Yessir."

"Then you know that this won't be easy, and since I'm runnin' the cooperage, you have to do what I say. I report to Lord Blackwood, and you report to me. Understood?"

Thomas nodded in agreement. Unsure of what he had gotten himself into, he knew this was a chance to learn a trade that might one day grant him an independent future.

"What's your name, boy?"

"My name is Thomas," he replied. Across the building, the other men murmured and snickered, pointing at him. Anger rose within him, but he swallowed his pride, determined to make an excellent first impression.

"Alright, Thomas, but you need to know there's more to barrel making than meets the eye. Now, follow my lead, and let's get started."

Samuel walked over to a half-finished barrel. "First thing, you need to learn how to shape the staves. See these?" He pointed to the wooden planks. "They must be tapered just right, or the barrel will leak."

Thomas nodded, watching intently.

"And don't think this is just about cuttin' wood,"

Samuel continued. "You need to feel the wood, understand it. Each piece is different. You got that?"

"Yessir," Thomas replied, trying to absorb everything.

Samuel handed him a stave and a plane. "Start with this. Smooth it out, but be careful not to take too much off. We need a snug fit."

Thomas took the tools, feeling the weight of responsibility settle on his shoulders. He set to work, aware of the eyes still on him but focused on doing his best.

"Remember," Samuel said, "patience and precision. That's the key. You rush it, and you'll ruin it. Take your time, lad."

Thomas nodded, his determination growing. "I'll do my best, sir."

"Good," Samuel replied with a slight nod. "Now, let's see what you've got."

The air in the cooperage was thick with sawdust as Thomas watched Samuel's skilled hands at work. Samuel picked a piece of straight-grained oak and explained that it was essential for making a robust and watertight barrel. Following the wood's natural curve, he carefully used an adze and drawknife to shape the stave.

Samuel lifted a curved adze. "Every barrel begins with the staves," he said.

Thomas watched intently as Samuel demonstrated how to shape and bevel oak staves. "It's been years since I carved anything," Thomas admitted, his hands itching to try the tools himself.

"Well, today's your lucky day," Samuel said with a grin. He handed Thomas the adze. "Give it a go."

Thomas took the tool and began working the wood, feeling a thrill as he carved.

"Not bad," Samuel said, nodding. He then started assembling the staves into a barrel. "See how the pieces fit together, just right?"

Thomas watched closely. "I see. It has to be precise."

"Exactly," Samuel said, slipping iron hoops over the barrel and hammering them into place. The other coopers paused their work to watch.

"Samuel, breakin' in a new pup?" a barrel-chested man with a bushy beard called out.

"That I am, John. Lad's keen to learn the cooper's trade," Samuel replied.

John strolled over and gave Thomas an appraising glance. "Eager to get those hands dirty, are ya?"

"Yes sir, very eager," Thomas replied respectfully.

"Good," John said. "But remember, it's not just about eagerness. You've got to get it right."

Samuel stepped in. "Once you have all the staves shaped, you'll need to fit them together using the iron hoops. This step is crucial. If the hoops ain't tight enough, the barrel won't hold under pressure."

Thomas felt a knot of doubt in his stomach. What if he messed it up? What if he wasn't good enough?

"Think you can handle it?" John asked, a hint of skepticism in his voice.

"I'll do my best," Thomas said, trying to sound confident.

"Your best better be good enough," Samuel warned. "We don't have time for mistakes."

Thomas nodded, the pressure weighing on him. He

picked up a hoop and started fitting it over the staves, his hands shaking slightly.

"Steady now," Samuel said, watching him closely. "Take your time, but make it tight."

Thomas carefully hammered the hoop into place.

"Not bad," Samuel said, giving a slight nod. "Keep at it."

Thomas felt a small surge of relief. Maybe he could do this after all. "Thank you, sir," he said, determined to prove himself.

"You've got a lot to learn," Samuel added, "but you've made a good start."

Thomas nodded, committing the information to memory. He felt the weight of responsibility that came with this craft. Even the slightest mistake could have enormous consequences. If the barrels were made incorrectly, the tobacco stored in them would be ruined. It was essential to be precise and careful. His first attempt assembling a barrel ended in a mess of splinters and curses. The second and third tries were no better. Each time, he picked up the pieces, studied his mistakes, and asked Samuel or one of the other coopers for help. They shared their wisdom grudgingly.

As the hours passed, Thomas's skills slowly improved. His staves aligned better, his edges became crisper, and the barrels, though still rough, began to hold together. The other coopers nodded in approval, some patting him on the back as they passed.

Across the room, a rough-looking man with years of experience and an apparent disdain for newcomers watched Thomas with a sneer. "Watch this," he muttered to a fellow cooper, picking up a misshapen stave from a pile of discarded pieces.

As Thomas reached for a new stave from the stack beside him, he stealthily swapped it with the defective one he had picked up. The flawed stave, poorly balanced and full of knots, would make it nearly impossible for Thomas to achieve a clean finish. Unaware of the switch, he began to work on the stave. His mallet strikes grew increasingly frustrated as the wood splintered under his tools.

"Need some help there, lad?" the man called out mockingly, drawing the attention of the other coopers. Some chuckled, while others shook their heads, disapproving but hesitant to intervene.

Thomas struggled with the misshapen stave, trying to make it fit. Sweat dripped down his face, and his heart pounded in his chest. The stave refused to cooperate, and Thomas could sense the man leering at him.

"Looks like you're in over your head, boy. Maybe stick to what you know, if you know anythin' at all," he said, his voice loud enough for everyone to hear. The room filled with mocking laughter. Thomas fought back tears of frustration, his vision blurring.

Samuel finally stepped forward. "Let me see that, Thomas," he said in a firm but gentle tone. Thomas handed over the stave, his hands trembling. He examined the stave, his gaze shifting knowingly towards the man. "This piece ain't fit for work," he announced. Then, turning to him, he added, "Why don't you show us how it's done, Robert, since you have such a keen eye?"

The man's smirk faded. "Sure, boss," he said, taking the

stave. But as he worked, it became clear that he struggled with the flawed piece.

Samuel's eyes never left the man. "Looks like even the best can have a hard time with bad wood," he said pointedly.

The man grunted, embarrassed but unwilling to admit defeat. "Just needs more effort," he muttered. He scowled and turned away, but Thomas could feel the tension easing slightly. He had a long way to go but was determined to prove he belonged.

The afternoon bell rang, signaling it was time for a short lunch break. The midday sun hung high, beating down mercilessly on the plantation, its relentless rays turning the dusty earth into a baking oven. Sweat dripped from Thomas's brow as he joined the other indentured servants, trudging wearily to their usual resting spots, eager for the moment of relief. He sat under the branches of a large tree. The cool shadows beneath the tree provided a fleeting comfort, a momentary escape from the sun's brutal assault. He sank onto a discarded barrel, its rough surface creaking under his weight, and pulled a chunk of stale bread from his pocket. The bread was hard and dry, but it was all he had. As he gnawed on it, the taste of dust and sweat lingering on his tongue, his eyes wandered across the field.

And then he saw her. Marianne Doyle. The young woman he had met when he first arrived at the plantation.

At that moment, Thomas forgot his aching muscles, parched throat, and even the unforgiving sun. Her grace transfixed him, especially how the light caught the delicate strands of her red hair escaping her tied bun. He knew then, as he had known since he first saw her, that he would do anything—bear any hardship, endure any pain—to steal a few brief moments in her presence. He was surprised to see her near the cooperage but felt happy at their unexpected reunion. Marianne looked equally surprised as she caught sight of Thomas across the yard.

"Thomas! I didn't expect to see you here," Marianne exclaimed, a hint of a smile on her lips.

"Nor did I expect to find you, Marianne," Thomas replied, his voice thick with exhaustion but lightened by their chance encounter. "I started work at the cooperage today."

"Ah, so you're learnin' the barrel-maker's trade." She eyed his calloused hands. "It's honest work, it is. How are you findin' it?"

"Challenging," Thomas admitted, rubbing his sore fingers. "But I'm determined to master it."

Marianne nodded, her gaze softening with empathy. "So, where are you from, Thomas?" she mused, her lilting accent weaving a thread of connection between them.

"London, over in England," he said, remembering the filth of London's slums and the agony of losing his family.

"I remember when I first came to this plantation, just a scared little girl all alone," she said.

"Just like my first days in the city after my folks died," Thomas said, his voice low and sad. "But we both made it through, didn't we?"

"Against all odds," Marianne agreed. She had a defiant smile on her face. "But I hope for somethin' better than this."

As they swapped tales of their pasts—the cold nights

against damp brick walls, the hard work that left them bruised—they found comfort in each other's words. In these shared, vulnerable moments, their bond grew stronger, quietly acknowledging the unbreakable spirit within them both.

"Time to get back to work. Lady Constance's got me cleanin' the windows today, and with this heat, it ain't gonna be easy," Marianne said as the break ended all too soon. "Hope to see you again before too long."

"See you soon, Marianne," he said, his heart fluttering. He nodded towards the cooperage, took one last look at her, and returned to his work.

Break time ended, and Thomas trudged back to the cooperage, his muscles aching with every step. The steady thud of hammers and the whir of saws welcomed him like an old friend, drowning out the voices in his head and the butterflies in his stomach. He found solace in the rhythm of his work, a bit of peace in turning rough staves into something useful.

Samuel noticed Thomas's downtrodden demeanor and clapped him on the back. "What's got you down, lad? Girl troubles?" he asked, a twinkle in his eye.

Thomas blushed and returned to work, his hammer striking the iron hoops with new energy. Samuel chuckled and walked away, but not before giving Thomas a pat on the shoulder, a rare show of camaraderie.

Hours slipped by as the sun sank below the horizon, signaling the close of another grueling day. Thomas stretched his sore back and surveyed his work. Five sturdy barrels stood in a neat row behind him, each a testament to his growing skill. He allowed himself a brief, satisfied smile. As the other coopers left the sweltering workshop, they patted his back and offered gruff words of approval. His heart swelled with pride, but the thought of a pair of emerald green eyes kept him company as he trudged back to his quarters.

Chapter Fifteen

The autumn air was pleasantly warm. Thomas sat on a stone bench beneath a peach tree, enjoying the cool breeze, which was a welcome relief after hours of working. Typically, the air smelled of tobacco, but it carried the sweet scent of jasmine tonight. In the distance, crickets chirped a soothing lullaby. His body was tired and sore, and his clothes, once neat that morning, were rumpled and dusted from sawdust from his first day as a cooper.

He couldn't stop thinking about Marianne. She wasn't just beautiful; she had a spirit he admired. Like him, she had been through tough times but never let it break her. He could see she was a fighter, and she was always laughing. The thought of seeing her again filled him with a deep sense of longing. She made him feel alive in a way he hadn't in years.

Thomas pulled the carved wooden soldier from his

pocket, reflecting on his circumstances. His father had hoped he would carry on the family's woodworking tradition, and now here he was, an indentured servant, learning the very trade his father had envisioned. The irony wasn't lost on him. He rose from the bench and went to his quarters, only to find them empty. Hearing chatter and laughter from another cabin, he stepped outside to see what was happening.

Elijah waved him over with a grin. "Hey, Thomas," he called out with a tired but warm smile. "C'mon over, we're havin' fun. Don't be shy now. Don't make me come drag ya over here like a mule!"

Thomas stumbled into Elijah's cabin, where he saw the whole family gathered. He paused, letting the rich, comforting smell of stew simmering in the pot fill his nostrils and lift his spirits.

"Evenin', Thomas," Henrietta greeted, her voice carrying a warmth despite the fatigue etched into her features. Her hair, streaked with gray, was neatly tied back in a simple, practical bun. Her dress was a deep, faded blue, with patches and repairs adding character to its fabric. Though weathered and calloused, her hands moved with practiced ease as she stirred a pot of stew hanging above the hearth.

"Evening, ma'am," Thomas replied, managing a weak smile despite being exhausted. His legs felt like lead as he dragged himself into the main room.

Inside, William, James, and Elijah were gathered around a rough-hewn table, their faces glowing in the soft flicker of candlelight. Tired smiles welcomed Thomas as he entered the warm, dimly lit room. The air was thick with the gentle murmur of conversation. Candlelight cast dancing shadows on the walls, making the small space cozy. It was like stepping into a different world, a brief escape from the day's hard work.

"How'd it go with the barrels today, Tom?" Elijah asked, his eyes full of genuine concern.

"Exhausting," Thomas said, sinking onto a stool. He rubbed his aching hands, the palms raw from handling the unfamiliar tools. "Spent the day shaping staves and fitting them into barrels. Blackwood's demanding we speed up and get more barrels done than we usually do."

"Sounds like a bloody hassle, that does," James muttered, shaking his head.

"That it is," Thomas agreed. "It's different from the fields, but I enjoy it. Reminds me of watching my Pa back in England carving wood in his workshop."

"Got blisters to show for it?" William teased.

"Plenty," Thomas chuckled, holding up his hands. They all laughed, a brief reprieve from the reality that they were bound by chains they couldn't see but felt every day.

"Least you learnin' a craft," Elijah said thoughtfully. "Better than the fields, maybe a way to earn you a livin' one day."

"Maybe," Thomas echoed, though doubt lingered in his voice. Dreams of earning his way seemed distant, like stars barely visible through a cloudy night sky.

"We all need somethin' to hold on to. Keeps us goin', even when the days is tough," Elijah replied.

"Guess so," Thomas murmured. He looked around the

room, feeling the unspoken bond among them. Each carried scars from their struggles but found strength in each other's company.

"Food's ready!" Henrietta announced, breaking the somber mood.

They hurried to the table, their stomachs growling in anticipation. As they gathered around, the soft scrape of wood on the floor accompanied the sound of chairs being pulled out. The earlier conversation settled into a comfortable hum. Thomas sank into his chair, feeling the day's exhaustion settle into his bones. Just as he reached for a piece of cornbread, a sudden burst of color flashed across his vision. His heart skipped a beat. He blinked, trying to make sense of it. He forgot his weariness for a moment, replaced by a spark of curiosity and surprise.

Marianne stepped into the room, her hair pulled back into a simple braid that tumbled gracefully over her shoulders. Her presence infused the space with a vibrant energy, making everyone pause in appreciation. Thomas sat up a little straighter, his heart quickening at the sight of her. She moved with a grace that belied the hardships she had endured. Each step was confident and poised, her eyes sparkling with life and her warm smile radiating warmth. Thomas felt a surge of admiration and a longing he couldn't quite name. She was like a breath of fresh air in a room that had grown stifling with the day's weight.

"Evenin', folks," Marianne greeted, her voice carrying a lilt that could lift the heaviest of hearts, and there was an unmistakable spark between them. She glanced at Thomas, her eyes sparkling with curiosity and warmth.

"How's the new cooper? Are you managin' to keep those barrels from fallin' apart, or did you invent a new art form in splinters?"

Thomas's smile widened, a glint of amusement in his eyes. "I guess you can say I'm surviving," he replied. "Though I might be able to start a business from the extra sawdust I'm spreading around."

Marianne laughed, a melodic sound that seemed to dance through the room, "Oh yeah? Well, if you keep this up, you might be settin' new trends. Just be sure not to get buried under a mountain of wood shavings."

His weariness eased as she sat beside him. Moments later, the door creaked open again, and Harriet and Emily stepped inside.

"Good to see you all!" Harriet exclaimed.

"Harriet, Emily," Henrietta greeted. "Join us." She gestured to the table.

"Thank you, Henrietta," Emily said softly. She and Harriet settled into seats around the table.

Bread, stew, and a small wheel of cheese sat on the table. The rich smell of herbs and vegetables wafted up in tantalizing waves. The flickering light from the fireplace danced across the room, casting warm shadows that played on their faces. Thomas reached for a wooden spoon, as the rich aroma of the stew made his stomach grumble louder than he wanted.

"Dig in!" Elijah said, chuckling. "We done earned it. Momma's the best cook I've ever known."

"You just sayin' that cause I'm your Momma. They gon' think I paid you to say that 'bout my cookin'."

"No, ma'am, it's the truth."

"Alright, y'all go 'head and eat and stop talkin'."

As Thomas took his first bite, the flavors melted on his tongue, comforting him. The stew was rich and hearty, full of herbs that burst in his mouth.

"Did I ever tell you about the time James tried to catch a chicken with his bare hands?" William asked, breaking the silence with a mischievous grin.

"Only about twenty times," Emily replied, rolling her eyes but smiling.

"Well, for those new to the tale," William began, a twinkle in his eye. "It happened in London. James thought he could catch a chicken with his bare hands. He chased it through the streets, knocking over barrels and scaring the neighbors. He tripped over his own feet and landed face-first in a puddle. That chicken, smart as it was, flew right over him and perched on a fence, clucking like it was laughing. James looked like a drowned rat, and the whole street was in stitches."

"Careful, William," Harriet chided gently, her eyes twinkling. "You'll have us believe you're some hero next."

"Hero? More like a fool," James interjected, shaking his head. "But a well-fed fool tonight, so carry on."

The banter flowed easily, lifting their spirits and easing the heaviness of plantation life. Their burdens seemed to melt away as shared stories and laughter filled the room. Thomas joined in more freely than he had in days, the warmth of the gathering seeping into his bones. Marianne sat beside him like a bright flame in the dim light. Her laughter was infectious, and his heart skipped a beat whenever she smiled at him.

"To shared moments," Marianne said, raising her cup in a toast.

"To shared moments," they echoed, clinking cups and savoring the moment.

Thomas's mood shifted, his gaze fell, and his eyes shadowed with sadness. "And to Charlie. He was on the streets with William, James, Emily, and I back in London. He was scared when we were kidnapped and put on that ship, and I promised to protect him. I'm angry with myself that I couldn't keep him safe."

A hush fell over the room. Marianne reached out, her hand resting on Thomas's. "We all miss him, Thomas."

Thomas nodded, his voice cracking. "He was planting in that hot sun, and I should've ensured he got out of the heat. But I didn't make him, and he paid the price. I should've done more."

Harriet spoke softly. "We all wish we could've done something more. Charlie was like family to us all."

James placed a comforting hand on Thomas's shoulder. "Charlie wouldn't have wanted us to be sad. We can't change the past but can hold on to the good times we shared."

Thomas wiped a tear from his eye, nodding slowly. "You're right. I miss him, that's all."

The room fell silent, but a gentle shift happened as the night continued. Elijah stood, stretching his legs, as he cleared dishes from the table. "Let's move some of this out of the way," he suggested. "Then, let's sing some songs for Charlie."

They rose, their chairs scraping the floor. Thomas gathered the empty bowls. Marianne stacked the bread plates, her fingers brushing his as they worked together. Elijah wiped down the table, and Emily put the leftover cheese away.

They pushed the table aside, creating a small open space. Someone started humming a familiar tune, and soon, everyone joined in, weaving a melody that struck a deep chord. Thomas felt a warmth spreading through him, more intense than the firelight. Marianne's voice rose above the rest, clear and sweet, stirring emotions he couldn't quite name. They moved to the rhythm, their worries momentarily forgotten, lost in the simple joy of the moment.

"Come on, don't be shy," Marianne urged, grabbing Thomas's hand and pulling him into the center of the space. Her touch was both grounding and electrifying.

"Alright, alright," Thomas chuckled, giving in as the rhythm began to seep into his muscles. He let himself sway to the music, the folk songs evoking memories of simpler times and a world outside the confines of the plantation.

They sang of old homes and distant lands, their voices rising and falling harmoniously. For a moment, the room transformed. The walls faded away, and they were in places of freedom and hope. Thomas could almost see rolling hills and open skies and smell the fresh air of distant fields. Marianne's voice soared, filling the room with bittersweet longing. They were no longer just tired souls in a dim room; they were dreamers, united by the music and the memories it evoked.

"Keep it goin'!" Emily shouted, clapping her hands to keep the beat.

Thomas glanced at Elijah, who gave a nod of encouragement, then caught Marianne's eye again. Her smile was radiant, her spirit unshakable. As he danced with her, he felt a spark of true joy.

"Sing it out, Tom," William encouraged.

And so he did, letting the words flow, feeling them connect him to everyone in the room. They weren't just surviving; they were truly living. Thomas watched Marianne as she danced, her fiery red hair bouncing with each step. Her movements were graceful and full of life. The two of them joined hands, and for a moment, the world narrowed. The music swirled around them, guiding their movements. They danced in perfect harmony, their feet instinctively finding the rhythm. Thomas marveled at how natural it felt to dance with her as if they had been partners all along.

Her touch was warm and electric, sending shivers down his spine. Her smile, a beacon in the dim room, drew him irresistibly closer. Each step they took together felt like a promise, a glimpse of something brighter beyond the shadows. Their bodies pressed closer as they danced, the heat between them undeniable. His hand rested on the small of her back, feeling the soft curve of her waist. She leaned into him, her breath warm and comforting against his neck.

Their eyes locked, and the world around them faded even more. His heart pounded, not just from the dance but from the intensity of their connection. This was more than just a dance; it was a moment of shared longing and unspoken desire. In that fleeting moment, the harshness of their world melted away, leaving only the fire of their shared passion.

"You're not half bad," Marianne teased, her eyes twinkling with mischief.

"Thanks," Thomas replied, a shy smile tugging at his lips. "I've had some practice in my dreams."

Marianne laughed, a sound so pure and free it made Thomas's heart pound. They spun together, and for that moment, the weight of their reality seemed to lift. It was just music, movement, and the warmth of her hand in his. Around them, the room began to fill with others joining the dance. James grabbed Emily's arm, pulling her into the circle. Harriet clapped along to the beat, her eyes shining with a rare lightness. Even William, typically stoic, let loose a hearty laugh as he twirled Henrietta around.

The atmosphere buzzed with joy. Laughter echoed off the walls, mingling with the lively tunes. Each step and twirl was a small act of rebellion against the oppression that bound them together on Blackwood Plantation. As the night wore on, the dancing slowed. Breathless and flushed, the group settled into a circle on the floor, their faces beaming with happiness.

"Who wanna start? Not me, 'cause y'all know how I love to talk. We'll be here all night if I get goin'." Elijah asked, his voice still carrying the echoes of laughter.

"Lawd have mercy, don't get him started," Henrietta laughed. "Well, I've got one," she said, her voice rich with nostalgia. "Back when I was a just a young'un in Africa, we'd dance around the fire every full moon. The village would come together, and the night would be filled with stories and songs, just like magic."

"That sounds beautiful," Marianne said, her eyes wide with wonder.

"It was," Henrietta continued, her gaze distant as if she could see it all again. "The firelight would flicker, throwin' shadows on the trees. Drums' would be beatin', and we'd dance 'til we was too tired to move. Elders would spin tales of our ancestors, and us young'uns would sit with wide eyes, takin' in every word."

"Did you have a favorite story?" Thomas asked, leaning in.

Henrietta smiled. "Yeah, there was one 'bout a mighty warrior who saved our village from a dreadful drought. He traveled far and wide, searchin' for a magical spring that never run dry. His courage and willpower was a true inspiration to us all."

"Sounds like a real hero," William said, nodding.

"He was," Henrietta agreed. "And them nights, with the fire and the stories, they brought us all closer. It was a time of unity and joy, no doubt."

The group fell silent, picturing the scene Henrietta had described. The fire's warmth, the drums' rhythmic beat, and the shared sense of community. It was a powerful image.

"Thank you for sharing that, Henrietta," Thomas said softly. "It sounds like a wonderful memory."

"It is," she replied, her voice full of emotion. "And it's good to remember them times, 'specially when things get tough. It reminds us who we are and where we come from. This place been my home for seventeen tobacco harvestin' seasons, but Africa will always be in my soul."

The room came to life as Henrietta shared folk stories passed down through generations. As the night went on, more stories emerged—simple tales of daily struggles and memories of happier times. Despite their lack of freedom, they clung to their cultural heritage and identities, refusing to let people like Lord Blackwood erase who they were. For a brief moment, within the walls of Elijah's home, they were not the property of another; they were simply human.

Chapter Sixteen

Hoofbeats echoed sharply across the dirt path before coming to a sudden stop. The abrupt silence that followed was filled with an almost tangible tension. The loud barking of dogs shattered the quiet of the night, their frantic yelps cutting through the stillness. The sound of boots thudding against the hard ground grew louder. It was deep into the night, and the inky darkness seemed to envelop the small cabin where Thomas and the others were sound asleep.

The sudden commotion jolted them awake. Thomas's heart pounded as he listened to the chaos outside. There was a forceful pounding on the door. Each knock resonated through the cabin like an ominous warning. Heavy boots clomped across the front porch, their menacing rhythm accompanied by angry voices shouting, "Open up!"

Thomas scrambled out of bed, his mind racing with dread. This could only mean one thing. The patrollers had come. Just a few nights before, he and the others had given food and water to a runaway indentured servant who had sought temporary refuge near their cabin. Though the runaway had since moved on, hoping to put more distance between himself and his pursuers, the fear that their act of kindness had been discovered was overwhelming.

Looking out through the small window, Thomas's worst fears were confirmed. Outside stood five men armed with muskets and clubs. Their expressions were harsh, marked by scowls that radiated with contempt and authority. The flickering light from their lanterns cast eerie shadows across their stern features, accentuating the cruel lines etched into their skin. The patrollers had arrived without warning, as they always did when hunting for runaway slaves.

A cold gust of wind seemed to carry with it whispers of past atrocities, causing the hairs on the back of Thomas's neck to stand on end. Shadows outside the cabin contorted and twisted, distorting his vision. He could almost see ghostly figures moving within the darkness, their hollow eyes and bony hands reaching out as if to drag him into the abyss.

Thomas's pulse quickened. A tight sensation of impending doom wrapped around his constricted chest. The air around him grew colder, and he could feel a sinister presence creeping closer, thriving on his mounting dread. The barking dogs outside grew more frantic, as if they, too, could sense the malevolent aura surrounding the patrollers.

As the banging on the door grew more intense, Thomas knew they had to act fast. The others were roused from their sleep. Confusion and fear were etched on their faces. William, always quick to act, joined Thomas at the window. "What do we do, Tom?" he whispered urgently, his voice almost drowned out by the commotion.

Thomas's thoughts churned. They had no place to hide, no means of escape. "We have to open the door," he said, his voice steady despite the fear coursing through him. "If we don't, they'll break it down."

James stood frozen, his face drained of color and eyes wide with fright. "They'll take us," he muttered, his voice cracking. "They'll take us, and we'll never return."

"We need to stay calm," Thomas urged, trying to control his panic.

Thomas took a deep breath and moved towards the door, his hands trembling as he reached for the latch. The relentless pounding continued from the outside. He glanced back at the others, drawing strength from their presence. Slowly, he unbolted the door and swung it open. The cool night air rushed in.

As he peered through the doorway, the figure who confronted him was imposing. A man with a heavily scarred face stepped forward, the remnants of old wounds crisscrossing across his cheeks and forehead. His dark hair, perhaps once neatly trimmed, was unkempt. His eyes, a deep and penetrating dark, narrowed sharply as they locked onto Thomas. He introduced himself with a stern authority, "I'm Town Sergeant Eugene Jackson. Where is he?"

"What do you mean, sir?" Thomas replied, trying to keep his voice steady.

"Don't play stupid!" the sergeant snapped, backhanding Thomas hard enough to send him reeling backward. Pain surged through Thomas's cheek, but he steadied himself, standing firm and refusing to display any sign of weakness.

"We got word there is a runaway hidin' here," the sergeant continued, stepping into the cabin with authority. "And we're not leavin' until we find him."

The other patrollers shoved their way inside, their eyes scanning the room with cold precision. They started ransacking the cabin, overturning furniture, and rifling through belongings. Thomas remained motionless, willing himself not to crack. He was all too familiar with the tales of slave patrollers and their brutality. If a runaway slave was caught, their punishment was severe. Every plantation had a whipping post for punishing slaves at the master's whim. Just the previous year, a captured runaway had received fifty lashes with a horsewhip. His injuries were so severe he didn't survive.

"We have nothin' to hide," William said, stepping forward with his hands up.

"Is that so?" the sergeant asked, eyes narrowing. "We've got no time for games. If you're lyin', it'll be your neck. We know someone here has been workin' with the scoundrels, helpin' scum like you escape, and we ain't gon' stop lookin' until we find out who it is. We'll tear this place down if we have to."

For a moment, the sergeant's gaze pierced through Thomas, probing for any trace of deceit. However, after a brief pause, he gave a curt nod and spun around, exiting the room. The sound of his footsteps faded away. As the door shut behind him, Thomas exhaled, his heart pounding. He looked around at the others, noticing their faces flushed with relief. They had narrowly escaped disaster.

James, trembling with a mix of fear and anger, confronted Thomas. "What were you thinkin', openin' the door like that?" he hissed. "You could've gotten us all killed!"

Thomas met his gaze, trying to stay calm. "We didn't have a choice. They would've broken it down. It was the only way to buy some time."

"Time? For what?" James snapped, his eyes blazing. "They're tearin' apart every cabin now. You think we're safe? We're not safe. If they find out we helped someone who escaped, they'll skin us alive."

Thomas clenched his fists, feeling the weight of the situation. "We need to stay calm and think. Panicking won't help us."

A young girl's shriek from another cabin pierced the night. Thomas felt a chill run down his spine. The cries continued, and the sound of smashed furniture echoed through the night. The patrollers were relentless. Inside the other cabin, the patrollers forcefully shoved a young slave girl against the wall.

"Tell us where they're hidin' the runaway!" the sergeant shouted, his face twisted into a snarl. He raised his hand threateningly above the girl's head.

"Please, sir," she sobbed, "I don't know nothin'."

"Wrong answer!" One of the patrollers' hands came down hard, leaving the girl whimpering on the floor.

Rage surged inside Thomas. But he knew getting involved would only put them all in more danger. With his fists clenched by his side, he fought back the urge to intervene. Witnessing his friends and fellow servants being treated so cruelly made him want to scream. He thought of Marianne but knew she was safe inside the main house.

"Where is he?" demanded one of the patrollers, his voice sharp as he gazed at an elderly man trembling before him. The old man's grizzled hair and sunken eyes spoke volumes of a life spent in toil and hardship. The patroller's grip tightened on the old man's collar, his forearm muscles tensing visibly. "You're hidin' him, aren't you?"

"Please, sir," the old man stammered, tears streaming down his face. "I don't know nothin' about no runaway."

"Useless!" the patroller spat, shoving him roughly. The old man staggered and fell, gasping for air. His frail body shook as he crawled to the corner, clutching his chest.

The patrollers continued their rampage, heavy boots thudding on the wooden floorboards as they ripped through each cabin. Belongings were tossed aside, leaving a trail of disorder. When they reached Elijah's family's cabin, the patrollers moved like a storm, overturning beds and rummaging through chests.

"Get up, boy!" one of the patrollers barked, grabbing a young black slave by the arm and yanking him to his feet. The boy's eyes were wide with terror, his small frame shaking uncontrollably. He couldn't be older than three. His shirt was torn from the rough handling.

The patrollers kept searching, knocking over a table and scattering dishes everywhere. One kicked open a cupboard, sending its contents crashing onto the floor. The boy's mother sobbed quietly in the corner. Elijah stood helplessly, fists clenched, watching their home get torn apart.

"Where's the runaway?" the patroller snarled, shaking the boy again. The child whimpered, unable to speak, his tears mingling with the dirt on his face.

"Tell us where that runaway is, or you'll regret it!" The patroller's voice was a low, menacing growl, the threat hanging in the air.

"He don't know what ya'll talkin' about, sir," the boy's mother said, her eyes darting around the room, seeking escape. Her voice trembled with fear as she moved to put her arm around her son.

"Liar!" the patroller roared, raising his hand to strike.

"Get yo' filthy hands off'n him!" Henrietta's voice rang out, solid and transparent, as she stepped from the shadows. The other servants watched in awe, their eyes full of hope and fear.

"Who are you to speak to me like that, woman?" the patroller demanded, releasing the boy and turning to face Henrietta.

"Someone who knows what's goin' on here. You're terrorizin' him cause of the color of his skin," she replied, her gaze steely. "And I can tell ya none of these folks know where no runaway be."

"Is that so?" the patroller sneered, moving closer to Henrietta. "And how you reckon you know that?"

"Cause I been watchin'," Henrietta replied without a blink. "Every last one. They's scared of ya'll and yo' kind, and they wouldn't dare hide no runaway."

The town sergeant stared at her for a minute, his eyes dark and cold. Finally, he stepped back, but not before delivering a harsh warning. "If I find out any of y'all are lyin', you'll pay dearly. We ain't done here. We'll be back."

He turned his gaze to Thomas, eyes narrowing. "And you," he sneered, his eyes narrowing, "associatin' with these black folks goin'ta bring you trouble. You'd best watch yourself, boy."

Thomas met his gaze without flinching. "They're more of a friend to me than you'll ever be," he said, his voice steady. "You think you're something special, pushing people like us around. We might be property, but at least we don't treat other humans like dirt."

The town sergeant's lip curled with anger and contempt, but he said nothing. With that, the sergeant and patrollers turned and left, their footsteps echoing in the now-silent cabin. The door slammed shut behind them with a sound like a gunshot. The silence that followed was heavy, the tension thick.

Everyone slowly emerged from their cabins, gathering in the yard. The air was mixed with tension and disbelief as the servants gathered in small clusters, whispering among themselves.

The young boy, still trembling from the encounter, collapsed into Henrietta's arms, his tiny body shaking violently. His tear-streaked face pressed against her chest as he sobbed uncontrollably. Henrietta's eyes were a storm of sadness and anger as she gently stroked his back, her tears threatening to spill.

Thomas, his face pale and drawn, stepped forward. "Henrietta," he said quietly, his voice filled with gratitude, "thank you. You saved us. It could've ended badly for us."

Henrietta nodded, her expression firm. "We got to be careful now. They'll be watchin' us closer than ever," her voice warm but tinged with concern.

Henrietta squeezed the boy gently, her voice softening as she spoke to him. "It's gon' be alright, honey. They ain't gon' hurt you no more."

The boy nodded against her, his sobs gradually subsiding as he found comfort in Henrietta's embrace. The group began to disperse slowly, returning to their cabins as they cautiously looked over their shoulders. Henrietta settled the young boy onto a small cot, wrapping him in a blanket. She glanced around the room of her cabin, noting the disarray left by the patrollers. "We'll clean this up later," she said quietly, more to herself than anyone else. Her eyes lingered on the boy, who was now huddled under the blanket, his breathing slowly calming.

Thomas lingered near the doorway, his gaze distant as he took in the scene. "We need to stay alert. They won't give up easily, especially if they know we helped that runaway."

Henrietta nodded, her mind racing with plans to keep their community safe. "We gonna stick together," she said firmly. "That's our strength, and that's what they tryin' to take from us."

She then turned to Thomas, her expression softening with genuine gratitude. "Thomas, I wanna thank ya for standin' up for us to them patrollers," she said, her voice warm and sincere. "For seein' us as more than they do. It means more than words can say."

Thomas met her gaze, a faint smile touching his lips. "It's the least I could do. You're like my family. You, Elijah, and the others have always been there for me, for us. I can never repay you for how you cared for Charlie before he died. It means a lot to me, Henrietta."

As he spoke, Thomas reached over and gave her a heartfelt hug. The embrace was tight and warm, a silent gesture of deep gratitude and solidarity. Henrietta returned the hug, holding him close a moment longer before pulling back. Her eyes glistened with appreciation as she whispered, "We got a long road ahead of us. But with folks like you standin' with us, we'll find a way through."

Chapter Seventeen

Thomas stirred from his bed before the first rays of dawn could grace the winter sky. It was 1773, and three years had passed since Thomas and his friends were brought to Blackwood Plantation. He was settling into his role as a cooper. The biting chill of the morning air gnawed at his bones as he wrapped himself in the blanket that served as his only defense against the cold.

He rose and splashed his face with icy water from the basin. His reflection—a boy turned into a man with unkempt brown hair and a strong frame—gazed back with piercing eyes that had seen too much. He dressed quickly, pulling on his leather apron, its surface scarred with the marks of his hard work.

Stepping outside, the morning air's chill was biting, a sharp reminder that winter had arrived. Frost clung to the edges of the grass, and a thin layer of ice had formed over the puddles on the path, crunching under his boots. On his way to the cooperage, the lane opened up from the dense woods, revealing a pasture blanketed in a light frost on one side and an orchard wall, its trees bare and branches etched against the cold sky on the other. The entire plantation lay under a cloak of frost, the icy grip of the season apparent in the stillness in the air.

As time passed, minor improvements made life more bearable. Harriet, still primarily working as a servant in the main house, also embraced the role of a part-time schoolteacher. A modest one-room cabin was constructed on the plantation to serve as a schoolhouse, marking a new chapter and a chance for a different future. When not hired to teach the children of neighboring plantation owners, she dedicated her time to educating the servants in reading and writing. Every other Sunday, following church services, they were granted a few hours of leisure. Sometimes, they ventured into town; other times, they enjoyed a picnic beside the James River, which flowed near the plantation.

The workshop was filled with the scent of freshly cut wood, blending with the earthy smells of the farm. Thomas hauled planks and staves, his shoulders straining under the weight. At eighteen, his body had been toughened by years of hard labor.

As the sky brightened, the other coopers appeared, wiping sleep from their eyes. Thomas was already at work on his first barrel, his adze carefully carving smooth arcs into the wooden staves. Alongside him, the others began their tasks, their muscles flexing as they bent over their barrels. Sawdust filled the air, creating a thick haze, as the workshop buzzed with activity—the sharp scrape of drawknives and the clattering of truss hoops blended with grunts of exertion.

Thomas focused intently on his barrel, his hands moving with the precision of extensive practice. Despite his youth, he had mastered his craft, developing a feel for the wood and tools. Unlike other coopers who relied on brute force to shape the staves, Thomas worked with finesse. He carefully selected each piece of wood, reading its grain to determine where pressure was needed. With a few deft strikes of his adze, he tapered the edges perfectly, forming the classic bulge of a cask. As he worked, Thomas became absorbed in his craft, finding satisfaction in transforming rough planks into expertly crafted barrels.

"Mind the angle there, lad," said a voice roughened by years in the cooperage. It was Old John, whose back bent not from age but from decades shaping oak and elm. "You've got a keen hand, Thomas. Aye, you'll carve your name into this trade yet."

"Thank you, John," Thomas replied without looking up, his focus unbroken as he measured and cut with an artisan's touch. The older coopers had come to respect him, not just for his evident skill but for the quiet tenacity that clung to him like the sawdust on their aprons.

Next to him, Marcus, a robust man with knuckles as gnarled as the wood they shaped, nodded in approval. "You're on your way to becomin' a master cooper," he said, his voice a gruff murmur amidst the workshop's clamor. "Your barrels hold, and that's more than I can say for some."

"Means a lot comin' from you," Thomas replied, allowing a smile to cross his face though he kept his eyes on his work. The camaraderie in the workshop was built on shared purpose and mutual respect for their craft. They were both teachers and learners, exchanging knowledge as seamlessly as they passed around their tools.

With a skilled thump, Thomas drove the iron hoop into place, the sound echoing through the workshop. He wiped his forehead, smearing a streak across his tanned skin. Then, he noticed Lord Blackwood standing in the doorway, his overseer looming behind him like a shadow.

"Everhart," Blackwood called out, his voice piercing through the clamor of hammering and sawing. Thomas straightened, his heart racing but his expression calm.

"Yes, my lord?" Thomas replied, stepping forward.

"Your barrels have been deemed superior once again," Blackwood announced, his eyes scanning the row of stout wooden vessels. "They command a fine price in England. Your craftsmanship is proving invaluable."

"Thank you, my lord," Thomas said, bowing his head slightly. He took pride in his work and appreciated the recognition, yet he could sense the envious glares from the other coopers.

Once Lord Blackwood departed, Samuel barked at everyone, clearly annoyed by the disruption, "Get back to work—no time for dawdlin'. We have five more barrels to complete. And, Thomas, don't let the praise get to your head. Remember, I'm the one who ensures these barrels are ready on time. I'm the one in charge here."

Thomas looked down at the floor, not wanting to provoke Samuel further. The air was tense and heavy with rivalry, and the other coopers stared him down, lounging against the rough wooden walls of the workshop. Their laughter rang sharply against the backdrop of the tools and barrels. Arthur, leaning back with a confident smirk, eyed Thomas provocatively.

"Word around is that Marianne is Lord Blackwood's mistress," he taunted, eliciting snickers from the group.

Thomas's jaw clenched, his face flushing with rising anger he struggled to suppress. His hands balled into fists, knuckles turning white. The image of Marianne's bright red hair, the way she smiled at him, and the sound of her laughter were all precious memories. Now, they were being sullied by crude insinuations of the men around him.

Eager to stoke the flames, John sneered, "I swear I've seen her comin' out of his bedchamber when Lady Constance isn't around. That bright red hair of hers is hard to miss."

Thomas's simmering fury reached a breaking point. The room seemed to shrink, funneling his anger directly at Arthur and John. He marched towards Arthur and said sharply, "You better shut your mouth and take back what you said."

Arthur's eyes narrowed. His expression was one of disdain. "Or what? What are you goin' to do about it?"

Thomas's right hand shot out without another word, delivering a solid punch to Arthur's jaw. The force of the blow sent Arthur reeling backward against the workbench, scattering tools onto the floor. The room fell silent, punctuated by the heavy breathing of the two men.

Arthur quickly regained his composure, rubbing his jaw with a grimace. His eyes icy with spite, he growled, "You'll regret that," and charged at Thomas, fists raised.

Thomas sidestepped the first blow, seized Arthur's

arm, and twisted it behind his back, pinning him against the workbench. "Enough!" he shouted. "Speak of her that way again, and next time, it won't just be a punch."

Arthur writhed, his face contorted with pain and fury. Eventually, he gave a reluctant nod, and Thomas let him go, stepping back. The room was hushed, the other coopers watching in stunned silence. Thomas scanned the room, his gaze challenging anyone else to remark. The room stayed silent; the message was clear.

Previously smirking, John shifted uncomfortably, his eyes darting between Thomas and Arthur. The intensity of Thomas's stare silenced any further snickers or slurs. With a final stern look at Arthur, Thomas exited the workshop. As he walked away, he replayed the confrontation, trying to steady his racing heart. His fists still throbbed from the strike, and his breath came in short bursts, fueled by residual anger.

"Nothin' good comes from rumors, men," Samuel said, breaking the silence. He reached over and smacked Arthur and John on their heads. "Get back to work, or I'll release you for the day, which will be to your disadvantage if we fall behind."

Arthur muttered something under his breath, but the sting of Samuel's rebuke and the humiliation of being overpowered by Thomas kept him subdued. Meanwhile, John hastily resumed his work, casting uneasy glances toward the door where Thomas had left.

Outside, the cold air did little to calm Thomas's simmering anger. He paced back and forth, attempting to regulate his breathing and gather his thoughts. The plantation was a brutal environment, with frequent high tensions, but this incident felt different. The insults about Marianne had deeply offended him, sparking a fierce protective instinct. As he calmed down, Thomas made his way to the edge of the field, where he expected to find Elijah working on a plow. Sure enough, Elijah was there, working hard.

"Elijah," Thomas called, walking up to his friend. "I need to talk."

Elijah looked up, worry etched on his face. "What's wrong, Thomas? You look like somethin' heavy weighin' on ya."

Thomas shook his head, a bitter smile on his lips. "You could say that. Arthur and John were talking nonsense about Marianne. I couldn't just let that be."

Elijah's gaze grew steely. "Them fools never know when to hush up. You did good standin' up for her, but watch yourself. Arthur ain't the type to let things slide."

"I know," Thomas replied, absentmindedly rubbing his knuckles. "But I couldn't stand by and let them disrespect her like that. She doesn't deserve it."

Elijah nodded, placing a reassuring hand on Thomas's shoulder. "None of us deserve the cruelty we face here. But we got to be smart about our battles. You took a stand today, and that counts for somethin'. Best you get back to work 'fore Samuel runs tellin' Mister Lawson."

Thomas sighed. "You're right. Thanks, Elijah. Catch you at dinner tonight? Hope your Ma is cooking some of her fine stew."

"Hope so, too. See you later," Elijah replied, turning back to sharpen the plowshare.

Thomas returned to his work with renewed vigor. The

familiar sounds of metal clanging and wood thudding filled the air. John and Arthur concentrated on their tasks and didn't bother him again, the earlier confrontation seemingly forgotten, at least for now. Samuel paid him no attention, but the displeasure on his face was a silent reminder of the simmering tensions.

As the day drew to a close, the sky transformed into a canvas of orange and pink, its vibrant colors softening the rigid contours of the fields and buildings. Thomas set down his tools with a slight smile on his face. Despite the day's hard work, he felt accomplished. He looked around at his friends and fellow workers. Elijah gave him a nod of encouragement. Marianne walked toward him, her red hair catching the sunset's glow, and her lips curved into a welcoming smile.

"Elijah told me what happened. You held your own today, Thomas," Marianne said softly, her voice laced with admiration. "Thank you for defendin' me."

A warmth unfurled in Thomas. "I couldn't just stand by while they spoke about you that way," he responded, his tone firm.

As the day wound down and twilight settled over the plantation, the servants began gathering at Henrietta's cabin, drawn by the inviting smell of stew. The warmth of the small, flickering fire in the hearth cast a cozy glow as Henrietta stirred the large pot as spices and herbs emanated through the cabin. Wooden bowls were set out, and soon, everyone sat together on whatever makeshift seats they could find. Laughter and conversation bubbled up as they enjoyed one another's company.

As the last of the sunlight vanished below the horizon,

casting long shadows across the plantation, everyone started to head towards their quarters. Nightfall brought a fleeting respite from the day's toils. Thomas paused for a moment, taking in the twilight. The sky was painted a deep purple and twinkled with the first stars. He felt a sense of peace, a rare and precious thing in their harsh reality.

Before heading back to his cabin, he sought out Marianne. Finding her near the fading embers of the fire, he gently took her hand, asking softly. "May I walk you back to your quarters?"

Marianne's eyes lit up, and she nodded, "Yes, that would be nice." Together, they walked toward the main house where her quarters were located, their steps slow, savoring the night's cool night air.

Outside the front door, Thomas paused, turning to face her. The soft glow of the main house's lights illuminated their final moment together for the night. "Goodnight, Marianne," he whispered, leaning in to give her a gentle kiss. Her response was tender, her lips meeting his in a sweet, fleeting connection that made the stars above shine brighter.

With a final squeeze of her hand, he stepped back, watching her disappear into her quarters with a soft smile. Thomas then returned to his cabin under the starlit sky, the serene moment with Marianne leaving a lingering warmth in his heart, a beautiful end to the day. Settling into bed, he replayed the night's tender goodbye. As sleep claimed him, Thomas thought about Marianne. He dreamed of them being together all the time, far away from Blackwood Plantation.

Chapter Eighteen

Thomas and Marianne found their secret haven under an ancient oak, its gnarled branches weaving a protective canopy above. The sprawling roots of the massive tree burrowed deep into the earth, forming a natural seat amidst a bed of fresh spring grass. Enriched by the vibrant greenery, they found a quiet world away from their daily struggles. The air was filled with the scent of blooming honeysuckle, adding a sweetness to their private meetings.

Thomas reached out, his fingers brushing a stray hair from Marianne's face. Her eyes sparkled with warmth and affection. He gently caressed her cheek. His rough skin contrasted with her softness, but she leaned into his touch, her green eyes shimmering with the colors of twilight.

"Marianne," Thomas whispered, his voice thick with emotions held too long in check. His eyes, intense, locked onto hers.

She returned his gaze, her eyes alight with desire and

vulnerability. "I worry I'd lose myself without these moments," she confessed, her voice quivering as her fingers wove between his, binding them together. Her voice trembled, each word a fragile thread connecting their souls.

Feeling a deep, visceral connection, Thomas was driven by a mix of protectiveness and raw desire. "You are the light that banishes my shadows," he breathed out, his eyes burning with an intensity as vivid as the setting sun. Slowly, he drew her closer until their foreheads touched. The warmth of her breath mingled with his, enveloping them in a shared cocoon.

His hand reached up to caress the curve of her neck, his fingers tracing the delicate lines leading to her shoulder. The gentle yet deliberate touch sparked a shiver that ran through her body, heightening their electric connection. Marianne leaned into his touch as his fingers lingered on the nape of her neck, her breath quickening.

Thomas's other hand found the small of her back, pulling her closer and diminishing the space between them. Marianne's hands moved to his chest, feeling the rapid beat of his heart through his thin shirt. With a boldness fueled by their mounting desire, she began to unbutton it, her fingers trembling slightly as they worked their way down.

As each button came undone, the anticipation surged, electric in the air between them. Thomas's hands mirrored hers, slipping to the hem of her simple dress, fingers grazing her skin as he lifted it, inch by inch. Their gaze locked in a silent exchange filled with longing and tacit consent. The rustling of fabric and their soft, quickened breaths blended with the whispers of the evening breeze, driving them irresistibly toward a point of no return.

Her lips curved into a serene smile, yet suggestive smile. "Promise me, Thomas," she whispered. "promise we'll escape this life together."

He nodded, his eyes burning with the same fierce desire and determination. As he leaned in to kiss her forehead tenderly, his hand ventured further, exploring with a gentle boldness that drew a soft gasp from her lips. "I promise," he murmured against her skin. His fingers continued their daring journey, igniting a deep, resonant pleasure that mirrored the sincerity in his words. His heart swelled with determination to make their dream a reality, no matter the obstacles.

But soon, the harsh reality of their circumstances crept back in. The distant shouts and the clatter of activity on the plantation pierced their bubble of isolation. Reluctantly, they pulled apart, their hands parting, yet fingers brushing in a final, lingering caress that spoke of promises and plans yet to be fulfilled.

A horse's whinny shattered the silence, quickly joined by the eager barks of dogs. Thomas and Marianne paused, their intimate moment disrupted by the sudden commotion. They saw a groom rushing forward to grab the reins from a striking-looking gentleman on a sleek, dark horse. His russet brown hair peeked out from under a felt hat worn at a rakish tilt, his eyes twinkling with a playful glint.

The gentleman dismounted with ease, his movements fluid and confident. He exchanged a jovial remark with the groom, eliciting laughter that echoed through the courtyard. After a hearty slap on the back and flipping a coin into the groom's palm, he strode across the cobblestones, his boots clicking with each step.

Marianne nudged Thomas, her eyes wide with curiosity. "Who do you think he is?" she whispered.

Before Thomas could respond, the door to the main house burst open, and Lady Constance emerged, her elegant figure framed by the doorway. She wore a flowing emerald gown, its fabric shimmering in the sunlight, with lace trim at the sleeves and neckline. "Peter!" she exclaimed, her voice a blend of excitement and relief. "You have arrived, finally!"

The gentleman's countenance brightened into a cordial smile, his presence authoritative and cordial. "Pray, compose yourself, dear sister. Our separation was but brief," he said, his tone both rich and calming.

"I understand, but it remains a pleasure to see you," she said, embracing him warmly. Their genuine affection was evident, a sharp contrast to Lady Constance's usual reserved demeanor.

Peter's gaze lingered on his sister, then shifted to the bustling fields. He observed the workers diligently performing their tasks, planting seeds in the freshly thawed soil.

His expression became pensive as he continued to survey the scene. "And how fare all matters here? Does Reginald keep things in order?"

Constance's smile waned somewhat, a shadow flickering across her features. "As well as one might anticipate," she replied, her voice carefully neutral. "You are familiar with his ways."

Peter looked at her more closely, noticing a subtle change. "Constance, are you...?"

She nodded, her hand resting gently on her abdomen. "Indeed, I am with child. Reginald and I are overjoyed."

A joyful commotion erupted at the front door as Lord Blackwood's dog bounded through, leaping enthusiastically onto Peter. Laughter filled the air, easing the tension as Peter tried to calm the exuberant animal. Lord Blackwood appeared in the doorway soon after, his face breaking into a wide smile. "Ah, Peter! What a pleasure to see you!" He exclaimed, clapping his hands together as he greeted him. Together, the three of them headed back towards the house.

As they walked, Peter spoke up, his voice tinged with regret. "Regrettably, my visit must be brief, for I am bound to return to England shortly on business matters."

Thomas and Marianne watched the exchange from a distance, their curiosity piqued. "Who is he?" Thomas wondered aloud, his eyes fixed on the new arrival.

"He must be Lady Constance's brother," Marianne said. "He seems different from Lord Blackwood. Kinder, perhaps."

Thomas looked at Marianne, giving her hand a reassuring squeeze as they watched the exchange. This was the first time he'd heard Lady Constance being with child. Rumors had swirled around the plantation about her struggles to provide an heir, which reportedly strained their marriage. Memories of the coopers' jeers and the whispers of an affair between Lord Blackwood and Marianne flashed through his mind. He pushed the thoughts away, refusing to dwell on them.

The sharp ring of the overseer's bell cut through their brief escape, echoing across the field and calling them back to their tasks. They paused for a moment, their eyes locked in a silent promise. Sharing a quick, stolen kiss, they savored a fleeting moment of intimacy. Then, with one final glance that carried a silent vow, they reluctantly parted ways.

Thomas walked back to the cooper's shed, his mind full of Marianne. Sunlight streamed through the open door, casting dusty rays over the workbench. He picked up a curved stave and slotted it into place with the others, forming a new barrel's skeleton. He struck the iron hoop with a mallet. Each blow made a satisfying 'thunk,' echoing off the shed's worn wooden walls. The floor vibrated with each hit. Sweat trickled down his forehead, cutting through the grime and sawdust on his skin.

John looked up from the barrel he was working on. "I heard Lady Constance is with child."

Thomas paused mid-strike, the mallet hovering in the air. "Her brother arrived today. I saw them talking earlier."

"Oh yeah?" John frowned, glancing toward the manor house. "He hasn't been here in years. Wonder what brought him to the plantation."

Thomas resumed his work, the mallet's thunk filling the silence. "Maybe it's not just the baby," he said, eyes narrowing. "I've heard whispers about old debts and family secrets."

Samuel pounded his fist on his workbench. "That's enough. This isn't a gossip hall. Stop worryin' about the affairs of our master and mistress and get to work. Lord Blackwood needs twelve barrels completed before the end of the month. A new shipment is headin' to London, and we're already runnin' behind."

Suddenly, a loud commotion broke out in the tobacco fields. The overseer's yelling cut through the servants' chatter, capturing Thomas's attention. He excused himself from the workshop and walked towards the disturbance, his curiosity aroused. His heart sank when he spotted James being hauled away by the collar of his worn shirt by Lawson. James's eyes burned with defiance. His jaw set as he spat out words at the man restraining him.

"I won't do it! I won't work another day in this godforsaken place!" James yelled, his voice echoing across the plantation. The other servants stopped their work, their frightened eyes darting between James and Lawson. Thomas's stomach twisted. He knew this wouldn't end well for James.

Lawson growled to one of the slaves nearby, his eyes cold as steel. "Twenty lashes should teach him a lesson in obedience!"

Thomas's blood ran cold. Everyone watched him, waiting to see what he'd do. His friendship with James put him in a tough spot. If he stepped in, he'd face the same punishment, maybe worse. But if he did nothing, he'd see himself as a coward.

As James was dragged away, Marianne appeared beside him, her face pale as snow. "Thomas, you mustn't!" she hissed under her breath. "You'll only get yourself whipped, too!"

His gaze met James's, and in that moment, they both knew. Thomas couldn't risk it. With a final, apologetic look, he turned away, his heart heavy with guilt. His heart lurched as the men dragged James toward the dreaded post. He dropped his mallet, the sound swallowed by the chaos. His hands trembled with rage and dread. The usual hum of work stopped. Every servant stood still, faces filled with fear and silent sorrow. They knew what was coming, and it made them fear for James.

Lawson's leather boots at the whipping post stirred up dust clouds as he circled James, securing his wrists with coarse rope and tying him to the post. James's shirt was ripped away, leaving his back exposed. Thomas watched, his throat tightening, as his friend held his head high despite the restraints. Fear gripped Thomas's heart, each beat pounding with dread for what would happen.

Lawson stepped forward, his voice cold and menacing, "Are you property, boy?"

James's response was defiant yet weak, "No."

Lawson flexed the leather whip, its coiled length casting ominous shadows on the ground. "We'll see about that."

Lawson uncoiled the whip with chilling precision and stepped back a few feet from James. His arm swung forward and snapped back, creating an arc with the whip. The whip cracked through the air, its echo slashing through the tense silence before landing a vicious strike across James's back. The sound was sickening, a sharp snap followed by the raw, anguished screams that tore from James's throat. Again and again, the whip descended, each lash leaving a fiery trail of welts and bloodied stripes. Raw, wet wounds reached across James's back, each one separated by an inch or two of untouched skin.

Thomas clenched his jaw, his muscles taut with anger

and powerlessness. Beside him, Marianne trembled, her hand gripping his shoulder, her eyes wide with horror. Thomas briefly met her gaze, desperately seeking some comfort. But there was none to be found. The horror of the moment was too overwhelming. Lash after harrowing lash landed across James's back.

Finally, Lawson stepped back, wiping his brow, satisfied with the brutality he had inflicted. James hung limply from the post, his breathing shallow and uneven, his back a canvas of raw, bloody stripes. Around them, the other servants watched in stunned silence, their faces etched with shock and deep sorrow.

"James, we're here," Thomas said, his voice thick with emotion as he rushed over and touched his friend's arm.

"You'll heal, brother," Elijah whispered. "My momma gon' make some ointment for them wounds. Them times I got lashed, that stuff she made healed me up quick. She learnt all 'bout healing herbs from her momma."

James groaned, his eyes barely open. "I'll be fine. Just need a moment."

Marianne knelt beside him, her hand gentle on his arm. "We'll get you to Elijah's cabin for medicine and rest."

They helped James to his feet, supporting his weight as they led him toward the cabins. As they walked, Thomas wondered if he'd ever know true freedom. Or if the Virginia colony was doomed to be where dreams went to die, like so many before them.

Chapter Nineteen

The spring sun shone brightly on the small servants' garden, casting golden rays upon the vibrant green plants. Henrietta knelt among the herbs and vegetables, her fingers skillfully selecting what she needed for her ointment. She carefully gathered yarrow leaves and comfrey stems, placing them gently into her apron. Each plant was familiar to her. She knew their uses and potency well. This knowledge had been passed down from her mother, who had learned it from her mother. It was wisdom that was meant to heal, not harm.

She moved methodically through the rows, her apron growing heavier with each handful of herbs. Pausing at a patch of calendula, she brushed the petals with her finger-tips before picking the brightest blossoms. Standing up, she surveyed the garden, ensuring she had all she needed. With her bag filled, she headed back to her small quarters. Her expertise in herbal remedies had earned the respect and trust of her fellow servants. She was determined not to disappoint them, especially James, who needed relief from his wounds.

Inside, she emptied her apron onto the rough wooden table, carefully sorting through the roots, leaves, flowers, and stems. Taking up the mortar and pestle, she began grinding the herbs into a fine powder, her shoulder muscles flexing with the effort. Years of being enslaved had made her strong and resilient. The servants received no medical care, so they had to learn to treat themselves. Henrietta's knowledge of herbal remedies was crucial for their survival.

Next, she mixed the powder with lanolin and olive oil she had saved from the big house kitchen. The room filled with the pungent smell of the salve as she blended the ingredients. This was her purpose, her gift—to heal and soothe, to bring relief where there was pain. She was more than an enslaved woman; she was a healer. She recalled the time, long ago, when an elderly slave woman had a severe burn on her arm from the kitchen. She had quickly prepared a soothing balm using calendula and comfrey, applying it gently to the burn each day. Within a week, the angry, red skin had calmed, and new, healthy skin began to form. The woman's pain had eased, and Henrietta's heart swelled with pride. She would use her knowledge to care for those who needed her, now and always.

James sat hunched in the corner. Angry red welts from the whip oozed and seeped across his shoulders and back. He clutched his knees to his chest, trying to make himself as small as possible. His face was etched with pain. His eyes were squeezed shut to block out the agony. It was a terrible sight.

Henrietta approached slowly, her footsteps soft on the dirt floor. She had seen many wounds like these over the years, but it never got easier. In a gentle tone, she said, "Let me tend to you, child."

James glanced up at her, his eyes wide with hope and fear. Henrietta saw the depths of his suffering, and her heart ached for him. He was about the same age as her son, Elijah, and a maternal instinct rose within her. The orphans had arrived four years ago, in the summer of 1770. Since then, Henrietta devoted herself to being a mother figure for them, offering them the love and care they desperately needed.

"James," she whispered, kneeling beside him, "I'm here to help. I got some medicine that'll heal you right up."

"What is it?" James choked out, his voice barely a whisper, strained and hoarse from the overwhelming pain and exhaustion. His body trembled with each breath, and the agony in his eyes was almost unbearable to witness. Over the years, he had grown into a strong young man in his twenties, his once boyish features now lined with premature age, showing the resilience of someone who had endured far more than his share.

"An ointment," Henrietta replied, holding a small clay jar. "It should help ease your pain and heal your wounds."

Henrietta removed the lid from the jar as she spoke, revealing the earthy, fragrant salve inside. The scent of herbs filled the air, mixing with the acrid smell of sweat and blood that clung to James like a shroud.

"Will it hurt?" he asked hesitantly, his eyes flicking between Henrietta and the jar. His body trembled, expecting more pain.

"Jus' for a moment," she promised, her voice steady. "But the relief gon' be worth it."

James nodded weakly, giving her permission. Henrietta scooped some salve onto her fingers. Its texture was smooth and cool. As she moved closer, she saw the tension in his muscles, the way he braced himself for the sting. Henrietta's touch was light but firm as she applied the ointment to the worst lacerations.

"God above!" James gasped as the salve touched his wounds. He clenched his teeth, the initial sting sharp and biting, but he endured it with grim determination.

Henrietta clucked her tongue in sympathy. "That evil man," she muttered, fire sparking in her voice. "But we gon' heal these wounds. We done suffered much, Lord. Please, preserve our lives accordin' to your word."

She dabbed on more salve, her hands gentle but firm. "They treated us like cargo on them ships, packed so tightly we could scarce breathe. Many died on the way, their bodies tossed overboard without a care. And here on the plantations, they work us to the bone, beat us without mercy, and treat us like animals."

James winced but listened, the pain momentarily forgotten.

Henrietta smeared the ointment over each welt and cut. The room was quiet except for James's ragged breathing and Henrietta's gentle, comforting words. "You're doin' alright, James. The worst done passed now."

Bit by bit, he felt the fire in his wounds ease up, replaced by a cool, numbing sensation spreading through his body. His breathing got easier with each strip of linen wrapped tight around his ribcage. By the time she tied off the last bandage, he had let go of his stiff tension.

Henrietta gently clasped James's shoulder. He looked up at her, his eyes filled with gratitude. In that simple act of care and compassion, Henrietta had done more than heal his physical wounds. She had restored a small measure of his dignity and hope.

"Thank you, Henrietta," he whispered. Despite the lingering soreness, he knew that without her help, he might have succumbed to infection or worse.

"Rest now," she told him with a small smile, placing the jar back into her apron pocket.

"Your hands work miracles, Henrietta," Thomas said, admiring her.

"Thank you, child," she replied modestly, wiping her hands on her apron. "But it ain't my hands; it's the power of nature's remedies."

James nodded. "I owe you my life, Henrietta."

She smiled gently, her aged face lighting up. "We look out for each other. That's how we make it through."

As James slowly rose to his feet, grimacing from the pull of the freshly applied bandages, the other servants came close. Harriet and Emily approached first, their expressions filled with sympathy and admiration for Henrietta's healing skills. Elijah hung back, his tall and muscular frame taut with tension.

"Bless you, Henrietta," Harriet said, her voice filled with genuine emotion. "God knows we need your gifts in these times."

Henrietta nodded solemnly, her weathered face folding into a sad smile. "That we do. We ain't gon' get no mercy from our masters. We got to give it to ourselves."

The room's mood shifted as Elijah stepped forward, his voice carrying a new weight. "We can't just accept this as our lot, Momma. We deserve better than this. And what about them?" He gestured toward Thomas and the other indentured servants. "Their servitude ends. Ours don't. They count years. We count generations."

Thomas shifted in his seat. It was the first time he had seen Elijah visibly upset, and the raw intensity in his words made him uneasy. Yet, deep down, he knew that Elijah was right. Their indenture, though harsh, had an expiration date, a stark contrast to the perpetual bondage of slaves.

"I understand your anger, Elijah," Thomas spoke up, his voice hesitant but sincere. "It's true we have a date when we can hope to be free, but you're bound for life. It's not fair. We see that."

"Fair?" Elijah's voice rose slightly, his frustration palpable. "It ain't about fair. People talk about bein' free, but I dunno what that means. I ain't never been free. I was born a slave."

Henrietta, always the voice of reason, interjected. "We need each other if we're goin' to change anythin' 'round here. Whether it's a few years or a lifetime, sufferin' is sufferin'."

William nodded. "That's the truth. We might not share the same chains, but we share the same burdens, the same overseer, the same fields. We got to use that to bring us together, not push us apart."

The room grew quiet. Elijah looked around, his gaze

meeting both indentured and enslaved. "I guess so. We're all under the same boot. If we're gon' lift it, we need every hand we can get. Your end date might be comin', but I'll be damned if we don't have the same one day."

As the discussion heated up, the sharp whistle of the overseer sliced through the air, silencing everyone. His sneering presence loomed over them. "What's this? A meetin' of minds? Plannin' a little rebellion, are we?"

Marianne stepped forward bravely. "No sir. Just tendin' to James's wounds, like any good Christian would do." Her voice was firm but calm, betraying no hint of fear that fluttered in her chest.

His eyes narrowed, sweeping over the group with distrust. "Make sure that's all it is. Any sign of trouble, and it'll be the whip for every last one of ya." His warning hung heavy as he stalked off, leaving a cold silence.

As night fell and the overseer's steps faded in the distance, the group slowly dispersed, each person retreating to their quarters. Thomas carefully helped James to his bed despite the pain that grimaced across James's face with every move. The rough blankets did little to cushion the hard surface against his back. James winced, the bandages pulling at his skin.

Thomas lay awake for a long while, staring at the outline of the wooden beams above his bed. He wished there was something he could do to change their circumstances, but for now, he would bide his time, waiting for the right moment to make his move.

Chapter Twenty

The halls of the grand manor buzzed with activity as the house servants scurried from one opulent room to another. The glow from the chandeliers cast warm light over their tasks: polishing heirloom silverware until it was flawless, meticulously straightening the white tablecloths draped over the long dining table, and aligning each place setting with perfection.

Anxiety was etched on their faces, and their hands trembled as they arranged the delicate crystal glasses and polished silver cutlery. The usual chatter that accompanied their preparations was absent this evening, replaced by a heavy silence that thickened the atmosphere. This dinner party was unlike any other they had served before—it was charged with a palpable, unspoken tension.

The head butler double-checked every detail, his sharp eyes catching the slightest misalignment or smudge. "Everything must be perfect," he reminded everyone in a hushed tone that underscored the gravity of the evening. "Tonight's gathering will set the course for the future. Our master and mistress have high expectations for the party. We must not disappoint. We needed an extra pair of hands, and Lord Blackwood has requested that Thomas fill that position. He will be working with us tonight."

The kitchen staff worked in a controlled frenzy. The aroma of roasted meats filled the air while Henrietta directed the kitchen staff. As the final touches were added to the dining hall, Emily adjusted a centerpiece of freshly cut flowers from the garden, ensuring they were symmetrical. She glanced around, taking in the scene as Marianne nodded her approval.

The grand clock in the foyer ticked louder as the hour drew near, and the first carriages could be heard rolling up the gravel outside. The servants took their positions, each aware that the night's events would be discussed for years. As the distinguished guests began to arrive, cloaked in their finest attire and masked with polite smiles, the servants stood ready, their eyes flickering with anticipation. Rumors had circulated that among the night's attendees were two prominent gentlemen named George Washington and Patrick Henry.

Marianne paused outside the dining room, a tray of hors d'oeuvres balanced in her hands. She took a deep breath, steadying her nerves. Tonight was important—a chance for the servants to prove themselves to the master's distinguished guests. They were promised a few extra hours of leisure time if everything went well.

She smoothed her apron, pasted a pleasant smile, and

entered the dining hall. The candlelight cast eerie shadows on the walls, giving the opulent space an otherworldly feel. She took a deep breath and stepped in, carrying a tray of neatly arranged appetizers. At the head of the table sat Lord Blackwood, an imposing figure in his embroidered waistcoat, made from a deep, rich burgundy fabric adorned with intricate gold thread that caught the light with every movement. He wore a crisp, white shirt beneath, its high collar stiff and pristine. His dark breeches were tailored perfectly, and a gold pocket watch chain dangled from his vest. His presence commanded the room, every detail of his attire adding to his air of authority and power.

"Marianne," Blackwood said with a nod, his voice smooth and commanding. "Our guests have been eagerly awaiting these delicacies."

"Of course, my lord," she replied, her gaze skimming over the assembly of influential figures. She felt the weight of their eyes on her as if they could see straight through her practiced calm.

"Allow me to introduce you all to Patrick Henry and George Washington of the House of Burgesses," Lord Blackwood announced, gesturing grandly toward the two esteemed gentlemen. A murmur of interest rippled through the crowd.

Marianne felt a surge of curiosity. Who were these men, with their meticulous clothing and commanding presence?

"Serve them well," Blackwood said, his eyes fixed on Marianne. "Tonight must be perfect."

"Yes, my lord," she answered, moving with careful

grace to offer the tray of appetizers to the guests. The men spoke in hushed tones about things like revolution and freedom, which were foreign to her. She lingered near them, trying to catch snippets of their conversation.

Sitting tall and composed, George Washington addressed the table of distinguished guests. Washington wore a dark blue coat with brass buttons tailored to perfection and a high collar that added to his imposing presence. Underneath, he had a waistcoat of a lighter shade, typically buff or cream, which contrasted elegantly with the darker coat. His breeches were made of fine wool or linen, tucked into knee-high leather boots that bore the marks of use, showing that Washington was a man of action, not just words.

His hair was pulled back and powdered in the day's fashion, tied neatly at the nape of his neck with a black ribbon. His powdered wig was styled without the excessive curls favored by some, giving him a dignified yet practical appearance. The careful simplicity of his attire highlighted his features—sharp eyes, a firm jawline—making him the leader of men in every bit.

"The colonies shall not remain shackled under the weight of the king's tyranny," Washington said, his voice low but resonating with fierce determination. "We must break free, no matter the cost. Liberty is worth the fight. Our cause is just."

The room hushed to absorb his words. It was then that Patrick Henry spoke, "Yet, let us also consider the manifold complexities this path unfolds before us. To break from the crown is no small undertaking—it is a venture fraught with peril, one that demands the utmost sagacity and fortitude from all who embrace it."

Pausing to ensure his words had taken hold, he continued, "Should we, as stewards of these colonies, lead our people into a fray so formidable without assurance of aid and alliance? Is this promise of liberty sufficient to justify the inevitable toll? We stand at a precipice, gentlemen, and our actions henceforth must be guided not solely by the justness of our cause but by the prudence it necessitates."

Marianne's heart raced at his bold words. She looked up and caught Lady Constance's eye. For a brief moment, she felt a silent understanding between them, a flicker of something deeper and more dangerous that passed in a heartbeat. Hope flickered in Marianne's heart. Was change coming? Inside, her thoughts raced. She had glimpsed the fervor brewing beneath the polite conversation, a passion that mirrored her secret desire to be set free.

As she pushed through the swinging doors and returned to the bustling kitchen, the clamor of pots and pans greeted her. Henrietta manned the large, blackened stove, hair strands escaping her bun. Her hands moved precisely, stirring a bubbling pot of rich, aromatic stew that filled the air with its enticing scent. Nearby, Emily and Harriet stood at a large, worn wooden table covered with colorful vegetables. They chopped in smooth, rhythmic motions, their heads bent in concentration. Despite the chaos, everything moved like a well-oiled machine. The kitchen buzzed with energy, each person playing their part in the night's orchestrated dance.

"Better hurry. Lord Blackwood expects everythin' to

flow on time," Henrietta paced the floor, clenching and unclenching her fingers.

"Marianne, is all well out there?" Harriet asked without looking up from the vegetables she was chopping.

"Fine, Harriet. The gentlemen are deep in conversation," Marianne replied, placing the empty tray on the counter. "But they're talkin' about things like revolution and freedom from the king."

Harriet paused in her chopping, her eyes narrowing. "Dangerous talk," she murmured, glancing cautiously at Emily.

Emily nodded, her face serious. "Be careful, Marianne. Listenin' to that kind of talk can get us into trouble."

Marianne nodded, understanding the gravity. "I know. But it's hard not to hope when you hear them talk about a different future."

Harriet went back to chopping, looking thoughtful. "Hope's powerful, child. But we should be careful. We're already under watchful eyes."

Thomas entered the kitchen, adjusting his collar. "What are they saying out there?" he asked, curious.

"Revolution and liberty," Marianne replied. "It's like a whisper of somethin' new, somethin' possible."

Thomas's eyes brightened with intrigue. "Perhaps it's a sign. Perhaps things are changing."

"Let's not get ahead of ourselves," Harriet cautioned, her voice softening. "Those people speak about freedom, but it's their freedom, not ours.."

Thomas hovered just outside the dining room, peeking through the doorway as Marianne moved gracefully among the finely dressed guests. His servant's garb felt foreign and scratchy, but he kept his shoulders back and head high, trying to look confident. The room buzzed with conversation, and snippets reached his ears, fueling his curiosity.

"The taxes they impose are simply unacceptable," Lord Blackwood grumbled, his voice low and seething angrily.

"Quite right," Patrick Henry replied, his voice rising with each word. "The colonies have had enough!" His fist struck the table with a sharp crack, making the crystal glasses tremble. "We must not stand for this ill treatment any longer. It is time for us to take a stand and show them we refuse to be pushed around."

George Washington leaned in, his gaze intense and his voice low and imbued with a gravitas that demanded attention. "Indeed, gentlemen, your points hold merit. However, let us proceed with utmost circumspection. The king's agents are manifold and mingle unseen amongst us. One slip, one inadvertent revelation, could spell ruin for those present and our noble cause itself."

He paused, allowing his words to resonate in the hushed atmosphere, his eyes scanning the faces of the compatriots. "We stand on the precipice of an endeavor that will either liberate our people or lead us to the gallows. Thus, every step must be as silent as it is firm, every plan as secure as it is bold. Let us not falter under the illusion of safety, for the walls have ears, and the shadows may harbor those with allegiance not to our cause but to the crown."

Lord Blackwood, somber and thoughtful, acknowledged Washington's prudent warning with a slight incline of his head. After a moment of reflection, he addressed the assembled group. "General Washington, your counsel illuminates the dark path we tread with the wisdom of prudence. We are indeed encircled by peril, much like the beleaguered fortresses of our olden tales. Your words, sir, serve as a clarion call to the discretion and secrecy this lofty enterprise demands."

Lord Blackwood paused, ensuring his words were met with understanding and acceptance. "It is with a heart steadfast in the cause of liberty, yet mindful of the labyrinthine dangers we navigate, that I pledge my support to you gentlemen and this noble cause set before us."

The tension in the room was thick, every word hanging in the air. Marianne stood at the edge, her heart pounding. Thomas inched closer, straining to hear as the noblemen's debate grew louder. Words like freedom, independence, and rebellion cut through the din. His pulse quickened with their zeal, igniting a spark of longing for liberty within him. A hand on his shoulder made him flinch. He turned to see Harriet's concerned face.

"Best not to linger too long," Harriet whispered, nodding towards the kitchen.

Thomas nodded, reluctantly stepping back. He couldn't shake the feeling that he was on the brink of something monumental, a tide of change about to sweep them all away. He quietly left the dining hall, his mind buzzing with talk of change in the colonies. The longing for his freedom burned bright within him. If only fate would allow him to seek the same for himself. He blinked, returning to the moment. For now, duty called. He straightened his shoulders and got back to work.

Thomas took a deep breath to steady his nerves and reentered the dining room, balancing a large silver platter with the main course. The savory aroma of roast duck made his mouth water. As he navigated through the room, the platter felt heavy in his hands, both physically and symbolically.

Beside him, Marianne and the other servers moved in careful synchronicity, their faces tense with concentration as they served the guests. Thomas noticed a faint tremor in Marianne's hands, showing her nervousness. He wished he could offer some reassurance but now was not the time.

As Thomas placed a duck breast on Lord Blackwood's plate, he felt eyes on him. He looked up and met Lady Constance's gaze from across the table. Her eyes were full of unspoken emotions as she watched the servants. Though her jeweled gown marked her as nobility, her expression held a deep empathy that transcended status. Thomas saw her gaze shift to Marianne. A flicker of sadness crossed her delicate features. She looked back at Thomas, offering the faintest hint of an understanding smile before turning her attention to her dinner companions.

Marianne took a deep breath as she entered the kitchen, leaning against the door for support. Dinner had been a whirlwind of nerves and tension. She remembered bits of the guests' heated political talks. She only caught fragments while serving, but it was evident significant changes were coming. The thought excited and scared her.

"You alright, dearie?" Harriet asked with concern in her voice.

Marianne opened her eyes to see Harriet looking at her with sympathy. The older woman's face, dusted with flour, was lined with worry from a lifetime of hard work. But her eyes were warm and wise, something Marianne found comforting.

"Just overwhelmed," Marianne admitted, tucking a strand of hair back in place.

Harriet nodded. "Things are heating up. Best we can do is take it one day at a time."

The door swung open, and Thomas stumbled in, his face red from the kitchen's heat. He gave Marianne a look. They'd talk later. For now, there was work to do.

Hours passed, and the busy evening slowly wound down. The kitchen grew quieter as the servants drifted off to their quarters for the night, one by one. When the last of them had gone, Thomas slipped out to the small pantry. He found Marianne huddled there in the dim light.

"Well, that was somethin'," Marianne said, her eyes wide with excitement and apprehension as she leaned forward to give Thomas a quick, comforting hug.

Thomas returned the gesture, but his expression was pensive, his mind elsewhere. He glanced around cautiously, making sure they were alone. "I'm shocked at what we overheard tonight," he admitted, his voice barely a whisper. "Revolution and independence. The guests didn't hide their hatred for British rule. Not too long ago, I was living in England myself. Now, I'm here on a plantation working for people who want to fight the king."

Marianne nodded, her face serious as she pulled back to look at him. "It's all a bit overwhelmin', ain't it? To think, the air we breathe is thick with talk of rebellion, but we get the whip if we don't do as we're told."

Thomas frowned, his mind racing. "Yeah, makes me

despise them with their hypocritical speeches. They speak of liberty while denying us the same rights."

They stood silently, the flickering candlelight casting long shadows on the walls.

"Whatever comes, we'll face it together," Marianne said, her eyes locking onto Thomas's with an intensity that underscored her conviction. She reached out and grabbed his hand. "You're the one good thing that's come of this place, and I must say you looked quite handsome tonight," she added, a playful smile curving her lips.

Thomas, standing stiffly, relaxed at her touch and smiled, his earlier anxieties momentarily forgotten. He looked down at his modest attire, a simple but well-fitted jacket borrowed from another house servant for the occasion, and chuckled softly. "Handsome, is it? I suppose this old thing does look better in the candlelight," he joked, his tone light but his heart warmed by her compliment.

Marianne laughed, her gaze appreciative. "It's not just the candlelight," she teased back, her eyes twinkling with mischief. "It's who is wearin' it. Tonight, among those high-flown guests and their fineries, you're the one who made my heart flutter. It ain't the clothes, Thomas. It's the way you carry yourself. You have a strength about you that doesn't need silk or jewels to be seen."

Her words seemed to hang in the air, a testament to the bond that had grown between them. Thomas felt a surge of gratitude for Marianne's presence in his life. As he gazed into her eyes, the soft glow of the candlelight illuminating her features, a deeper emotion stirred within him.

"Thank you, Marianne," he replied, his voice steady and sincere yet carrying an undercurrent of emotion. "For seeing me as I am and for being by my side. No matter what tomorrow brings, having you here makes everything manageable. You were as beautiful as ever tonight."

Marianne's face softened, and she stepped closer, her hand reaching up to gently touch his cheek. "And, thank you, my love, for being my anchor in this storm. I don't know what I would do without you." Her voice was a whisper, her breath warm against his skin.

The air around them seemed to hold its breath, the usual sounds of the house fading into a hushed silence. Thomas reached out, his hands framing her face, bringing her closer until their foreheads touched. There was a tenderness in his touch, a promise of something profound that neither dared to voice until now.

"Marianne, in a world as uncertain as ours, one truth remains clear to me," Thomas confessed, his eyes locked onto hers. "You have become more to me than just a companion. You are the heart of my days, the peace in my nights."

Her eyes shimmered with unshed tears, a smile touching her lips. "And you, Thomas, are my courage, my reason to face each day with hope." She leaned in, her lips brushing his in a kiss that sealed their unbroken vows.

At that moment, surrounded by the echoes of revolution and change, Thomas and Marianne's romance grew deeper.

Thomas glanced at the moonlit fields as they slipped back to their quarters. The plantation was silent, with only the occasional dog barking. He took a deep breath; the night air contrasted with the kitchen's heat. He knew their journey wouldn't be easy, but the thought of freedom pushed him forward.

"Ready for this?" Marianne whispered beside him, her eyes shining in the moonlight.

Thomas nodded, a smile tugging at his lips. "Ready as I'll ever be."

Chapter Twenty-One

Thomas leaned against the old maple tree near his cabin, its gnarled branches throwing speckled shadows on the grass. It was September, and the air around him hummed with chatter and laughter. Harriet braided Emily's hair, her fingers working quickly as they gossiped. James and William played cards, their faces shifting between focus and amusement. Nearby, Elijah dozed, his head bobbing with each breath, a soft snore escaping now and then.

Thomas watched them, feeling a wave of calm washing over him. These simple moments, the everyday routines, offered a slight sense of comfort in the face of uncertainty. He took a deep breath, letting the sounds and sights around him ground his thoughts.

"Hey, Thomas, want to join us?" James called, waving a card.

Thomas shook his head with a smile. "Maybe later."

He glanced at the sky, noticing the sun's descent.

There was work to be done and plans to be made, but for now, he let himself enjoy this rare moment of peace. No overseers shouted orders or cracked whips. The sun warmed the soil while they rested in the shade. It almost felt like freedom.

Almost.

He tilted his face upward, soaking in the sun's warmth. A gentle breeze wafted the sweet scent of jasmine, mingling with the earthy aroma of tobacco and soil. In the distance, the rhythmic tapping of a woodpecker on a tree trunk melded with the rustling leaves and chirping birds, crafting a soothing symphony. For a moment, he felt a brief escape from their harsh reality.

"You're staring again, Thomas," Harriet teased.

Thomas blinked, pulled from his thoughts. "Just thinking."

"Dangerous habit," James chuckled from his card game.

"Leave him be," Elijah said, poking James on the shoulder. "A man's entitled to his thinkin', even if it ain't much to think on," he added with a wry grin, sparking a chuckle from those nearby.

Thomas chuckled. Elijah had been the first to offer him kindness when he'd arrived, a skinny boy with hollow eyes. Now, they were good friends. He always made Thomas laugh, which was always needed in their circumstances.

Suddenly, the sound of boots crunching on gravel pierced the air. Thomas's shoulders tensed. He feared it might be the patrollers again, but it was just Lord Blackwood and Lady Constance taking a stroll. Relief washed over him, but he remained alert, curiosity piqued by their conversation as they passed by.

Blackwood's voice drifted over, low and firm. "Constance, my love, we must confront some arduous decisions. The plantation suffers financially due to the prevailing unrest, which compounds our difficulties. We must take measures to curtail our expenditures."

Lady Constance's voice, though softer, carried a firm undertone, "What are you proposing, Reginald?"

"We must consider the sale of some of the servants," Blackwood stated plainly. "It is the sole viable strategy to regulate our expenditures."

Thomas felt cold dread settle in his stomach. Selling servants meant tearing families apart and sending people to unknown fates. He strained to hear more.

"Whom do you have in mind?" Constance asked, her voice laced with apprehension.

"It matters not whom," Blackwood responded brusquely. "We require the funds, Constance."

Constance stopped walking, turning to face her husband. "Reginald, these souls are not mere figures upon our ledgers. They possess lives and families. Such a decision cannot be taken lightly."

Blackwood's expression grew stern, his gaze sharpening. "This matter extends beyond the reach of sentiment, Constance. It is a question of survival. Our estate cannot continue to support itself under these current strains."

From his discreet vantage, Thomas saw a shadow of sadness and frustration clouding Lady Constance's countenance. "Surely there exists an alternative," she persisted.

"We might discover other methods to curtail expenses and enhance the tobacco yield."

Blackwood shook his head, his expression unyielding. "I have weighed every potential course." He declared with finality. "This is our only recourse."

As the grave reality took hold, Thomas felt a coldness creep over him despite the sun's warmth. Those who would be sold off faced separation from their friends, possibly forever. He could almost hear the heart-wrenching cries of mothers torn from their children and friends ripped away from one another. The thought was unbearable.

Constance's voice softened, almost pleading. "Reginald, I concede the necessity of practicality, yet we mustn't forsake our compassion. These determinations bear upon real lives."

Blackwood's gaze softened a bit, but his resolve stayed firm. "Compassion, whilst noble, is a luxury we cannot presently entertain, Constance. The continuance of our estate and the well-being of our family hinge upon these difficult decisions."

Constance paused, choosing her words with deliberate care. "If we are compelled to sell anyone to stabilize our finances, perhaps we should consider Marianne. It might protect the others, particularly those with young children." Although she had never openly challenged her husband about the whispers of his affair with Marianne, her suggestion subtly aimed at removing Marianne from the estate, influenced by these underlying tensions.

They continued walking, their voices dwindling into the distance, leaving Thomas heavy-hearted. He glanced at the other servants. What was once a peaceful moment now seemed overshadowed by the looming threat of separation, especially the separation from Marianne. The laughter and chatter around him now felt distant, subdued by the heavy reality of what he had just overheard.

As the sun began to set, casting long shadows across the field, Thomas knew the illusion of peace was shattered. The bonds of friendship and kinship they had formed were at risk. The harsh reality of their existence pressed down on him. He had to share what he had heard. They deserved to know.

He was at a loss for how to shield himself and his friends from being sold, and the thought of losing his friends filled him with dread. The other orphans were his only family. Losing them would mean losing a part of himself. What if it was Emily? They were too young to survive on their own. He always protected them, but this situation was out of his control. And Marianne? The thought of losing her was unbearable. He looked around at his friends. He took a deep breath, ready to share the news he'd overheard.

"Everyone, listen for a moment," Thomas began. "I overheard Lady Constance and Lord Blackwood talking. They're planning to sell some of us. There must be something we can do," he said, looking to Harriet.

A gasp rippled through the group. James was the first to break the silence. "Who? When?" His eyes were wide with alarm.

Thomas shook his head, his expression grim. "I don't have all the details, but we can't just sit here waiting for it to happen. We need to take action."

Emily twisted her apron between her fingers, her voice quivering with fear. "But what can we do, Tommy? We're indentured servants, bound by our contracts."

James's fists tightened, his face contorting with anger. "We can't let them treat us like cattle! There has to be somethin' we can do to fight this."

Harriet raised her voice. "Remember what we heard in the main house about the colonists and their struggle against the British?"

William scoffed. "And what's that got to do with us?"

Harriet lifted her hand, her voice filled with a hopeful naiveté. "It's bigger than we think. This whole fight of theirs, well, they say they're fighting for dignity and the right to freedom," she said, her eyes meeting each of theirs. "In a way, our freedom is linked with theirs."

James scowled. "That makes no sense, Harriet. You just heard Tom say they are goin' to sell some of us. So how can their fight help us? We're nothin' but servants here. They don't care about us."

Harriet shook her head. "Calm down, James. They may not think their fight is our fight, but if they win, it might change things for us, too."

Elijah leaned forward. "So what do we do? How do we help?"

"We stay informed," Harriet said. "We listen, we watch, and when the time comes, we act."

Thomas nodded. "We need to stay united, like a family. We can't let them break us apart."

Marianne added, "We need to find out who they might be lookin' to sell. Henrietta, Harriet, Emily, and I are workin' in the main house. We can listen in, maybe catch some talk about who they're plannin' to sell. Then, maybe we can hide 'em or find some way to protect 'em."

As evening settled in, casting a gentle dusk over the grounds, Harriet pulled a worn newspaper from her pocket, carefully unfolding the brittle pages. She gathered the group closer, her voice steady and clear against the chirping crickets. "Listen to this," she urged, pointing to a faded article as everyone leaned in. "It talks about the colonists' mounting troubles with the British—taxation without representation, unfair laws, and all that. They're fighting for their rights, much like we dream of doing. It makes you think. Maybe we're not so different in our struggles."

"What does 'taxation without representation' mean?" Emily asked, her brows furrowed in confusion.

Harriet looked at her thoughtfully before responding, "It means the colonists are being forced to pay taxes to the British government, but they don't have any say in the government's decisions. They're paying for policies they have no control over—just like we toil under rules we didn't choose."

Thomas nodded, adding, "The colonists want to have a say in how they're governed. They want to make their own choices, like we wish we could."

Elijah said, "And if them colonists can fight back against bein' treated wrong, maybe we can too."

Harriet continued, "It's a different kind of fight, but the desire for freedom is the same. If they can stand up and demand their rights, perhaps one day we can too."

"Yeah, I guess you got a point, Harriet," James added.

Thomas's mind drifted back to his conversation with

Marianne after the dinner party when George Washington and Patrick Henry discussed unrest with Lord Blackwood. They had spoken of running away. Marianne had been passionate, her eyes bright with hope, whispering that if things got worse, they should consider escaping. She had told him stories of people making it to the North, where slavery had been abolished. He had felt a mix of fear and excitement at the idea. Running away meant leaving everything behind, but it also meant a chance at a new life. Then he remembered Henrietta's talk about the Friends of Freedom who helped hide runaways. She said they had safe houses and routes to the North. She said they would help us if we needed them.

As he listened to Harriet, Thomas realized they might need to act sooner than he had thought. The revolution brewing among the colonists could be their chance. They just had to be ready to take it. Murmurs rippled through the group. Thomas pulled Marianne closer, wrapping his arms around her.

"There are many important figures in this fight against tyranny. One man you should know is George Washington, a respected military leader who has shown great courage against the British. Some of you will remember him from the dinner party not long ago. Then there's Patrick Henry," Harriet continued, her voice growing stronger. "He's a passionate speaker who has rallied the colonists with his powerful speeches. When the colonists were forced to pay taxes to England without having any say in things here, the House of Burgesses was formed, an assembly of elected representatives challenging the Crown's authority."

Thomas's heart pounded. He wanted to be brave like Washington and Henry, to fight for freedom and justice. He knew their fight was his fight, too.

"Are these men fightin' for people like us also?" William asked, voicing the question that lingered in all their minds.

"Perhaps not directly," Harriet said, her eyes fierce. "But that doesn't mean we have to accept this. We deserve a say over our own lives, too."

"And don't forget all of these wealthy men own slaves," Thomas said, "But, we can't let that hold us back. I say we do what's necessary."

Murmurs rippled through the group. Thomas met each person's gaze, seeing his hope reflected there. Maybe their dream of freedom wasn't so far-fetched after all. If they stood united with the rebels, how could they fail?

Chapter Twenty-Two

It was the winter of 1774, and Virginia was heating up in the growing revolutionary sentiment. Tensions with the British government had exploded as colonial grievances hit a boiling point. Virginia, with its influential leaders like George Washington, Thomas Jefferson, and Patrick Henry, was at the forefront of the movement toward independence. The royal governor dissolved the Virginia House of Burgesses, but its members continued to meet in defiance, contributing to the call for the First Continental Congress.

On the Blackwood plantation, unrest mirrored Harriet's secretive actions. After Lord Blackwood finished reading it every morning, she would sneak the *Virginia Gazette* from the garbage. As the only servant who could read and write, Harriet became a crucial source of information for the others. She read aloud the news of revolutionary activities, the calls for resistance, and the proclamations of liberty that inflamed the hearts of many.

Thomas eagerly looked forward to their secret evening gatherings in the servant quarters. Harriet would carefully unfold the crumpled newspaper and read the news aloud. Her steady voice brought to life stories of colonial defiance and the calls for liberty and justice. The servants, their faces illuminated by flickering candlelight, listened intently, their eyes wide with hope and fear. Through Harriet's readings, they learned about the bold actions of the Virginia House of Burgesses, the solidarity with Boston, and the fiery speeches of leaders like Patrick Henry and George Washington.

Life on the Blackwood plantation had been unforgiving since Thomas arrived. Under strict orders from Lord Blackwood, the overseer enforced a brutal regimen. Whips cracked in the fields, and even minor infractions were punished severely. Although the law allowed a maximum of thirty-nine lashes, the overseers routinely ignored this limit, and Thomas had heard stories of people dying from their injuries. Now nineteen, Thomas had become proficient as a cooper, his hands rough and calloused from years of labor.

Thomas had witnessed his friends and family torn apart by the overseer's cruelty. Many were sold to other plantations. Arthur, the man he used to brawl with in the cooperage, was the latest to be sold off. He couldn't shake the memory of Elijah and James, stripped and whipped, their screams echoing in his mind. He longed for freedom, but his indenture still had years left. Even then, there was no guarantee he would be granted his freedom at the end. Plantation owners had sneaky ways to keep their servants indentured for life, and the stories he'd heard terrified him.

Tonight, Lord Blackwood and Lady Constance were hosting another dinner party. Since the colonists started defying British rule, the Blackwood Plantation had become a hotspot for Virginia's elite and members of the House of Burgesses. Lord Dunmore, the royal governor of Virginia, had not supported the colonists' position against the King's policies. As royal governor, he endorsed unpopular measures such as the Coercive Acts, setting him at odds with the colonists.

Amidst the social gatherings over the past year, tensions also escalated on another front. The colonists were engaged in a battle with the Shawnee and Mingo tribes in what was known as Lord Dunmore's War. This conflict, instigated by Dunmore, had further strained the already tense relationship between the colonists and the British government, exacerbating the discord sparked by his dissolution of the Virginia House of Burgesses during a day of fasting and prayer by the colonists. His actions were intended to suppress the growing spirit of rebellion but only deepened the colonists' resolve for independence.

For Thomas and the others, it was a challenging but thrilling time. The air was thick with rumors that the British might offer freedom to the enslaved if they joined the fight against the colonists. Amidst this turmoil, they were frustrated to hear the frequent talks of independence that stirred among the elites and politicians, talks that spoke of liberty and rights yet conspicuously failed to include them. This irony was not lost on them; while their masters debated the chains of tyranny from across the ocean, they faced the literal chains of bondage, equally longing for a freedom that seemed just as distant.

Thomas stood in the main foyer, the heavy scent of beeswax mixing with the faint smell of tobacco. The old house creaked with history, its dark wood beams and fancy furniture showing off centuries of wealth and power. He tugged at the stiff collar of his servant's uniform, the rough fabric rubbing against his sunburned neck.

Thomas, now grown taller and standing with the stature of a man, shifted uncomfortably in his servant's uniform. Though finer than his usual garb and neatly tailored attire, the attire felt tight and constricting around his broadening shoulders. "Nicer clothes, but still a shackle," he grumbled under his breath, his voice low and tense. The meticulously kept uniform featured a crisp white shirt under a dark, buttoned vest and polished black shoes—a stark contrast to his feelings of restraint and unease.

With her striking features and lively eyes, Marianne gave Thomas a wink. Her servant's dress, though simple, was immaculate and form-fitting, tailored to echo the modest elegance of her figure. The deep navy fabric was complemented by a crisp, white apron that accentuated her neatness.

"You look handsome," she complimented, her voice light and playful.

Thomas, momentarily taken aback by her presence, managed a small smile. "And you, in that dress—it suits you better than it does me," he responded with a laugh.

The servants' kitchen door groaned upon its hinges, and Lady Constance entered, her presence unmistakably commanding despite the unspoken sorrow reflected in her deep blue eyes. Her grief was fresh, a silent burden she bore after the loss of her unborn child. Her steps were measured, each seeming to echo the loss that had quietly hollowed her out.

As she surveyed the room, her gaze was meticulous and all-encompassing, and her attire mirrored the grace of her high standing. She was clad in a richly embroidered gown of deep green silk, which flowed elegantly about her as she moved. The dress was fitted at the bodice and flared gracefully at the skirt, accentuated with delicate lace at the cuffs and collar. Her movements bore the elegance of the aristocracy, yet Thomas perceived a certain heaviness in her stride as though she, too, was burdened by unseen fetters.

"Tonight holds great importance," she said in her usual crisp and authoritative tone. "I require your service to be executed with utmost precision and discretion." Her eyes paused on Thomas, and he met her stare with unwavering determination. "Our guests this evening are gentlemen of the highest reputation. George Washington, Patrick Henry, Thomas Jefferson, and George Mason will grace our halls. It is imperative that they depart with naught but the most exalted opinion of our estate."

The names took Thomas aback. They had served Washington and Henry before, but the other men were also the subject of quiet talk among the servants. These were men who embodied the hopes of freedom. His heart raced, and he struggled to keep his composure.

"Remember," Lady Constance said, "your conduct reflects upon us all. There is no margin for error." Her gaze momentarily softened, revealing a touch of empathy before she resumed her austere expression. She then turned and left the room, leaving them to their thoughts and preparations.

As the servants straightened their uniforms for the final time, Thomas reflected on the irony of serving men who might be allies in his struggle for freedom. He observed the faces of his friends, marked by hardship and determination. Harriet caught his glance and gave a subtle nod that spoke volumes.

"Are we prepared?" Marianne asked.

"Ready as I'll ever be," Thomas replied firmly. He took a deep breath, feeling the weight of the moment. Tonight, amid the grandeur and pretense, seeds of change might take root. He would now play his part, waiting for true freedom.

With one last look at his friends, Thomas stepped forward, ready to face the evening and whatever it might bring.

Thomas balanced the tray of roasted pheasant, the rich scent of rosemary and sage enveloping him. Tonight, the tray felt unusually heavy. He was worn out, body and soul. Leading the procession of servants into the dining hall, he stepped into a room alive with subdued conversations and the gentle clink of silverware, all under the warm, soft light of candles reflecting off the polished mahogany surfaces. Nearing the head of the table, Thomas caught snippets of a spirited debate, with Patrick Henry's impassioned voice resonating with conviction.

Patrick Henry stood with a commanding presence, his fiery spirit evident in his words and demeanor. His face was marked by a determined jawline and piercing eyes that seemed to challenge every listener in the room.

He was dressed like a Virginia gentleman, wearing a deep blue coat tailored to perfection over an intricately embroidered cream waistcoat. His white cravat was neatly tied, accentuating his strong voice as he declared, "We must not suffer these injustices to persist. Taxation without representation is naught but tyranny!" His passionate proclamation resonated sharply through the dining hall.

With his tall and imposing figure, George Washington stood as the embodiment of resolution and dignity. His face, a visage of stoic contemplation, was framed by his powdered wig, lending him an air of gravitas. Clad in a finely tailored military uniform of deep blue with buff facings, his presence commanded attention and respect.

Washington nodded solemnly in response to Patrick Henry's impassioned words. "Verily," he began, his voice deep and deliberate, "the moment for resolute action approaches swiftly. The King's peace is but enslavement. It behooves us, as gentlemen, to cast off the yoke that diminishes our stature as free men."

Thomas tiptoed, placing the tray on the table, but he couldn't help listening to their words. The room was tense, and he knew this night could change everything. His eyes flicked to Marianne, who poured wine into Lord Blackwood's glass as she moved with a dancer's grace.

Lord Blackwood stood, his stature commanding as he spoke with an enthusiasm that filled the room. He was impeccably dressed in a coat of midnight blue, his vest intricately patterned with subtle golden threads that caught the candlelight and reflected his wealth and position. "Liberty must be our cause, gentlemen," he declared, his voice resounding with deep-seated passion. "We owe it to our progeny that shall follow."

He paused, his eyes sweeping across the room, his expression of steely resolve mixed with a trace of defiance. "Amidst the oppressive policies enacted by Lord Dunmore, which seek to bind and subjugate us, we find our cause ever more justified. His measures, which impose severe constraints and unjust taxation upon us, serve only to fuel our zeal for freedom. It is not merely for ourselves we fight but for the liberty of all who will come after us."

The words resonated with Thomas, stirring his dreams. He stepped to the side, waiting for George's next signal, his mind racing. Could these powerful men understand his longing for freedom as an indentured servant? Or were their struggles worlds apart from his?

In the bustling kitchen, Henrietta presided over a pot of stew. The scent of savory meat and vegetables filled the air. Beside her, Emily busied herself with chopping herbs, and Harriet rolled out dough for bread with precise, practiced motions. Harriet's gaze occasionally drifted towards the door that led to the dining hall, her mind wandering to Thomas and the others in service there.

Together, the three women toiled, the kitchen acting as a tense haven where their hands crafted meals and a semblance of solidarity. The clanging of pots and the sizzle of boiling water filled the air, yet beneath the noise lay an unspoken connection.

Henrietta's eyes flickered with worry. "Almost ready, Harriet? Emily?"

"Just about," Harriet replied, placing the bread on a

tray with a tired sigh. Emily chopped herbs nearby, her hands moving quickly.

"Keep movin'," Henrietta urged. "We got to be sharp. Remember what Lady Constance tol' us 'bout how important tonight's dinner be. We's got to do our best an' make no mistakes."

Harriet slammed the tray down harder than necessary. "Freedom? They're talking about freedom out there," she said, her voice thick with anger. "What do they know about our kind of freedom? They're fighting for their rights while we have none ourselves."

Emily nodded, her hands still busy. "Ain't it the truth? They want liberty, but they don't see us, not really."

Henrietta shook her head, her anger simmering. "One day, things gon' change. One day, they'll see us."

As Thomas stepped back into the kitchen to grab another tray, he exchanged a glance with Harriet. With a new tray in hand, Thomas's resolve deepened. He was determined to listen in on the dinner guests' conversations, intent on learning as much as he could about the current unrest and the political winds shifting outside their kitchen walls. Each snippet of dialogue he could overhear was a piece of the larger puzzle, potentially offering insights that could affect their futures.

As he stepped back into the dining hall, the clinking of crystal and murmur of conversation filled his ears. Thomas moved through the room with practiced grace, his tray expertly balanced. Tonight, each step seemed more burdensome, every movement charged with the heightened awareness of watching eyes. He paused to serve a dish to one of the esteemed guests, catching another fragment of heated talk about colonial unrest. It was a dangerous dance—listening without appearing to listen, understanding without showing it.

"Lookin' good, Thomas," Marianne whispered, the serving tray in her hands and a determined glint in her green eyes. Her fiery red hair was tucked neatly under her cap, but a few rebellious strands framed her face. Their eyes met, and an unspoken bond tightened between them in that fleeting moment. They shared no words; their silent communication spoke volumes. Over the past year, their romance had blossomed, and Thomas was deeply in love with her. He'd have married her by now, but their indenture terms forbade it.

As they moved past each other, Thomas felt a surge of strength. Marianne's presence was a beacon amid the sea of demands and expectations.

The air thickened with tension as the evening wore on. Thomas could feel it. There was a shift in Lawson's demeanor. His gaze lingered longer. His footsteps echoed louder. Marianne stumbled slightly as she poured wine into a goblet, earning a harsh glare from Lawson. His eyes narrowed. Suspicion was etched into every line of his face.

"Careful," Lawson said in a low, menacing whisper. His gaze lingered on Marianne in a way that made her visibly uncomfortable, and the intensity of his stare carried an unsettling undertone.

Marianne mumbled an apology, her hands trembling slightly, a clear sign of unease. Thomas clenched his jaw, anger, and helplessness rising within him as he noticed Lawson's eyes lingered on her. His dislike for Lawson deepened, repulsed by the man's unsettling gaze. Nearby,

Lawson tightened his grip, attuned to the undercurrent of tension among the servants. Every nervous glance and hesitant step seemed to fuel his suspicion and readiness to assert control.

Henrietta's instructions became sharper in the kitchen, her voice carrying an urgency that mirrored the mounting tension. She, too, could sense the change. What was once a sanctuary now felt like a powder keg, primed to detonate at the slightest spark.

Thomas returned to the dining hall with another tray, his mind racing. He ducked into a narrow hallway, his heart pounding. The dim light from the wall sconces cast long shadows, making the corridor feel like a maze of secrets and whispered plans. He signaled with a quick nod, and Marianne slipped into the hallway.

"Quickly now," Thomas whispered, his voice barely audible over the distant clatter of dishes and muffled conversations from the dining hall. "What did you find out?" he asked, his eyes darting around to ensure no other listeners were around.

Marianne leaned in closer, her voice equally hushed. "They're plannin' somethin' big, somethin' about a new tax protest. It could happen any day now," she replied, her eyes reflecting the seriousness of the information.

Thomas nodded, absorbing the gravity of her words. "We need to be ready, then. Anything else?"

She glanced back towards the kitchen briefly before continuing. "Yes, there's talk of a meetin', a secret gatherin' of the leaders tomorrow night. They think it might be the spark they need. Speakin' of that, the old bastard, Lawson, is comin' this way."

Lawson stood ominously at the end of the corridor, his eyes narrowing into slits as he surveyed the scene. His presence was a dark cloud, suffocating.

"What's goin' on here?" he barked, his gravelly voice echoing off the walls.

"Just fetching more wine, sir," Thomas replied, keeping his gaze respectfully lowered though every fiber of his being screamed to meet his stare head-on. He could feel the overseer's scrutiny, the man's suspicious nature probing for any hint of rebellion.

"Get to it, then," Lawson growled, turning away but not without casting one last lingering look over his shoulder.

As Thomas resumed his duties, he saw his friends, each focused on their tasks. Yet, beneath the surface, their determination to be free grew stronger.

They would escape. They had to.

Chapter Twenty-Three

The blistering summer heat bore down on the fields of Blackwood Plantation, stretching long shadows over the tobacco rows. Servants snapped off ripe tobacco leaves and tossed them in rough-hewn sacks on their backs. Years of relentless toil had hardened their fingers, leaving them calloused and green-stained from the plant sap. Once occupied with the cooperage, Thomas now found himself reassigned to the tobacco fields due to a downturn in barrel-making work. He labored diligently, side by side with his fellow workers, each day blending into the next under the relentless sun.

The morning bell rang early, waking them and marking another day of hard work in the fields. There was no break, no leniency, just endless labor driven by the overseer's commands. It was 1775, and the stirrings of freedom that spread through the colonies only heightened Lord Blackwood's paranoia about his servants escaping.

Thomas, who had seen countless slaves toiling without freedom, felt the sting of this irony deeply.

"Faster!" Lawson's command cut through the stifling heat like a whip. Positioned atop a small hill, he surveyed the workers with the intense focus of a predator. His presence loomed over the field like a dark cloud, a stark reminder of the iron grip that held them captive. With thick arms crossed over his chest, he radiated menace. A jagged scar ran down his right arm, mirroring the harshness of his spirit. His wide-brimmed hat cast his eyes into deep shadow, hiding them from view, yet Thomas could feel the piercing intensity of his gaze.

"Don't think I haven't noticed you draggin'," the overseer sneered, locking his gaze on Thomas. His voice was laced with malice. Each word meant to intimidate. "You think you're clever, hidin' behind those plants? Get back to work now!"

Thomas clenched his jaw but lowered his eyes. It was clear Lawson took twisted pleasure in his role, thriving on the power he wielded over the vulnerable souls under his watch. His heavy boots crunched on the dry soil as he roamed the fields, ever vigilant for any hint of defiance or weakness. The sharp crack of his whip cut through the air, a harsh reminder of his control.

"Remember your place," he growled at another servant who had paused to wipe the sweat from his brow. The man's shoulders sagged further as he hurried to comply, the weight of despair almost visible.

Thomas glanced at his fellow workers, seeing the emptiness in their eyes. Their silent pleas for mercy were ignored. They shared a common bond of suffering, yet each faced their struggles alone. Life for them had dwindled to mere survival.

As the afternoon sun climbed higher, its heat sapped their strength. Summers in Virginia were hot, and it was common for workers to faint from heat-related illnesses. Thomas felt his shirt cling to his back, drenched in sweat. Every breath felt heavy, the air thick with dust from the fields. Yet, within him, a fierce desire for freedom still blazed. His mind was consumed by thoughts of escape, of fleeing this torment. The risk was high, but the prospect of remaining under Blackwood's rule was worse. His hands trembled as he heaved another sack onto the cart, his muscles protesting.

Lawson's voice cut through the air once again. "Faster! You lazy dogs, faster!"

The fury within Thomas intensified with each shout and each brutal flare from the overseer. He yearned to turn the tables, to make Lawson feel the sting of being bound and whipped thirty-nine times.

"It's as hot as hell out here," William's weak, strained voice interrupted his thoughts.

Thomas turned to see William staggering slightly under the weight of a heavy bundle of tobacco leaves. He couldn't help but crack a wry smile and a quip, "Well, if it's hot as hell, at least we know they grow tobacco down there. Maybe we should send them a note asking for lighter bundles, eh?"

"What's this?" Lawson's boots thudded as he approached, eyes narrowing at William's faltering steps. "You're slowin' down."

"Sorry, sir. I'm just thirsty," William gasped, trying to straighten up, but his legs buckled, sending him crashing.

"Get up!" Lawson bellowed, wielding his cane with savage force. The first strike landed across William's back, drawing a sharp cry of agony that reverberated in Thomas's ears long after it ceased. The second hit followed quickly, ruthlessly, and Thomas felt his nails press into the palms of his hands.

"Don't hit me again. I'm not here for you to push around," William said, his fists clenched tightly.

"You're right. You're nobody. You're property," Lawson sneered, delivering another vicious strike. "You'll work, or you'll die out here, understand?"

The overseer's words lingered heavily in the air, heavy and suffocating. Rage clouded Thomas's vision, his lips turned white, and his jaws clenched shut. Every fiber of his being urged him to act, to rebel. Yet, he compelled himself to remain still, to wait for the right moment. Any rash move could doom them all.

"Get up, you worthless scum!" Lawson yelled at William, his voice laced with sadistic glee. William's cries seemed only to spur his brutality. Another strike followed, then another.

Thomas heard the sickening thud of the cane, the grim sound of wood striking flesh. He stood powerless as William's body jerked with each hit, his screams mingling with the oppressive heat and the stench of sweat and dirt.

"What are y'all looking at? Get back to work!" Lawson barked at the rest of the servants, who had stopped to watch in horrified silence. The threat in his tone was unmistakable.

Thomas swallowed hard. He could feel the tremble in his fists, clenched at his sides, as a wave of helpless anger flooded him. The sight of William's agony left a deep, burning mark on his mind. He rushed over to William, who had collapsed on the ground, breathing shallowly and unevenly. Gently, he helped him to his feet, taking on most of his friend's weight as he supported him to stand.

"Easy now, Will," Thomas said, trying to offer him comfort. "Let's get you to the shade, at least. This sun isn't doing you any favors. I'll have someone get you some water."

William managed a weak nod, leaning heavily on Thomas as they went to the meager shade provided by an old, gnarled pine tree nearby. Once there, Thomas eased his friend against the trunk.

"I shouldn't have let you carry that tobacco alone," Thomas said, his voice laced with guilt as he wiped a bead of sweat from his brow.

William gave a weak chuckle. "And what? Have both of us flattened under those cursed leaves?" He tried to muster a grin. "No, Tom, it's this place and this damn heat and everything else piled on top. I would've beaten the overseer if I knew it wouldn't bring down hell upon everyone else here."

As the day ended, Thomas and the others carefully carried William back to their cabin. Henrietta carefully dressed William's wounds inside the cabin, applying her homemade remedy to ease the pain and ward off infection. Meanwhile, the others prepared a simple dinner of cornbread, collard greens, and beans. After they ate, they settled down for the night, sharing stories and laughter.

Once the cabin had settled into silence, Thomas slipped out, merging with the shadows of the night as he made his way toward the forest. Throughout the day, he had been formulating a plan. Now was the time to carefully observe the guards, identifying any lapses in their patrols. It was vital to craft their escape strategy meticulously.

The evening mist hugged the earth as Thomas crept along the forest's edge. He observed the shadows, tracking each guard's movements. Hidden by the dense foliage, Thomas didn't count on luck. Every step was deliberate.

From his concealment behind a cluster of bushes, Thomas watched a guard pause to light a pipe. He marked the place in his mind—a lapse in vigilance. Another guard paced back and forth, his boots crunching on the gravel, his eyes scanning the horizon but missing the shadows where Thomas hid. He crept forward, heart pounding, and pressed himself flat against the damp earth as another guard ambled past, oblivious to his presence.

In these fleeting moments, Thomas found his peace. The wilderness spoke to him in ways the plantation never could. It whispered secrets of secret trails and sanctuaries, hints of where freedom might still be possible. His hand caressed the rugged bark of an ancient oak, drawing strength from it. Surrounded by nature's embrace, a flicker of hope ignited within him. The rustle of leaves and distant calls of night creatures filled the air, cloaking his movements. Thomas knew that every second counted, and every inch gained brought him closer to freedom. The guards' idle chatter and the occasional flicker of their lanterns were reminders of the danger that lurked and the opportunity that awaited.

As the first light of dawn painted the sky, Thomas made his way back towards the servant quarters. He slipped inside just as the morning bell rang, signaling the start of another grueling day. He exchanged brief, meaningful nods with his friends as they gulped down their morning breakfast of hoecakes and molasses.

The day dragged on, each hour stretching out as they toiled in the fields. Finally, as dusk settled and the plantation quieted, he and his friends gathered in a secluded corner of the barn. The air was thick with the scent of hay and sweat as they huddled close, speaking in hushed tones. In this hidden enclave, they shared their hopes for the future as they planned their escape.

"Any news?" Elijah asked, his eyes wide with anticipation.

"The guards are getting lazy," Thomas replied, his voice low but firm. "We might have a chance if we time it right."

James leaned in closer, his face etched with determination. "Are you sure?"

Thomas described the scene he had witnessed—the guard lighting his pipe, the routines he noted, and the instances of the guard's lack of attention. "They lack the vigilance they think they possess. Near the south fence, there's a gap during the shift change. For about ten minutes, the area is not watched."

Elijah nodded. "Ten minutes. That's all we got. It's risky but the best chance we had in months."

William listened intently, his usually cheerful face

serious. "What about the others? Shouldn't we tell them too?"

Thomas hesitated, glancing at each of his friends. "We can't risk it, Will. The more people know, the more likely someone will slip up. We start with us. If we make it, then we come back for the others."

James's jaw tightened. "I don't like leavin' anyone behind, but Tom is right. We need to be smart about this."

Elijah placed a reassuring hand on James's shoulder. "We'll come back. We ain't leavin' them behind. But we need to be free first before we can help anyone else."

A determined silence fell over the group. They all knew the risks and the consequences, but the thought of freedom was seared in their minds.

"What about supplies?" James asked, breaking the silence. "We can't just run with nothin'."

Thomas nodded. "I've been stashing some food and water. Not much, but enough to get us started."

Elijah's eyes sparkled. "We need a signal. Somethin' to tell each other when it's time to make our move."

They exchanged ideas for a moment before Thomas spoke up. "Three short whistles. We'll practice it so we all know the sound."

Suddenly, a noise shattered the stillness—a creak of wood, the unmistakable crunch of footsteps on gravel. Thomas's heart leaped into his throat. He spun around, eyes wide with alarm.

"Who's in there?" a gruff voice cut through the silence, sending a jolt of fear through Thomas's veins. The overseer stepped into view, his gaze sweeping the barn with suspicion.

Thomas froze, his mind racing. Had he overheard their plans? Or worse, discovered their stash of supplies? Lawson's eyes narrowed, and it seemed as though the air held its breath for a moment.

"Just checkin' on things," Lawson muttered, though his tone suggested otherwise. He turned, casting one last glance over his shoulder before disappearing into the night.

Thomas exhaled shakily, every muscle tense. "We're running out of time," he whispered to himself. Lawson was onto them, and the stakes were higher than ever.

A sense of urgency gripped his heart as the barn door closed behind him. Their opportunity to leave was closing, and the plantation's shadow loomed. The escape plan teetered on the edge of discovery. Thomas and his friends had no choice but to act soon.

That night, as Thomas lay on his bed, the gravity of their plans weighed heavily on his mind. The stars outside his window shimmered brightly as if encouraging him forward. Closing his eyes, he visualized the forest path, the coarse bark under his touch, and the diminishing sound of the guards' footsteps. Freedom was tantalizingly close, and he was prepared to seize it.

Chapter Twenty-Four

Thomas was scouring for useful items for their escape when he stumbled upon a faded parchment tucked away in the manor's library. The inked words became apparent in the dim light as he unrolled it. The document was titled "Freedom Certificate," penned in meticulous, formal script. Constance Jackson leaped off the page, followed by a statement of her indenture, the name of her master, the terms of her indenture, and the date of her freedom. A life that was utterly unbefitting a noblewoman. This revelation—that the lady of the house had once been bound by indenture—shook Thomas to the core, his heart racing with implications.

Marianne had let him into the main house, taking advantage of the rare moment when Lord Blackwood and Lady Constance were away. The usually imposing halls felt strangely vulnerable without their presence, and Thomas, encouraged by the quiet, had dared to search deeper. Now, with this document in his hands, he was faced with the undeniable proof that even those who seem to hold power were not always born into it.

Astonishment washed over Thomas as he absorbed every word on the page, his mind spinning. Lady Constance, a woman of such elegance and status, had once endured life as a mere servant. It was almost beyond belief. She had been deprived of her liberty and compelled into servitude, her identity bound by the terms of a contract.

He envisioned her elegant hands, now graced with jewels, once forced to scrub floors on raw knees. He pictured her majestic figure, currently swathed in silk, reduced back then worn rags as clothing. A bitter taste filled his mouth as he imagined the humiliation she must have endured, hidden behind the polished exterior she presented to the world now. Lady Constance was more than she appeared. She was a kindred spirit, once bound by servitude, and this revelation changed everything. Thomas's heart raced as new possibilities sprang to mind. Carefully, he returned the parchment, his hands trembling. He knew he must safeguard this secret at all costs.

Thomas purposefully walked through the manor, his thoughts churning with the startling discovery. The revelation that Lady Constance, once an indentured servant, had ascended to the ranks of nobility by marrying Lord Blackwood struck him as an extraordinary twist of fate. Such a transition from servitude to the upper tiers of society was exceptionally rare, stirring both suspicion and curiosity about their relationship. Was their marriage founded on love, or was it merely a strategic alliance? This enigma deepened his intrigue about Lady Constance, driving him to seek direct answers from her to understand the layers beneath her poised exterior.

As he stepped outside, the low-hanging afternoon sun cast a golden hue across the manicured lawns, its rays shimmering in the warmth of autumn. He walked the garden paths with determined strides, the uneven cobblestones clicking familiarly under his worn boots. The humid air was perfumed with the scent of blooming magnolias and roses, offering a fragrant mask over the underlying earthiness of the plantation's grounds. Cicadas buzzed loudly, their chorus rising and falling in the thick summer air, adding to the sense of urgency and weight that pressed on him as he made his way to confront Lady Constance.

There she stood, the lady of the manor amidst the vibrant hues of her garden. Lady Constance Blackwood, her golden hair elegantly pulled back, maintained a posture befitting her noble status. Yet, as she tended to her roses, a softness in her actions seemed at odds with her aristocratic role. Thomas observed as she carefully pruned a thorny stem, her movements precise and confident. The vibrant roses contrasted with the secrets concealed in their caretaker's heart. Among these blooms, tenderly cultivated by her hands, the layers of her identity began to peel away, revealing a woman who had experienced both servitude and sovereignty.

The weight of his discovery pressed heavily on him, yet it did not crush his growing empathy. His gaze lingered on her, feeling an invisible thread of shared hardships. As he prepared to bridge the gap between servant and mistress, he knew his words must be as carefully chosen as the roses she tended. He cleared his throat, signaling the start of a pivotal conversation that would entwine their fates more closely than either could have imagined. Stepping forward, the crunch of the gravel underfoot punctuated the garden's quiet. He paused, observing her pale fingers against the dark soil as she tenderly cradled a rose, its petals gently unfurling in her grasp.

"My lady," he began, his voice puncturing the serene stillness of the garden.

Lady Constance straightened, a flash of surprise crossing her features before she composed herself with practiced calm. Yet her eyes, transparent and reflecting the vastness of the sky, betrayed a flicker of alarm. Thomas noticed the quickening pulse at the base of her throat, throbbing like a bird fluttering its wings in captivity, eager to escape.

"Thomas, what brings you here." Lady Constance asked.

Thomas paused, the weight of his discovery tempering his response. How should he broach such delicate matters, especially with a noblewoman?

"Something has come to my attention," Thomas began, his voice unsteady as he struggled with his thoughts. Her gaze locked onto his. "It's about your past, my lady." The sentence hung in the air, heavy and foreboding as a storm cloud.

Her lips quivered slightly as a flicker of vulnerability crossed her face. Struggling to maintain her composure, she faltered only slightly. "What exactly is it that you think you know, Thomas?" she asked, her voice trembling.

He paused, feeling the weight of the moment settle

around them. "Your indenture," he stated softly, his words both a revelation and an indictment, peeling back the layers of grandeur to expose a raw, shared truth. She recoiled slightly, her eyes flashing with surprise. At that moment, Lady Constance's facade crumbled, exposing the resilient woman who had endured great trials and risen adorned with dignity.

"Thomas," she whispered, her voice unsteady. Surrounded by roses, their thorns symbolic of life's dual nature--beauty interwoven with pain—they both stood, bound by circumstance. In that instant, the garden transformed into a sanctuary of truth, with the flowers bearing witness.

"There are chapters in life marked by hardship, pages we wish never to revisit," she said.

For Thomas, every word fell heavy. His chest tightened, a knot of fury and sorrow entwined like the brambles around them. He felt the sharp prick of thorns—the injustice of their bondage—piercing through his tattered existence. He gazed directly into her eyes and asked, "How does a person go from being a servant to nobility?"

Lady Constance paused. "I completed my servitude," she revealed, her voice a soft murmur against the rustle of the roses. "It was arduous, but it shaped me. After being free, I vowed never to endure such indignity again." She paused, her gaze drifting to a nearby rose, its bloom bold against the thorns. "I worked, saved, and slowly built a new life. It was then I met Lord Blackwood."

Her eyes met Thomas's again, shimmering with reflections of a past life. "We fell in love, truly so, despite society's disdain." A small, knowing smile curved her lips. "At first, society shunned me, the former servant now dressed in a lady's silks. But as time passed, they accepted me—some grudgingly, others genuinely. My journey was not just mine but a testament to what can be endured and overcome. Does this answer your question, Thomas?"

Thomas absorbed her words. He nodded slowly, respect dawning in his eyes. "It does, my lady," he replied, conveying new understanding. "And it shows me the strength of your character. Not many could walk such a path and emerge with grace."

He hesitated, choosing his following words carefully. "But tell me," he continued, his curiosity piqued, "how did you maintain your integrity and sense of self? And how did you forge a new identity in a world that seeks to define us by our past?"

Lady Constance's expression softened. "It wasn't easy, Thomas. Every day was a fight to prove not just to others, but to myself, that I am more than my beginnings. Love, resilience, and a bit of stubborn defiance helped me carve out the space I now hold." Her eyes twinkled slightly. "And having a husband like Lord Blackwood, who saw me for who I truly am, made all the difference."

Thomas listened intently, absorbing the dichotomy of her experiences and her current status. His brow furrowed as a new question formed, spurred by a lingering doubt. "If Lord Blackwood understands and respects your past as a servant, why does he continue to treat his own servants so harshly? It seems contrary to the kindness he showed you."

Lady Constance sighed, a trace of sadness crossing her features. "Thomas, that is a question I too have wrestled with. The truth is that Lord Blackwood is very much a product of his upbringing and the expectations set upon him by society. He manages his estate as he was taught—firmly and without showing the vulnerabilities he reveals in private. It is not an excuse but a reality of our times."

She paused, her gaze distant. "He has a gentler side, one not often seen by those outside our private life. He has supported me in changing some of our practices, though change comes slowly. He is not cruel but a man of his era, often bound by its conventions and role."

Thomas nodded. "Thank you for sharing your story. I hope you are correct about change, and maybe one day, the future will be different." He lingered for a moment and cleared his throat softly, breaking the silence between them. "My lady, if your heart truly aches for those shackled by servitude, maybe you can help us? Help us find our freedom?"

Her hand paused on the rose's stem, thorns pressing against her skin. "Help you?" The words were a whisper, voicing a notion fraught with risk.

"Escape," Thomas urged. "You know the estate, the patterns of the guards." His eyes, intense, imploring, met hers. "Your influence with Lord Blackwood could change our fate."

Lady Constance turned away, her gaze lost in the roses. Remorse lined her brow. "I have ignored these truths for too long," she admitted, her voice trembling. "My silence has made me complicit in the suffering of souls no less deserving of freedom than I."

Thomas watched as her noble facade crumbled, revealing raw determination beneath. "Then stand with us," he urged.

Her eyes, blue as the sky, met his with a clarity that spoke of storms weathered and survived. "I will do what I can, Thomas Everhart," Lady Constance said, her words granting her a courage she hadn't felt in years. "I vow it upon my honor."

At that moment, the garden seemed to hold its breath, the scent of roses thick in the air. A pact was forged, not of ink and paper, but of shared scars and silent rebellion. Lady Constance's hands, once soft, now bore the grit to reshape destiny.

Thomas lingered behind the rosebushes, his heart pounding. The fading sun cast long shadows, cloaking them in secrecy as they discussed their escape plan. Lady Constance glanced toward the manor, her resolve firm before entering. Moments later, she returned with a parchment and a quill in hand. She began to draw a rough sketch of the plantation.

"Through here," she said, her voice barely rising above the rustling leaves. "The north wall is unguarded at night. But you must be very quiet."

Thomas nodded, etching every word into his memory.

"Once beyond the wall," she added, "you can make for the forest. It will cover your tracks until dawn."

Right then, there was no more master and servant, no noblewoman and orphaned boy—only two souls bound by the yoke of oppression, yearning to break free.

"Promise me," Thomas implored, "that no harm will come to the others because of my actions. Promise that you will care for Emily, Harriet, and Henrietta."

"Upon my life, I swear it," Lady Constance promised.

"Meet me at the old barn tomorrow night, and I'll bring you some provisions."

She raised her hand, tenderly brushing a stray lock from her face—a simple gesture yet heavy with the weight of their pact. As she turned to leave, her silhouette merged gracefully with the shadows of the night. Watching her departure, Thomas felt a newfound kinship with the noblewoman who had seemed as distant as the stars.

As she walked away, Thomas felt a profound sense of duty. The document revealing her past, a tattered remnant of a life once shackled, was now his to safeguard. It was not merely parchment and ink but the crucible of their burgeoning trust. In the stillness, he felt his own transformation. No longer was he simply an orphan scrabbling for survival; he was now a conspirator against oppression, an architect of freedom.

As Thomas navigated his way back to the servants' quarters, his mind was a whirlwind of thoughts spurred by Lady Constance's commitment to their cause. This new hope bolstered him, yet he was acutely aware of the dangers ahead. Once they executed their escape, he knew Lord Blackwood would unleash his hounds and patrols. His heart pounded as he ducked behind hedges and slipped through shadows. Every creak of the manor, every rustle of leaves, made him jump. The escape plan was fragile, and one misstep could mean capture—or worse.

The thought of Lord Blackwood's wrath chilled him. The man was relentless and would stop at nothing to retrieve what he considered his property. Thomas knew they had to move swiftly and smartly, leaving no trace behind. The stakes were higher than ever, but so was their determination to taste freedom.

As he slipped inside the cabin, his friends looked up with expectancy. Thomas kept his voice low, swiftly recounting his conversation with Lady Constance.

"But how can we trust her?" Marianne whispered. Skepticism was etched on her tired face. "She's one of them now."

Thomas shook his head. "I found a document that showed she was once an indentured servant. She's had her chains—believe me, she wants to break free of her past as much as we do. She said she would give us provisions, and she drew this map and told me which way to go to avoid the guards."

William nodded slowly, brow furrowed in thought. "If she can get us supplies, maybe we have a chance."

"It won't be easy," Thomas cautioned. "We'll need to move fast once we run and stay hidden. It's a long way to freedom."

"I don't care how hard it is," Marianne declared with fire in her eyes. "Anything's better than this."

Thomas felt his determination swell. "We leave in three nights. Tell no one else—the fewer that know, the safer we'll be. Just be ready."

As the night drew to a close, Thomas replayed his earlier conversation in his mind. The plan was bold and dangerous, but with Lady Constance's assistance, freedom shimmered on the horizon. The following day seemed to stretch on endlessly as he awaited nightfall. They had agreed to meet at the old barn at the edge of the estate under the cover of darkness. The hours were filled with dread and anticipation, knowing that tonight could change everything. Later in the evening, after others had settled in for the night, the moon's light streamed through the open window as Thomas crept across the manor grounds. The air was thick with tension. Lady Constance appeared silently from the shadows, holding a burlap sack.

"I've gathered some supplies—dried meat, bread, blankets. I've also given you two pounds to help you when you arrive at your destination," she whispered, handing him a bag. "It's modest, but it will have to suffice."

Thomas accepted the bag with a respectful nod. "It's more than enough. Thank you, my lady. Your help means a lot to us, and we understand your risk."

Lady Constance gave a slight shake of her head, her expression sad. "This is the least I can do. After all that you've been through, I wish there was more that I could offer."

Thomas placed a reassuring hand on her shoulder. "You've already done so much. We couldn't have come this far without you. The kindness you've shown to all of us."

In two nights, under the veil of darkness, Thomas, Marianne, Elijah, James, and William would make their escape. Lady Constance was to distract the guards at the main gate, fabricating a story to hold their attention. Meanwhile, Thomas and his companions would quietly dash across the fields and disappear into the dense, welcoming forest.

"We'll follow the stars north," Thomas said, excitement and fear churning. "We'll make it to the next township before they know we're gone."

Lady Constance squeezed his hand, her eyes glistening. "Be careful, Thomas. I will pray every day for your safety."

Thomas blinked back tears, overcome with gratitude. "I won't forget this. It's my wish that one day we shall all be free."

"You must be quick and silent," Lady Constance emphasized. "Any noise could ruin it all."

Thomas nodded, determination hardening his gaze. "We will be. And when this is over, we'll come back for the others. Please take care of them."

Lady Constance smiled through her worry. "You are brave, Thomas. Remember that. Courage will see you through."

"Courage and hope," Thomas whispered. "We have plenty of both."

As they parted ways, Thomas felt a new spring in his step. The future was suddenly bright, filled with hope. Their journey would be long and dangerous, but freedom was within reach with allies like Lady Constance. He watched her disappear toward the manor house, her pale blue dress blending into the night. He let out a long, shaky breath, the weight of their plan settling on his shoulders. So much could go wrong. If they were caught, it meant certain death. But living as property, never knowing true freedom—that was worse.

Quietly, Thomas slipped into the small cabin he shared with the others. Inside, James and William looked up, waiting.

"Lady Constance gave us some supplies. We need to tell Elijah and Marianne so they can be prepared," Thomas said, his voice tight and urgent.

The three of them exchanged tense glances. "She's going to help us?" James asked, uncertainty lacing his words.

Thomas nodded. "Lady Constance will distract the guards as we make our escape."

He clasped their shoulders, trying to steady his nerves. "In two nights, we make our stand. Whatever happens, we look only forward, never back. I'll tell Marianne. Will one of you tell Elijah for me?"

"I'll tell him," William responded, his voice wavering slightly.

They had suffered too much to turn back now.

Thomas slipped out of the cabin and walked through the shadows toward Marianne's quarters. The night air was cool, carrying the scent of earth and the distant murmur of the forest. His footsteps were nearly silent on the well-worn path. When he reached Marianne's door, he knocked softly. The door creaked open, and Marianne's worried eyes met his.

"Thomas, what's wrong? It's late," she whispered.

"I've got good news," he said gently. "Lady Constance has given us supplies. I already told William and James. In two nights, we will run from this place, this hell. I hope you're still planning on going with me. I can't imagine leaving you behind. I want to build a life with you. I love you, Marianne."

Marianne's eyes widened, a mix of fear and hope. "Thomas, I want to be with you. I'll follow you anywhere you go. I hate this place, and just thinkin' about livin' free somewhere, with my own house. Maybe a little garden too. With you by my side. I can't think of nothin' better than that."

"We have a real chance at freedom, Marianne. We can't stay here any longer. I believe this is the right thing to do," Thomas replied.

She nodded slowly, her resolve strengthening. "I'll be ready, Thomas."

Thomas pulled her into a soft embrace. "Goodnight, Marianne. I love you. I can't wait."

"Me too, Thomas. I love you too," Marianne said, her tone soft.

As the evening drew to a close, Thomas lay on his bed, eyes shut but unable to sleep. His mind buzzed with Lady Constance's revelation. She was one of them—an indentured servant. It changed everything. They had suffered under her command for years, never imagining she understood their plight. Yet she had endured the same hardships in her youth and had faced the same cruelty.

Thomas thought back to their first meeting. She had inspected the new arrivals with cool detachment. He had disliked her then, seeing her as just another privileged oppressor. How wrong he had been. Now, she had vowed to help, to use her power for good. Together, they would fight against the injustice that had shaped them both.

He knew the risks. If they were caught, the consequences would be dire. Everything had to be perfect; there was no room for error. The gallows loomed over the disobedient like a shadow. But they had lived too long without freedom. It was better to die trying than to live in chains. He could almost feel the heartbeat of the land beyond the plantation, a rhythm that beckoned him to rise and seize the destiny he deserved. As the moments ticked by, their escape plan grew clearer in Thomas's mind. The risks were significant, but he knew that dawn often follows the darkest hours. He clung to that hope, letting it strengthen his spirit as he plotted each step of their path to freedom.

Chapter Twenty-Five

Thomas stood motionless, the parchment slipping from his grasp. The roughly sketched map that charted their path to freedom danced in the air before settling on the dusty barn floor. His heartbeat thundered in his chest, a relentless drum heralding a looming catastrophe. Outside, the crunch of heavy boots on gravel grew ominously close, each step a harrowing echo that spiked fear through his veins, chilling him to the marrow.

He pressed himself against the barn wall, every muscle tensed. The flicker of a lantern's light danced through the cracks in the wooden planks, growing brighter as the steps came closer. Thomas held his breath, his mind racing with thoughts of capture and the gallows that awaited. The footsteps stopped just outside the barn door. He could hear the creak of leather as the intruder shifted their weight, the metallic clink of keys or chains. Thomas's pulse quickened, a cold sweat breaking out on his forehead. He silently cursed himself for not hearing them sooner, for being so careless.

Slowly, he crouched down, his fingers scrabbling in the dirt for the fallen map. His heart thundered louder, the barn's silence amplifying every sound. Just as his fingers brushed the parchment, the barn door groaned open a crack, sending a sliver of light slicing through the darkness.

It was the overseer, Lawson.

Thomas's heart hammered against his ribs. There was no time to hide the evidence. He whipped his head toward the others, who stood frozen beside him. Their wide eyes met his, reflecting the same dawning horror.

They'd been discovered.

The barn door opened. Lawson's hulking silhouette blocked the waning evening light. Thomas's mouth went dry as Lawson's flinty eyes scanned the interior, nostrils flaring.

"Evenin' boys and gal," Lawson rumbled, each word coated in menace.

"Evenin'," Thomas replied. He knew that it wasn't the time to show anything but deference to the overseer. Any sign of disobedience would cause him to search the barn, putting their plans in danger.

"Now tell me, what devilry are you three plannin'?" Lawson snarled.

Thomas met his livid gaze without flinching. "The only devilry here is your cruelty. We aren't doing anything but talking."

Lawson backed away from the scene with a twisted grin, careful not to alert the conspirators. He would bide his time, letting them think they had escaped detection.

Then, when they least expected it, he would strike. Thomas's mind raced as the overseer stormed from the barn, no doubt to gather men to hunt them down. They had mere minutes to flee into the night.

"We have to go now. We don't have time to wait. They're onto us," Thomas said, his voice steady despite the fear gripping his heart.

His friends leaped into action, grabbing their satchels. Thomas ran to the cabin and snatched his old coat from beneath his bed. Though frayed and worn, the woolen fabric would shield him from the chill of the night. He quickly scanned the room, ensuring they left no trace of their plans. Satisfied, he motioned his friends toward the door. As they slipped outside, the shout of men echoed from the main house. The urgency in Thomas's heart pushed them forward. They hurried through the darkness to Henrietta's cabin, their footsteps muffled by the soft earth.

Henrietta stood at her door, eyes wide with worry. "What's happenin'?" she asked, her voice trembling.

Elijah stepped forward, his expression grim. "Momma, we have to go. Now. They're onto us. The overseer came to the barn where we were talkin' and plannin' our escape."

Henrietta's face paled. "But are you ready for what's comin', Elijah?"

"We've got a plan, Momma. I promise," Elijah assured her, his voice low. "We're goin' to head north. We're goin' to find the Friends of Freedom you told us about. Hide there."

Henrietta grabbed his hand, squeezing it tight. "You be careful now, Elijah. Don't you dare get caught up in no trouble. I'm mighty proud of you. I love you, son. Don't you ever forget that."

Elijah pulled her close, holding her tight. "I promise, Momma. We gon' make it. And one day, I'm comin' back for you."

Thomas glanced back, the distant shouts growing louder. "We have to move," he urged.

Henrietta released Elijah, tears glistening in her eyes. "Go on now, son. Don't you turn back."

Thomas led the way, his friends following close behind. They moved swiftly through the shadows, hearts pounding. The promise of freedom was their guiding star, pushing them onward into the unknown.

As they neared the edge of the property, the hounds' baying grew louder. Thomas's breath came in short, sharp gasps. "This way," he whispered, leading them toward a narrow path through the woods.

Under the blanket of night, they crept across the fields, the tall grass whispering against their legs. The baying of hounds pricked Thomas's ears, louder than his heart pounding. He dared not look back. They reached the shelter of a towering oak and paused, gasping for breath. The momentum that had driven their flight was fading, leaving them shaken and exhausted. But there was no time to rest—the hounds' baying still echoed faintly in the distance.

Thomas scanned the dark horizon, his eyes wide with fear. "We can't stay here," he whispered, his voice barely audible. "They're getting closer."

James nodded, his face pale in the moonlight. "Just a

moment more," he panted, leaning against the oak's rough bark.

Marianne clutched Thomas's arm, her eyes pleading. "What if they find us?"

"We keep moving," Thomas said firmly, though his fear threatened to choke him. "We can't stop now."

They pushed on, slipping through the shadows, the hounds' cries growing fainter but never disappearing. Every step was a gamble, every rustle of leaves a potential betrayal. The promise of freedom was still far away, but they had no choice but to keep going.

"We need to keep on movin'," said James, his eyes darting nervously.

Thomas nodded, though his legs ached to lie down on the leaf-strewn earth. As they moved deeper into the woods, Thomas strained his ears for any sign of pursuit. An owl hooted mournfully in the distance. The rustle of tiny creatures in the underbrush set his nerves on edge. He flinched at every snapped twig and stirring leaf, half-expecting to see the overseer and slave patrollers crashing through the trees at any moment.

Every shadow seemed to hide a threat, every sound a possible alarm. Thomas's heart pounded in his chest, and each beat was a reminder of the danger they were in. He glanced back at his friends, their faces tense with fear. They had to keep moving, keep pushing forward, no matter what. Freedom was just ahead, but so was the risk of capture.

When the first light of dawn crept over the horizon, Thomas finally let the group stop and rest. As the others collapsed in exhaustion, Thomas kept watch. They were still in danger, hunted men in hostile territory. But seeing the weary faces of his friends, he couldn't bring himself to wake them. Just a few precious moments of rest—that was all they had.

Thomas settled against a sturdy tree trunk, listening to the morning songbirds greet the sun. Somewhere out there, the overseer raged at their escape. Somewhere, Lord Blackwood's wrath would be terrible. But for now, bathed in the golden glow of dawn, Thomas allowed a spark of hope to flicker in his heart. He felt free.

Suddenly, gunfire shattered the silence like rogue lightning strikes, each blast a death knell. Thomas's heart thundered in his chest, a frenzied drumbeat echoing the panic. They had to leave. Fast.

"Get up!" Elijah's urgent whisper cut through the chaos. "They done found us."

Marianne scrambled to her feet. Her eyes were wide with fear. "How did they catch up so fast?" she gasped, her voice trembling.

"No time to question it now," Thomas said, grabbing her hand. "We need to move. Now!"

James, already on his feet, scanned the surrounding woods. "This way," he pointed, leading them toward a denser part of the forest. "We can lose them in the thick brush."

They dashed through the undergrowth, footsteps and angry shouts growing louder behind them. Thomas glanced back, his heart sinking at the patrollers closing in. The mud sucked at their boots as they fled through the murky wilderness, twigs snapping beneath their desperate steps. The shouts of their pursuers clawed at the shadows, relentless as hunting hounds on the scent of fear.

"Keep goin'!" he urged, pushing William ahead. He stumbled but caught his balance, determination on his face.

"Elijah, do you see a way out?" Thomas called, his voice straining with urgency.

Elijah nodded, his eyes sharp with focus. "There's a stream up yonder. If we stick to it, might throw 'em off our scent."

Marianne's breath came in ragged gasps as she clung to Thomas's side. "I can't keep this pace," she admitted, her strength waning.

"You have to," Thomas said, squeezing her hand. "We all do."

"Hurry up now! They right on us!" Elijah's urgent voice cut through the noise, a beacon amidst the chaos.

But fate was a cruel mistress. A solitary shot rang out, its echo a harbinger of doom—a sound distinct from the rest, carrying the weight of finality. Time slowed, the moment stretching taut as a bowstring. Elijah's eyes met Thomas's, and in that brief exchange, volumes were said—of camaraderie, of shared dreams now teetering on the brink.

"Thomas!" Elijah cried out, his voice laced with pain.

Time seemed to slow as Thomas turned to see Elijah fall to his knees, blood blossoming like a dark flower on his chest. Thomas sprinted back as Elijah crumpled to the ground, eyes wide with shock.

"No!" Thomas skidded to his knees. Blood seeped between Elijah's fingers, stark against his shirt.

Elijah gazed up at him, lips parted. "Go on now," he rasped. "Don't stop."

Thomas grasped Elijah's hand, his pulse pounding. They had come so far, sacrificed everything for a taste of liberty. Sweat trickled down Thomas's face, mingling with the dirt and grime of their desperate flight. His heart ached with the weight of their shared struggle, the promise of freedom so close yet perilously distant. He could see the fear in Elijah's eyes, mirroring his own.

Thomas could only stare in horror at the scene unfolding before him. His friend, the man who had become his brother, had been struck down in cold blood. The world around him blurred as shock and grief threatened to overcome him. The shouts grew louder and closer. Elijah squeezed his hand with the last of his strength. "Live free, brother."

The words shattered Thomas's heart. He clutched Elijah's hand, a sob catching in his throat. They couldn't end like this. Not after all they'd endured.

"I won't leave you," he said fiercely.

Elijah smiled, eyes dimming. "You must."

After a few minutes, Elijah's chest rose and fell in a rattling sigh. Thomas shouted, grasping his friend's hand. Elijah's eyes flickered open, gazing up at the stars.

"The sky sure is so bright here," he whispered. "So beautiful, it is."

Thomas squeezed his hand, emotion choking his throat. "We will be free, Elijah. I promise you."

The faintest of smiles touched Elijah's lips. "I know you will, brother."

He drew another rattling breath, his eyes finding

Thomas's. "My momma...she got a locket, silver with green clasp. Please give it to her. Tell her I love her."

Thomas blinked back tears, nodding. "I will, Elijah. I swear it."

Elijah's eyes drifted shut, a look of peace softening his features. His chest stilled, his hand growing limp in Thomas's grasp.

Thomas bowed his head, grief and anguish warring within him. The escape was a desperate move, driven by a need only those in servitude could understand. They moved in the dark, captive souls clinging to the fragile hope of freedom. But the night turned on them, filled with the sharp cracks of musket fire and the cries of men bred for conflict. Elijah Weston, his friend, was killed by their captors. At that moment, Thomas stood at the edge of a harsh truth: the cost of liberty could be measured in blood and tears.

Thomas's hands trembled as he knelt beside Elijah, the soil beneath them cool and unforgiving. His eyes brimmed with sorrow that threatened to spill forth like a stormy sea. The air hung heavy with despair, wrapping its tendrils around his heart and squeezing without mercy. The woods loomed ahead, cloaked in shadows. Thomas steadied his nerves and glanced at the others. Their faces, etched with sorrow, still held a hardened resolve in their eyes.

Thomas nodded. "We must go on. For Elijah and all the others."

"Damn it!" William choked out, slamming his fist into the earth. "He was our brother! This isn't fair!"

"Life ain't fair," James murmured, his voice rough with emotion. "But we've got to keep movin'."

"James is right," Thomas said, wiping the tears from his cheeks. "We have to lay him to rest and get the hell out of here fast. Lawson and the patrollers are still on our trail."

They hurriedly laid Elijah to rest in a shallow grave, their hands trembling as they covered him with earth. The moment was brief. Their sorrow mingled with the urgent need for escape. As they finished, the distant crack of gunshots echoed through the trees, a stark reminder of the danger closing in. With heavy hearts and fear driving their every step, they quickly abandoned the spot, knowing they had no time for proper mourning. The sound of gunfire spurred them onward; their only solace was the hope that Elijah's sacrifice would not be in vain.

Chapter Twenty-Six

The evening sun dipped low on the horizon, casting long shadows across the autumn landscape as Thomas and his companions reached the swollen banks of a river. The recent rains had transformed the usually tame waterway into a roaring torrent, its waters glinting ominously in the fading light. Branches and debris rushed past, carried by the relentless current. Mosquitoes nipped at their skin, leaving itchy welts on their arms and legs.

"We can't wait for the river to calm. It's now or never," Thomas said, his voice barely audible over the rush of water.

Marianne's face was pale in the moonlight, her eyes wide as she stared at the surging river. "Tom, it looks too dangerous," she whispered, clutching his arm.

Thomas glanced at James and William, who nodded grimly in agreement with Marianne. The decision weighed heavily on him. They could hear the distant baying of hounds, a haunting sound that urged them to quicken their escape. "If we stay, they'll catch us by dawn," Thomas replied, his tone resolute despite the fear that gnawed at his insides. "We must cross. We have no other choice."

William stepped forward, squinting as he assessed the river. "I saw a spot up the way that's a bit narrower. Might give us a better shot at crossin'."

Without a word, the group retraced their steps along the muddy riverbank to the spot William had mentioned. The river was indeed narrower here, but the current appeared even swifter. Thomas tested the edge with a long branch, watching as the turbulent waters quickly snatched it away.

"Let's find some willows," Marianne said, eyes scanning the nearby grove. "Their branches are strong but still bendy enough for weavin'. I've seen the folks back on the plantation makin' rope from willow branches. Maybe we can use somethin' like that to help us get across."

James nodded, leading the way to a cluster of willow trees, their slender trunks bending gracefully toward the river. The group quickly gathered several long, thin branches, stripping them of leaves and smaller twigs.

"We need to twist these real tight. This is how Henrietta showed me to do it," Marianne instructed. Her hands were already at work. She showed them how to lay three branches parallel and twist them around one another, periodically adding more branches to extend the rope's length.

Thomas and William followed her lead, their fingers working deftly despite the urgency pressing upon them. "Like braidin' hair," Marianne commented, a faint smile breaking her focus as she glanced at Thomas, who was awkwardly trying to manage the slippery switches.

Gradually, the makeshift rope took shape, growing in length and strength as they interwove more willow branches. After a tense hour, they had a sturdy rope long enough to span the river's width.

"Let's secure it," Thomas said, tying one end of the rope around a large, anchored tree. They stretched the rope across the river, battling the fierce pull of the current. William waded into the water, using a heavy stone to anchor the rope on the opposite bank.

With the rope in place, they tested its strength, pulling and tugging to ensure it would hold. Satisfied, Thomas looked at his friends, a grim determination settling over the group. "This is it," he said. "Let's get across before those hounds catch up."

The icy waters surged around their legs as they each grasped the rope, pulling at them with a terrifying force. Despite their efforts, the river claimed one of their bags early in the crossing, sweeping away precious supplies and leaving them with barely any food and clothes on their backs. The loss heightened the tension among them, and soon, James and William were at odds, each blaming the other for not securing the packs tightly enough.

"You should've checked the knots more than once!" James shouted over the river's roar, his voice laced with frustration.

"It's not just my job to check every little thing!" William retorted, his face flush with anger and exertion.

The argument escalated, their voices growing louder against the backdrop of rushing water until Marianne intervened. "Enough!" she cried, her voice cutting through the tension. "Arguin' won't bring our supplies back or get us across this river any safer."

Her words struck a chord, and the group fell silent, the only sound the ominous rush of the river. With a deep breath, they refocused on the task, gripping the rope tightly as they resumed their precarious journey across the swollen river. Marianne felt her foot slip on an unseen underwater ledge. Her grip on the rope slackened momentarily as the current yanked at her legs, threatening to drag her downstream. "Help!" she gasped, water splashing into her mouth as she struggled to regain footing.

Thomas reacted instantly, tightening his hold on the rope and reaching out to grab her arm with his free hand. "Hold on!" he shouted, pulling her back against the powerful current. The scare galvanized the group, and they moved more carefully, inch by inch, fighting against the river's pull.

The cold water numbed their limbs, making each step feel heavier and more dangerous. Shivers racked their bodies, and their teeth chattered almost inaudibly against the noise of the river. But the fear of being caught, or worse, kept them moving forward, their eyes fixed on the safety of the opposite bank. Finally, after an eternity battling the merciless river, they made it to the other side. They clambered up the bank, exhausted and soaked to the bone but alive and still free. Thomas helped Marianne up the last few feet, their eyes meeting in a moment of shared relief.

"We made it," Marianne said, her voice weak but filled with gratitude. They all gathered in a huddle, trying to share body heat, their breaths visible in the cool air of the early evening.

"I know we're tired. Let's take a few minutes to rest, and then we need to keep moving," Thomas said after a moment, his voice steady despite the ordeal. "We need to put as much distance between us and the overseer and the patrollers as we can before dark."

Nodding in agreement, the group set off through the thick underbrush, the last rays of the setting sun filtering through the trees. The dense forest eventually gave way to a clearing, a slight reprieve from the relentless wilderness around them. Here, the ground was flatter, and patches of grass peeked through the leaf-littered floor. They decided this was as good a place to camp for the night.

James and William quickly gathered firewood, finding enough dry branches and twigs to start a small fire. The warmth was a welcome relief from the chill that had seeped into their bones during the river crossing. Thomas, taking on the role of cook, found a relatively flat stone to set near the fire and placed their last can of beans on it to warm. While the beans heated, Marianne carefully rationed out the remains of their salted pork, their previous substantial piece of food. The smoke from the fire mingled with the scent of warming beans and cooking pork, filling the clearing with a comforting, meager aroma.

As they sat around the fire, they passed the can of beans and pork strips, each taking a share. It tasted like a feast after the day's harrowing escape and exhausting river crossing. They ate slowly, savoring each bite. Laughter and light conversation began to replace the tension of the earlier arguments. Once they finished eating, they carefully extinguished the fire, mindful of leaving no trace of their presence that could be spotted from a distance. Using their bags as pillows, they settled down for the night under the canopy of stars peeking through the clearing's open space.

Marianne and Thomas huddled close, sharing a small coat they had managed to keep dry, its fraying edges barely warding off the night's chill. The rest of the group, wrapped in whatever scraps they could scavenge—thin blankets, torn shirts, even sacks—shivered as fatigue crept into their bones. The day's stresses were etched deep in their faces, their bodies slumping under exhaustion, every breath a slow, quiet struggle.

As the others began to settle in for the night, the wind howling softly through the trees, Marianne turned to Thomas. "Who will take the first watch?" she asked, her voice barely above a whisper, though the tension in her tone was clear.

Thomas straightened, scanning the makeshift camp. James and William were already stretching out on the ground, making themselves as comfortable as possible. "I will," he replied, his gaze unwavering as he glanced at them. "I'll wake Will for the next shift. We can't afford to let our guard down. Not tonight."

William, overhearing the conversation, nodded in agreement without opening his eyes. "Just nudge me when it's time," he murmured, his voice muffled by the coat he used as a pillow.

James, who was beginning to doze off, added sleepily, "And I'll take the last one before dawn. Just make sure to wake me up."

Thomas nodded silently, his senses heightened as he prepared for the long night ahead. As the night deepened, the sounds of the forest grew louder. Thomas sat with his back against a tree and adjusted his position slightly. His eyes scanned the dark tree line. His mind replayed the day's events, planning their next moves while savoring the small victory of having made it through another day.

Chapter Twenty-Seven

A couple of days passed since they made it across the river. Thomas lurched through the thick woods, each step a struggle to keep himself from collapsing. He grabbed at the trees to stay upright, his hands grimy and scraped. Behind him, his friends dragged themselves in a weary line. They were hungry, and their supplies were running low. They had managed to escape the overseer's hounds but now found themselves going in circles in the dense forest, unsure of their exact location since the map had been lost with their bag during the river crossing.

Ahead, a sparkle of sunlight on the water caught Thomas's attention—a narrow stream meandered through the forest, bordered by mossy rocks. Eager for a drink, Thomas sped up, his dry throat begging for water.

"Finally," Thomas breathed out, collapsing to his knees by the stream. His hands shook as he scooped the cool water to his dry lips. It felt like a healing salve on his cracked mouth, soothing the soreness that had tormented him for days.

"Thank God," James said, his expression filled with relief. Marianne and William lined up behind them, each taking a turn to drink. The water seemed to bring them back to life, even for a little while, giving them a brief respite.

When Thomas opened his eyes again, his worn-out face stared back at him from the water. But beneath the grime and exhaustion was a determined sparkle—a fierce resolve of someone who had been through a lot but refused to be beaten. He was determined to lead his friends to freedom. He drank deeply, scooping up another handful of water, steeling himself for the arduous journey ahead.

A wolf's distant howl cut through the dense forest, a chilling reminder of the dangers still to come. Instinctively, Thomas grabbed a jagged rock, his knuckles turning white as he gripped it tightly. Next to him, James picked up a sturdy branch, and Marianne held a sharpened stick, her eyes filled with fear.

"Stay close," Thomas hissed, his voice almost drowned out by the rustling leaves and the heavy silence around them.

But the quiet didn't last. Suddenly, the forest exploded with fierce war cries, startling the birds into flight. Thomas's head shot up, his heart pounding. Through the trees, a dozen Indians rushed toward them, their faces painted for battle, weapons raised.

"Ambush!" Thomas shouted, leaping to his feet.

Thomas tensed as the first warrior barreled toward him, a stone club swinging at his head. He ducked and slammed his shoulder into the warrior's stomach. They crashed to the ground, limbs flailing. Thomas cracked his rock against the warrior's head, knocking him out cold. Around him, his friends fought hard, the forest echoing with grunts and shouts. A spear flew past Thomas's ear as he jumped up. He needed to gather his friends; they were outnumbered and struggling.

"Protect each other!" Thomas roared, his arms flailing. His voice cut through the fear, snapping his friends into formation. They closed ranks, forming a solid wall. Thomas grabbed a fallen club, swinging it in broad, desperate arcs to hold back the encroaching attackers. Step by shaky step, they edged away from the stream.

But then, catastrophe. With a brutal war cry, a warrior hurled James to the ground. Thomas dove to assist, but the forest seemed to devour the others in that split second. Suddenly, Thomas was alone, enemies closing in. A crushing blow to his back knocked him to the dirt. Staggering, he saw nothing but the empty, mocking trees—his friends had vanished.

"James! William! Marianne!" Thomas screamed into the chaos. Only the mocking jeers of the warriors answered back. His only option was to run. Clutching his club, he plunged into the underbrush. Thorns tore at his skin, but he pushed on, driven by raw fear, as if the devil himself was on his heels. When his lungs seared and his legs buckled, Thomas collapsed behind a fallen oak to catch his breath, his mind spinning. He had to find his friends. Time was running out.

Leaning against the rough bark, Thomas fought for air, his chest heaving with deep, desperate breaths. His eyes flicked around, scanning for any sign of pursuit. Silence hung heavy, punctuated only by the thudding of his heartbeat. Slowly, his breathing eased. He risked a cautious glance around the oak's thick trunk. There were no warriors in sight, but they couldn't be far. He needed to find a hiding place to wait out the search.

Thomas scanned his surroundings, his eyes landing on a dark, gaping hole in the rock face—a cave. Clutching his club, he bolted for this possible refuge. He squeezed through the narrow entrance, batting away the musty cobwebs that clung to him. Inside, the cave widened into a larger chamber. Thomas slid down the damp wall, the cool, enveloping darkness a brief respite. Here, he could catch his breath and muster his strength. His friends were out there somewhere, possibly hurt. He had vowed to protect them, no matter the cost. He couldn't abandon them now.

Thomas bowed his head, despair nipping at his resolve. So much had gone wrong on this cursed expedition. If only he had been wiser, stronger. But regrets were a luxury he couldn't afford. He had to believe they could still survive despite the dire odds. Clenching his fists, he promised to find his friends or die trying.

Night fell, and a chilling stillness gripped the wilderness, broken only by the distant howl of a wolf. Thomas cautiously stepped out of the cave, alert to any hint of danger. The forest lay in deep shadows, the moon casting strange, shifting patterns on the leaf-covered ground. An owl's eerie call echoed in the distance, adding to the night's menacing atmosphere.

Thomas's heart pounded as he crept forward, club in

hand, ready for any threat. He had to find his friends. He needed to know if they were alive.

During his search, Thomas stumbled upon a narrow, overgrown game trail. Hidden among the leaves and branches, he spotted animal and human tracks. It was a small beacon of hope in the dark. Following this trail might lead him back to his friends.

Clutching his club, Thomas hurried down the winding path, moving quickly yet quietly, stopping often to listen. The forest seemed to tighten around him as he delved deeper. Tangled branches overhead blocked out the moon's light. Thomas refused to surrender to fear. He had to press on for his friends and himself. This trail could be their only shot at safety. He was determined to follow it wherever it led, guiding his friends out of this wild if it killed him. They had given up too much to quit now.

After an eternity weaving through the thick woods, Thomas broke into a clearing and found his friends resting. Relief flooded through him at the sight of their familiar faces.

"Tom!" Marianne called out, her face lighting up with surprise and joy. "You found us!"

"Thank God," James muttered, rising to his feet. "We were startin' to think you weren't alive."

"Is anyone hurt?" Thomas asked, his eyes scanning their weary faces.

"James's leg got nicked," William said, nodding towards James.

Thomas turned to James, concern etched on his face. "Can you still walk?"

James gritted his teeth and nodded. "Aye, I'm okay to keep movin'."

Thomas took a deep breath, gathering his thoughts. "Listen, we need to keep moving. The Indians, the constable, and the patrollers are all still looking for us, and we can't stay in one place for too long."

James nodded. "We barely escaped the last attack. They know this land better than we do."

"I know," Thomas replied, "but I found something. There's a cave not far from here. It might be a good place to hide and regroup."

"A cave?" Marianne echoed, her brow furrowing. "Are you sure it's safe?"

"It's our best option right now," Thomas said. "We need to move before they catch up to us."

The group caught Thomas's urgent look and immediately grabbed their things, following him as he pushed toward the cave, their hoped-for sanctuary. A storm hit like a curse from a vengeful spirit. One moment, the night was clear; the next, dark clouds swarmed over them, unleashing a torrential downpour.

Fat raindrops hammered down on them. Within moments, their soaked and heavy clothes clung to them, sending shivers through their bodies. Lightning tore through the sky in jagged flashes, lighting up the drenched wilderness, while thunder boomed, each roar shaking the earth beneath their feet.

"This way!" Thomas shouted over the thunder, pointing toward a rocky outcropping visible through the downpour.

They rushed toward the shelter, feet skidding in the

slippery mud. By the time they reached the overhang, they were soaked through, their hair and clothes clinging to their wet skin. Yet, it was better than facing the storm's full fury outside. Huddled under the rock ledge, Thomas and his friends clung to each other for warmth, their teeth chattering and bodies shaking from the cold.

"I don't think we're goin' to make it," Marianne said, her voice quivering with the effort. "It's lookin' bad out there. Hopefully, the storm will pass over soon enough. Then we can find some food. I'm starvin' and don't know how long I can go on." Marianne started crying.

Thomas reached out and gently touched Marianne's shoulder, trying to offer some comfort. "The storm will pass. When it does, we'll find something to eat." He hugged her. Inside, his spirit battled against the storm's wrath, determined not to break. Hours dragged by as Thomas watched the storm raging across the rocky terrain. His sharp, alert eyes pierced through the downpour, desperately seeking a break from the relentless assault. Suddenly, a dark gap in the forest caught his attention. It was the cave!

"Over here!" he yelled above the howl of the wind, gesturing wildly for the others to follow. They stumbled across slippery boulders, battling the fierce wind and biting rain that lashed at them like whips. Finally, they slipped into the cave, collapsing from sheer exhaustion.

Inside, the storm's roar softened to a distant murmur, and the air became eerily quiet, almost suffocatingly still. Their drenched and heavy clothes clung to their skin, chilling them to the bone.

"We need to get out of these wet clothes," Thomas

suggested, his voice echoing slightly in the cave. He started stripping off his soaked shirt. The others quickly followed, wringing out their garments, their movements quick and desperate for warmth in the cold, shadowy cave.

Huddled together for warmth, skin pressed against skin, Thomas wrapped his arms around Marianne, trying to still her shivering. Gradually, their combined warmth began to fill the small space. Thomas felt the knot of anxiety in his chest start to unwind. They had found shelter, a temporary sanctuary from the storm outside. Silently, he gave thanks for their haven.

As he glanced around, the last rays of daylight streamed into the cave, signaling the approach of night. They would need to stay here until the storm abated. For now, they were safe; the storm's wrath couldn't reach them here. Thomas tightened his hold on Marianne, then let his eyes close. Sleep overtook him swiftly, comforted by the rhythmic sound of rain tapping outside.

When Thomas awoke the following day, a dull ache of hunger gnawed at his stomach. It felt like ages since they'd had a proper meal. He pushed the hunger aside, knowing worrying wouldn't help. Food had been scarce for days.

Blinking in the dim morning light, Thomas gently pulled away from Marianne's embrace. She and the others needed more rest, and he'd let them have it while he explored the cave. The rocky walls, slick with moisture, caught the faint light from the entrance. Thomas ran his hand along the cool, gritty surface as he walked deeper into the darkness.

As he rounded a corner, he paused, squinting into the

shadows. Was there a slight gleam ahead? Moving cautiously, he approached the source.

In a small rocky nook, he discovered a cluster of berries. Thomas's heart surged with hope. Were they safe to eat? He knelt, inspecting the plump berries with their deep purple skin. Carefully, he picked one and took a tentative bite.

The berry burst in his mouth, flooding it with sweet juice that eclipsed any meal Thomas could recall. Barely able to contain his excitement at their luck, Thomas gathered handfuls of the berries and rushed back to share his find.

As the group stirred from sleep, Thomas greeted them with a grin, offering the berries with a flourish. "Wake up, everyone! Look what I've found!"

Rubbing the sleep from their eyes, they reached for the fruit. The rich taste burst on their tongues. Their hunger, momentarily forgotten, was replaced by the simple joy of the unexpected feast.

As they finished the last of the berries, Thomas stood, energized by the food and a newfound hope. "Come on, the storm's cleared. It's time we moved on."

He led the way to the cave's entrance, where the light of a new day was spilling in. Stepping out, they were greeted by a sky washed clean by the night's storms. Thomas turned back to his friends, his voice steady and sure, "Let's keep going. We've got a lot of ground to cover."

As they pushed on through the wilderness, the taste of sweet berries still lingered on their tongues. The recent storm had cleared the air, leaving it crisp and refreshing—a welcome relief for their weary bodies. They trekked for hours, the forest seemingly endless as they maneuvered through dense undergrowth, rocky places, and rough terrain that tested their stamina. Their feet stumbled over roots and stones while they fought through thick bushes and brambles that snagged at their clothing. Eventually, the dense forest opened to a clearing as the sun climbed higher in the sky. They stopped short, taken aback by the sight before them. A small encampment, arranged around a smoldering fire pit, appeared at the edge of the clearing. Thomas's muscles tensed. Friend or foe? He had no time to decide.

A man emerged from one of the structures, tall and imposing with a feathered headdress and long, dark hair. His headdress, adorned with brightly colored feathers arranged in a fan shape, framed his strong, angular face. Around his neck hung a necklace crafted from beads and animal bones. His bare chest, marked by the sun, showcased intricate tattoos narrating the story of his life and his people. A soft deerskin cloak draped over his shoulders, secured with a polished bone clasp. A belt woven from plant fibers, holding a knife sheathed in a leather pouch, cinched at his waist. His eyes widened in surprise at the sight of Thomas and his friends, assessing the strangers with curiosity and caution.

"Wait here," Thomas whispered to his companions. With cautious steps, he advanced towards the man, his hands open and held at his sides to clearly show he was unarmed.

The chief, a tall man with a dignified presence, stepped forward. "I am Chief Nacotchtank of the Patawomeck," he said, calm and measured. "Who are you? What are your intentions here?"

Thomas hesitated but then stepped forward, trying to appear non-threatening. He wasn't sure if this Indian tribe was connected to the ones that attacked him, and he wasn't taking any chances. "My name is Thomas," he replied cautiously. "We're runaways, escaping from a plantation where we were held as servants. We mean no harm. Our only intention is to find safe refuge."

Chief Nacotchtank studied Thomas for a long moment, his deep-set eyes searching for truth in his face. The silence was heavy as the chief weighed the situation. Finally, he gave a slow nod. "Safe refuge is a difficult thing to find in these lands. You seek safety, but you must understand that our people have seen much, and we protect what is ours. If you wish to roam among us, you must prove you are worthy of our trust."

To Thomas's surprise, the man gestured for him to come forward. The invitation was clear: Come, sit, and share our fire. After a brief hesitation, Thomas accepted and settled beside the fire. The man handed him a bowl of stew, its rich aroma making Thomas's mouth water. As he ate, more tribe members gathered around, eyeing him with curiosity. Thomas kept his gaze steady and his movements deliberate and calm, ensuring he appeared non-threatening.

Chief Nacotchtank nodded, his expression thoughtful. "You have nothing to fear from us. We have encountered your kind before and understand your plight."

Thomas, still wary, asked, "How do you speak our language so well?"

The chief smiled slightly. "I learned from the Quakers who came to trade with us many years ago. They taught me your language and customs."

After the meal, Chief Nacotchtank gestured toward the edge of the clearing, where the others watched cautiously. Understanding the chief's intentions, Thomas called them over. "Come on, it's safe," he encouraged, inviting them to join the circle.

As the others approached, they took in the unique surroundings of the Patowemeck village. Nestled along the banks of a winding river, the village featured small boats shaped in gentle curves with flat bottoms, a design Thomas had never seen before. Tall, sturdy palisades encircled the settlement, providing a formidable defense against potential threats. Inside the walls, the village buzzed with activity. The homes, called yehakins, were constructed from wooden frames covered with woven mats or bark. Wisps of smoke curled from the tops of larger dwellings, signaling cooking fires within. Around the village, small garden plots thrived with corn, beans, and squash—the staple crops known as the Three Sisters.

The group moved forward hesitantly, drawn by the lingering scent of the meal and the genuine warmth in Thomas's voice. As they neared, members of the Patawomeck tribe stepped forward with smiles, extending their hands in friendship. The village women approached eagerly, their hands expressive and eyes inquisitive as they spoke in their own language. They presented plates heaped with remnants of a feast—cornbread, smoked fish, and wild vegetables—offering a taste of their hospitality.

Chief Nacotchtank spoke again. "You are welcome to

share our fire and our shelter," he declared, sweeping his arm towards a cluster of nearby huts crafted from the earth and adorned with the vibrant symbols of the tribe.

The visitors were ushered into a large communal hut at the heart of the settlement. The floor was covered with soft animal hides and handmade mats, providing comfort and warmth against the evening's chill. A small fire crackled in a stone hearth at the center of the hut, casting flickering shadows on the walls and bathing the space in a gentle, soothing light. The tribe members showed them where they could sleep, arranged additional blankets, and offered the best of their accommodations. The atmosphere was marked by mutual respect and curiosity, with the Patawomeck people eager to share their way of life and learn about their guests.

As they settled in that night, Marianne whispered to Thomas, "Can you believe this? Just when I thought we couldn't take another day out there."

Thomas smiled, the fire's glow reflecting in his eyes. "It's like we've stumbled into a whole new world. These people, they're nothing like the other tribe that attacked us."

"Yeah," Marianne agreed, tucking the blanket tighter around her. "But I'm not sure we should let our guards down. They might attack when we least expect it."

Overhearing the conversation, James added, "We should take turns keepin' watch. Just in case."

William nodded. "I'll take the first shift."

With a tacit understanding, they settled in for the night. Enveloped by the encampment's soft murmurs and the comforting warmth of the fire, Thomas and his friends succumbed to a deep, restful sleep, their anxieties momentarily forgotten. As morning dawned, the tribe was already bustling with activity. Children played and laughed, their joyful sounds filling the air, while women tended the fires and men readied themselves for the day's hunt.

Waking up and rubbing the sleep from his eyes, Thomas was greeted by Chief Nacotchtank, who presented him with a bundle containing dried meat, nuts, and bread—provisions for the journey ahead. Thomas accepted it with heartfelt gratitude. Around him, his friends received similar bundles from the Patawomeck people. This display of unexpected kindness brought tears to Thomas's eyes, moved by the generosity they were shown.

Chief Nacotchtank placed a firm hand on Thomas's shoulder, his expression solemn as he spoke. "There is a path through the forest that leads to a Quaker settlement," he advised. "Follow the stream to the east for two days, and you will find them. They are good people and will offer you shelter."

Thomas looked up, tears welling in his eyes. "Thank you," he managed to say, his voice thick with emotion.

The chieftain's grip tightened slightly, conveying a silent promise of safety and well-being. No words were spoken, yet the intent was clear—a heartfelt wish for their protection and prosperity. Tears welled up in Thomas's eyes as he clasped the chieftain's hand with both of his, the connection between them deep and sincere.

"May the spirits guide you," Chief Nacotchtank said softly. "Travel safely."

With one final, lingering look at the tranquil village,

where smoke gently curled up from the fires and the soft hum of everyday life resonated in the background, Thomas and his friends set off. The kindness shown by the Patawomeck tribe had become a beacon of hope, illuminating their uncertain path ahead.

Chapter Twenty-Eight

Shortly after Thomas and his friends left the Patawomeck tribe's territory, tension gripped the camp. The soft, whispering rustle of leaves underfoot heralded the arrival of unwelcome visitors. As the sun sank low, casting elongated shadows across the land, the Constable and his slave patrollers emerged, their boots thudding ominously against the forest floor.

The Constable, a broad-shouldered man with eyes as cold and unyielding as the steel of a sword, stepped forward with an air of menacing authority. The tribe members gathered, wary but persistent, as he surveyed them with a dismissive glance.

"We know you're hiding them," he snarled, his voice thick with contempt and the assuredness of power. "Tell us where they are." His hand rested on his pistol, a silent threat that spoke louder than words.

Chief Nacotchtank stood firm, his voice steady though the fear in the eyes of his people was palpable. "We have no quarrel with you. The ones you seek were here, but they left," he declared, meeting the Constable's icy gaze with quiet defiance.

Unmoved, the Constable's men pressed the Indians with sharp, insistent questioning. Though momentarily satisfied with the responses, they were not deterred. The Constable and his crew eventually withdrew from the encampment, the determination to track down the runaways etched in their grim expressions.

A day had passed since Thomas and the others left the Patawomeck tribe. Long, sinister shadows stretched through the dense Virginia woods as the sun dipped below the horizon. Cooler weather had arrived, and Thomas knew they needed to find the Quaker settlement before Winter. He and his friends pushed through the underbrush, gasping for breath, their faces etched with terror. Behind them, the furious shouts of the Constable and the patrollers tore through the eerie calm, with the chilling baying of bloodhounds close behind.

"Keep going!" Thomas panted, his legs screaming in agony. Stopping was not an option.

"We can't keep this up, Tom! We're too tired!" William argued, his voice strained with exhaustion.

"We have no choice!" Thomas shot back, his eyes scanning the darkening path ahead.

Marianne's sobs suddenly pierced the air, her body shaking with each cry. Thomas slowed momentarily, reaching out to soothe her. "We have to keep moving, Marianne. We can't be too far from the settlement now."

"Everything aches, and they're closin' in on us," Marianne whimpered, wiping tears from her cheeks as she struggled to regain her composure.

Thomas pulled her close briefly, his voice soft but firm. "I'll steady you. Hold onto my arms, and I'll lead the way."

Nodding through her tears, Marianne took a deep breath and leaned on Thomas for support. As twilight deepened in the forest, their plight grew ever more desperate. The howls of the hounds, sharp and hungry, echoed off the trees, drawing closer with each passing moment. Thomas clenched his teeth, fighting through the biting pain and exhaustion. He was painfully aware that mercy would be the last thing they'd find if caught.

Just as despair threatened to overwhelm them, a figure emerged from the shadows—Chief Nacotchtank. Standing tall, his eyes blazing with fierce resolve, he moved with lethal precision. In a flurry of swift, decisive actions, he shot the advancing hounds. One by one, their menacing cries were abruptly silenced, and the forest fell quiet once again.

"Come," Chief Nacotchtank called, smiling warmly. "I will guide you."

Thomas met the man's eyes, a surge of gratitude washing over him. At that moment, he realized that their path to freedom would not be traveled alone.

"Thank you," Thomas whispered, his voice trembling. Chief Nacotchtank nodded, his eyes showing he understood the profound meaning behind those words.

Together, they turned north and moved deeper into the wilderness, putting more distance between themselves and the Constable's frustrated posse. Having narrowly escaped, Thomas glanced back and let out a relieved sigh upon seeing the fading figures of their pursuers, now beaten and retreating. The air, once thick with tension, grew lighter, infusing them with a sense of tentative hope.

"I can't believe it," Marianne said, her voice quivering. "We owe you our lives."

"Indeed, we do," James added, his eyes fixed on the chieftain.

With a humble nod, Chief Nacotchtank accepted their thanks. "You are brave to have come this far. Let me help you find the freedom you seek. I know the way to the Hopewell Friends settlement, where you seek refuge. I have helped many like you find the way."

"Lead the way," Thomas said firmly.

As they adjusted toward the east, they journeyed further into the Virginia wilderness. The shadows deepened, the towering trees casting veils over the path ahead. The man led effortlessly, skillfully guiding them through the challenging terrain.

"Stay close," he warned as they maneuvered along narrow paths, ducking under branches and stepping over gnarled roots. "This land is as unforgiving as it is beautiful."

As Thomas gazed at the vast wilderness stretching before him, he felt a profound surge of freedom, a stark contrast to the constraints of his past life. For the first time in years, he felt truly alive, invigorated by the untamed beauty of the landscape around him.

"Are you alright?" Marianne asked, catching his contemplative look.

"Never better," Thomas responded, his eyes fixed on

the lush greenery enveloping them. "I feel truly free for the first time in my life."

"Freedom," James chimed in, his eyes bright with hope. "It's a beautiful thing, ain't it?"

"Watch out for that snake. It is a poisonous one," their guide warned, nodding toward a serpent coiled among the roots. They edged around it, their hearts racing from the near miss.

As they passed, Thomas noticed something unusual about the snake. As the snake moved, a strange, segmented object rattled at the end of its tail. He had never seen a snake like that before. The chief, noticing Thomas's curious gaze, spoke up.

"That is a rattlesnake," the chief explained, his voice calm and steady. "That rattle warns you to keep your distance. It's a powerful creature, respected by my people. We take heed when it makes that sound."

Thomas tightened his grip on his walking stick, following their guide further into the forest. The trees crowded close, barely letting sunlight through the thick canopy above. They climbed over mossy logs, ducked under branches, and pushed through thickets of thorny brush. The uneven ground, strewn with rocks and concealed sinkholes, challenged every step. Thomas stumbled often, his legs burning with fatigue.

As a faint but unmistakable growl of a wildcat echoed in the distance, Thomas felt a surge of genuine fear. Out here, danger was ever-present, and help was far from reach. His mind raced with thoughts of the beasts that might roam these woods—bears, wolves, panthers. Yet, the chieftain appeared unfazed, maintaining a steady pace. Thomas drew comfort from knowing they were in capable hands. He paused, gasping for breath and leaning heavily against a towering oak, its thick roots sprawling across the forest floor like gnarled tentacles clutching the rocky soil. Glancing back, he saw the path they had forged through the dense undergrowth, now just a narrow tunnel disappearing into the green expanse. In this maze of trees and vines, losing their way seemed all too easy.

Thomas's thoughts drifted to the plantation they had left behind, with its endless fields of corn and tobacco. It seemed like another lifetime—a place where he had dreamt of freedom, ready to risk it all to live and die on his terms. Now, surrounded by the beauty and menace of the untamed wilderness, he pondered the future that awaited them if they managed to reach it. Where would they go? How would they survive? Could they ever indeed be free?

Thomas glanced up at the canopy of leaves overhead, allowing himself a moment of quiet reflection. It was miraculous that they had made it this far. If not for the intervention of Chief Nacotchtank, he and his friends would likely be shackled in irons by now, dragged back to the hellish plantation. But here they were, miles away, breathing free air. It seemed almost too good to be true. Thomas said a silent prayer of thanks for the stranger who had appeared just when they needed him most. Without his help, their bid for freedom would have failed before it began. He knew they still had a long and dangerous road ahead. But Thomas felt a glimmer of hope. This land held promise—the promise of a new life.

As he ducked under a low-hanging branch, Thomas turned to look back at his companions. Marianne offered him a weary smile. Beyond her, James and William trudged onward, their faces set with determination. They would make it. They had to believe that.

Up ahead, their guide paused and turned back. "Not much further now," he said, gesturing toward a clearing visible through the trees. "We will rest there."

Relief washed over Thomas as he nodded. Soon, they could rest their aching feet and fill their empty bellies. Despite the creeping exhaustion, anticipation for what lay ahead energized him. In the vast wilderness, anything was possible—this was a place of freedom. Taking a deep breath, he stepped into the clearing, blinking against the late afternoon sunlight that filtered through the canopy above. Despite the ache in his legs and the gnawing hunger, a profound sense of peace washed over him.

Thomas surveyed their makeshift campsite as the others wearily trudged into the clearing behind him. A small creek burbled along one edge, ideal for refilling their water skins. The tall grass offered a promise of softer sleep than the hard planks back at the cabin, and the surrounding forest was abundant with edible plants. They had all the essentials for survival right there.

James dropped his pack to the ground with a heavy thud. "Never thought I'd be so glad to stop walkin'," he grumbled, rubbing his sore shoulders.

"We've come a long way already," Thomas replied, looking around at their small haven. "Let's make the most of this place for now."

The chieftain, silently observing their setup, approached Thomas. "You are adjusting well to the freedom of the forest," he noted, a slight smile breaking through his stoic expression.

Thomas nodded, his eyes meeting the guide's. "It's a different kind of freedom we're still learning to understand. Out here, it feels like we really can make our path. Thank you for showing us that."

Chief Nacotchtank looked out over the clearing, his gaze thoughtful. "It is a hard path but a worthy one. The land teaches us that freedom is not just about escaping what holds us back but learning to live with what lies ahead."

Thomas absorbed the words, feeling the truth resonate with his burgeoning feelings of liberation. "Thank you for your help," he responded.

As the evening shadows deepened, Thomas and his friends prepared their camp. They gathered wood from the nearby forest, the crackle of dry branches breaking the stillness of the dusky woods. They built a fire in a small cleared area, the flames casting a warm glow that pushed away the creeping chill of the night air. James and William ventured into the undergrowth to forage for edible plants and roots. They returned with hands full of leafy greens and a few hardy tubers, adding to the modest provisions they had carried with them. Marianne and Thomas went to a nearby creek to gather some water.

As the fire grew, casting light in the darkness, they arranged a small clearing, creating a temporary home in the wilderness. The warmth of the fire and the promise of a hot meal bolstered their spirits. Together, they cooked a simple meal over the open fire, the scent of cooking greens mingling with the smoky air. As they ate, their conversation was light but meaningful. The air grew colder, and Thomas wrapped his arms around Marianne to keep her warm. Noticing his friends shivering slightly, he couldn't help but throw a teasing suggestion into the mix, his eyes twinkling with mischief.

"If you lads feel chilly, just wrap your arms around each other. That should do the trick!" Thomas joked, a broad grin spreading across his face.

William laughed heartily, shaking his head. "Oh, I guess James would keep me warmer than this fire, but I'll pass this time!"

James joined in the laughter, adding with a mock, serious tone, "Well, I'm always here if you change your mind, Will. But let's stick to the fire tonight, shall we?"

The laughter subsided, and the men settled into a more reflective mood as the fire crackled before them. Thomas turned to Chief Nacotchtank, who had been listening quietly, his face illuminated by the flames.

"Chief Nacotchtank," Thomas began, "would you share more about the Patawomeck people? We're grateful for your help and would love to understand more about your tribe and its history."

He paused, looking into the fire as if it might reflect scenes from the past. "Our history is marked by peace and conflict, with neighbors and newcomers alike. We have always strived to be strong, wise, and brave in the face of challenges, upholding the traditions passed down from our ancestors."

Thomas listened intently, captivated by the chief's words that painted a picture of a vibrant culture deeply connected to the earth and its cycles. The chief's pride in his heritage was evident, and his words brought a deeper understanding of the Patawomeck tribe to the small group gathered around the fire.

Chief Nacotchtank's expression grew more somber as he continued. "In recent times, our encounters with the white man have brought both opportunities and hardships. Some tribes within the Powhatan Confederacy have seen the newcomers as allies, trading and sharing knowledge. My tribe has chosen the path of peace, believing coexistence can bring mutual benefit. We have traded with the settlers, providing them with food and furs in exchange for tools and other goods."

He sighed deeply, the weight of history evident in his eyes. "However, not all tribes share this view. Some see the white man as a threat, an invader who brings disease and takes our lands. Conflicts have arisen, battles fought to protect what is ours. Blood has been shed on both sides. My people have been caught in the middle, trying to maintain peace while others around us go to war."

The chief's gaze moved from the fire to the faces of the boys, his eyes filled with hope and sorrow. "The Patawomeck have always sought to balance the old ways with the new. We honor our ancestors by preserving our traditions and adapting to survive. This land, our home, has seen much change. We have welcomed those who come in peace and stood firm against those who bring harm."

Thomas felt a profound respect for the chief and his people. "Thank you, Chief Nacotchtank, for sharing your story with us. We have much to learn from your wisdom and resilience."

Chief Nacotchtank smiled faintly, his pride in his

people evident. "May the spirits of our ancestors guide us all to a future of understanding and peace." The fire crackled, and the night deepened, wrapping the group in a shared sense of history and hope for a better future.

As the sun disappeared behind the trees, they prepared for the night. Darkness wrapped around the wilderness, with only their small fire casting a flickering glow. Despite the eerie nocturnal sounds of the forest, Thomas found himself enveloped in an unexpected peace. Nestled in his makeshift bed of grass, his body cried out for rest, but his mind was alive with thoughts of the future. What challenges would they face? Could they find a place to call home? These questions swirled endlessly in his head. This was merely the beginning. Thomas was sure of that.

Chapter Twenty-Nine

The moon was a stark white disc in the ink-black sky as Thomas, Marianne, William, and James followed Chief Nacotchtank through the wilderness. They were covered in dirt, their clothes plastered to their bodies. Every step was a battle against exhaustion, but Thomas pressed on, fueled by a flicker of hope. Beside him, Marianne's red hair had lost its luster to the grime of their journey, yet her spirit remained undimmed. She glanced at him and managed a weary smile, her usual sharp wit quieted by fatigue. The long days on the move were taking their toll, but the hope of reaching the Quaker settlement kept them moving, one painstaking step at a time.

"Thank you for helping us," Thomas rasped, his voice hoarse from days of fleeing and hiding. Their guide nodded, his stoic presence a reassuring beacon on their treacherous journey. Renowned among the Quakers for his dedication to aiding escapees, he had become essential to many seeking freedom.

Thomas glanced back at his friends, noting the weariness on their faces from their long journey since escaping the plantation. As they crested a small hill, the Quaker settlement unfolded before them. Lanterns swayed gently outside quaint wooden houses, casting warm, welcoming glows on the cobblestone paths. The sound of laughter and voices carried through the air, wrapping Thomas in a comforting embrace and easing the tight knot of fear in his chest. He felt a surge of hope in this haven without chains or cruel overseers. For the first time in what seemed like forever, Thomas sensed that true freedom might be within reach.

Marianne's eyes widened, her fatigue momentarily forgotten. "I can't believe we made it," she whispered, a joyful sob breaking through. She clutched Thomas's hand, and he gave her a comforting squeeze. Although the future remained uncertain, this moment offered solace—they were safe, at least for now.

With a final nod of gratitude to Chief Nacotchtank, Thomas and the others entered the heart of the Quaker settlement. They were greeted with welcoming smiles. The sound of children's laughter, darting past, acted as a balm to Thomas's weary soul, infusing him with joy. As they moved further into the settlement, a kind-faced man and woman approached, their eyes radiating warmth.

"Welcome, friends," the man said. "My name is Reuben Turner, and this is my wife, Abigail."

Reuben Turner stood tall, his presence marked by a quiet dignity. He wore simple but sturdy clothes typical of the Quaker community: a plain, dark brown coat over a cream shirt loosely tied at the neck with a simple cord. His trousers were a matching dark hue, and he wore sturdy leather boots that spoke of many hours spent working outdoors. His face was gentle, framed by a neatly trimmed beard and hair peppered with gray, showing his experience and wisdom.

Beside him, Abigail Turner presented a comforting figure. Her soft brown curls were pulled back from her face, accentuating her warm, welcoming blue eyes, which sparkled with kindness. She wore a modest dress of soft blue fabric, covered by a clean white apron neatly tied around her waist.

Abigail stepped forward with a warm smile. "We are glad to have you here," she added. "Please, feel at home. You must be tired after your journey."

"Thank you, Reuben, Abigail. It's been a long road, and your welcome brings more comfort than you know," Thomas replied, his voice thick with emotion.

As they spoke, other community members gathered, curious and eager to meet the new arrivals. The adults offered quiet nods and handshakes while the children peeked from behind their parents, shy but interested. Reuben continued, "Let us show you around and get you settled in so you can rest. You must be exhausted."

Abigail and another woman gently led Marianne away while Reuben gathered the men.

"Welcome to Hopewell Friends settlement," Reuben said, gently touching Thomas's shoulder. "Let me show you where you will be staying and where you can wash up and rest. Once you're finished, we will gather for community Bible study and dinner."

Thomas nodded. He was exhausted and wanted a bath and a clean change of clothes. He followed Reuben to a small cabin with four beds and a wash basin.

"There are clean clothes in the chest there," Reuben gestured. "Take as long as you need to settle in and get comfortable."

"Thank you, sir," Thomas said.

"Of course, son," Reuben smiled. "I'll give you some privacy. When you're ready, find me, and we'll formally introduce everyone here."

Once Reuben left, Thomas peeled off his filthy shirt, wincing as it clung to his wounds. Slowly, he cleaned himself, scrubbing away the blood and grime. For the first time in weeks, he felt human again. Dressed in soft, clean clothes, Thomas sat on the edge of the bed. A wave of peace washed over him. For now, he and his friends were safe. Tonight, they would sleep without fear.

As the evening drew near, Thomas and the others made their way to the community hall, a large, welcoming structure at the center of the settlement. When they arrived, the hall was already bustling with activity. Children played quietly in one corner while adults set up tables and arranged seating. The smell of stewed vegetables and apple pie filled the air, mingling with the soft hum of conversation.

Reuben greeted them at the door with a warm smile. "Friends, you are just in time. We are about to begin our Bible study before supper. We gather here each evening to share and reflect upon our faith," he explained, guiding them to a circle of chairs where several community members were already seated.

Thomas sat among the others, feeling slightly out of place yet welcomed. The Bible study began with a moment of silence, which the Quakers held dear as a time for inward reflection and spiritual communion. Reuben then read passages from the Bible, and members of the community shared their thoughts and insights. The discussion was gentle and thoughtful, focusing on peace, forgiveness, and the inner Light that Quakers believed resided in every person. Thomas wondered to himself if that were true. He found it hard to believe that someone like Lord Blackwood had light within.

After the study, the group moved to the adjoining dining area, where tables were laden with simple, wholesome food. Thomas was introduced to various community members, each greeting him with the same kindness and openness he had received from Reuben and Abigail. Thomas found himself amidst a whirlwind of conversation as they gathered to eat. With a gentle voice and wise eyes, an elder named Jacob turned to Thomas as they passed a bowl of stewed vegetables.

"Thomas, our settlement here began as nothing more than a vision for peace in a time of unrest," Jacob began, his voice rich with the weight of memory. "We've faced many trials, from harsh winters to scarce resources, but our commitment to each other and our faith has seen us through."

Across from them, a woman named Sarah, whose laugh was as bright as the lanterns above, chimed in. "And don't forget the celebrations! Harvest feasts, weddings, and even the simple joy of a new calf born in the spring. We find every reason we can to celebrate life's blessings."

The warmth in her words and the genuine smiles around the table drew a laugh from Thomas. "It sounds like you've built more than just a community here," he responded, feeling the truth of his own words. "You've built a family."

Reuben leaned in with a look of curiosity on his face. "Thomas, could you share more about your life before coming here? We understand you worked on a plantation?"

Thomas exchanged a glance with his companions. Clearing his throat, he began, "Yes, we were indentured on a plantation, and life there was challenging. We were brought over from England, kidnapped as youths, and sold into servitude to Lord Blackwood."

A murmur of sympathy went around the table as the community members absorbed the gravity of Thomas's words. Reuben's wife, Abigail, placed a comforting hand over Thomas's. "That sounds like a grievous burden to bear," she said softly.

Thomas nodded, appreciating the empathy but wanting to paint a fuller picture. "It was, but it was also there that we found strength in each other. We supported one another, and over time, we did more than survive; we helped others when we could."

"Runaways?" asked another member of the community, an older man named Samuel.

"Yes," Thomas confirmed, "Once a runaway came through seeking freedom from slavery. Despite the dangers, we couldn't look the other way. We helped him as best we could by giving him food and hiding him for a night. It was a great risk, and we almost got caught. Not long after that, we decided to risk our lives to escape the plantation. One of the slaves, Henrietta, told us one night about the Friends and your desire to help those seeking freedom, and that's when we began planning."

Reuben nodded thoughtfully. "It's a testament to your spirit, Thomas. Here, we believe every person has that of God within them, and it's our duty to act accordingly, helping others, regardless of the law, when it's unjust."

Abigail added, "Indeed, we strive to live by peace and justice here. We might not face the same dangers, but we support each other and advocate for those outside our community who suffer injustice."

As the conversation continued into the evening, the room was filled with warm, gentle light from the oil lamps, casting soft shadows against the wooden walls. Community members shared their experiences and thoughts on justice, peace, and community living. Eventually, the gathering began to wind down. People started clearing the tables, stacking chairs, and saying their goodbyes. Thomas felt a deep sense of contentment as he listened to the final few exchanges, feeling more connected to this community than anticipated.

"Thank you, everyone, for such a warm welcome and for sharing your thoughts and lives with us tonight," Thomas said, standing up from his chair.

Reuben and Abigail walked Thomas and his friends out, the night air cool and crisp under the starlit sky. "We're pleased you could join us tonight. Rest well, friends," Reuben said, his voice warm.

Thomas and the others made their way to their cabin, the path illuminated by the soft glow of lanterns hanging outside each doorway. As they reached their cabin, Thomas paused, looking up at the stars, feeling a sense of peace. He looked at Marianne, gave her a quick smile, and pecked goodnight on her cheek.

The following day, Thomas awoke to the scent of freshly baked bread and the murmur of voices. For a split second, he thought he was back at the plantation, stirred by the morning bells. But then it all came rushing back—the daring escape, the grueling journey, Elijah's sacrifice, Chief Nacotchtank, and the Quakers who had taken them in. Sitting up, he took in the cabin around him. James and William were already awake, silently pulling on their boots. Marianne stood in the doorway with a shy smile on her face. Seeing her safe made Thomas feel a tiny spark of hope ignite within him.

"Good mornin'," she said. "Breakfast is ready."

Thomas followed her outside into the crisp morning air and the community dining hall. A long table was piled high with bread, cheeses, preserves, and pitchers of milk. Thomas's mouth watered at the sight.

As they ate, Reuben approached. "Good morning, friends. I hope you all slept well."

They nodded, murmuring their thanks between mouthfuls of food.

Reuben continued, his voice gentle yet firm. "Friends, you are welcome to remain here for as long as your needs require. I am well aware that your journey has been arduous and filled with trials. Let this place serve you as a sanctuary of rest and peace. Yet, we must exercise great diligence and caution so that your presence among us may remain hidden from those who seek to do you harm."

Thomas swallowed a bite of bread and said, "Thank you, Reuben. Last night was the first full night's rest we've had since we left the plantation."

Reuben offered a gentle smile. "We strive to create a welcoming refuge for all who seek freedom and fellowship," he said, reflecting a deep sense of purpose. His expression grew solemn as he continued, "These are indeed troubled times, with the weight of political strife heavy upon us. Yet, we must trust God's guidance and remain steadfast in our commitment to His will."

William spoke up. "We've heard talk about the colonies fightin' back against the British. Is it true?"

Reuben nodded thoughtfully, his voice carrying the weight of years of wisdom. "Aye, it is true. The seeds of violence have already taken root in Massachusetts, and I fear Virginia stands on the edge of the same dark path. There is much talk of the colonies seeking independence, but we must approach such matters with great care and discernment, ever mindful of the principles of peace and the guidance of the Inner Light."

"What does that mean for us?" Thomas asked.

Reuben spread his hands gently, his voice calm and measured. "I cannot speak with certainty on what lies ahead. For oppressed people, the prospect of revolution holds both hope and peril. As a community, we stand firm in our commitment to peace, refraining from violence and war. We seek to walk the path of neutrality, guided by the Spirit within, and trusting in the Lord's wisdom in these troubled times."

James nodded, his voice dropping to a hushed tone. "Word's goin' round that they might give us our freedom if we fight. Could be our shot at breakin' free for good. But listen, we're still runaways. To them, we're just property. If they catch us, we're goin' back, and it'll be bad, real bad."

Thomas scratched his head, thinking over Reuben's words. "I get what you're saying, Reuben, about staying neutral about it and all. I know peace is important. But the idea of being free, really free, it's something else. Not having someone else telling you what to do daily and controlling you. That's worth a lot. We have to think about what matters most here—whether this might be our one shot to break free from our chains finally." He met Marianne's worried gaze, his uncertainty mirrored in her eyes. Was this the freedom for which they had risked everything?

After breakfast, the group quickly integrated into the daily routines. William and James helped Reuben repair a section of the fence damaged in a recent storm. Thomas, skilled in carpentry, helped build a new barn. He carefully measured and sawed the lumber, his hands moving surely as he followed the Quaker carpenters' guidance. Together, they raised the barn's frame, the sound of hammers echoing through the settlement. Thomas felt deeply satisfied as the structure took shape, each nail and plank bringing them closer to completion. While the men labored, Marianne joined the women of the settlement by gathering fresh eggs from the henhouse and chopping vegetables for dinner.

Reuben looked up at the sun, noticing its high position in the sky. "Friends," he began in a gentle, measured tone,

"I believe it is time we take a moment to rest. Your labor has been a great service, so I sincerely thank you. Truly, your dedication is a testament to the strength of our community and the light that guides us all." He paused, wiping the sweat from his brow with a soft smile. "Let us refresh ourselves, and may we continue in this spirit of unity and purpose."

As the day went on, they found their places in the community. The work was hard but a welcome distraction from the dangers they'd left behind. William and James climbed up to fix the meeting hall roof, carefully replacing broken shingles. Marianne learned to preserve fruits, canning under the guidance of the older women. With his knack for carpentry, Thomas was asked to help carve new chairs for the dining hall, a task he took on with pride.

By late afternoon, the settlement buzzed with activity. Children played in the fields, their laughter mixing with the sounds of adults working and chatting. Fresh bread baked in outdoor ovens wafted through the air, blending with the scents of blooming flowers and tilled earth. Thomas laughed with James as they fetched water from the well, while Marianne shared stories with the women as they kneaded dough and tended the garden.

As evening descended, the group assembled in the large meeting hall. Despite their exhaustion, the day's work had buoyed their spirits. Thomas stared into his bowl of stew, the savory aroma wafting up, yet it did little to soothe his troubled thoughts. His dreams of freedom had been with him since he was torn from his home in London, confined in a ship's hold, and sold into bondage. He had been reflecting on their earlier discussion about the promise of freedom if they joined the militia, wrestling with the idea in his mind. Could he do it? Could he leave the safety of this settlement, leave Marianne behind, and step into the unknown? Glancing at William and James beside him, he saw a flicker of hope in their eyes, mingled with the weariness of years spent toiling at the plantation.

After dinner, as they returned to their cabin, the air was heavy with tension and the chill of the approaching night. Inside, the cabin was warm, the fire crackling softly in the hearth, casting a comforting glow but doing little to ease the brewing storm.

Thomas broached the subject first. "We should consider joining the militia," he said, his voice steady but his hands betraying his nerves as they fidgeted with a wooden cup.

"Dunno, Tom. It's a big risk, innit? We've finally got a bit of peace here. Why go and stir up trouble?" William sighed, leaning back against the wall.

"But think of the freedom it promises, Will. This could be our chance to change things, not just for us but for the others still stuck in chains," James said.

William shook his head, his expression troubled. "And what if we die out there? What then? Freedom ain't much use to the dead."

Thomas's frustration flared. "So, we just sit here? Live quietly while others suffer the same fate we escaped? That's not enough for me. At any time, the patrollers can show up here and find us. Then we're back where we started."

The argument heated, voices rising as each man laid bare his fears and hopes. Looking at them, Thomas felt a spark ignite. Whatever this war brought, they would face it together. Their fate was bound as brothers, just as it had been in chains. With his jaw set, Thomas looked at Marianne's gentle face. He would find his freedom and then return to build a life with her. For her, he would be brave. He loved her and knew that staying put them at risk of being caught and sent back to the plantation. That was the last thing he wanted. They had fought too hard to escape Blackwood Plantation, and he would do whatever it took to keep their freedom.

Marianne's eyes welled with tears as she listened to Thomas, William, and James discuss joining the fight for independence. She understood it might be their only chance for freedom, but the thought of Thomas going off to war made her heart ache deeply.

She pulled him aside, her voice shaking. "Must you go? This war could take you so far away. What if. . ." Her words trailed off, and she was unable to voice her deepest fear.

Thomas took her hands. "Marianne, this is the only way I can escape my indenture. This is our chance." He lifted her chin, his eyes full of determination. "When it's over, we can start a new life together."

Marianne threw her arms around him, holding him tightly. "Just promise me you'll come back. Even if this war lasts a lifetime, it won't change how I feel about you, Thomas," she whispered, her heart breaking at the thought of him leaving.

"I love you, Marianne. Nothing could keep me from you. I'll be back. I promise," Thomas vowed, tilting her face and kissing her.

After deciding, the group spent a few more moments in quiet camaraderie, reflecting on the significant step they were about to take. As the night deepened, they each made their way to prepare for bed, the cabin filled with a sad yet determined silence.

"Goodnight, Marianne," Thomas said gently, reaching out to gently touch her cheek. His voice carried a depth of gratitude and affection, a reassurance in the simple words. "Thank you for being here, for everything. Sleep well."

Marianne looked up at him, her eyes reflecting the flicker of candlelight. "Goodnight, Thomas," she replied, her voice soft. "Sleep well."

The night passed with uneasy dreams for Thomas, visions of battlefields mingling with the peaceful images of the settlement. At dawn, he rose, feeling the burden of what was to come and the ache of impending departure. Later that day, Thomas sought out Reuben and Abigail to share their decision. Finding them in their garden, he explained their decision to join the militia.

Reuben listened intently, his face showing both sadness and respect. "Your courage is commendable," he said after a moment, his hand resting on Thomas's shoulder. "This settlement will hold you in our prayers. Remember, the Light within you is stronger than the darkness without."

Abigail, ever the nurturing presence, added, "We'll prepare some supplies for your journey. It's the least we can do."

Grateful for their support, Thomas thanked them and returned to Marianne, who was waiting by their cabin, anxiety etched on her face.

"When will you be leavin'?" Marianne asked, her voice shaky as tears welled up in her eyes.

Thomas held Marianne close, feeling the warmth of her body against his, a stark contrast to the cold dread of the days ahead. His fingers gently traced the curve of her back as if trying to memorize the feel of her in his arms. "In a few days," he whispered, his voice thick with emotion. "After we've rested and prepared. I promise you, Marianne, I'll return to you." He kissed her forehead tenderly, his lips lingering as if sealing the vow. "Wait for me, love. We'll have our time again."

Marianne's eyes glistened as she clung to him, the silent plea in her heart echoing in the stillness around them. She managed a small, trembling smile through her tears, reflecting her trust in him. Deep down, she knew that Thomas would keep his promise, no matter the distance or the time apart. Her heart, unwavering and steadfast, would remain with him until the day he returned to her embrace.

The next few days were a blur of preparation. Thomas, William, and James gathered supplies, checked their equipment, and received well-wishes from other members of the community. Reuben and Abigail helped them pack, providing dried food, medical supplies, and warm clothing.

On the morning of their departure, the air was crisp, with a delicate mist clinging to the earth. Thomas held Marianne close, feeling her body tremble in his embrace. Their farewell was laden with emotion, tears mingling with whispered promises of a safe return and heartfelt declarations of love.

Marianne clung to him, her voice trembling as she

whispered, "Keep safe, Thomas. Please come back to me. I can't live without you." Her words were laced with fear and love, her tears falling silently as she looked into his eyes.

"I will, my love," Thomas vowed, kissing her forehead. He gently wiped the tears from her cheeks with a tender touch. Then, with a heavy heart, he stepped back, his eyes alight with determination. With one last, heartfelt glance at Marianne, he turned and joined William and James. Together, the three of them slowly disappeared into the morning mist, their silhouettes fading as they marched toward an uncertain future, fueled by the hope of making a difference and the dream of freedom.

Chapter Thirty

The line of worn and weary men stretched around the corner, packed together like fish in a suffocating sea. Thomas stood among them, his heart pounding to the slow, steady beat of the drums echoing through the air. Beside him were his friends William and James, their faces showing the same determination that he felt. They exchanged nods of silent encouragement. It was now or never, but they weren't alone in this.

The recruitment office loomed ahead, a grim reminder of the choice they were about to make. The smell of ink, parchment, and the sweat of desperation filled the air as they moved closer to the large oak door. Thomas's stomach churned with anticipation and fear, his mind clouded with uncertainty. Alongside him stood men who were farmers, shopkeepers, artisans, fishermen, doctors, lawyers, freemen, and indentured, white, black, illiterate, educated, young, and old. All were there to join the cause for the colonies.

Finally, they stood before the clerk, an older man well past his prime, with a back slightly hunched from years of bending over desks and records. His hair, what little was left of it, was thin and gray, sticking out in uneven tufts that looked like they had long since stopped caring about propriety. His eyes, pale and watery, peered out under heavy lids, their dullness suggesting they had seen more than their fair share of eager young men like Thomas and his friends. The faint smell of ink and parchment filled the small room as the clerk dipped his quill, the soft scratching sound echoing with finality as he recorded their names and the meager belongings they carried. Thomas took a deep breath, his chest swelling with pride as he and his friends were sworn in as soldiers and militia members.

"Raise your right hand," commanded an officer, his tone solemn and firm.

Thomas raised his hand, feeling the rough calluses that marked years of hard work. Beside him, William and James did the same, their hands steady despite the weight of the moment.

"Do you swear to serve in the Continental Army, to defend the cause of liberty, and to faithfully obey the orders of your officers and the Continental Congress?"

"I do," Thomas said, his voice firm. He glanced at William and James, seeing the same fire in their eyes.

"To stand by your brothers-in-arms, no matter the cost?"

"Yes," they replied in unison. Thomas felt the words

bind them together, a pact sealed with their voices and very souls.

"In the Year of Our Lord, March 1776, you are now placed under orders and discipline. You shall muster on the green at the sound of the drum. Welcome to the 1st Virginia Regiment, commanded by Colonel William Woodford."

The officer's words hung in the air as they lowered their hands. Thomas was excited but also frightened. They were soldiers now, and their lives forever changed. He glanced at William and James, drawing strength from their presence. They had chosen this path together, and together, they would face whatever came next.

As they exited the recruitment office, the sun seemed brighter, the air crisper. Thomas took a deep breath, feeling the weight of his new identity settle. They were no longer just three young men trying to escape their pasts; they were part of something bigger, something that could change history.

"To freedom," he whispered, more to himself than anyone else.

"To freedom," echoed William and James, their voices blending into the promise of what lay ahead.

Thomas couldn't help but wonder what trials awaited them on the battlefield. Would they stay united, or would war tear them apart, perhaps through death in battle or by being sent to different units? Their fates were now tied to the cause they fought for, and there was no turning back. He lingered for a moment, reflecting on his life's path. He thought back to the countless days spent laboring under the crushing weight of poverty, struggling to survive in a world that seemed determined to break him. And yet, here he was—a soldier with a purpose, a chance to fight for something greater than himself. It wasn't just a rebellion against tyranny; it was a chance to redefine who he was, to carve out a place in history.

"Come on, Tom," urged William, clapping a hand on his shoulder. "We've got work to do."

With one last glance at the empty room, Thomas turned and followed his friends into the unknown, ready to face whatever challenges lay ahead in their fight for freedom.

By mid-morning, Thomas and the others had arrived at their new camp. The sun rose steadily over the untouched landscape, casting long shadows across the training camp on the outskirts of Williamsburg, Virginia. The camp was on a fifty-acre plantation that had once belonged to a loyalist. The position provided an excellent vantage point for observation. The grounds were expansive, with a stately mansion standing at its center, surrounded by a serene pond, a sturdy barn, workshops, and a hothouse now repurposed for storage. Everywhere he looked, he saw soldiers preparing for the trials ahead, their footsteps crunching on the gravel paths that crisscrossed the plantation-turned-camp.

Prominently displayed amidst the disciplined arrangement of tents was the flag of the 1st Virginia Regiment. This striking banner featured a rich, crimson field, symbolizing the profound courage and sacrifice of the troops. In the upper left corner, a blue canton adorned with thirteen white stars represented the unity of the original colonies. A vibrant green wreath at the center encircled a golden

Roman numeral I, denoting the regiment's designation. Beneath the wreath, a white scroll carried the bold inscription "VIRGINIA," proudly proclaiming the state's commitment to the struggle for independence. This flag served as a constant source of inspiration for the men, reminding them of their duty and the support of their fellow Virginians as they prepared for the challenges ahead.

The following day, muskets fired, and men shouted, jolting Thomas from his restless sleep. He lay there for a moment, taking in the scene. The smell of damp earth and sweat filled the air inside the makeshift tents. The ground was hard beneath him, the thin blanket offering little comfort. As he sat up, he saw other soldiers stirring, their faces marked by exhaustion and determination. The camp buzzed with the sounds of training, a stark reminder of the battles to come.

"Let's go, lads! There's work to be done!" a burly sergeant bellowed, kicking the side of their tent.

Thomas, William, and James scrambled to their feet in the dim light of the dawn, hastily pulling on their dirty clothes. The air was cool, and the earth was damp as they dressed. The boots they had been issued upon arriving at the camp weren't comfortable; they were too large for James, slightly too small for Thomas, and just a misfit for William. Despite the poor fit, they were grateful for the protection against the rough, unforgiving ground. The leather was stiff and unyielding, chafing against their feet with every step. Yet, it was far better than going barefoot across the thorn-strewn paths surrounding their encampment.

"Alright, men," the sergeant called out, his voice firm. "Enough idle chatter! We've a war to fight, and today we'll see if you have the steel to stand in the ranks of the Continental Army!"

Thomas gritted his teeth as the drills began, pushing himself to keep up with the sergeant's grueling pace. His muscles ached, but he refused to let fatigue win. The trio marched across the uneven terrain, their boots sinking into the soft soil. They twisted their bodies through the rigorous drills, bayonets thrusting and parrying invisible foes. Sweat ran down Thomas's spine, his hair sticking to his forehead. Despite the exhaustion gripping his limbs, he pushed forward, driven by an unyielding resolve. This was his chance to make a difference.

Weeks passed in a blur of drills and training. The ragged group of recruits transformed into a disciplined unit. Their bodies grew more muscular, their movements sharper. Waking before dawn, the men would form ranks, their breaths forming clouds in the cold air. They drilled until dusk, practicing musketry, bayonet drills, and formations with unyielding intensity. The sergeants were relentless, barking orders and shouting obscenities that echoed across the camp.

Discipline was enforced with brutal methods. A careless mistake or a moment of insubordination could result in the lash—a leather whip that bit into the skin with a crack that made the others wince. Men who faltered under the weight of their gear or lagged during a march were sometimes met with the flat of an officer's sword across their backs or shoulders. For more severe infractions, a recruit might find himself trussed up to a wooden frame, enduring hours in the stocks as a warning to others. Each day pushed them harder, but they kept going, driven by the need to prepare for what lay ahead. The punishments, though harsh, forged a sense of resilience in the men, hardening them not only in body but in spirit. They knew the stakes were high, and the price of failure would be paid in blood on the battlefield.

One evening, after a grueling session, the men were assembled around a roaring campfire. The sergeants announced that they would be assigning tradesmen to specialized roles.

"Everhart, Thomas, step forward," a grizzled sergeant barked.

Thomas's heart raced as he stepped forward, the fire's heat warming his exhausted body.

"We know your trade, lad. Report to the quartermaster's tent at first light. You and your friends too," he gestured to William and James, who exchanged surprised looks.

"Sir, yes, sir!" Thomas barked, hope glimmering in his eyes.

The next morning, at the quartermaster's tent, they were given tools of their trade. Instead of muskets, they received saws, hammers, and axes.

"We need good lads like you to keep our supplies safe and wagons rolling," the quartermaster said, slapping Thomas on the back.

In the following days, Thomas worked under the master cooper's watchful eye, crafting barrels and learning how to repair wagons. It reminded him of his time at the plantation, crafting the tobacco barrels. Each morning, they reported to the cooper's workshop, a large barn filled with the scent of fresh-cut wood.

"That looks good, Tom," William said, running his fingers along the smooth edge of the barrel. "Should hold up proper, that should." He nodded in approval, a rare smile creeping onto his face. "Yer getting' right handy with that."

"Thanks," Thomas replied, his eyes meeting William's with a hint of satisfaction. "It's coming along."

The master cooper, a grizzled veteran named John, walked over to check their progress. "Good work, men," he grunted, nodding his approval. "Remember, a well-made barrel can mean the difference between preserved supplies and spoiled goods. Pay attention to every detail."

Thomas nodded, feeling a deep sense of pride in his craftsmanship. Each barrel he made was a critical piece of the war effort, destined to store vital supplies like gunpowder, salted meat, and fresh water. He knew that his work, though removed from the front lines, was essential for the soldiers' survival.

He watched as William and James worked beside him. The barn echoed with the sounds of saws cutting through wood, hammers driving nails, and the steady scrape of planes smoothing rough edges. Thomas took a moment to admire the sturdy and well-crafted barrels they had completed. He knew that each would play a part in the fight for freedom, whether it held the gunpowder that powered their muskets or the food that kept them marching.

During breaks, the men would gather around the workbench, sharing stories and news from the front lines. Their conversations often centered on the recent Battle of Great Bridge.

"Lost three good men from our regiment," lamented a burly man with deep-set eyes that seemed to carry the weight of every story he told.

Despite looking worn out, an older man with a quick grin said, "Heard they fought like lions, they did. Made the British tuck tail proper. Ain't got no control over Virginia no more, thanks to us."

"Did you hear about the latest scuffle up north?" James asked one afternoon, wiping sweat from his brow. "Word is, the British got a right kickin'—took heavy losses, they did."

"Seems like we're givin' 'em a good fight. Every barrel we bang out here, every wagon we patch up, it all adds up," William replied, adjusting his grip on the hammer.

Thomas paused, looking at his friends. "Do you ever think about going to the front lines?"

James nodded slowly. "Every day, mate. Part of me wants to be out there, fightin' for our freedom proper."

William sighed, setting down his hammer. "Aye, I feel the same, but we're doin' our part here. Without these supplies, the soldiers wouldn't stand a chance."

Thomas picked up the plane again, running it along the barrel stave. "I know we're helping, but a part of me wants to stand and fight. To see the enemy, to know we're pushing them back."

James wiped his brow and leaned against the workbench. "I think about Elijah a lot, and ya know how he gave everythin' so we could have this shot. Sometimes, I wonder if he'd want us out there on the front lines."

"Marianne worries, you know," Thomas said, his voice softening. "She understands why we're here, but the thought of us going to fight... it scares her. She's been through so much already. The plantation, the escape..."

William nodded. "We all have, mate. But that's why we keep fightin', any way we can. Elijah's sacrifice, Marianne's courage, and even Emily's. They're our reasons. We owe it to them to keep pushin' forward."

Thomas looked at his friends, seeing the same determination in their eyes. "We'll keep building these barrels and fixing those wagons. We'll do our part here. And if the time comes to take up arms, we'll be ready."

"Think we'll get these done by nightfall?" James asked, wiping his hands on his breeches.

"With any luck," Thomas replied, glancing at the setting sun.

Just as they finished their tasks and prepared to retire for the evening, a rider approached in a hurry, dust kicking up from his horse's hooves.

"Urgent news!" he called out, dismounting quickly and heading straight for the quartermaster. After a brief, intense conversation, the quartermaster turned to Thomas and his friends.

"New orders, men," the quartermaster declared with authority. "There's been an engagement at the front, and we're in need of every man. You're to report to the main encampment without delay."

Thomas felt a knot form in his stomach. "Are we to fight, sir?" he asked, trying to keep his voice steady.

"The British are pressing hard, and reinforcements are needed at Gwynn's Island," the quartermaster stated with a grave tone, urgency apparent in his voice. "Lord Dunmore's forces have entrenched themselves, and if we don't act swiftly, we'll lose our strategic advantage."

Thomas exchanged glances with William and James, the reality sinking in. They had been ready to support the war effort from behind the lines, but now they were being called to face the enemy directly.

"We need to gather our tools," Thomas said, trying to keep his voice steady.

"Make haste," the quartermaster urged. "You'll be issued muskets and ammunition at the encampment."

They quickly gathered their tools and made their way back to the encampment. The looming threat of battle now overshadowed the camaraderie of their recent days of hard work. Upon arrival, they were issued muskets. The cold metal felt heavy in their hands, a stark reminder of the reality ahead.

"Move out!" the quartermaster barked, and the group began their march towards Gwynn's Island. The path was rough and uneven, winding through dense forests and across open fields. The scent of pine and earth filled the air, mingling with the salty tang of the nearby Chesapeake Bay. Birds scattered from the treetops as they passed, their calls a stark contrast to the grim silence of the marching men.

As they neared Gwynn's Island, the landscape began to change. The dense forest gave way to more open terrain, and the sound of the waves crashing against the shore grew louder. The air was cooler here, the breeze carrying a hint of salt and seaweed. They could see the island in the distance, a small, strategic point now their destination.

"Keep moving!" the quartermaster shouted, his voice cutting through the weariness that hung over them.

Once they arrived, the men immediately set up camp. As night fell, the camp settled into a tense quiet. Fires were lit, casting flickering shadows on the tents and the weary faces of the men. The scent of burning wood mingled with the salty sea air. Thomas thought about the battle ahead. It was his first battle as a soldier, and he was nervous.

"Tomorrow, we face whatever comes," Thomas said quietly, breaking the silence. "But we face it together."

A few days passed at camp, but then the call for battle sounded. As they marched towards the front lines, distant gunfire and the smell of gunpowder filled the air. Thomas clutched his musket tightly, his heart pounding in his chest.

"Stay close," William whispered, his eyes scanning the horizon. "Let's try to stay together."

The battlefield was chaos. Smoke hung thick in the air, and the cries of wounded soldiers echoed around them. Thomas and the others took their positions, loading their muskets with trembling hands.

"Fire!" came the command, and they raised their weapons, aiming at the advancing redcoats. Thomas pulled the trigger, the recoil jolting through his shoulder as the musket ball flew towards the enemy.

The ground shook with the impact of artillery, and the cries of the wounded and dying created a haunting symphony of war. Thomas saw men fall around him. Musket balls and cannon fire struck down comrades. Blood soaked the earth, and the once-green field became a grim scene of death and destruction. Hours passed in a blur of smoke and gunfire. The heat of battle was relentless, with waves of British soldiers clashing against the American lines. Thomas's arms ached from the constant reloading and firing, but he fought on, driven by a fierce determination to survive.

James was next to him, his face grim and focused. A British soldier charged at them, bayonet fixed. Thomas swung his musket like a club, knocking the attacker down. Nearby, William fired shot after shot, each one finding its mark. The intensity of the fight seemed unending. Men screamed in pain, and the ground was littered with the fallen. Thomas saw a young drummer boy, no older than twelve, crumpled on the ground, clutching his wounded leg. He wanted to help, but the chaos of battle left no room for mercy.

When the battle finally ended, the field was littered with the fallen. Bodies lay in twisted heaps, and the once booming battlefield fell eerily silent except for the groans of the wounded and the cries for help. Smoke still hung heavy in the air, obscuring the sun and casting a pall over the scene.

Though exhausted and shaken, they had survived. They stood amidst the carnage, breathing heavily, their faces smeared with black powder, dirt, and sweat. They looked around at the devastation, the reality of war stark and unforgiving.

"We made it," James muttered, his voice shaky. "But just look at the cost. All our lives, we fought to stay alive, to get some grub. We fight our own demons to stay decent, and now we're fightin' someone else's battle so we can be free."

William, standing beside him, let out a deep sigh. "Harsh as it is, it's not about survivin' anymore. It's about livin' free. And that's a fight worth fightin' for."

Thomas nodded in agreement, his gaze drifting towards the battle remnants across Gwynn's Island. "We've come this far," he added. "And we've seen it through. We defeated Lord Dunmore here, drove him and his forces off the island," he observed, the victory bittersweet as his gaze fell on the bodies of fallen comrades. "And yet, the price of this victory is steep. The sight of our fallen is a sobering reminder of the brutality of war."

What dangers lurked ahead for these three young men? What trials and tribulations would they face as they continued their fight for freedom? And most importantly, would their bond, tempered by the fires of war, endure the harsh winds of change that lay in store?

Chapter Thirty-One

The battle at Gwynn's Island had finally drawn to a close, and though weary and battered, Thomas and his comrades made their way back to their encampment, seeking some respite from the relentless fighting. As time passed, they were called upon to defend against British raids on Virginia's shores, a task that demanded constant vigilance and left little room for rest.

Amidst these demands, Thomas, who had been serving as a cooper for the army, found himself stretched thin. The dual responsibility of crafting necessary supplies while guarding against sudden raids became increasingly unsustainable. Recognizing the toll it was taking, he was compelled to request a temporary leave from his duties as a cooper after a particularly close encounter during one of the raids.

One crisp evening, as they huddled around a crackling fire for warmth, their conversation naturally drifted toward the recent monumental events reshaping their world.

"Have you heard? They've gone and declared independence," James said, his tone a mixture of awe and apprehension, reflecting the gravity of their struggle.

Thomas, poking at the fire with a stick, watched the embers spark and ascend into the night. "Yes, I overheard some officers discussing it. They're calling it the Declaration of Independence. Seems like our fight has just found its true north," he mused, the glow of the flames lighting up his thoughtful face.

William chimed in, a trace of pride coloring his voice as he spoke of their new leader. "And Patrick Henry is our first governor. 'Give me liberty, or give me death!' Remember when he was at Blackwood Plantation, and you were servin' that dinner party, Tom?"

"Yeah, I remember. The world's a strange place, that's for sure," Thomas sighed.

Winter wrapped its icy fingers around the encampment as the months wore on. The once lively green canvas of tents was now blanketed in snow, transforming the camp into a stark, frosty haven. The men fortified their spirits against the biting cold, bolstering each other's resolve. Amidst the harsh winter, their thoughts occasionally escaped to warmer days, to the springs they once knew.

The following fall, a stirring directive reached them. They were needed in Pennsylvania. "Looks like we're moving out soon to join the fight near Chadds Ford," Thomas announced to his friends, his voice steady despite the biting cold and the looming uncertainty of their journey. "It'll be several weeks' journey in this frost, but we march at dawn."

As they packed their gear and prepared for the long

trek, Thomas found himself haunted by the vivid memories of battles past. The roar of musket fire, the anguished cries of the dying, and the chaos that had engulfed him were imprinted deeply in his mind. He packed each item with solemn reverence as if the routine itself might help dispel the ghosts of war around him.

With each step towards Pennsylvania, Thomas steeled himself to continue their fight for freedom, carrying with him the hopes ignited by the Declaration of Independence and the visionary leadership of men like Patrick Henry. Their journey was not just a march across geography; it was a march towards destiny, shaped by the ideals they fought to uphold. As they moved forward, each mile traversed brought physical distance from their last encampment and a symbolic move towards a future they all believed in sincerely.

Upon reaching Chadds Ford, Pennsylvania, the weariness of their long march was momentarily lifted by the sight of the encampment site. Thomas and his comrades began the meticulous process of setting up their camp, a task that had become all too familiar yet was approached with renewed urgency given their proximity to General Sir William Howe's forces. The campsite was strategically chosen near the ford, offering them a crucial vantage point over the creek that meandered through the landscape.

The soldiers worked together, unrolling heavy canvas to erect their tents, the fabric snapping in the autumn wind that swept through the valley. Each tent was methodically placed, forming neat rows that transformed the rugged terrain into an organized military settlement. The smell of wood and smoke soon filled the air as fires were kindled, their glow casting a warm light against the encroaching dusk. Cooks busied themselves preparing meals, their pots and pans clattering over the fires as they cooked enough to feed the weary and hungry men.

The sounds of hammers and muffled commands blended with the rustling leaves, creating a bustling atmosphere of preparation and anticipation. Sentry posts were established, with guards rotating shifts to ensure their readiness against any surprise maneuvers by the British. As night fell, the camp settled into a guarded stillness, with only the occasional crackle of firewood or the distant call of a night bird piercing the silence.

The brief peace of the night was abruptly shattered at dawn. A rider, his horse foaming, and panting galloped into the camp with urgent news from General Washington's headquarters. The British were advancing more quickly than anticipated, and every soldier was called to march to the nearby fields of Brandywine. The urgency was palpable; there was no time to waste as the reality of the impending battle set in.

Thomas and his comrades scrambled to break camp. The morning sounds were no longer just the serene whispers of nature but were now marked by the clanging of metal, shouting of orders, and the hurried footsteps of soldiers preparing for combat. The camp, so meticulously set up the day before, was swiftly dismantled. Tents were struck, and supplies were loaded with practiced efficiency.

As they formed ranks, the officers moved along the lines, ensuring each man was equipped and ready. Thomas checked his musket, feeling the familiar weight in his hands, and looked around at the determined faces of his fellow soldiers. They knew the battle ahead would be crucial, not just for the control of Philadelphia but also for the morale of the Continental Army.

With their gear secured and spirits bolstered by the gravity of their task, Thomas and his unit marched out from the encampment, leaving behind the relative safety of their temporary shelter. The crisp morning air was soon filled with the rumble of marching feet as the Continental soldiers moved towards Brandywine, their flags fluttering in the early breeze, signaling their readiness to confront whatever awaited them on the battlefield.

After hours of marching, they arrived at the chosen site to set up camp near Chadds Ford along the Brandywine Creek. The landscape was both beautiful and ominous, the gentle flow of the creek contrasting with the tension that hung in the air. Rolling hills and dense woodlands surrounded them, offering strategic cover and the looming threat of hidden enemies. The men moved with purpose, setting up tents and fortifications, their hands working quickly yet methodically despite the weight of fatigue.

As evening fell, the campfires flickered in the gathering darkness, casting long shadows on the soldiers as they huddled around for warmth and camaraderie. The scent of cooking fires mixed with the earthy smell of the creek and the ground's dampness, creating an atmosphere heavy with anticipation. Thomas could feel the anxiety of the men around him, each one silently contemplating the battle that would surely come.

It wasn't long before their worst fears were realized. Just as the soldiers began to find some rest on the first of September, they were roused from sleep by the ominous sound of British war drums echoing through the early morning mist. Once still and quiet, the air was filled with the rhythmic, foreboding beat that signaled the enemy's approach. Officers rushed through the camp, barking orders to get the men into formation.

Thomas felt his heart pound in his chest as he grabbed his musket and joined his comrades. The soldiers, still groggy from sleep, scrambled to line up, their faces pale in the dim light of dawn. The sounds of the British forces grew louder, the drums accompanied by the distant clatter of hooves and the low murmur of thousands of voices. The tension in the air was palpable, like a taut string ready to snap. The cold morning air and the heat of their rising fear created a sense of dread weighing heavily on every man's shoulders.

As they stood there, the reality of the situation began to sink in. There would be no time to steady their nerves or gather their thoughts; the enemy was almost upon them. Thomas exchanged a glance with his comrades, whose faces were set in a determined grimace, though Thomas could see the flicker of fear in their eyes. The moment hung in the balance, stretched thin by anticipating the violence to come.

And then, without warning, the world erupted into chaos.

The roar of musket fire and the screams of the dying filled the air as Thomas was thrust into the heart of the storm. The battle raged around him, a swirl of death and chaos that spared no one. His musket felt heavy in his hands, and fear clung to his heart. His eyes darted left and right, trying to make sense of the chaos. Smoke clouded his vision, and the acrid smell of gunpowder stung his nostrils. All around him, men fell like autumn leaves, some with gaping wounds, others collapsing without warning. The air pulsed with the fury of musket fire, and the ground trembled with each cannon blast.

"Stay together!" James shouted over the roar of battle, his voice cracking with terror. But his words were lost in the chaos, and Thomas was separated from William and James as the tide of war swept them away like debris in a raging river.

"Over here!" William gestured toward a shallow trench hastily dug into the earth. They threw themselves into it just as another explosion shook the ground, sending a shower of dirt and debris raining down. For a moment, Thomas lay still, the weight of the earth pressing down on him, grounding him in the harsh reality of their situation.

Thomas lifted his head, peering over the edge of the trench. The scene before him was a nightmare. Soldiers clashed in brutal hand-to-hand combat, their cries mingling with the constant noise of battle. Blood stained the ground, turning the once-green field into a grotesque mix of red and brown.

"Keep your head down," James warned, pulling Thomas back into the trench. But Thomas couldn't look away. He saw a young man, no older than himself, fall to the ground clutching his chest. The young man's eyes met Thomas's for a fleeting moment, and in that brief exchange, Thomas saw the same fear and desperation that gnawed at his soul.

"Move!" James shouted, yanking Thomas from his thoughts. They crawled through the muck, slow but steady, passing bodies—friends and foes alike. Thomas's mind raced.

Ahead, an explosion ripped the ground apart, sending shards of metal flying. Thomas ducked, feeling the sharp sting of artillery slice across his arm. He bit back a scream, knowing any sound could give away their position.

"Almost there," William muttered, his voice tight with strain. Thomas saw the remnants of a stone wall ahead, a potential refuge in the chaos. They made a final dash, feet slipping on the blood-slicked ground, and collapsed behind the wall, panting and gasping for air.

As they huddled together, the sounds of battle raged on, a relentless reminder of the danger surrounding them. Thomas clenched his fists, feeling the rough texture of the earth beneath his fingers. In this storm of violence and death, he realized that every moment was a precious gift, one that could be snatched away without warning. He thought of Marianne and the promise he made to return to her. That promise gave him the strength to keep fighting, to survive this hell and find his way back to her. He shifted his weight against the rough stone wall, ignoring the searing pain in his arm. William and James flanked him, their breaths coming in ragged gasps. The battle raged on, but the wall provided a brief respite, a fragile barrier against the unending storm.

"Ready?" Thomas mouthed to William. A curt nod

was all he received in return. They exchanged glances with James, whose eyes betrayed a mixture of fear and resolve.

"Go!" William signaled, and they sprang up together, darting from their cover into the chaos. Musket balls whizzed past, but they moved instinctively, weaving through the debris-strewn field. Thomas's heart pounded like a drum, each beat reminding him of his mortality.

Ahead, a soldier fell with a strangled cry, clutching his stomach. Without hesitation, James veered off course, dragging the wounded man towards another fragment of wall. "I've got you," he murmured, his voice calm amidst the clamor. Thomas felt a surge of pride and sorrow; bravery often came at such a high price.

"Keep movin'," William barked, urgency lacing his tone. They pressed on, navigating the deadly landscape.

To their left, a group of soldiers formed a human shield around a fallen comrade, musket balls ripping through flesh and fabric, but they held firm. Their sacrifice allowed others to advance, a powerful display of courage and selflessness. Thomas's throat tightened.

"Cover me," Thomas hissed. William nodded, firing his musket with precision, while James, now free from his earlier rescue, provided additional cover.

The earth shook as another round of artillery fire exploded nearby, sending dirt and debris raining down on them. They pressed themselves against the ground, hearts pounding. The acrid stench of gunpowder hung heavy in the air, mingling with the scent of blood and sweat.

"We have to keep going," Thomas yelled, his voice barely audible over the noise of battle. He pushed himself up, muscles protesting with every motion.

Each step forward was a struggle. Thomas's legs felt like lead, his body battered and bruised. Fear gnawed at the edges of his mind, whispering doom and despair. He glanced at William, whose face was set in grim determination, and at James, who wore an expression of steely resolve. They were mirrors of each other, reflections of shared suffering and unspoken fears.

A musket ball whizzed past Thomas's ear, so close he could feel its heat. Instinctively, he ducked, his breath catching in his throat. Time seemed to stretch and distort, moments blending in a haze of terror. He saw a fellow soldier fall, clutching a gaping wound in his side, and the sight sent a jolt of horror through him.

"James! Watch out!" William's shout cut through the chaos, and Thomas turned just in time to see an enemy soldier lunging toward James with a bayonet. James moved faster, deflecting the blow and striking back with lethal precision. The enemy crumpled to the ground, lifeless.

"Thanks," James panted, giving William a quick nod. There was no time for more discussion.

Everywhere Thomas looked, there was destruction and death. The ground was littered with bodies, and the cries of the wounded pierced the air like a mournful chorus. He saw men sacrificing themselves, throwing their bodies into the path of gunfire to save their comrades. Acts of heroism played out in brutal, fleeting moments, leaving behind only echoes of bravery and sacrifice.

"Stay close," Thomas urged, leading the way through a maze of shattered trees and crumbling fortifications.

"Artillery, to arms!" someone yelled, and Thomas barely had time to react as another explosion rocked the ground beneath them. He was thrown off his feet, landing hard on his back. Dazed, he struggled to regain his bearings, blinking away the dust and smoke clouding his vision.

"Thomas!" William's voice reached him through the haze, and he felt a hand grasp his arm, pulling him up. He met William's gaze, seeing the same exhaustion and desperation in his friend's features.

"Thanks, brother," Thomas said, his voice hoarse. He glanced at James, noting how his hands trembled despite the firm grip on his musket. A sense of unease settled in the pit of his stomach. James had always been the most resilient among them, keeping their spirits determined even in the darkest times. But today, there was fear in his eyes, a vulnerability that made Thomas's heart clench.

Suddenly, a roar filled the air as an enemy cannonball struck a supply wagon nearby, sending shards of wood and twisted metal flying. Thomas hit the ground hard, the impact knocking the wind out of him. Dazed, he struggled to his feet, blinking away the dust.

"James? Will?" he called out, panic rising in his chest.

"Here!" William's voice came from behind a smoldering wagon. Thomas staggered toward it, relief flooding through him when he saw both of his friends crouched behind the meager cover.

"That was too close," James muttered, wiping sweat from his brow. His face was pale, his expression haunted. Thomas reached out, gripping his shoulder in silent reassurance.

They pushed onward, the battle raging around them. Time lost meaning as they fought, and the world was reduced to a nightmarish blur of violence and survival.

Thomas's muscles screamed in protest, but he ignored the pain, driven by sheer willpower.

"Up ahead!" William pointed to a strategic position on a small hill. "If we can take that, we'll have the advantage."

"Let's go!" Thomas led the charge, determination fueling his steps. They climbed the incline, ducking under fire and weaving through the chaos.

Just as they neared the crest, a sudden, chilling silence fell over the battlefield. Thomas froze, his instincts screaming danger. He turned to see James standing a few paces behind, his eyes wide with shock.

"James, get down!" Thomas shouted, but it was too late.

A single shot rang out, impossibly loud in the eerie quiet. James staggered, clutching his chest. His musket slipped from his grasp, falling to the ground with a dull thud.

"NO!" Thomas's scream tore through the air as he lunged forward, catching James before he could collapse entirely. William was beside them in an instant, his face contorted in anguish.

"Hold fast, James," Thomas pleaded, his voice choked with emotion. He pressed his hands over the wound, desperate to stem the flow of blood. But James's eyes were already glazing over, the light fading.

"Thomas—." James's voice was a faint whisper, barely audible above the chaos. "I regret—."

"Don't speak of regrets, James," Thomas said fiercely, tears streaming down his face. "You must hold on. You will see this through."

But even as he spoke, he knew it was a lie. Life was

slipping from James's body, leaving only a hollow shell in its wake. With a final, shuddering breath, James went still.

"James!" William's cry was a raw, guttural sound, echoing the agony in Thomas's heart. They knelt there, cradling their fallen friend and brother, as the battle raged on around them, the world reduced to a maelstrom of grief and loss.

In that moment, time stood still. The war, the fighting, and the chaos all faded into the background. All that remained was the profound, unbearable truth: James was gone, and nothing would ever be the same again.

Thomas dropped as a musket ball whizzed past his head, inches from ending him. His heart pounded in his chest, and for a moment, he lay there, frozen by fear. But the thought of Marianne pushed him forward. With gritted teeth, he lurched to his feet and kept moving. As he stumbled on, Thomas saw a fallen comrade clutching his belly, blood seeping into the already-soaked earth. The man's eyes met his, full of a desperate plea. Thomas knew he couldn't help. He'd been taught to trust no one but himself, and stopping meant certain death. Torn between compassion and survival, he hardened his heart and moved past the dying man.

As the smoke began to clear, the enemy retreated, leaving their dead and wounded behind. Thomas dropped to his knees, the weight of what he had just experienced pressing down on him. The cost of freedom had never seemed so high, so terribly dear. Surrounded by the carnage of war, he hunched over and retched, the reality of his new life as a soldier hitting him like the grapeshot that had torn through the man beside him.

"They say there's freedom in our muskets, but this ain't nothin' other than butchery," a grizzled voice growled behind him, snapping him out of his daze. The speaker spat tobacco juice onto the ground, not even glancing at the lifeless bodies around them.

Thomas wiped the bile from his mouth, bracing himself for what was to come.

Chapter Thirty-Two

Smoke from the campfire curled into the night sky, its wispy tendrils disappearing among the twinkling stars. Thomas sat on a log near the flames, the firelight dancing across his face. He hunched over his ration of hard tack, picking at it listlessly. Beside him, William, his only friend in this war, prodded the fire's dying embers. The year of fighting took its toll on them. Beneath the grime caking their faces, Thomas and William looked gaunt, their eyes hollow and filled with a weariness far surpassing their years. Chewing the dry biscuit took all the strength they could muster.

"Another day in this godforsaken war," Thomas muttered, his breath fogging in the frigid air.

William sighed, the sound hollow and defeated. "I'm not sure how much more of this I can take. The fightin', the hunger, the death. . .it haunts me. Do you ever dream of home, Tom?"

Thomas nodded slowly, staring into the fire. "Every night. Keeps me going."

"Me too," William said softly, poking at the embers again. "I just hope we make it out of here to see it again."

Thomas glanced up, his eyes reflecting the flickering firelight. "I dream of being back at the Quaker settlement. The work was hard, but it was peaceful. Hell, even being back at the Patowemeck village would be better than seeing friends blown apart." He swallowed the hard tack with difficulty, the memories tasting sweeter than the meager rations.

William closed his eyes, a faint smile tugging at his lips. "I'd rather be workin' at the settlement than sittin' here."

Thomas nodded, his expression hardening. "I miss James. This stupid war took his life, and none of it seems fair. Why do we have to die for our freedom? What kind of world is this?"

Both young men fell silent, lost in their memories of a time before the war.

"Remember when we didn't have to think about muskets and cannon fire?" Thomas said quietly. "Before the endless marches and the cries of the dying?"

William nodded, his eyes distant. "Yeah, I remember. The screams of the wounded and dying—I can still hear 'em."

Thomas sighed. "And the friends we've lost. . .the sacrifices we've made for freedom. It all feels so heavy."

William looked at Thomas, new lines of worry etched on his face. "Bein' in this war has changed me, made me appreciate life more."

Thomas nodded. "We've been through a lot."

"Do you ever wonder if it's worth it?" William asked suddenly, voicing the doubts that sometimes crept into Thomas's mind late at night. "All the hunger, the cold, watching friends die. Sometimes, I wonder if we should have stayed on the plantation. Goin' to war to fight for a word they call liberty, a word I've never had my whole life." His voice trailed off.

Thomas tossed a stick into the flames, watching the sparks swirl upward. "We're fighting for something bigger than ourselves," he said. But even as he spoke, he felt a nagging doubt. Was it worth it? Would they ever be free?

William sighed, leaning back against a tree trunk. "You're right. We have to keep believin' that freedom is waitin' for us on the other side of this war. That all of this hasn't been for nothin'."

Thomas nodded, though he was losing faith. How much longer could they endure this endless fight? William rose slowly, his joints creaking. Across the camp, a commotion was brewing near the fire. Raised voices drifted through the crisp morning air as soldiers argued. Tempers were brewing in the camp. Soldiers were hungry, and many were suffering from dysentery.

"Tom, look at them bastards," William muttered, nodding toward the group of soldiers huddled together in heated conversation. "They're arguin' about rations again. Can't they see we're all in the same boat? We're all foragin' for food, tryin' to find food wherever we can. I heard some of the soldiers talkin' about desertin'. They're hungry and tired. It doesn't help that we haven't been paid our dues as promised."

The argument grew louder. The soldiers' voices were laced with anger and frustration. The hardships of war had taken their toll on everyone.

"Looks like we're not just fighting the enemy," Thomas said, his eyes narrowing.

"Those fools will tear this camp apart if they don't let go of their damn bickerin'," William grumbled, his hands clenched tightly into fists.

Thomas frowned, worry gnawing at his empty stomach. Hunger and short supplies had been fraying tempers in the camp. This wasn't the first clash over food. As the argument heated up, Thomas felt compelled to intervene.

William grabbed his arm. "Let 'em sort it out."

Thomas pulled away. "We can't waste energy fighting each other when we have a bigger battle. Someone could get hurt. I need to calm this down before it gets out of hand." He strode toward the angry mob, heart pounding. He understood their rage and fear, but letting it tear them apart would only lead to ruin.

As Thomas drew nearer, the air crackled with tension, the harsh exchange of words slicing through the atmosphere like a knife. "You overstepped, you thieving bastard!" one soldier snarled, his voice thick with fury, veins bulging in his neck as his face contorted with rage. The threat of violence hung in the air, heavy and palpable, as fists clenched and eyes narrowed in barely restrained anger.

"I took what was due to me, as any man would," another retorted, fists clenched. "Shall we settle this in the way of gentlemen?"

The first soldier lunged forward. Thomas quickly

stepped between them, raising his hands. "Enough!" he shouted, his voice cutting through the chaos. "This isn't helping anyone. We're all hungry, but fighting each other won't solve our problems."

"Hold your tongue, Thomas," the first soldier spat. "This ain't your business!"

Thomas's temper flared. "It is my damn business! We're all suffering here, but we need to stand together, not tear each other apart. The real enemy is out there, not among us."

The second soldier glared at Thomas, but then his shoulders sagged. "He's right," he said reluctantly. "We're at each other's throats when we should be stickin' together."

The first soldier looked around at the faces of his comrades, their expressions weary and hollow. He let out a frustrated sigh and stepped back. "Fine. But we can't keep goin' like this."

Thomas nodded. "I know. We'll talk to the quartermaster in the morning and see if we can get more supplies. But for now, let's try to get some sleep."

The soldiers dispersed, muttering under their breaths. Thomas turned back to William, who had watched the entire scene unfold.

"I ain't sure I would've handled that as well as you did," William said.

Thomas's thoughts were interrupted by boots crunching on the ground. He looked up to see an officer striding past, his face etched with exhaustion and disbelief. The men exchanged glances, and a low, ominous murmur began to spread through the camp.

"What do ya think it means?" William's voice trembled, showing fear for the first time in months.

Thomas straightened his shoulders, trying to look confident. "We'll find out soon enough. For now, get some rest. Dawn's going to come early, and we've got another day of this cursed war to endure."

They settled on the ground, their thin blankets barely helping against the evening chill. The fire crackled and popped, the only sound in the night. The weight of the war-torn world pressed down on their shoulders, threatening to crush their very souls. But they would endure, these boys turned men, because they had no choice. The dawn would bring another day and, with it, another chance to fight for the broken pieces of their shattered lives.

As Thomas closed his eyes, he thought of the settlement, its simple comforts, and the promise of peace. In his mind's eye, he saw the faces of those he had left behind, their gentle smiles, and the rustling of their plain clothes as they moved about their chores. He thought of Marianne and her flaming red hair and green eyes. He remembered his parents and his father's words: "You'll make a huge impact on the world one day." It was a vision of hope, a light in the darkness, and he clung to it with a desperation born of survival.

The night dragged on, with the men's sleep broken by the cries of the injured carried on the breeze. Dawn came with a sudden urgency as the camp woke to the sound of trumpets. The familiar call to arms cut through the crisp morning air, rousing the men from their restless slumber.

"What now?" Thomas muttered, still bleary-eyed as he struggled to sit up.

Already awake and dressed, William handed him a piece of hard tack, their meager ration for the day. "Looks like we've got a job to do, mate."

Scanning the camp, Thomas spotted an officer with a roll of parchment barking orders to the men.

"Alright, lads, hark at me!" the officer hollered, his voice booming across the clearing. "We've got a problem. The supply convoy's delayed, and we must build a bridge across this blasted river by nightfall!"

The men, weary from the night's skirmish, groaned in unison.

"I know, I know," the officer shouted over the noise, "but we're low on rations, and the recruits won't march on empty bellies. We have no other choice."

Resigned, the men gathered their tools and formed a ragged line, Thomas and William among them.

The river, swollen from the recent rains, churned angrily, its currents treacherous and unforgiving. Ahead of them, felled trees lay waiting, their glistening trunks a testament to the hard work ahead.

"Looks like we're in for a real treat," William grumbled, hefting his ax.

Side by side, the two friends got to work, chopping trees, trimming branches, and carving out the joists for the bridge. As the day wore on, blisters formed on blisters, and the river's taunting flow dared them to stop. But Thomas gritted his teeth and pressed on, pushing his weary body with sheer willpower. Finally, the last nail was driven into place as the sun dipped below the treetops. The men stepped back, hands on hips, gasping for air as they surveyed their handiwork.

"Not pretty, but it will do," the commanding officer muttered with grudging respect. "Tomorrow, we will start on the planks. Get some rest, boys. You have earned it."

The rhythmic sound of hoofbeats approached. Thomas looked up and saw a tall figure on horseback approaching the camp. It was General George Washington. His uniform was crisp despite the long ride, and his posture was ramrod-straight in the saddle. Awe washed over Thomas as he watched the respected figure make his way through the soldiers, who parted like the waters of the river they sought to bridge.

"Attention!" shouted the superior officer who had assigned them their task.

The soldiers snapped to attention, eyes on General Washington as he dismounted and walked to the center of the camp. His piercing gaze swept over the men, and Thomas felt pride at serving under such a respected leader.

With a discerning eye, Washington surveyed the unfinished bridge, his gaze then settling on the assembled men. "Stand at ease, gentlemen," he commanded with a firm, authoritative tone. "I am here to appraise the progress of your labors on this construction."

"The men have completed the foundation, Your Excellency," the superior officer said respectfully. "They have yet to lay the planks."

General Washington nodded approvingly. "Your diligence is commendable, gentlemen. The strategic importance of this bridge cannot be overstated, for it serves as a vital artery to our supply lines. The success of our cause may very well hinge upon the steadfastness of your efforts here."

At this, the soldiers shuffled their feet, the weight of responsibility settling over them.

"Gentlemen," General Washington continued, his voice deep and resonant, "I address you today not merely as your commander but as a comrade in arms, united with you in our noble struggle for liberty."

Thomas listened intently, feeling the weight of each word as it echoed through the camp and settled in his heart.

"Each of you has endured hardships most severe and sacrifices profound," General Washington continued, his tone solemn, "yet, I entreat you once more to summon even greater fortitude and resolution from within, that we might persist and prevail in this most sacred cause." He paused, allowing the gravity of his words to sink in before continuing. "This bridge you labor upon transcends mere timber and iron. It is a testament to our resolve, collective spirit, and unwavering conviction in a brighter destiny. Each nail driven and plank laid embodies our steadfast desire to triumph."

Thomas felt a shiver run down his spine as General Washington's words stirred something deep within him. He glanced at William, who stood rigid beside him, his eyes shining with newfound determination. Washington's presence was like a lightning bolt, igniting a spark of hope and resolve in the weary men. His uniform gleamed in the fading light, and his voice carried the weight of experience and authority. Thomas straightened his back to impress the general. He wondered if he remembered him from the dinner party at Lord Blackwood's plantation.

"Bear in mind, gentlemen, your struggle is not solely for your liberty but for that of posterity," General Washington declared, his voice resonant with fervor. "Reflect upon those who have already laid down their lives in this conflict. Let the recollection of their sacrifice impress upon you the cost of our freedom, and may your endeavors this day honor their memory."

A renewed sense of purpose coursed through Thomas's veins as Washington finished his address. Their hardships seemed to fade away in the face of the general's rousing speech, replaced by a fierce resolve to continue the fight for freedom.

"Thank you, Your Excellency!" one of the soldiers called, his voice breaking the silence over the camp.

General Washington raised a hand in salute. "Godspeed, gentlemen!" he replied, his voice strong and clear. Then he turned and strode back to his horse, the respect and admiration of the soldiers following him. Thomas watched him go, feeling a fire that hadn't been there before.

Chapter Thirty-Three

In early October 1777, General George Washington and the Continental Army received orders to move their encampment closer to Germantown, Pennsylvania, in preparation for a surprise assault against the British forces stationed there. The crisp autumn air was heavy with anticipation, and the sharp scent of falling leaves mixed with the damp earth signaled the change of seasons in Pennsylvania. As the troops marched under a sky mottled with clouds that promised colder days ahead, a sense of urgency propelled them forward.

The plan to attack at dawn took shape just days after their arrival. As the first light of day crept over the horizon, the Colonial forces began their coordinated assault on the unsuspecting British troops. The morning was cool and misty, with a light fog that hung low over the fields, shrouding movements and muffling the sounds of soldiers preparing for battle. The damp earth underfoot and the chill in the air made the soldiers' breath visible as puffs of white, blending into the morning mist. As they moved forward, the silence was palpable, punctuated only by the occasional clink of gear and the soft thud of boots on the soft ground.

Suddenly, the relative quiet of the dawn was shattered by the first shots of the engagement. A musket ball whizzed past Thomas's ear as he ducked behind a cannon, instinctively seeking cover. His heart hammered against his ribs as explosions rocked the ground, sending tremors through the field. The air quickly filled with the acrid smell of gunpowder and smoke, reducing visibility and adding to the chaos of the morning's battle. Across the battlefield, through the haze of smoke, he saw his friend William locked in deadly combat with a redcoat. The intensity of the fight was magnified by the smoke and mist, making each movement seem surreal and disjointed.

The air reeked of sulfur and blood. Men screamed in agony around him as lead tore through flesh and bone. Thomas steeled himself and leaped back into the fray, dodging a bayonet thrust from a wild-eyed enemy. Cannons roared, spewing flames. Muskets barked endlessly, their smoke clouding the air and blocking out the sun, casting the battlefield in a hellish hue. The stench of gunpowder hung heavy, mingling with death and destruction.

The ground shook with the thunderous footfalls of clashing infantry as red-coated lines met the enemy. Bayonets flashed. Men screamed in agony and defiance. Thomas's heart raced like a wild stallion, numbing him to the chaos around him. His world had shrunk to the clash of steel and the desperate cries of dying men.

Through the smoke and mayhem, he saw his comrades, their faces etched with fear. Men like himself were thrust into the inferno of war, their dreams and innocence shattered. His gaze locked with William's briefly, and they shared an unspoken understanding. They were the thin line between a life of servitude and a slim chance at a better tomorrow as free men.

Suddenly, a gap appeared in the enemy ranks, and the order to charge was given. With a roar of desperation, the ragged line of soldiers surged forward, bayonets leveled, as one unstoppable force. Thomas was swept along with the tide. Lead whizzed around him, and the cries of the fallen added to the chaos. He felt a hot sting across his cheek as a passing musket ball grazed his skin, but he ignored it. His entire focus was on the enemy before him, a faceless blur of red and bayonets.

As the two lines collided, the air was filled with the shrieks of tearing metal and the sickening sound of flesh giving way. Thomas's world became a blur of brute force and instinct. The dance of death had turned primal. The earth beneath his boots was crimson with the blood of the fallen.

In the chaos of battling at the British fortification of Cliveden, also known as Chew House, Thomas saw William struggling with a burly redcoat. Amid the sturdy walls and defensible positions of the fortification, the combat was intense and personal. Their bayonets were entangled as they grappled like enraged beasts, each desperately seeking the advantage amidst their comrades' relentless gunfire and shouts. With a last Herculean effort, leveraging the tight space around them that left little room for maneuvering, William freed his weapon, impaling his opponent through the heart. But it was a Pyrrhic victory. A second, unseen assailant nearly came close to plunging his blade into William's arm. Thomas reacted instinctively, lunging forward and tackling the attacker to the ground. The redcoat's knife sliced across Thomas's arm, a hot line of pain, but he managed to wrest the weapon away. Gasping for breath, Thomas looked at William, who gave a nod of thanks before they both turned back to the raging battle around them.

Thomas's world narrowed to a pinpoint of searing rage. Fury roared through his veins, giving him strength he never knew he had. With a guttural roar, he wielded his musket like a club, laying waste to the redcoats in his path. He was a wrathful specter, avenging the loss of James and many others. Once a maelstrom of violence, the battlefield fell into an uneasy silence. Thomas stood panting, his chest heaving. Around him, the cries of his fellow soldiers rose. He felt William's hand clasp around his shoulder, grounding him.

Just then, General Washington gave the order. The situation had become untenable, and with a heavy heart, Washington commanded a retreat. This decision was driven by the overwhelming strength of the British fortifications at Cliveden, which had proven impervious to the American assaults. As the retreat was sounded, Thomas and William quickly disengaged from the immediate fray, pulling back with their fellow soldiers in a disciplined withdrawal, leaving the stronghold behind but preserving their forces for future battles.

"We made it, mate," William murmured, his voice thick with emotion.

Thomas nodded, unable to speak. The weight of the moment settled on him. Beside him, William leaned against a splintered cannon wheel, trembling from exhaustion. They exchanged a glance, silently acknowledging the bond forged in combat. Thomas looked around, his heart heavy. Faces he had come to know, men who had shared bread and stories, now lay still or writhed in pain.

"Good fightin' out there," William said.

Thomas nodded, wincing as he inspected a bloody gash on his arm. "We did, but at what cost? We've lost a lot of good men."

He thought of the friends and comrades who had bled and died beside him over the harsh years of war. He thought of James, of Elijah, and about their loss—a lump formed in his throat.

William bowed his head. "Their sacrifice won us this victory."

Their conversation was interrupted by the sound of footsteps crunching through the snow. Their commanding officer approached, his breath visible in the cool air. "We're to retreat to camp to prepare ourselves for a march onward. We're to head toward Perkiomen Creek at first light. It's going to be a long march. Get your rest."

Thomas looked at William, concern etching his features. "That's miles away. Our shoes are barely holding together," he muttered, glancing back at the officer.

William nodded grimly, tightening his grip on his musket. "It won't be easy, but it's what we signed up for. Just wish it was over already. If we don't go, they'll hunt us down for desertin', and you remember how they lashed them blokes at Brandywine for tryin' to leg it,' he replied.

Thomas sighed, his breath forming a cloud in the frosty air. "Yes, I know. It's hard to keep marching away from one fight only to head into another. When does it end?"

"The end will come when we've got our freedom," William replied. "Every step gets us closer. Valley Forge ain't goin' to be easy, but our enlistment's almost up, Tom. We just got to hang on till then."

With that, the two soldiers spent the remaining hours of darkness checking their equipment and mentally preparing for the journey ahead. The thought of joining their compatriots at Valley Forge bolstered their spirits, providing a glimmer of hope amidst the harsh realities of war.

Chapter Thirty-Four

Washington's forces retreated initially to Perkiomen Creek in Pennsylvania, about twenty miles northwest of Philadelphia, following their defeat at Germantown. The area provided a secluded spot for the troops to regroup and recover from the battle's toll. They remained there briefly, taking the time to reassess their strategies and tend to the wounded.

By mid-October, the Continental Army's need for a more defensible position was evident. It moved strategically near Whitemarsh, about thirteen miles northeast of Philadelphia and not far from Germantown. This new position offered significant advantages for defense and enabled General Washington to keep a watchful eye on British movements in Philadelphia. The elevated terrain at Whitemarsh provided a panoramic view of the surrounding area, making it an ideal spot to monitor enemy activities and prepare for potential engagements.

After spending a few weeks at Whitemarsh, where the

troops continued to train and strengthen their fortifications, a new set of orders arrived. The Continental Army was instructed to prepare for another move; they would march to Valley Forge this time. The news came as winter began to set its grip on the region, promising even harsher conditions for the weary soldiers.

The orders specified that the march would commence the following day, giving the men little time to prepare for the journey ahead. As night fell, the camp was abuzz with activity; soldiers packed up their limited possessions, checked their equipment, and tried to gather as much warmth as possible from the dwindling fires. The atmosphere was tense. Valley Forge was renowned for its strategic position and harsh and unforgiving landscape. Each soldier understood the importance of this next phase, aware that the winter at Valley Forge would likely test them to their limits.

Wrapping a worn blanket tighter around his shoulders, Thomas turned to William, who was methodically checking the flint in his musket. "It's going to be a hard march tomorrow and even harder when we get there," he said, his breath visible in the cold air.

William nodded, securing his musket and picking up another blanket. "True, but we've faced hard marches and cold nights before," he replied, offering a wry smile." At least this time, we know exactly what we're walking into."

Thomas chuckled softly, the sound muffled by the wind. "Do you think the forge will live up to its name?"

"With General Washington leading us? It has to," William responded.

Their conversation was momentarily interrupted as

their commanding officer walked by, nodding at the preparations. "Rest up while you can, men. Tomorrow, we march towards our destination," he declared, his voice carrying over the murmurs of the camp.

The following day, the camp buzzed with activity as soldiers packed their belongings for the march. Thomas and William helped their comrades, ensuring everyone had what they needed. As they set off, the wind was relentless, biting their faces and hands. But there was a sense of determination in the air, a feeling that this march could be the turning point they'd been waiting for.

Days turned into weeks as they trudged through snow and ice, their progress slow but steady. The journey to Valley Forge was grueling, but Thomas kept thinking of Marianne and the future they'd build together. Each step brought him closer to home, to freedom. As they marched, the harsh winter winds cut through their already-worn garments, chilling them to the bone. Despite the biting cold, there was a fire within them that not even the frigid temperatures could extinguish. One night, as they made camp in a sheltered valley surrounded by towering pines, Thomas and William sat by the fire. Their bodies were weary, but their spirits were high. The flickering flames cast a warm glow, providing a brief respite from the relentless cold.

"We're getting closer," William said, his voice filled with hope as he poked at the fire with a stick. "I can feel it."

Thomas nodded, a smile spreading across his face. "We'll make it. We have to," he responded, his eyes reflecting the fire's glow.

Their conversation was suddenly interrupted by a

commotion on the other side of the camp. Shouts and cries filled the air as soldiers rushed to see what was happening. Thomas and William hurried over, their hearts pounding in their chests. They arrived to find a group of soldiers surrounding a man lying on the ground, blood seeping through his uniform. The quiet of the night was shattered by the urgency of the moment.

"What happened?" Thomas asked, pushing his way through the crowd.

"He was attacked by a scout," one of the soldiers replied, his voice tense. "Came out of nowhere."

Thomas knelt beside the injured man, his hands shaking as he tried to stop the bleeding. "Stay with us," he urged, his voice filled with urgency. "We'll get you to the surgeon."

But it was too late. The man's eyes fluttered closed, his breath escaping in a final, shuddering sigh. Thomas felt a wave of despair wash over him. They had lost so many, and the war seemed to stretch on endlessly. But as he looked around at the faces of his comrades, he knew they couldn't give up. They had to keep fighting for those who had fallen, for those who still believed in the cause.

"He deserves a proper buryin'," William said, placing a hand on Thomas's shoulder.

Thomas nodded, his resolve hardening. "We'll honor him," he said quietly. "And we'll keep fighting. We owe it to him and the others who've fought and died."

After several grueling days on the march, the Continental Army finally arrived at Valley Forge. The landscape that greeted Thomas, William, and their fellow soldiers was bleak and barren, stripped of its autumn colors by the biting winter chill. It was snowing heavily, with stinging sleet that scraped their faces. As they trudged into the encampment area, their boots crunched on the frost-hardened ground, a stark reminder of the harsh conditions they would face.

Setting up camp began immediately, with officers directing soldiers to designated areas where they would construct their winter quarters. The air was filled with the sounds of axes and saws as men cut down trees and fashioned them into rough logs. Others gathered stones and mud to chink the gaps, striving to make the makeshift huts as insulated as possible.

Thomas and William worked side by side, their breaths visible in the freezing air as they heaved logs into place. "We need to make these shelters strong," Thomas grunted as he positioned a heavy beam. "General Washington says they need to last us through the winter."

William nodded, wiping sweat and frost from his brow. "And keep the wind out. I ain't keen on freezin' in my sleep," he replied, half-joking but with a serious undertone.

Despite their exhaustion, the men had a determined energy; each knew the importance of quickly establishing a secure camp. As the structures slowly took shape, the camp began to resemble a rudimentary village, albeit one born of necessity rather than design. The huts were arranged in orderly rows, with officers' quarters positioned centrally to maintain discipline and oversight.

By the time they had finished setting up the basic structures, darkness had enveloped the camp. Thomas and William, both exhausted, joined their comrades around a newly kindled fire. The flames crackled weakly, its small flames casting a flickering light on Thomas's and William's faces. Huddled close to the meager warmth, they sat on rough-hewn logs, their shoulders hunched against the biting wind. Thomas rubbed his hands together, feeling the rough calluses scrape, trying to coax some warmth into his fingers. He looked up at the sky, where stars glittered icily, indifferent to the suffering below. The winter night seemed endless, each second stretching out like a string pulled taut. The air was frigid, sharp as glass, cutting through their threadbare coats. Their breath rose in wisps, quickly disappearing into the cold night. The camp lay in silence, broken only by the occasional murmur or cough from other soldiers.

"Cold enough to freeze a man's soul," William muttered, his voice barely audible above the wind's mournful howl. He pulled his blanket tighter around his thin frame, his face pale and etched with fatigue.

"Feels colder every night," Thomas muttered through chattering teeth. The icy wind cut through his thin uniform like a knife. He longed for the heavy woolen coat he left behind at the Quaker settlement. Even that wouldn't keep out the chill that had seeped into his bones after the long, brutal campaigns they had endured the past few months.

Beside him, William shuddered, pulling his blanket tighter around his shoulders. "If this cold keeps up, we'll freeze to death before the redcoats even get a chance to shoot us," he said nervously, trying to lighten the mood.

Thomas nodded, a faint smile touching his wind-chapped lips. As he gazed into the glowing embers, his thoughts drifted to Marianne. He imagined her waiting for him back at the settlement, her gentle face and loving embrace beckoning him home. The vision of her kindled a spark of warmth in his chest, fueling his spirit through the darkest nights. No matter how long this war dragged on, he vowed to survive—for Marianne, for the chance to build a new life together. He gritted his teeth against a fresh gust of icy wind and edged closer to the fire. Just a little longer, he thought. Freedom is waiting.

Thomas rummaged through his pack, taking inventory of the few supplies he had left. A half-eaten loaf of hard bread, a small wedge of moldy cheese, and a few shriveled apples. It would have to last at least a week.

Beside him, William picked at his food, trying to make each bite count. "I wonder sometimes if it was all worth it."

Thomas looked at his friend, seeing the doubt and exhaustion in his eyes. He felt that same uncertainty gnawing at him during the long, cold nights. But then he remembered Marianne's words as he marched off to war. "Fight bravely. Build us a better world. Come back to me."

"It will be," Thomas replied. "We'll get back home. Start new lives. It'll all be worth it in the end."

William managed a small smile. "I hope you're right."

Thomas gazed into the flickering flames. "I miss her," he said softly. William didn't need to ask who 'her' was.

"I know you do," William replied. "But you'll see her again, mate."

Thomas nodded, clinging to that hope. "I keep imagining the life we'll build together—a little cottage on the edge of the settlement. I'll use my skills as a cooper. She'll tend to her garden and heal the sick. We'll raise a family." His voice trailed off wistfully. The cold night air suddenly seemed warmer as he imagined Marianne's arms around him, her lips against his.

William smiled. "She's lucky to have you. I know you'll build a good life together."

Thomas felt a swell of gratitude for his friend. "And you, William? Any plans after this?"

William chuckled. "Find a pretty wife, I reckon. Settle down, maybe get me an apprenticeship, like we always talked about. Maybe our kids'll play together one day," William said with a hopeful grin.

Thomas grinned at the thought. He stared into the dying embers, the fire's warmth barely cutting through the icy chill that had settled into his bones. He pulled his blanket tighter, though it provided little comfort against the bitter cold. "I don't know how much more of this I can take," he said, sighing. "My feet are numb, my hands shake so badly. I can barely hold my musket."

He poked at the dwindling fire with a stick, watching as embers flared briefly before dimming again. Sparks danced into the night sky, swallowed by the darkness. He pulled his coat tighter around him, trying to fend off the biting cold that gnawed at his bones.

"Think there's any chance we might get some fresh rations soon?" William asked, rubbing his hands together over the dying flames.

"Unlikely," Thomas replied. "Colonel Woodworth said it's been difficult to get what we need because of the snow and ice. We'll have to make do."

Soon, the call would come to form ranks. Thomas stood, his limbs stiff from the cold night air. But his eyes blazed with renewed determination as he shouldered his musket.

As the soldiers assembled, a figure rode through the rows of huts, drawing curious glances. It was Baron von Steuben, a Prussian officer recently appointed to train the Continental Army. His arrival at Valley Forge had been a significant boon; his reputation as a seasoned military tactician promised much-needed discipline and expertise.

Baron von Steuben dismounted briskly and walked along the ranks, his keen eyes assessing the troops. "Gentlemen," he began, his voice carrying across the assembled men, "we begin today. Your training will be rigorous, and your discipline must be unwavering. We have much to accomplish if we are to stand against the British effectively."

Thomas exchanged a look with William, both understanding the importance of this moment. The training they were about to receive from such an experienced soldier could change the tide of the war. Inspired and somewhat daunted, they watched as Steuben demonstrated the first drill, his commands crisp and his movements precise.

Under Steuben's watchful eye, the days became filled with intense training sessions. He introduced them to a series of drills and maneuvers that were entirely new to the Continental Army. From the proper handling of their muskets to complex marching formations, Steuben's methods were transformative. The camp, once a scene of disarray, soon throbbed with the energy of a disciplined military force.

The days passed in a blur of frigid marches, endless drills, and bone-chilling nights. Each step felt like a battle against the biting cold, each breath a struggle against the freezing air. Thomas, William, and their comrades trudged onward, their spirits lifted only by the thought of the freedom they fought for. One evening, as the sun set behind the snow-covered hills, Thomas and William sat by the fire again, trying to find comfort in its weak warmth.

"Remember when we first joined up?" William asked, a wistful smile on his face. "We thought it'd be over in a few months. We had no idea what we were in for."

Thomas chuckled, though there was little humor in it. "Seems like a lifetime ago. We were so eager, so full of hope."

"Do you think we'll ever feel that way again?" William's voice was soft, almost lost in the crackling of the fire.

Thomas stared into the flames, the flickering light reflecting in his eyes. "I don't know," he admitted. "We've put in our time. The long years of fighting and bloodshed—they're coming to an end for us."

"The quartermaster mentioned today our enlistment's up soon," William said.

Thomas nodded slowly, his gaze fixed on the fire. "Yeah, he did. Said we can re-enlist or head home. It's our choice now," he sighed, poking at the fire with a stick. "We've done our time in battle, but what now? Do we go back to what was, as if all this," he gestured broadly at the camp around them, "never happened?"

Looking over at William, he saw the flickering light reflecting in his friend's eyes. "I don't know," Thomas admitted. "What about you, Will? What's pulling you more—home or the fight?"

William sat back, a pensive look on his face. "I keep thinkin' about what we're fighting for, Tom. It's bigger than us. If we leave now, will I ever be able to shake the feelin' that I could have done more?"

Thomas nodded, understanding the internal conflict his friend faced. "And if we stay, we risk everything again. It's not just our lives on the line—it's missing the chance to rebuild what we left behind."

The conversation faded as both men lost themselves in thought, weighing the lives they could return to against the cause they had fought so hard for. The crackling of the fire filled the silence, a reminder of the time passing and the decision that awaited them.

As the night deepened, the resolve in Thomas's voice grew stronger when he finally spoke again. "Whatever we choose, we do it together, right? Either way, we're brothers, bound by more than just this war."

William smiled slightly, clapping Thomas on the shoulder. "That's right. Brothers in arms, in peace, or war. We'll make this decision as we've faced everything else—together."

Thomas turned to his friend, a faint smile touching his dirt-smudged face for the first time in ages. "Just think if we were back at the settlement. No more cold camps and marching for days on end."

"Sleep in a real bed, eat a hot meal," William added wistfully.

Thomas clapped him on the back. "You've dreamed of nothin' but food for months, mate!"

They shared a weary chuckle. It felt good to laugh after so long at war.

Looking upwards, Thomas took in the open sky, clear and blue now that the haze of battle, despite the freezing weather. "I want to farm again, but this time as a free man."

As dawn broke over Valley Forge, the cold morning air was crisp and invigorating, bringing with it a sense of clarity and resolve. Thomas and William woke early, emerging from their makeshift shelter to rekindle the campfire that had dwindled overnight. They huddled close to the flames, warming their hands as they prepared a modest breakfast of salted pork and hardtack softened with a bit of water. They ate in silence for a few moments, each lost in his thoughts about the decision they faced. The warmth of the fire and the first meal of the day brought a semblance of comfort, easing the weight of their conversation from the night before.

"They say the hardest decisions are the ones that set us free," William finally said, breaking the silence as he tossed a small twig into the flames.

Thomas nodded, glancing up at the clear, blue sky that stretched above them—a stark contrast to the grey and turmoil-filled days of battle they had grown accustomed to. "I want to farm again, but this time as a free man with Marianne by my side," he declared, the determination evident in his voice. "It's time to go home, Will. We lost Elijah and James. Time to start anew, with everything we've learned and all we've become."

William smiled, feeling relief washing over him as he met Thomas's gaze. "And me to my workshop. I've missed the wood's grain more than I realized. We've done our part here and fought the good fight. Let's carry that spirit back to rebuild our lives. The war ain't over, and it'll still be here if we get the desire for fightin' again."

With their decision made, they finished their meal and packed up their few belongings. As they walked towards the commanding officer's tent, the camp around them slowly came to life with the sounds of other soldiers beginning their day. Thomas and William felt a bittersweet mix of anticipation and nostalgia; they were leaving a brotherhood forged in adversity but stepping towards a future they had fought to secure.

Upon reaching the commanding officer, they stood firm. "Sir, we've come to inform you that we will not be re-enlisting," Thomas stated clearly, with William nodding in agreement. "We're grateful for the chance to have served, and now it's time we returned home."

The officer looked at them both, his expression somber yet tinged with understanding. "Your service has been honorable, and your decision respected. You'll leave with our blessing and our thanks. Godspeed, gentlemen," he replied.

With that, Thomas and William turned back towards the camp, their steps lighter than they had been in months. The reality of their newfound freedom slowly sank in. They were going home, not as the men who had left, but as soldiers returning from the forge of war, ready to build their lives anew in peace. It was a moment they had dreamed of and fought for, and now, it was finally here.

"We're free men now, Will," Thomas said quietly, the weight of the words settling in his heart.

"Yes, we are," William replied. "Let's make the most of it."

Chapter Thirty-Five

As dawn broke over Valley Forge, Thomas and William woke to a frigid morning, the cold biting through their blankets. The air was still, and the silence was a stark reminder of the life they were about to leave behind. Sitting up, rubbing their hands together for warmth, they decided to set their path in a new direction.

"We've received our pay for the enlistment," Thomas said, pulling a small leather pouch from his belongings. "It's not much, but it might just be enough to tide us over for a while."

William nodded, his breath visible in the cold air. "Virginia's too far to travel in this cold. What if we head to Philadelphia instead? We could wait out the winter there."

The idea resonated with Thomas. He had heard stories about Philadelphia, its bustling streets and growing commerce, and how it offered opportunities that the war-ravaged countryside could not. "I want to hurry up and return to Marianne, but you're right. The trip is too far and will be difficult in this weather. It's settled then," he replied, a hint of excitement in his voice. "We'll go to Philadelphia and see what the city has for two former soldiers. Might take us a few days to get there. We've got enough supplies to hold us over."

The journey to Philadelphia was arduous. The winter cold was relentless, and they often had to trudge through snow that blanketed the roads. Despite the harsh conditions, they pushed forward. Upon their arrival, Thomas and William were struck by the contrast between the wartime scarcities they had grown accustomed to and the relative abundance of the city. Philadelphia was a hive of activity, with stores brimming with goods and the streets alive with people from all walks of life. The cityscape was a mix of new constructions and old buildings.

Eager to start anew, they used some of their meager funds to secure a room in the Indian Queen Tavern on the bustling Market Street. The city, alive with the hum of commerce and conversation, starkly contrasted the silent, snow-covered fields they marched through during the war.

The following days were spent exploring the city, each man seeking apprenticeship opportunities in trades that could use their skills. With his knack for carpentry, Thomas sought work with local woodworkers, while William, drawn to the land, looked for work that could lead back to farming or similar pursuits.

It wasn't long before they secured work as an apprentice. Thomas in a busy carpentry shop, and William found work with a market gardener who supplied produce to the city. As they settled into their apprenticeships, Thomas and William became part of the vibrant community life in

Philadelphia. The city was a melting pot of ideas and cultures, with frequent tavern gatherings where men debated politics and the new nation's future. On Sundays, the streets were quieter, with families heading to various churches, the bells ringing across the cobblestones.

After a hard day's work, Thomas and William sometimes joined their fellow apprentices and workers at a local city tavern in the evenings. Over mugs of ale, they exchanged stories of their days, shared news, and discussed everything from the price of tobacco to the latest gossip about the Continental Congress.

One evening, as they sat near the fire in the crowded tavern, Thomas leaned over to Thomas, a grin spreading across his face. "You know, I never thought I'd find peace in the sound of a hammer or the smell of sawdust," he said, raising his mug.

William laughed, nodding in agreement. "And I didn't think dirt under my nails would feel so right after all that gunpowder," he replied. "Seems we're findin' our way, eh?"

"Aye, that we are," Thomas said, clinking his mug against William's.

As spring approached, the harsh chill of the Philadelphia winter began to recede, replaced by the new season's milder breezes and warming sun. The city, always bustling, seemed to awaken further with the warmer weather, its streets and markets more vibrant and lively. Trees along the avenues blossomed, adding color to the brick and cobblestone cityscape.

During this change, William became increasingly captivated by a young woman he encountered at the market where he bought wood supplies. Her name was

Eliza, a seamstress known for her quiet charm. What started as a casual acquaintance at the market soon flourished into a deliberate courtship, as they began meeting serendipitously at the market and intentionally at various social gatherings around town. Their strolls along the bustling streets of Philadelphia became a regular fixture, and it was noted that William walked with a newfound spring in his step.

As William's relationship with Eliza deepened, Thomas found himself reflecting on the life and love he had left behind. Watching William's budding romance, Thomas couldn't help but think of Marianne, whose memory still burned brightly in his heart. Although he had found camaraderie and purpose in Philadelphia, returning to Virginia to reunite with Marianne increasingly filled his mind. With each passing day, his longing for home and her intensified, stoked by the changing seasons that reminded him of the cycles of planting and harvest—the very essence of the farm life he once knew.

One evening, over dinner, after sharing a toast to new beginnings, Thomas turned to William with a more serious tone. "It's been good here, learning and growing," he began, "but I miss her, Will. I miss Marianne and the life I had planned to build. It's warmer now with spring's arrival, and travel should be easier."

William nodded, understanding his friend's heartache. "Then you should go back, Tom," he said. "Spring is a time for starting new. This city has given us plenty but can't replace where you truly belong."

Thomas gazed into the fire, pondering William's words. The notion of leaving was daunting, especially after finding a semblance of peace following the turmoil of the war. Yet, the prospect of seeing Marianne again and returning to the familiar rhythms of the settlement offered him a deep, comforting sense of solace.

"Maybe it's time," Thomas finally said. "Time to go home to Virginia and start the life I've dreamed of since I left."

William nodded, a mixture of happiness and sadness in his eyes. "And I'll be staying here in Philadelphia," he added, his voice steady but filled with emotion. "Eliza and I have plans here, and I think I've found a place to build somethin' lastin'."

The two friends sat in silence for a moment. Then, almost instinctively, they began to reminisce about their shared past, from their early days as street urchins, scrounging for food and dodging trouble, to the years spent toiling side by side as indentured servants on the Virginia plantation.

"Remember how we used to dream of a day like this?" William chuckled his tone light despite the heavy undertone. "Dream of bein' our own masters, of choosin' our own paths?"

Thomas smiled, the memories flooding back. "We've come a long way, haven't we? From those two scrawny kids stealing apples to soldiers fighting for freedom. We've seen a lot together."

"And we've survived," William added. "Survived through sheer stubbornness and because we always had each other's backs. It's goin' to be different, not havin' you just a shout away."

"I know," Thomas replied, the reality of their

impending separation settling in. "But we're not really leaving each other, are we? We'll keep part of these times with us, no matter where we are."

William nodded, clapping Thomas on the shoulder. "Always. And you and Marianne always have a place here, with me and Eliza. Don't you forget that."

"And you're always welcome in Virginia," Thomas said. "Who knows? Maybe our paths will cross again. Life has a funny way of bringing people back together."

Their conversation drifted late into the night, filled with laughter and quiet moments as they shared stories and reminisced about their adventures. When they finally parted, it was with a deep, unspoken understanding that their friendship, forged through hardship and solidified through loyalty, would endure the miles and changes ahead.

A few days had passed since Thomas and William had shared their heartfelt conversation by the fireside in Philadelphia. With his decision made, Thomas spent those days preparing for his journey back to Virginia. He gathered his belongings, carefully selecting what he would need for the long ride. Supplies were packed, including some dried food and essential tools, and he secured a sturdy horse from a local dealer, knowing the reliability of his mount would be crucial for the arduous journey.

On the morning of his departure, the air was crisp, a gentle reminder of the change in seasons and the new chapter beginning in his life. Thomas saddled up his horse, his movements tinged with excitement and melancholy. The city of Philadelphia, a sanctuary and a forge for his new self, now felt like a fond memory he was about to leave behind.

William accompanied him to the city's outskirts, both men walking in companionable silence. As they reached the edge of the town, Thomas turned to his friend, his emotions apparent. "You've been more than a brother to me," Thomas said, his voice steady but thick with emotion. "I won't forget what we've been through together, and I won't forget James and the others."

William clasped Thomas's hand, his own emotions mirroring his friend's. "And you'll always have a part of my story here with me," he replied, smiling. "Safe travels, Tom. Give Marianne my best when you see her."

With final clasps on the shoulder and nods of understanding, Thomas mounted his horse. He took one last look at William, memorizing the scene, then nudged his horse forward, beginning the long journey south to Virginia.

The ride was long and, at times, challenging. Early spring weather fluctuated between mild and wild as Thomas traversed the diverse landscapes of the Mid-Atlantic states. Yet, with each mile, his anticipation grew. Thoughts of Marianne and the life he hoped to build kept his spirits high and his focus clear.

After weeks of travel, Thomas finally arrived at the Hopewell Friends settlement where he and Marianne had once dreamed of their future together. The sight of the familiar landscape, with its rolling hills and the simple, sturdy homes of the Quakers, filled him with an overwhelming sense of homecoming. The settlement was alive with the signs of spring—fields being plowed, gardens being tended, and the distant sound of children playing.

He dismounted at the edge of the settlement, his heart pounding with anticipation. Walking his horse along the familiar paths, he spotted Marianne. She was in the garden, her hands buried deep in the soil, just as he had pictured countless times. She looked up in disbelief at the sound of his approach, her face lighting up with a broad, radiant smile. For a moment, time itself seemed to pause. Then, with a joyful shout, she dropped her tools and ran towards him.

Thomas opened his arms just in time to catch Marianne as she threw herself into his embrace. He held her close, his face buried in her hair, inhaling her familiar scent. A tear slid down his cheek, a release of all the pent-up fear and exhaustion from the years gone by. He was home—truly home—in the place and with the person where his heart had always lingered. The hardships of war and the burdens of distance dissolved as he stepped into Marianne's loving arms.

Chapter Thirty-Six

Thomas looked around him, his heart full. "I'm home," he whispered to Marianne, holding her close. "I must be a sight for sore eyes. The journey has been long and difficult, but I returned."

Marianne looked up at him, tears in her eyes. "You're as handsome as ever. I knew you'd come back to me," she said, her voice choked with emotion.

"I've missed this—missed you," Thomas said, brushing a stray tear from Marianne's cheek. "Tell me everything I've missed here."

Marianne laughed softly, a sound that Thomas realized he had longed to hear. "First, tell me about the others. How is William doing? And James?"

Thomas sighed, the joy of his return tempered by memories of them. "William has settled in Philadelphia," he explained. "He stayed behind to build a life there. He's found someone special, a woman named Eliza. They plan to marry next spring. He's made a home for himself there."

"And James?" Marianne asked gently, sensing there was more he hadn't shared.

The weight of the news he carried suddenly felt heavier, and Thomas took a moment before he could speak. "James didn't make it, Marianne. He died in one of the battles. He fought bravely and saved many lives. But it cost him his own." His voice broke slightly, the pain of loss still sharp.

Marianne reached out, squeezing his hand tightly. "I'm so sorry, Thomas. I know how close you were. Come. You must be starving and exhausted."

"I am. I could use some warm food and a good sleep," Thomas replied.

Marianne led Thomas to a large table under the main hall. It was full of food—freshly baked bread, roasted meat, hearty stews, and an array of fruits and vegetables. The sight and smell of the feast made his mouth water. He hadn't seen that much food in years. Reuben, the respected elder of the Quaker settlement, approached the table with a measured tread. His expression was polite but reserved, reflecting the community's well-known stance on nonviolence and their discomfort with the war that Thomas had been part of.

"Thomas, welcome back," Reuben said. "We are relieved to see you returned to us safely. How fared your journey?" His eyes briefly flicked to the musket Thomas had set aside at the door. He bowed his head and intoned a brief prayer, thanking God for Thomas's safe return.

"Thank you, Reuben. The journey was long and not without its trials," Thomas replied, acknowledging the elder's unspoken concerns. "But I am glad to be back, done with the war, and here again."

Reuben nodded, his eyes searching Thomas's face. "And the war? What is your heart's condition regarding what you have witnessed and done?"

Thomas took a deep breath, aware of the critical eyes upon him. "The war was difficult in many ways," he began slowly, carefully choosing his words. "It challenged many things I believed in. But it also affirmed my desire for peace, Reuben. I hope to find healing here, among friends and family."

Reuben's expression softened slightly at this. "Then you are welcome at our table, Thomas. Let the peace of this community be a balm to you, and may the Lord bless you with this bounty." He gestured towards the food. "Please, join us. Let us share in fellowship and begin the process of rebuilding."

Marianne squeezed Thomas's hand again, giving him an encouraging smile as they took their seats at the table. The food was as delicious as it looked, and Thomas felt the weariness of the road begin to lift with each bite.

After the meal, Reuben guided him toward his new living quarters, a modest cabin at the edge of the clearing. "You may rest here. There are fresh clothes for you to change into and a basin for you to bathe," he said, pushing open the door.

The cabin was unpretentious but sturdy, its wooden beams resilient against time. The inside was humble yet inviting. Thomas looked around, a sense of peace settling over him. "I'm grateful. Thank you, Reuben."

Thomas stepped inside the cabin, the scent of fresh

pine filling his senses. The interior held only the essentials: a rough-hewn table, a pair of simple beds, and a few shelves. He moved to the window, gazing out at the Hopewell Friends settlement. Outside, life carried on. A woman gathered herbs in the garden, her movements deliberate and gentle. A man repaired a broken wheel near the barn, the sound of his tools echoing softly. Children played with makeshift toys in the yard, their laughter a sweet counterpoint to the serene surroundings. This was a world far removed from the cruelty of the battlefield, a world grounded in the Quaker beliefs of peace and community.

The next evening, Reuben invited Thomas to a small gathering where the settlement discussed spiritual matters and community concerns. As they sat in a circle, the elder addressed Thomas directly. "You have seen much war, Thomas. How do your experiences align with the Light within?" Reuben's question was not accusatory but reflective, urging Thomas to explore his inner conflicts.

Thomas paused, the weight of the elder's question pressing upon him. "In truth, Reuben, the war challenged everything I believed in. Yet, it also showed me the preciousness of peace. I have witnessed too much suffering and too much loss. I wish only to live quietly, to forget the sounds of cannons and cries of the wounded. As you know, I joined the battle to secure my freedom from indenture. This settlement told me about that possibility." Thomas couldn't help but feel as if he was being accused.

After a few minutes, Reuben nodded, his face showing compassion and concern. He spoke of forgiveness, the Light in every person, and the profound belief in non-violence that guided their lives.

As the weeks rolled by, Thomas became increasingly caught between the peaceful life he yearned for and the unresolved threads of his past. The quiet days, filled with labor and the simple joys of community life, did much to soothe his spirit. Yet, the shadow of what had been left unfinished gnawed at him. Thoughts of Henrietta and the pouch Elijah had asked him to give his mother and the unresolved injustice meted out by Lord Blackwood haunted his quieter moments.

One morning, Thomas knew it was time to act. He could no longer ignore the need to confront the past and seek some measure of closure for himself and those who had suffered alongside him. He decided it was time to visit Blackwood Plantation to deliver news to Henrietta and confront Lord Blackwood.

After a simple breakfast, Thomas approached Marianne, who was tending the garden. "I need to go to Blackwood Plantation," he said, his voice steady despite his inner turmoil. "There are things left unsaid, actions left undone. Henrietta deserves to know Elijah's fate, and Lord Blackwood must be held accountable for his part in what happened."

Marianne looked up, her hands pausing in their work, soil clinging to her fingers. The lines of worry etched across her brow. "But why must you go? Haven't we had enough of violence and vengeance? What if something happens to you?"

Thomas felt a stir of frustration. "I can't let it rest, Marianne. I must confront him for James, Elijah, and everyone else he's hurt. What kind of man would I be if I turned away from seeking justice for those wronged?"

Their voices rose, the tension between them palpable. "And what about us, Thomas? What about the peace we have here? You speak of justice, but I'm afraid it's vengeance you want. What if you get yourself killed?" Marianne argued, her voice trembling.

Thomas took a deep breath, trying to temper his rising emotions. "I promise, I seek only closure, not vengeance. It's something I must do, not just for me but for all who can't."

Marianne looked away, her body tense. "Then go," she said quietly, "but remember what you're leaving behind."

Thomas felt a pang of guilt as he walked away from Marianne, her words echoing in his mind. Later that evening, as he made his way to his quarters, he couldn't shake the confusion that clouded his thoughts. The fight had unsettled him, but his determination to go to Blackwood Plantation remained unwavering. He needed to confront the ghosts of his past, even if it meant risking everything.

That night, Thomas lay in bed, his mind filled with thoughts of Marianne. Her concern for him, her fear, and her love were all tangled together, making sleep elusive. He stared at the ceiling, replaying their argument repeatedly, trying to find some peace in the chaos of his emotions.

The following day, Thomas awoke with a sense of resolve. He dressed in the dim light of dawn, the early morning chill seeping through his clothes. The air was crisp, biting at his skin as he moved about the small room. The faint light of the rising sun cast long shadows across the floor, the promise of a new day tinged with the weight of his decision.

After a quick breakfast, he began to prepare for his journey. The simple meal sat heavily in his stomach, a reminder of the task ahead. Despite their argument, Marianne helped him pack, her movements efficient but cold. The silence between them was thick with unspoken words, the tension palpable. As she handed him his belongings, the rustling of fabric and the clinking of metal were the only sounds that broke the stillness of the morning.

Thomas glanced at Marianne as she worked, her face a mask of concentration that barely concealed her worry. The smell of her lavender soap and fresh pine from the forest outside created a bittersweet aroma that clung to his senses. When it was time to leave, they embraced stiffly, the warmth of their earlier reunions replaced by a chill of uncertainty. Marianne's arms were tense around him, her breath warm against his neck, but her body rigid with fear and concern.

"Be safe," she whispered, her voice barely audible over the morning breeze.

"I will," Thomas replied, his voice equally soft. He pulled back slightly, looking into her eyes, trying to convey the depth of his feelings without words.

Marianne's eyes glistened with unshed tears. "Be careful, and don't be gone long. I'll await your return," she said, her voice trembling.

"I will. I promise," Thomas said, his heart heavy with knowing what he was risking. He squeezed her hand one last time before turning to leave, the weight of her gaze following him as he walked away.

The morning air was sharp and refreshing, filling his lungs with each breath. The sky was a pale blue, streaked with the first rays of sunlight, casting a golden hue over the landscape. The sounds of the forest waking up surrounded him: birds chirping, leaves rustling, and the distant murmur of a stream. Riding away from the settlement, Thomas felt a mixture of determination and doubt. He was committed to confronting Lord Blackwood to address the injustices of the past, but at what cost? The peaceful life he longed for with Marianne seemed suddenly fragile, balanced against the shadows of his old life he couldn't seem to escape.

Chapter Thirty-Seven

It took a few days to arrive at Blackwood Plantation. The familiar creak of the iron gates pierced Thomas's ears, a haunting melody that stirred long-buried memories. The hard days in the tobacco fields and the cooperage surged back, a bitter wave that left him momentarily breathless. He could almost feel the scorching sun on his back and the rough handle of the hoe in his hands. The white pillars of the plantation house loomed ahead. They seemed to leer down at him, their shadows long and dark, ghosts tormenting his weary soul. Each creak of the gates and whisper of the wind felt like the voices of the past, reminding him of the struggle he had endured to reach this moment.

His eyes scanned the grounds, searching desperately. By the old oak tree, he spotted a flash of calico. Henrietta. Thomas's heart hammered as he hurried over. Henrietta turned, her warm brown eyes meeting his, reflecting his pain. A silent understanding passed between them, acknowledging their shared grief. She rushed to him, wrapping her arms around him and holding him tight.

Thomas reached into his pocket, his fingers trembling. He pulled out a small leather pouch, the worn material soft beneath his touch.

"Thomas, how are you?" Henrietta's voice was soft but strained, a reflection of the nervous anticipation she felt.

Thomas took a deep breath, steadying himself for the difficult news he was about to deliver. "Henrietta, I'm managing, thank you," he replied, his voice carrying a heaviness he couldn't disguise. He paused, searching for the right words, knowing nothing he said could make what was coming any easier.

"And Elijah?" she asked, her voice hopeful yet filled with dread. Her eyes searched his face for clues, her hands clasped tightly in her lap.

Thomas's breath hitched, the moment of truth unavoidable. "He's gone, Henrietta," he said gently, his tone laden with sorrow.

"What are you sayin'? He's gone?" Henrietta replied, searching Thomas's eyes for meaning.

"He was shot while we were on the run, not long after we left the plantation. We buried him not far from here. Elijah wanted you to have this," Thomas said, his voice heavy with grief as he held out the small leather pouch to Henrietta.

Henrietta gasped, her hand flying to her mouth as tears filled her eyes. "No, no, that can't be—" her voice trailed off into a whisper as she collapsed to the ground. She took the pouch, her hands trembling. She traced her fingers over the intricate beading as if memorizing it by touch.

"Oh, Elijah, my son," she whispered, a tear slipping down her cheek. She held the pouch to her heart for a long moment, then looked up at Thomas, her eyes shining with gratitude and grief.

Thomas placed a comforting hand on her shoulder. "He loved you, Henrietta. This was his last wish."

She looked up at him, tears streaming down her face. "Thank you," she whispered through her sobs. "For comin' back, for givin' this to me—for everythin'. Elijah cared about you. You were his best friend."

Thomas nodded, a lump in his own throat. "He was a good man. I miss him, too. He'll always have a special place in my heart."

Henrietta wiped her eyes and managed a small, sad smile. "Come, let's sit for a while."

They settled beneath the shade of an old oak tree. Its branches spread wide like a guardian watching over them. Its leaves had turned a vibrant palette of autumn colors, with fiery red, burnt orange, and golden yellow hues that shimmered in the soft autumn light. Thomas leaned back against the trunk while Henrietta sat across from him, Elijah's pouch cradled gently in her hands. For a time, neither spoke, each lost in their thoughts. The distant sounds of the plantation faded away, and all Thomas could hear was the rustle of leaves above them. It was easy to let his mind wander back to simpler times here—the rare joy and kinship shared between him and the other servants. But so much has changed since he was last here.

Finally, he broke the silence, his voice soft. "Elijah could always make me laugh, even on the hardest days. He just had a way about him. Like this one time—."

Henrietta nodded, a sad smile on her lips. "Oh yeah, he always had a quick, clever word. His spirit couldn't be broken." She chuckled lightly. "I'll never forget the day he made instruments outta old buckets and spoons, determined we were goin' to have music."

Thomas grinned at the memory. "It was dreadful noise we made, but Elijah beamed with pride. For those moments, we forgot our sorrows and danced together under the stars."

"He brought light wherever he went," Henrietta said wistfully. She clasped the leather pouch to her heart once more. "I sure do miss his gentle soul." Her eyes searched his face, concern evident. "What about the others? William, Marianne, and James? How are they?"

Thomas's voice wavered. "William is in Philadelphia now. He found himself a woman, and he's getting married next spring. Marianne is safe at the Hopewell Friends Quaker settlement. They've found some peace. But James —." He paused, swallowing hard. "James died in battle."

Henrietta's eyes filled with tears. "Oh, James. He was always so brave. I remember when I healed his wounds from the lashin' Lawson gave him. Such a kind boy. He didn't deserve that."

Thomas nodded. "Yes, he was. We've all paid a high price, but we have to believe it was worth it. For the future, for those we love."

He lifted his eyes to meet Henrietta's gaze. "I have a lot of guilt for surviving when Elijah and James didn't. And I need to do something to honor their memory. Sometimes, I fear I'll never be free from the shadows that cling to my soul."

Henrietta touched his arm, offering a gentle, comforting touch.

"There's nothin' to be ashamed of, Thomas," she said firmly. "You were just tryin' to survive, like all of us. The evil that tore our loved ones away can't take away the light inside you."

Thomas placed his hand over hers, drawing strength from her compassion. Henrietta had been like a mother to him over the years, and he loved her just the same.

"We gotta carry each other through this darkness," Henrietta continued, "like we always have. Our bond won't ever break."

Thomas nodded, his eyes filled with determination. "Henrietta, tell me, how did everyone hold up here?"

Henrietta sighed, her eyes weary. "It's been hard, Thomas. After the four of you left, ole Blackwood got on a war path with everyone. It was rough for a long while. A lot of folks lost hope, but we kept goin'. And you? How's life with the Quakers?"

Thomas's face softened. "It's different, Henrietta. They're good folks. They treat me right. Got a chance to learn, to live free. Marianne and I are building something together. I love her and I want to build a life with her. They even asked if you want to come. They asked if you wanted me to bring you back. Said they'd take care of you."

Henrietta shook her head slowly. "I 'preciate it, but I'm too old for all that. My place is here, with my people. I'm glad you and the others got your freedom. Maybe one day they'll give folks like me freedom too, but I ain't countin' on it. Ain't nothin' gonna make me free but the grave, I reckon."

Thomas took her hand, his grip solid and reassuring. "I won't stop here, Henrietta. I promise I'll keep fighting for everyone's freedom. No chains will hold us forever."

Henrietta smiled, a tear slipping down her cheek. "You got a strong spirit, Thomas. You're goin' to make a difference. Just remember, we're all behind you every step of the way. And Elijah is lookin' down on you, givin' you his blessin'."

Thomas nodded, feeling the weight of their shared past and the hope for a brighter future. "I won't forget. I promise. I should return soon, but I'd like to speak to Lord Blackwood before I leave."

"He ain't here. Him and Lady Constance ain't supposed to be back for a few more weeks. What you wantin' to talk to him 'bout?" Henrietta replied.

Thomas took a deep breath, his eyes fixed on the horizon. "I'd like to speak to him about what it means to be a free man. I also want to visit Harriet if she's still here."

"She oughta be in the big house," Henrietta replied.

"I should get going before it gets dark. It was nice seeing you again, Henrietta. I'm going to miss you. If you ever change your mind, remember where you can find me," Thomas said, standing up to hug Henrietta.

A tear slipped down Henrietta's cheek. "I'm gon' miss you too, Thomas. You make sure to tell Marianne I said hello, and I'll be prayin' for you both to have a blessed life together."

Seeing Henrietta was more emotional than he expected. Returning to the plantation, seeing his friends still enslaved, was too much to bear. He had fought for freedom, but it didn't seem right that the talk of liberty didn't include those like Henrietta. He wondered what he was even fighting for in the end. It didn't make sense. And what was Elijah's sacrifice for when his mother remained in chains?

The time had come to face the demons of Blackwood Plantation. Thomas walked the grounds, revisiting places filled with painful memories—the cramped servants' quarters where he'd spent nights on dirt floors, the fields where he'd toiled under the relentless sun. Phantoms of the past seemed to peer at him from every corner, ghosts of his captors leering and jeering as if to challenge his right to be there. But Thomas refused to waver. Standing tall and proud, he would no longer be cowed by these specters of his mind. As he roamed the grounds, he felt the shadows retreat, dissipating like mist under the power of his conviction. The chains that once bound his body and soul now lay broken. He was no longer that frightened, vulnerable boy but a free man. By simply being there, Thomas was reclaiming his power and asserting his humanity in the face of those who had denied it. This place could haunt him no more.

After reflection, Thomas walked to the house to say goodbye to Harriet. The path to the mansion was lined with blooming magnolias, their sweet smell mixing with memories of hard days under the sun. He steeled himself for the final farewell as he neared the large doors. Inside, the house was a maze of familiar hallways and rooms, each holding good and bad memories. The polished wooden floors creaked under his feet, echoing like whispers from the past. Faded portraits of ancestors lined the walls, their eyes seeming to follow him as he moved through the mansion.

Thomas found Harriet in the servants' kitchen kneading dough. She welcomed him with a warm, motherly smile, easing some of the shadows from his heart. The kitchen felt like a sanctuary, filled with the comforting aroma of fresh bread and herbs, so different from the usual oppressive air of the plantation. The hearth crackled with a small fire, casting a golden glow over the room.

"Thomas," she said, embracing him. "It's good to see you." Her embrace was firm and reassuring, a reminder of the strength and care she had always given.

Thomas smiled, the tension in his shoulders easing slightly. "It's good to see you too, Harriet."

She wiped her hands on her apron and beckoned him to sit. "How've you been?" Harriet asked, her eyes searching his face.

"Better, now that I'm here," Thomas replied, his voice thick with emotion.

Harriet nodded. She placed a cup of tea before him, the fragrant steam curling into the air. "Drink up, it'll cheer you up."

Thomas wrapped his hands around the cup, savoring the warmth. As he sipped the tea, he looked around the kitchen, taking in the simple, homely details—the neatly stacked jars of preserves, the herbs hanging to dry, and the worn but well-loved utensils.

"This place hasn't changed a bit, and neither have you," he said, a touch of nostalgia in his voice.

Harriet chuckled softly. "Some things don't need to change, Thomas. They're good just the way they are."

Thomas nodded, the familiar surroundings and Harriet's presence bringing a sense of peace he hadn't felt in a long time. With its comforting smells and gentle warmth, the kitchen felt like a haven, a reminder of simpler times. They talked quietly, sharing memories and stories, their bond as strong as ever. For a moment, Thomas could almost forget his hardships, finding solace in their friendship.

"Harriet, I had to come back to see everyone and deliver something to Henrietta," Thomas said, his voice lowering slightly, his expression turning somber. "It's about Elijah. He didn't make it when we escaped. He was shot by one of the patrollers not long after we left."

Harriet's expression shifted instantly from one of comfort to concern. She reached across the table, placing her hand over his. "Oh, Thomas, that's terrible news. How are you holding up?"

Thomas sighed, the weight of the memories pressing down on him. "It's hard, Harriet. Elijah was one of us. We were good friends. He was brave to the end." He paused, collecting his thoughts. "And there's more. James, William, and I all joined the fight together. We fought with the Virginia militia under Colonel Woodworth until we were commanded to go to Pennsylvania. We fought at Brandywine and Germantown under General Washington. I'm sure you remember when he was here at the dinner party. Well, he didn't recognize us. Maybe that's for the best. James was killed in battle at Brandywine. After our enlistment, William and I went to Philadelphia, stayed there, and worked as apprentices. William met someone and stayed there, and I decided to return to the

Quaker settlement that sheltered us before we joined the war."

Harriet's eyes filled with tears. "I can't imagine how hard that must have been for you, losing James, seeing Elijah fall. I'm so sorry, Thomas."

Thomas placed his hand over Harriet's. "I've grown since then, learned so much more about life, what it means to appreciate life. Back at the Hopewell Friends settlement, life is good. Marianne is there, and I hope to build a life with her, settle down, and have a family one day."

Harriet's eyes twinkled with news. "I'm proud of you, Thomas. Emily gained her freedom. She's working for a family in another city now."

Thomas's heart swelled with pride. "That's great to hear. She deserves all the happiness in the world."

She placed a gentle hand on his cheek. "You've come a long way. Keep fighting for what's right."

Thomas nodded. "I will. I won't stop until we're all free. Some of us who fought got our freedom. But look around. There are still enslaved people. We were promised freedom from our oppressors. I don't see how that's real when so many remain in chains. And, I promised Elijah I'd keep fighting until everyone had their freedom."

"I know you will. You're a good man," Harriet replied.

"One day, I'll confront Blackwood free man to free man. Did you know Lady Constance helped us escape?"

Harriet nodded, her eyes reflecting the weight of the past. "I did. She has a kind heart."

"Please tell her thank you for me. What about you? Why did you choose to stay after your indenture was over?" Thomas said.

"I'll tell her, Thomas," Harriet promised. "My time was up with my indenture, and I was free to go, but I'd grown used to being here, working in the house, and teaching in the little schoolhouse. So, I decided to stay here as a free woman. Lady Constance treats me well. Now go and take care of yourself. Give Marianne my love."

He hugged Harriet, knowing he might never see her again. Saying his final goodbyes, he left the plantation. The walk back to the gates felt different, each step a small victory over the past. As he reached his horse, he paused and looked back one last time. Blackwood Plantation, with all its shadows and memories, was a part of him, but it no longer defined him.

Epilogue

Thomas ran his hand over the smooth wooden staves. The barrels he made in his cooperage were sturdy and watertight, perfect for storing and transporting goods. It was 1790, and the Revolutionary War had ended. Since returning to Virginia and marrying Marianne, Thomas had embraced a life far removed from the turmoil of his past. Together, they had established a comfortable homestead on a modest farm that sprawled across the fertile land near the Hopewell Friends settlement. The farm thrived with activity, boasting several cultivated fields that yielded corn, wheat, and vegetables, alongside a small orchard that Marianne nurtured with care.

Their home buzzed with their children's lively chatter and laughter—two spirited sons and a curious daughter—who filled their days roaming the expansive fields that stretched endlessly into the horizon. Beneath the vast sky, they chased each other through the tall grasses, their voices carrying across the countryside. Ever the nurturing presence, Marianne managed the household and garden with a gentle yet firm hand, ensuring their home was warm and welcoming, her touch evident in every lovingly tended corner.

Thomas paused, absorbing the tranquil scene around him. This was the life they had fought so hard to build, a future once only imagined in dreams. The gentle hum of the countryside and the sun's warmth on his face made everything feel surreal, almost too perfect to believe. Just then, tiny arms encircled his waist, pulling him from his thoughts. He looked down to see his daughter, Clara, her bright blue eyes—so much like his own—sparkling with a mischievous grin. His heart swelled with love as he returned her smile, grateful for this simple, perfect moment.

"Papa, I helped Mama pick apples today!" she said proudly.

Thomas ruffled her hair. "Did you?"

She giggled, her eyes sparkling. "Mama told me to bring you an apple, Papa!"

Thomas laughed. "My darling Clara, that apple looks delicious."

Clara giggled and scampered off, her curls bouncing as she disappeared around the corner. Thomas watched her fondly, his heart swelling with the love and pride fatherhood had brought into his life. As his gaze shifted back to his workbench, his eyes caught on the carved wooden soldier perched on a high shelf. The toy, worn but well-kept, had been with him for as long as he could remember—a relic from a time before his world had been torn apart.

His father carved it for him when he was just a boy, a symbol of their bond. It was one of the last things his father had given him before he died, a small token of comfort and strength that had seen Thomas through the darkest times.

Nearby, Marianne sat beneath the shade of a large maple tree, its leaves rustling gently in the warm breeze as sunlight filtered through the branches. She led their sons in song, her clear, melodious voice rising and falling with the melody. The boys' voices joined hers, high and sweet, a perfect harmony. He paused in his work, the adze resting in his hand as he let the music wash over him. The sound of their voices, so full of life and love, soothed his soul. He glanced over at them, his heart swelling with pride. Marianne caught his eye and smiled, her face glowing warmly and affectionately. The years had deepened their bond, and her gentle strength and unwavering support made her an extraordinary mother and wife.

He wiped the sweat from his brow as he sank beneath a tree, memories washing over him. He remembered the hunger on London's streets, the biting winter cold, the heavy shackles chafing his wrists. He had come so far and survived so much. But the past was not easily outrun. Some nights, he still woke from dreams of those dark days. Yet, with time, the burdens eased.

So much had changed since his arrival in Virginia. He recalled the momentous creation of the Declaration of Independence, a daring proclamation of liberty that resonated through the colonies. The excitement and hope that filled the air were palpable when George Washington was elected the first President of the United States, embodying the dawn of a new era.

His thoughts drifted to the secret meetings held at night, where he and other freedmen worked tirelessly to help those still in bondage. His skills as a barrel maker allowed him to create hidden compartments, providing safe passage for escapees. These underground efforts, often aided by sympathetic Quakers, were a lifeline for many, and Thomas was proud to be part of this cause.

One evening, he gathered with Friends in a concealed room beneath a barn. The air carried the scent of hay, mingling with the low murmur of cautious voices. They spoke in whispers, exchanging updates and strategizing their next steps. Maps, marked with safe houses and escape routes, were spread across a wooden table, illuminated by the flickering light of candles.

"Next week, we'll move a group through the southern route," a man whispered, pointing to a marked path.

Thomas nodded, his heart swelling with determination. "I've prepared a few barrels with false bottoms. They should help hide our friends."

Another woman with sharp eyes and a soft voice added, "We've got support in Williamsburg. They'll be ready to receive them."

Thomas felt a sense of purpose, knowing that each small action contributed to something far more significant. This was the fight that mattered now.

One day, Thomas received word that Henrietta had died. He felt a heavy sadness settle over him, knowing another link to his past was gone. Determined to honor her memory, he made a final visit to her gravesite at the plantation.

The journey was bittersweet. As he stood by Henrietta's grave, the wind whispered through the trees, carrying echoes of the past. He knelt, brushing away leaves and dirt from the simple headstone. Memories of the struggle and the fight for freedom flooded his mind. He recalled Elijah's laughter, Henrietta's comforting presence, and the shared dreams of a better future. Thomas vowed to keep fighting to end slavery, knowing that the spirit of independence that founded the nation had to extend to all its people.

"Rest in peace, Henrietta," he whispered, placing a small bouquet of wildflowers on her grave. "We'll keep fighting. For you, for Elijah, for everyone."

As he turned to leave, his resolve hardened. He could no longer stay silent. Marching up to the imposing mansion, Thomas's heart pounded with anger and determination. He found Lord Blackwood in his study, sipping brandy by the fire.

"Blackwood!" Thomas roared, his voice echoing through the room like a thunderclap.

Lord Blackwood looked up, startled, the glass of brandy nearly slipping from his grasp. "Thomas? What is the meaning of this intrusion?"

"The meaning?" Thomas spat, his voice trembling with barely contained fury. "The meaning is to confront you for the years of cruelty and horror you've inflicted. Every soul you've tormented—they deserved better than the nightmare you forced upon them."

Blackwood's countenance contorted into a contemptuous sneer. "You dare to enter my home and address me in such a manner? After all the endeavors I have undertaken to maintain this plantation, to provide clothing and sustenance for you and your friends?"

"Running on the blood, sweat, and lives of innocent people!" Thomas shouted, stepping closer, his eyes blazing. "Families torn apart, lives destroyed—all so you could sit here in luxury while others suffered. What right did you have to do that?"

"What right, you ask? I would scarcely expect someone of your station to comprehend," Blackwood said, his voice rising defensively. "It was my right, for I have duly purchased them, and yourself, if you recall."

"Not anymore," Thomas growled, his fists clenching. "This country was built on the promise of freedom for all, and we will see that promise fulfilled. Your days of ruling with cruelty and indifference are ending."

Blackwood stood, his face flushed with anger. "Depart from my home, Thomas. You are unwelcome here."

Thomas pushed his face toward Blackwood. "And what are you going to do about it, Blackwood? Get your gun and shoot me? I'm not afraid of you or your threats anymore."

"Shoot you? No," Blackwood smirked, "I shall simply claim Marianne. We shared a certain familiarity, as you are certainly aware. I am certain you have presumed as much but have chosen to disregard it."

Thomas's eyes glazed over with fury, and his cheeks turned crimson. He lunged at Blackwood, reaching for his neck. "You lay a hand on Marianne, and I'll kill you," he replied, his voice icy.

Just as Thomas's hands closed around Blackwood's collar, a firm grip pulled him back. Surprised, he turned to see Lady Constance, her expression stern yet tinged with worry. Her presence, unexpected yet commanding, forced a pause in the escalation.

"Thomas, stop this at once!" Lady Constance commanded. Her voice, usually so composed and serene, now carried a sharp edge that cut through the thick tension in the room.

Thomas, his chest heaving with ragged breaths, looked at her. Confusion and anger mingled in his gaze. "Why? Why do you defend a man like this?" he spat out, his gaze flickering dangerously between Blackwood and Lady Constance.

Lady Constance maintained her composure, though her eyes softened as she addressed Thomas. "There is a side to him that you do not see, Thomas," she said calmly. "A side not consumed by the bitterness and cruelty you know. I believe in the good in people, including my husband."

Thomas scoffed, his anger simmering just below the surface, but he made no move to shake off her restraining hand. "And what of the harm he's caused? To my friends, to all of us?"

"I understand your pain and anger, Thomas," Lady Constance continued, her tone earnest. "But I ask you to step back, not for his sake but mine. I see a path to change that needs encouragement, not further violence."

Her sincere plea reached Thomas. He stared at her for a long moment, grappling with the storm of emotions inside him. Finally, with a heavy sigh, he stepped back, releasing his grip on Blackwood.

"If it weren't for your respect, Constance," Thomas muttered, his voice low and strained, "I would not leave this be. For your sake, I will step away. But should he ever threaten Marianne or harm anyone I care for, no belief in redemption will stop me from protecting them. It is an abomination that one man holds another in bondage. One day, this practice will be abolished, and men like your husband will have to do their own work."

Constance's expression softened with a mix of sorrow and understanding. "Thomas," she began, her voice calm yet carrying an undercurrent of firm resolve, "your loyalty and principles do you credit, even in such trying times. I, too, dream of a day when such injustices are but memories of a misguided past. For now, I beseech you to proceed with caution. Your courage is noted, and your protection is cherished. Know that your actions, borne of good intent, hold my deepest respect."

Thomas turned and stormed out without another word, his words hanging heavy in the air. He mounted his horse, the animal sensing his rider's tension, and spurred it into a gallop. As the plantation faded behind him, Thomas felt a renewed sense of purpose. He finally confronted Blackwood and could now put the past behind him.

The ride home seemed shorter than he remembered, perhaps because his heart was lighter, having stood up for Marianne and their life together without resorting to violence. As he approached his farm, the familiar sight of the whitewashed fence and the smoke curling from the chimney made him smile. Marianne watched their children play among the autumn leaves in the garden. Her face lit up when she saw him, and she quickly wiped her hands on her apron before running to greet him.

"Thomas!" she exclaimed as she threw her arms

around him. Sensing the joyous mood, the children ran over and hugged his legs.

"Everything is alright," Thomas reassured her, hugging his family close. "I confronted Blackwood, and it's over now."

Marianne looked up at him, eyes full of questions, but she nodded, trusting his judgment. They walked back to the house together, the children chattering excitedly about their day.

Over dinner, Thomas shared more about his confrontation at the plantation, explaining how Lady Constance had intervened. Marianne listened intently, her expression a mixture of relief and concern. After the children were put to bed, they sat by the fireplace, enjoying the quiet of the evening.

"Thomas, I have something to tell you," Marianne said suddenly, her voice a mix of nervousness and excitement. Thomas turned to look at her, noting the seriousness in her tone.

"What is it, love?" he asked gently.

She smiled, her eyes filling with tears of joy. "I'm with child."

Thomas's heart swelled with happiness. He pulled her into a tight embrace. "My love, that's wonderful news! A new brother or sister for the children. They will be excited to hear the news," he whispered, kissing her forehead.

With Marianne's hand in his, they slowly made their way upstairs to their bedroom, the wooden stairs creaking gently under their weight. The house was quiet, with only the soft sounds of the night drifting in through the open window—crickets chirping and a gentle breeze rustling the leaves.

As they entered their room, the soft glow of the moonlight filtered through the curtains, casting a serene light across the quilt-covered bed. Marianne let go of Thomas's hand briefly to light a small lamp on the bedside table, its flame flickering into life and casting a warm, inviting glow. Thomas watched her, his heart full of love and admiration for the strength and grace she had shown through the years. They prepared for bed in comfortable silence, a routine they had perfected over the years.

Once in bed, they lay side by side, Marianne resting her head on Thomas's shoulder. He wrapped his arms around her, drawing her close. They lay there in the quiet, the warmth of their bodies mingling, the soft sound of their breathing filling the room.

"Are you happy, Marianne?" Thomas asked softly, his voice low in the quiet of the night.

"I am, Thomas. Truly content," Marianne replied in a gentle voice. "With you, our family, and the life we've created together—it's more than I ever imagined possible."

Thomas kissed the top of her head gently. "And there's more joy to come," he said, a smile in his voice.

They whispered for a while longer, sharing their hopes for the future, excitement about the baby on the way, and the simple joys of their everyday life. As the night wore on, their words became fewer until they finally drifted into sleep, content in the life they had built. Their hearts and dreams were intertwined, much like the branches of the oak tree under which they had once vowed to create a life together long ago.

Author's Note

A grim and often overlooked chapter in history unfolded in the seventeenth and eighteenth centuries. Street urchins, many orphaned or destitute, were kidnapped from the streets of England and Europe and shipped to the American colonies. There, they were sold into indentured servitude. Upon arrival, these children entered a harsh world where their labor was exchanged for passage, room, and board, bound by contracts for a set number of years.

This practice was historically significant because it shaped labor systems in the colonies and deeply affected those involved. Such people were treated as property, much like the enslaved, and their labor was essential for the colonies' economic growth. They toiled in harsh conditions on plantations, in homes, and emerging industries, often enduring severe mistreatment and exploitation.

The injustices they faced were severe. If these children tried to escape, patrols or bounty hunters hunted them down, much like runaway slaves. This reflected the harsh system of control in colonial labor practices. This pursuit and punishment showed their lack of rights and the brutal reality of their bondage. Many endured physical abuse, malnutrition, and a lack of medical care, leading to high mortality rates among indentured children.

As the American Revolutionary War neared, life for these people changed dramatically. Both British and Colonial forces, needing more soldiers, promised freedom to those who joined the fight. This offer of liberation was a strong incentive, leading many to take up arms, hoping to secure their freedom through military service. This shift underscored their desperate living conditions and their readiness to risk everything for a chance at autonomy.

These former indentured servants fighting in the Revolutionary War shaped American identity. Their involvement in the battle for independence added to the narrative of liberty and equality, even though these ideals were not fully realized for everyone. Their struggle for freedom became part of the larger quest for human rights and justice.

The exploitation and injustices faced by these people remind us of the deep-rooted inequalities in history. Their struggles highlight the enduring human spirit and the ongoing fight for freedom. Even after indentured servitude and slavery formally ended in the United States, their legacy continued to influence the battle for civil rights and equality.

Today, the fight against modern slavery and human trafficking continues worldwide. The story of kidnapped street children seeking freedom echoes today's efforts to end all forms of exploitation. Ensuring that everyone, regardless of their background, is free from bondage is crucial. The global commitment to human rights and abolishing all forms of slavery remains vital, highlighting the need for constant vigilance and action to protect society's most vulnerable members.

Acknowledgments

First and foremost, I must thank my family. For my husband, Reaves, your unwavering love and belief in me have been my guiding light. You are a warm ray of light in my life, and I will love you for eternity. Your support has been the foundation of my strength and courage.

To my children, Ashley (Josh), Abigail, Hannah, River, and Phoenix, and my grandson, Silas, nothing in the world has given me greater pride than being your mother, mother-in-law (Josh), and grandmother (Silas). You inspire me to be a better person, to keep fighting for justice and truth, and to keep reaching. You make this world a better place simply by being in it. I will love you forever and always.

To my parents, William and Gloria, I am forever indebted to the love you shared and the values you instilled in me. I remember the times we spent together, the lessons you taught me about the importance of justice and truth, and the love you showered upon me. Thank you for everything. I love you.

To my in-laws, Judy and Richard, thank you for being in-laws and welcoming me into the family with open arms. Your acceptance and love have made me feel part of the family. I love you and how you love others, always exhibiting the love that makes this world better.

Thank you to my friend Penelope Koutoulas for your undying support, time, and feedback as you read through the manuscript. You allowed me to bounce ideas and questions off you whenever I needed, and I'm very grateful for that.

Lastly, a huge thank you to my editor, Carol Trow, for your invaluable contribution in polishing this manuscript. Your red pen is mightier than the sword, and your keen eye for detail has truly brought out the best in my work.

About the Author

Melissa Cole is a writer with a deep commitment to historical research. Inspired by the forgotten victims of the Ukrainian famine known as the Holodomor, her debut historical fiction title, *A Grain of Hope*, captivated readers with its poignant portrayal of human suffering and resilience.

As a survivor of a life-altering heart attack in 2018, she brings a unique perspective to her storytelling, infusing her work with resilience, empathy, and an unwavering commitment to providing her readers with tales of survival.

Melissa Cole's professional journey is as diverse as her writing. With a Bachelor's Degree in Communications from the University of Florida, she has worked as a writer and editor at international advertising and textbook publishing companies. She has also published her own family-focused magazine. When she isn't reading, baking, or spending time with her family, she tirelessly advocates for the welfare of animals. She lives in Florida, USA, with her husband, children, and rescue cats.

Please visit: www.melissacoleauthor.com

Also by Melissa Cole

Thank you, dear reader, for embarking on this journey with me. I truly hope you found meaning in Thomas's story, a tale of resilience against the harsh realities of indentured servitude and slavery. Your support means the world to me, and I would be delighted if you could spare a moment to share your thoughts on your favorite bookseller's website or Goodreads. Your feedback is invaluable and helps me understand your perspective, enriching our shared connection through literature.

You might also enjoy my other book:

A Grain of Hope

Coming soon:

The Last Historian

www.ingramcontent.com/pod-product-compliance
Lightning Source LLC
Chambersburg PA
CBHW030603310726
48979CB00003B/553

9798989997657